Books by Mary Hoffman

THE STRAVAGANZA SERIES

Stravaganza: City of Masks

Stravaganza: City of Stars

Stravaganza: City of Flowers

Stravaganza: City of Secrets

Stravaganza: City of Ships

The Falconer's Knot

Troubadour

STRAVAGANZA
City of Secrets

MARY HOFFMAN

BLOOMSBURY

NEW YORK BERLIN LONDON

Copyright © 2008 by Mary Hoffman
First published in Great Britain by Bloomsbury Publishing Plc in 2008
Published in the United States of America by Bloomsbury Books for Young Readers in July 2008
Paperback edition published in March 2010

Published by Bloomsbury Books for Young Readers
175 Fifth Avenue, New York, New York 10010

The Library of Congress has cataloged the hardcover edition as follows:
Hoffman, Mary.
Stravaganza: city of secrets / Mary Hoffman. —1st U.S. ed.
p.   cm.
Summary: Seventeen-year-old Matt, painfully dyslexic and insecure, discovers that he can travel between
worlds after being transported to Talia, where he joins Luciano and other Stravaganti in trying to prevent the
di Chimici family's breakthrough to our world.
ISBN-13: 978-1-59990-202-9 • ISBN-10: 1-59990-202-8 (hardcover)
[1. Space and time—Fiction. 2. Renaissance—Italy—Fiction. 3. Adventure and adventurers—Fiction.
4. Dyslexia—Fiction. 5. Self-confidence—Fiction.] I. Title.
PZ7.H67562Svt2008   [Fic]—dc22   2007039000

ISBN 978-1-59990-451-1 (paperback)

Typeset by Dorchester Typesetting Group Ltd.
Printed in the U.S.A. by Worldcolor Fairfield, Pennsylvania
1 3 5 7 9 10 8 6 4 2

Acknowledgements

I want to thank Nigel Roche, Curator of the St Bride's Print Museum in the City of London, for his patient help and answering of queries about sixteenth century printing processes, and Dr Martin Maw, Archivist at the Oxford University Press for additional help and comments. The demonstration of a wooden press in action at the Plantin-Moretus Museum in Antwerp was a revelation. Thanks too to Mafra Gagliardi and her family for their interest and hospitality in Padua, Rose Sharp for her expert help on dyslexia, Alison Debenham for providing the invaluable plot-planning template and, as always, the completely wonderful London Library.

'A secret may be sometimes best kept by keeping the secret of its being a secret.'
Sir Henry Taylor, statesman, 1836

'There are no secrets except the secrets that keep themselves.'
Bernard Shaw, *Back to Methuselah*, 1921

Contents

Prologue: *Cloak and Dagger*

'I can't be apart from Luciano on my birthday,' Arianna told Barbara. 'You understand, surely? You wouldn't want to be separated from your Marco on such a day, would you?'

Her maid Barbara was in an agony of indecision. Her mistress, the Duchessa, was asking her to do something very dangerous indeed. Proud as Barbara was to be taken into the Duchessa's confidence, she knew she ought to tell Senator Rossi, the Regent, what his daughter was planning.

Still, the maid also thought the Duchessa's plan was desperately romantic and Barbara loved anything that smacked of romance. She was engaged, just like her mistress, only to a young footman called Marco, and the Duchessa had promised her an expensive dress and jewels to wear at her wedding. But this new scheme of the Duchessa's might mean Barbara lost her job long before her wedding day. And she'd be lucky if it was just her job she lost.

'Milady,' said Barbara cautiously, wondering how to dissuade her mistress without appearing disloyal. 'Forgive me but there are things an ordinary serving-woman like myself might be permitted to do that are not . . . fitting for a duchessa. And running off to Padavia to meet the Cavaliere when there is a state celebration for you here might be one of them.'

'But what if you were here to take my place at the celebration? You've done it before.'

That was when the maid had started to feel really afraid.

It was true that Barbara had impersonated her mistress once before and, on that occasion, had only narrowly escaped being murdered. Arianna had once sworn never to use a double but the longer she continued as ruler of Bellezza, the better she understood her mother who had been Duchessa before her. Silvia had used doubles for some state appearances for years. And on the final occasion it had saved her life.

The same was true for Arianna. She was only too aware that the last impersonation of her had led to a wound that would scar her maid for life, and could have killed her. After all, it was she, Arianna, who had stabbed Barbara's assailant, with her Merlino-dagger, before he could finish his attack. It still bothered her sometimes that she had never known the man's name or family.

Both the mistress and the maid were absorbed in their thoughts remembering that dreadful day.

'That was different, milady,' said Barbara at last. 'I didn't have to talk to anyone. I am sure the Regent and his wife would know in a moment that I was not Your Grace.'

Arianna decided not to press the point. She didn't really think that anyone would try to assassinate the Duchessa of Bellezza at her eighteenth birthday celebrations. Luciano – how she warmed just at the thought of him! – had told her that in his world eighteen was a very significant birthday and she had already planned to make his so for him, but it was not the case in Talia. Still, the city's ruler would have to have some kind of feast. And Rodolfo, her father and Regent, would be sure to make some very special fireworks. It was a pity she wouldn't see them.

*

It didn't look like a haven for someone on the run but that's what it was. The house in Padavia had lost its mistress and acquired a new tenant. The Widow Bellini had left for a new life in Bellezza with her new husband. And a tall slim young man, not yet eighteen, with black curly hair, now sat at the stone table in the garden, contemplating his future.

An elderly servant, rather flustered from the move to a new city, brought wine out to his master.

'Sit down a minute, Alfredo,' said the young man and the servant gratefully lowered his bulk on to a bench.

'Just for a minute then, Cavaliere,' said Alfredo, pouring the wine. 'There is so much to do. That housemaid Signora Bellini left behind has let the house go. It needs a thorough spring clean.'

'In October?' said his master, taking a deep draught of wine. 'I don't mind if it isn't spotless. I'm going to be spending most of my time at the University.'

Luciano smiled to himself, thinking about the kind of messy house-share or communal university hall he might have lived in if he had remained in his old life in his old world. By comparison, Silvia's house was a palace.

The smile turned to a sigh. It wasn't often now that he thought of might-have-beens but his move from Bellezza to university in Padavia was just the sort of rite of passage that brought his old life back to him with renewed vividness.

His mother Vicky and his father David would have pored over prospectuses with him, asking his views about where he wanted to go and what subject he wanted to study. He imagined them packing his belongings into the family car and driving him off to Brighton or York or Edinburgh, wherever he had got a place.

The application process had been quite different in the lagoon-city of Bellezza. For a start, he was a year younger than he would have been in England but that was normal for Talia; some students went to university at fifteen. Then again, he was engaged to the Duchessa. Thinking of Arianna brought the smile back to Luciano's lips.

There was no way he would ever have dreamed of asking a girl in his old world to marry him when they were both only seventeen but a lot was different about his new life. He was a Cavaliere, which his foster-father had explained was something like a knight in

Elizabethan England. And now that he was going to marry Arianna, he would soon be a duke.

That is, if he lived to see the day.

There was a warrant out for his arrest, signed by the Grand Duke of Tuschia. It accused him of killing the previous Grand Duke, Niccolò di Chimici. And it was true; he had done it. But it had been in a duel and Niccolò had played dirty, poisoning one of the foils. It wasn't Luciano's fault they had somehow been switched.

That had been nearly six months ago. He had escaped from the Grand Duke's city of Giglia, smuggled out in a crate with a marble statue of Arianna. And as soon as he had been released from the crate he had asked the subject of the sculpture to marry him.

There was something about life in Talia that speeded things up. Life expectancy was short: a phial of poison or a silent dagger could cut it off in its prime. People married young. Luciano had decided he just couldn't wait any longer to be with Arianna.

*

Professor Constantin was a Stravagante. And, oddly, he wasn't Talian; he came from an Eastern part of Europa and had settled in Padavia, where he taught Rhetoric at the University. He was a middle-aged, mild-mannered man with a neat grey beard but there was more to him than met the eye.

He was in charge of the Scriptorium, where all the books written by professors at the University were printed – a respectable extra job for a respectable-seeming man. But only Constantin and a chosen few knew that there was a concealed door at the back which led to a second Scriptorium where a hidden printing press made copies of books of secret lore.

He was an old friend of the Regent of Bellezza. And he had recently accepted from him an important charge.

'Luciano is as dear to me as my own child,' Rodolfo had told him. 'I want you to teach him what you can. And keep him from being killed.'

And it said a lot for their friendship that Constantin was as ready to accept the second commission as the first.

Chapter 1

Birthdays

It was a real downer having a birthday so close to the beginning of term, thought Matt, as he did every year. It should feel special, turning seventeen, legally able to drive a car, but starting his first year in the sixth form and being nearly a year older than some of his mates made him feel stupid, as if he had been made to retake a year. Matt was used to feeling stupid but that didn't mean he liked it.

It didn't help that his younger brother, Harry, was June-born and top of the class in every subject. But then Harry wasn't dyslexic. He was just a normal, rather bright kid.

'Being dyslexic doesn't mean you aren't clever.' That was a mantra Matt had been hearing ever since his problems had been discovered in primary school. His mother said it, his father said it and every ed psych he'd ever seen told him the same thing. He'd often wondered whether he should have it tattooed across his forehead or printed on a T-shirt. Whether that would help him believe it.

'Here you are,' said his mother, beaming as she slid a hot plate of bacon, egg, tomato and fried bread in front of him. 'Special birthday breakfast.'

'What about me?' complained Harry, but his own plate arrived before he could get into his stride.

'And me?' asked their dad, up unusually early and already waving his knife and fork as his wife produced his with a flourish.

'Anyone would think it was their birthdays too,' mumbled Matt through a mouthful of fried bread.

'Aah, diddums, would you like an extra tomato?' asked his mum. She wasn't having a cooked breakfast herself and she didn't usually wait on the rest of them, so that did make it special, even though she had chivvied the boys out of bed half an hour earlier than usual so they could eat a big breakfast before school.

Matt's mother contemplated her family with satisfaction. It was no mean feat to have raised two teenage boys in London without their ever having got into any trouble. Harry was doing really well at school and Matt was coping well with his dyslexia. Her husband Andy was smiling at her over his fried breakfast, his brown hair flopping into his eyes as it had when she had first met him twenty-two years ago. Jan noticed with a small pang that it was beginning to go grey.

'Don't eat a big lunch,' she told the boys. 'Remember we're going to the Golden Dragon tonight.'

But it was an unnecessary caution. Her sons could eat all day and still put away vast quantities of dinner.

On the morning of Arianna's eighteenth birthday, Luciano was missing her just as much as she might have wished. He had arranged for Rodolfo to give her a small package from him, containing the earrings he had chosen himself from the ducal silversmith, but it wasn't the same as seeing her eyes sparkle when she opened it.

He rode from Silvia's house near the many-domed basilica to the university building where he was due for a class in Rhetoric. He had to smile as he thought of it. If he had stayed in his old world, he might have studied Music or History. And when Rodolfo had first suggested sending him to study in Padavia, they talked about Alchemy and other subjects that might help a Stravagante to practise what Rodolfo called Science, though Luciano still thought of it as Magic.

But once he had asked Arianna to marry him, everything had changed.

'You must have the education of a proper nobleman,' Rodolfo had declared and, surprisingly, Luciano's foster-father, Doctor Dethridge, had agreed.

'Rhetoricke, Grammar, Logicke,' the old Elizabethan had said. 'Thatte wich we calle the Three-folde Waye will give ye a good grounding in al ye neede to knowe.'

Luciano wondered what his real dad would have said about those as a set of A level subjects!

'Grammar?' he queried. 'You mean like nouns and verbs? I think I know that already.' He remembered his Head of English at Barnsbury Comprehensive School, Mrs Wood, who had been a great stickler for grammar.

To his surprise, Rodolfo and William Dethridge had both burst out laughing.

'Harken to the ladde,' said Dethridge. 'Ye might as well saye thatte since ye knowe whatte a bricke be, ye canne build an house!'

'I don't know what Grammar means in your twenty-first century England, Luciano,' said Rodolfo, 'but at university here in Talia it includes the study of History, Poetry, all kinds of literature. Including reading it aloud.'

Luciano had a vision of himself standing up with his hands behind his back, reciting a poem he had learned by heart. It was his turn to laugh.

'I see it doesn't daunt you,' said Rodolfo, clapping him on the shoulder. 'We shall make you a complete sixteenth-century Talian nobleman, able to take his place beside any duke or prince in the land.'

Even a grand duke? thought Luciano to himself. He could never forget that he had made a powerful enemy of Fabrizio di Chimici. But he was content to do what his foster-father and his mentor wanted. He trusted them with his life. And he was secretly a bit relieved not to have to study Science, since he hadn't been very good at it in his old life.

He turned his horse up the street of the Saint towards his first class of the day, which was in the Palazzo del Montone, the building of the ram. Professor Constantin would be waiting.

'There's the postman,' said Jan as the rest of the family finished their breakfast. Matt jumped up from the table and fetched in a handful of cards and letters.

'No parcels?' asked Harry.

'Doesn't look like it,' said Matt, tearing open the biggest card. 'But, here's a huge cheque from grandma and grandpa. My kind of present.'

'They want you to put it towards your driving lessons,' said his father.

'What driving lessons would they be?' asked Matt innocently but he could see from his parents' faces that he was right about what they were giving him.

'All will be revealed at the sign of the Golden Dragon,' said his mother. 'But now you'd better get a move on. No, wait, you've missed one.'

There was one unopened white envelope in Matt's place, which he snatched up. 'I'll open it later,' he said. 'I have to hurry now.'

But he was in no hurry to open that card; he'd recognised the writing and he knew who it was from and what it was. His great-aunt Eva, his mother's aunt, sent him the same present every year: a twenty-pound book token.

It was a sore subject. Eva was a nice woman in her seventies, a bit vague but very loving. Jan's parents had both died young so Auntie Eva was the closest thing Matt had to a grandparent on his mother's side.

Eva lived alone in a big flat in Brighton and Matt had loved going there when he was little. He felt guilty now about how long it had been since he'd visited his great-aunt. She had always plied him and Harry with specially made meals and cakes but there was this great big rift between them: she assumed he was as much of a reader as she was.

Eva's flat was packed with books, arranged double on the bookshelves that lined every room – even the loo – and stacked in dangerous heaps up the sides of the stairs. New books came all the time, as Eva had taught English Literature at Sussex and still reviewed titles for several journals now she was retired. She had been told that Matt was dyslexic, of course, and even seemed sympathetic, but the information somehow just didn't stick in her head; like a lot of things she didn't want to remember, Jan said. And every birthday along rolled the generous book token.

Sometimes Jan gave Matt money for it, since she was always buying books herself, or she used to go with him to a shop and choose kids' books she thought he could manage. But that would have just been embarrassing now. He just shoved Eva's card into his duffel bag as he pulled his jacket on and then ran towards school. He didn't want to be late. It was bad news having a mother who taught at your school; it meant nothing you did wrong ever went unnoticed.

His girlfriend, Ayesha, was waiting for him at the gate and they just had time to snatch a kiss, to the delight of a few whooping Year 8 stragglers, before running in for registration. 'Happy birthday,' said Ayesha. 'See you at break.'

Matt felt really happy for the first time that day. He had to kick himself regularly to believe that Ayesha, the most gorgeous and the brightest girl in his year, liked *him*, Matt, the big stupid lunk. She had glossy black hair and eyes that looked as if she had been born with mascara and liner already applied. And, unlike him, she knew exactly what she was going to do about university next year. Go to Cambridge and become a high-flying lawyer. According to Matt's dad, she would probably end up as Attorney General, or at least a High Court judge.

Ayesha knew about Matt's dyslexia and, unlike Great-Aunt Eva, understood it. She said it didn't make any difference, that he was clever anyway and gorgeous with it. Matt didn't see it himself. When he looked in the mirror, he saw someone built like his dad, like a rugby forward, which is what he was. Matt, that is. Andy Wood had given up rugger years ago and put on quite a few pounds since. He was now a professional singer in the chorus at the opera house and couldn't risk any injury to his throat or chest.

It would have been even more embarrassing to have a parent who was an opera singer than one who was a teacher in your school, if Andy Wood had looked anything like that sounded. But anyone less ethereal and arty than Matt's father would have been hard to find. Six foot three and broad with it, with a full beard when he didn't have to shave it off for particular operas, Andy looked much more like a navvy than a singer, and only Matt's closest friends knew what he did for a living.

But his musical talent had passed Matt by. Harry was different; he played trumpet in the school orchestra and sang tenor in the school choir. Music came as naturally to Harry as sport did to Matt.

At breaktime, Matt went to the sixth-form centre, where several kettles were already boiling and mugs lined up for coffee and hot chocolate.

'Look at all that steam,' said an upper-sixth girl with red, black and white striped hair. 'We're probably contributing more to global warming at Barnsbury Comp than – I don't know . . .'

'A field of farting cows?' suggested a tall honey-coloured boy with dreadlocks.

A fair girl at his side giggled.

'It's true,' said the boy with dreads. 'The methane gas produced by all the cows in the world is causing more global warming than transatlantic flights.'

Matt knew this upper-sixth boy by sight and was sure he was doing Arts rather than Sciences, but the two girls were listening to him as if he were Al Gore.

'Well, I think we should get the school to buy us an urn,' said the stripey-haired girl. 'Then there would be only one lot of boiling water and one lot of energy.'

Ayesha came in then with a large fridge box under her arm. 'Birthday present, part one,' she said, opening the box. A wonderful waft of freshly-baked chocolate cake rose from it.

'Brownies!' said Matt and suddenly he became very popular indeed.

The Palazzo del Montone had once been an inn, with a ram's skull hung outside it to proclaim its name. But it was unusually big for an inn and, not so unusually, very popular with students in the city. So, as the University got itself established, more and more teachers drifted towards giving informal lessons there. That was more than a hundred years ago and the city had long since bought the inn and all the buildings in its block and turned them into the main part of the University. But it was still known informally as the Ram.

It made Luciano feel at home, remembering the time he had spent in the Twelfth of the Ram in Remora. And a winged ram was the emblem of his new home city of Bellezza. These days the university building had a sculpture of a ram's head outside with magnificently curled stone horns. Luciano ran up the stairs in the colonnaded great court two at a time but it was all right; Professor Constantin had not started his lecture.

The Professor was standing, talking to a couple of other students, and Luciano took time to look at him. He was totally unlike any other Stravagante he had met. No one would mistake him for anything other than he was supposed to be, a middle-aged university professor, with a neat grey beard. But Rodolfo had said that Constantin was one of their number, a powerful natural philosopher who had travelled to Luciano's own world.

Rhetoric wasn't as dry a subject as Luciano had feared. Professor Constantin had explained it was about the art of persuasion, of arguing a case in such a way as to make your audience agree with you, whether in reality you believed it or not. He set them topics to work on and then they had to persuade their fellow students to accept their viewpoint. Luciano's subject was to be 'When is it right to kill a man?' and he was looking forward to it.

Ayesha wouldn't walk home with Matt, saying she had to get changed for the family meal in the Chinese restaurant.

'But that's hours away,' he protested.

'I've got to look specially nice for your birthday dinner' was all she would say.

So he was dawdling along wondering what to do with himself. He should have been hurrying home to get his work done before the meal but there was nothing that couldn't wait and he rebelled at the idea of doing homework on his birthday; it had been bad enough being cooped up in school all day. He wished he'd had rugby practice or something else physical to do.

It was a fine sunny day, bright and cold with a blustery wind that made Matt think of Brighton. He remembered Eva's card and reluctantly dragged it out of his bag. He had been right – another book token. Matt found himself standing outside an antiques shop; it had some dusty old books in the window among all the candle-snuffers, silver mustard pots and china dogs and, on impulse, he pushed open the door and went in, having a vague idea that if he could get the shopkeeper to take the token, he might be able to buy a dagger or something.

The last thing he expected to see inside the shop was any other students from Barnsbury; it wasn't a typical teenage hang-out. But there, chatting away with the owner as if she'd known him all her life, was the stripey-haired girl with the thing about saving the planet. And the school's fencing champion, Nick Duke.

The whole school knew they were an item, even

though Nick was almost two years younger than his girlfriend. He didn't look it though, since he was almost as tall as Matt and well-muscled. He didn't have a rugby-player's build like Matt but was wirier, like the fencer he was. Matt remembered the girl's name now – Georgia something. She was sporty too, he thought, a keen horse-rider. They were the sort of people he could have been friends with but it hadn't happened, because one was in the year below him and the other in the year above.

The girl didn't look friendly now though. She was frowning at Matt, as if he had no right to be there. But the old man behind the desk was perfectly polite.

'Can I help you, young man?' he asked.

'Er,' said Matt. 'I was wondering if you take book tokens.' He waved Eva's card at the man.

There was a contemptuous snort from the girl.

'Of course he doesn't,' said Georgia. 'This is an antiques shop not a bookshop.'

'But I saw some books in the window,' objected Matt.

'He's quite right, Georgia,' said the old man. 'I certainly do sell books – old ones at least, but it's only the big shops that are part of the book tokens scheme. Was there a particular book you were looking for?'

If the others hadn't been there, Matt might have admitted to this friendly man that he wasn't really looking for a book at all, but he just mumbled something vague and saw out of the corner of his eye that Nick was whispering something to his stroppy girlfriend.

'Is it OK if I look round?' Matt asked, wishing he had never come into the shop.

'Of course,' said the owner. 'Take your time – and just let me know if you need any help.'

'Hi,' said Nick. 'You go to Barnsbury, don't you?'

Matt nodded. 'Yeah. Just started in the sixth form. Matt Wood.'

Now the girl came closer and said, 'Hi, I'm Georgia. You're the guy with the brownies, aren't you?'

'It's my birthday,' said Matt. 'My girlfriend made them.'

'Lucky you,' said Nick.

'Oh it's your birthday,' said the owner. 'Many happy returns. That explains the book token. And if we're doing introductions, I'm Mortimer Goldsmith. But call me Mortimer – Georgia and Nick always do. Now, I think I've got some chocolate biscuits somewhere. We should celebrate.'

He bustled off to the back of the shop and Matt relaxed a bit. Maybe Georgia wasn't as hostile as he thought. And she seemed very matey with this Mortimer.

'I didn't really want to buy a book,' he admitted.

'Not really your thing?' asked Nick.

'I'd rather have something like this,' said Matt, drawing out a rusty old sword from an umbrella stand.

'You like weapons,' said Nick. 'Ever thought of fencing?'

Matt shook his head. 'I don't think I'd be quick enough. Not built for it.'

'Put the sword away,' said Georgia quietly. 'You wouldn't want it if you'd seen what they can do.'

Matt was surprised but returned the old sword to its place. Maybe she was talking about fencing accidents. He was rummaging through boxes of odds and ends when Mortimer Goldsmith returned with a laden tray.

'I brought tea for everyone,' he said. 'I hope you don't mind, Matthew, but Nick and Georgia generally have a cup when they drop in.'

Matt wondered again how come the school fencing champion and a horsey eco-warrior were such pals with the old antiques shop owner; maybe he was the grandfather of one of them?

He put back the broken pocket watch he had been fiddling with and then found, to his surprise that he was holding a book after all. Not a modern paperback and not anything he could imagine exchanging a book token for. It was small and bound in brown leather with thin brown strips of leather wound around it to hold it shut. Matt wondered if it was blank inside, like the old-fashioned sketchbooks he'd seen when Jan took them to a Leonardo da Vinci exhibition. They were on sale in the exhibition shop, with thick creamy cartridge paper inside with rough edges; Harry had wanted to buy one but they were too expensive.

The book was still in his hand as he took a mug of tea and a chocolate Hobnob. It was awkward but somehow he didn't want to put it down. As soon as he was able to open it, he saw that this one wasn't blank at all; it was densely printed in old-fashioned heavy black type. The words meant nothing to him – Matt was used to that – but, curiously, the little book attracted him. He was suddenly sure that this was what he wanted to buy. He looked up and saw that both Nick and Georgia were staring intently at him.

Alfredo seemed agitated when Luciano got back home.

'There's someone here to see you,' he said. 'I couldn't get rid of him and he wouldn't give a name. He says he brings a message from Bellezza – otherwise I wouldn't have let him in at all. But what shall I do? Is it safe to let him see you? Suppose he's really from Giglia?'

'Let's not suppose anything till I've spoken to him,' said Luciano. 'If he does indeed come from Bellezza, he will be most welcome. Bring him out into the garden and fetch us some wine.'

When Alfredo brought their unexpected visitor through, Luciano knew straight away that this was no stranger.

The young man was little more than a boy of about his own age, tall and slender, wearing humble peasant clothes. A cap was pulled down over his eyes but his demeanour was not humble; in fact he had quite a noble bearing. Something about him made Luciano think of the first time he had stravagated to Bellezza.

There was an easy grace in the way the visitor accepted the seat he was offered which told Luciano the truth. Then the stranger pulled off the cap and a cascade of brown curls tumbled down.

'Happy birthday!' said Luciano, to Alfredo's amazement.

Chapter 2

In the Scriptorium

The Golden Dragon was the best Chinese restaurant in Matt's part of Islington. He knew the menu by heart from many family celebrations, so its dense type held no fears for him; he just took a cursory glance then ordered what he always had.

Ayesha was looking spectacular in a purple strappy top embroidered with sequins. Her glossy hair hung loose over her shoulders and Matt felt his throat tighten at the sight of her. Their table was a bit boisterous; Andy had ordered champagne. Even Harry had a small glass.

Jan gave Matt an envelope, which held a receipt for twenty driving lessons and the cardboard cut-out of a car key. On it was written in big black letters: I. O. U. 1 CAR.

'When you pass your test,' said Andy.

'Or on your eighteenth birthday,' added Jan. 'Whichever comes sooner.'

It was what Matt had wanted most. He was a bit nervous of the theory test but he was sure he could pass the practical. And then he would have a freedom he longed for. Street signs weren't hard to read and he would be equal to anyone else on the road.

'Thanks,' he said. 'That's fantastic.' And he even put up with Jan kissing him, right there in public. Ayesha smiled at his embarrassment.

In fact the evening would have been perfect if it hadn't been for two things. The first was that he still had the book he'd bought from Mortimer Goldsmith in his pocket. The old man had taken the book token after all, under a bit of pressure from Georgia. 'You can use it to buy a book on antiques,' she said. And Matt had left, having spent twenty quid on a book he couldn't read, couldn't have read even if he hadn't been dyslexic; it was in a foreign language, probably Latin.

The book fascinated him and – what was more peculiar – it seemed to intrigue Georgia and Nick as well. They hadn't taken their eyes off him once he picked it up in the old man's shop and he had an uneasy feeling that they were expecting something to happen to him because of it.

But the oddness of the book and the greater oddness of his attraction to it was the lesser of Matt's two distractions from his birthday meal. The bigger fly in the ointment was Jago Jones.

Jago was simply the person Matt hated most in the world – and by a huge stroke of bad luck he was in the Golden Dragon with a group of friends that night. Matt didn't know what they were celebrating and he didn't care; it was just a blot on the landscape that he was in the same room.

Jago was in the upper sixth and was the school's best English student. He was the editor of the magazine, star of every play put on in the last four years – he had even had *poems* published. In real magazines that paid money for them. If there was anyone Matt knew who was more of a words and language person than his mother, it was Jago.

And to add fuel to Matt's hatred, Jago used to go out with Ayesha. It had been the year before and she swore that she had dumped him, rather than the other way round but Matt didn't feel entirely secure about it. And as well as being word-smart, Jago was ridiculously good-looking in a blond, Jude Law sort of way. He and Ayesha had made a stunning couple, one that Matt had admired from afar, never dreaming that one day she would prefer him.

Jago had another girlfriend now – Lucy – who was in his year. She was sitting with him in the Golden Dragon but to Matt's sensitive eye it wasn't stopping him from casting admiring looks at Ayesha. Matt felt a sort of tight band round his chest constricting him and making it hard to swallow his Peking duck. Suppose Jago wanted to get back with Ayesha? Why would she prefer to be with a dumbo like him?

Perhaps it had been Jago who dumped her and perhaps he was regretting it now? Lucy was OK but she wasn't a beauty like Ayesha. And Jago must have known what a lovely person Ayesha was too. But then why would he have dumped her? Thoughts like these were running through Matt's head all evening and it was only with a huge effort that he managed to stop them spoiling his celebration.

The expression on Alfredo's face was a mixture of puzzled and appalled.

'Your Grace,' he said, making a deep bow. 'I'm sorry. I didn't know . . .'

'No one does, Alfredo,' said Arianna, shaking her hair. 'I'm in disguise.'

'You're crazy,' said Luciano.

'I think that's treason,' said Arianna. 'Even from a fiancé. Oh do stand up straight, Alfredo. I am not the Duchessa today.'

She stretched her arms and stuck her long legs in their coarse breeches out straight in front of her. 'It feels good,' she said. 'I feel like the old Arianna of the Islands.'

It was true, in her boy's clothes, she did look more like the wild girl Luciano had met in the Piazza della Maddalena more than two years ago.

'But what about Rodolfo and Silvia?' asked Luciano. 'I can't believe they let you come here on your birthday. And what about your bodyguard?'

Arianna shrugged.

'They don't know,' she said carelessly. 'And I didn't bring a guard – only Marco, my maid's betrothed. He's hanging about outside somewhere. Perhaps you'd let him in and give him something to eat, Alfredo?'

'Yes and bring us something too,' said Luciano. 'I was so surprised to see you I forgot my duties as a host.'

'But not host to a duchessa, please,' said Arianna. 'Just a peasant boy from Torrone. You can call me Adamo when I'm in disguise.'

'And when I kiss you?' said Luciano, taking her in his arms.

'Then you don't need to call me anything at all,' said Arianna, narrowing her violet eyes.

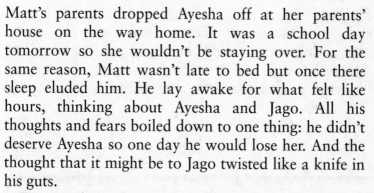

Matt's parents dropped Ayesha off at her parents' house on the way home. It was a school day tomorrow so she wouldn't be staying over. For the same reason, Matt wasn't late to bed but once there sleep eluded him. He lay awake for what felt like hours, thinking about Ayesha and Jago. All his thoughts and fears boiled down to one thing: he didn't deserve Ayesha so one day he would lose her. And the thought that it might be to Jago twisted like a knife in his guts.

He must have slept eventually because it was about 5.30 a.m. when he woke suddenly. He got up and went to the bathroom, then down to the kitchen for a glass of water. On his way back to bed, he stopped and took the old book out of his jacket pocket. By the light of his bedside lamp he tried again to decipher some of the words. The letters were in the normal alphabet so it wasn't Greek or Russian or Arabic, but it might as well have been.

Matt would have liked to be good at languages. His family often had holidays in France and he could imitate what he heard around him quite well. But he had no idea how anything was spelt and he couldn't recognise any of it when it was written down. So he had given up French at school as soon as he could. Maths and ICT were much easier for him.

He wondered for the umpteenth time why he had wasted his birthday money on the incomprehensible little book. And then he started to wonder what it would be like if he could understand it, what it would be like to be a scholar who understood many languages, living and dead. Perhaps if he were that clever, he would feel as good as Jago and worthy of the beautiful Ayesha.

Matt felt drowsiness creeping over him. He wound the leather straps round the book and tied them but before he could put it down sleep overcame him and he felt himself falling into a swirling vortex of words and ideas.

When Matt woke up, he had no idea where he was. It was a large but musty-smelling room as big as his school assembly hall and full of machines of some sort. At first he thought he was the only person in the room, but gradually, as his eyes adjusted to the dancing motes of dust in the weak rays of sunshine coming from the high windows, he saw some men working on the machines furthest away from him, near the big wooden doors at the far end of the room.

They seemed to be talking to each other and gesturing with their hands but he couldn't tell what they were saying for the noise of the machines, which was a sort of loud creaking, like wood on an old-fashioned sailing ship.

What a peculiar dream, thought Matt. He was used to dreams where you think you have woken up and then discover that's just another part of the dream.

The machine nearest to him was silent, as if waiting for someone to come and operate it. Beside it Matt saw a shallow box on a stand, with divisions inside it containing bits of metal, neatly arranged. He picked one up and examined it. It was small but heavy – a bit of lead, he thought. There was a raised letter 'b' on it or maybe a 'd'. Matt had a lot of trouble with letters that looked the same but turned into other letters if you reversed them.

He must have spoken out loud in his dream, because a voice said over his shoulder 'It's a "d".' Matt jumped and saw that a man had come up silently behind him. He was middle-aged with a neat grey beard. But what was odd about him was his clothes – they were old-fashioned, made of velvet and lace, like in a Shakespeare play or an old oil painting. And he wore a flowing scholar's gown on top.

'Do you know what it is?' said the man, taking the metal letter out of Matt's hand. 'It's a bit of movable type. The letter looks like a "b" because it's back to front – like an image in a mirror. When it's inked and pressed on to paper, it will give you a "d" though.' He spoke with an accent Matt couldn't quite place.

He put the letter back in the box. 'I'm Professor Constantin,' the man said. 'What's your name?'

Matt realised he'd never had a dream in which anyone asked him his name before, even as he said, 'Matt Wood.'

'Matteo Bosco,' said the man, rolling the syllables

round his mouth. 'That is a good name for you in Padavia.'

Matt had no idea what he might mean. 'Where is this?' he asked.

'It is the Scriptorium,' said Constantin. 'My Scriptorium, you might say. It used to belong to a monastery, where monks copied manuscripts. But now we have movable type and the books are printed. You could call it a "Stamparium" I suppose.'

He patted the nearest machine affectionately, as if it were a favourite dog.

'But you must come into my studio,' he said suddenly. 'I have clothes waiting for you.'

He took off his scholar's robe and threw it round Matt's shoulders. Matt looked down at himself, incongruous in his pyjama bottoms, his chest and feet bare under the heavy black gown. This was a very realistic dream.

It wasn't until then that he noticed he was holding the little leather-bound book in his hand.

But the Professor was leading him off towards a side door, beckoning him to be quick. Matt got the impression that Constantin didn't want the men at the far end of the Scriptorium to see him. He followed obediently, though he had no idea what was going on.

Constantin's 'studio' was nothing like what that word conjured up in Matt's brain and he was amazed that his sleeping mind could come up with such a scene. The only furniture was a large wooden desk, a wooden armchair and a couple of stools. But every surface was covered with books, parchments, rolls of paper and printed pictures.

There were no bookshelves, which would have been

the obvious solution to the clutter. Matt wondered how the Professor could find anything he wanted. There was no electric light or desk lamp but there were candle-holders on the walls and a big candlestick on the desk, which had dripped fantastic patterns of wax on to both wood and papers. And there was an unpleasant smell like old cooking fat. On one wall there was a religious picture that Matt somehow knew was called an icon. On the opposite one there was a cupboard built into an alcove. There was one window with a deep wooden window seat. Through it Matt could see a jumble of old buildings and narrow streets.

The view and the candles, together with Constantin's clothes, made Matt realise that he was dreaming of a distant past. The Professor was saying something, gathering up some clothes from a pile on a stool.

'Put these on,' he was saying. 'Of course, if anyone sees you haven't a shadow, your secret will be revealed. But at least you will be less conspicuous in these.'

He looked at Matt critically. 'Apart from your hair, of course. Why do you young men in the twenty-first century wear it so short? We'll have to find you a hat. I don't suppose you'd accept a wig.'

As he was rattling on, Matt looked down at the tiled floor of the studio. The light from the setting sun was streaming through the window on to him but as he twisted round to look, he saw that what Constantin said was true: he cast no shadow.

'What an odd detail for a dream,' he thought.

But the Professor was urging him into the clothes. Matt shrugged and put them on. It was not a bad idea to go along with things in dreams, he found. But the clothes were weird – sort of velvet trousers and a ruffled shirt. There were black leather shoes too with big silver buckles. What on earth must he look like? Constantin rummaged in the cupboard in the wall and triumphantly pulled out a dusty black velvet hat. He held it out to Matt.

'There!' he said. 'Now you can pass for a Talian.'

*

Barbara was petrified. It took away almost all the pleasure she felt in wearing the glorious turquoise silk dress and matching mask. Her hair was elaborately dressed, with turquoise ribbon threaded through it, and ornamented with butterfly pins of diamond and sapphire.

She was sitting between the Duchessa's father, the Regent Rodolfo Rossi, and his new wife, Silvia, at a banqueting table in the Ducal palace. Senator Rossi was making a speech but Barbara was too nervous to concentrate on what he was saying or on eating any of the fine food on her plate.

'Her Grace, my daughter, is unfortunately unable to address you all today,' said Rodolfo. 'Regrettably she is indisposed by a sore throat and has lost her voice . . .'

Barbara coughed elegantly into a little lace handkerchief. How on earth had milady ever thought they would both get away with this deception?

'. . . but she has asked me to thank you for your presence here to celebrate her birthday – and indeed your *presents*, which you in your generosity have showered upon her.'

He cast his eyes towards an oak table laden with boxes and jars tied with satin ribbons of every colour, while the guests laughed at his little jest.

Barbara thought longingly of what the contents might be – the jewels and lace collars, the writing-cases and scented bath oils. If only they were really for her! But she knew that the real Duchessa did not care about belongings – perhaps because she was so wealthy she could afford anything she wanted. The only gifts that meant anything to her were the ones from her parents and her fiancé. Barbara had seen how delighted she was when she opened Luciano's present of earrings. She wondered if they were having a happy time together now; it must surely be better than what she was going through.

*

'And now,' said Constantin. 'You must have questions you want to ask me.'

'Not really,' said Matt. 'I mean, this is a dream, right?'

'Is that your first question?' said the Professor. 'Good. We have started with an easy one. No, it is not a dream. You are in Talia, in the city called Padavia, famous for its University. It's the second oldest in Talia, after the one in Bellona. And I am a professor at this University.'

'OK,' said Matt, playing along. 'And are we in the University now? I mean I thought we were in the Scriptorium or the Stamparium or whatever.'

'The Scriptorium is part of the University now,' said Constantin. 'It is all that remains of an old monastery next to the main university building. And it was suitable in size for my enterprise of a printing press. I like to think, too, that it has always been a place where books were produced. And on your visits here we shall say that you are one of my apprentices.'

Matt couldn't help pulling a face.

'You don't like books?' said Constantin. 'I see you have one in your hand.'

Matt looked again at the leather-bound book he had bought at Mortimer Goldsmith's antiques shop. It was strange how solid and real it felt in his hand, just the way it did when he was awake.

'I like this one,' he admitted. 'I don't know why though.'

'Because it spoke to you,' said Constantin. 'It is your talisman and it found you. I have been waiting for it to do so for some time.'

The strangest feeling was growing in Matt that this wasn't an ordinary dream. The leather-bound book could well have come from a time and place like this. That was it, he thought: he had made up this whole dream-world to explain to himself where the book belonged. It couldn't hurt to tell this imaginary man the truth.

'I'm not good with books,' he said. 'I . . . I have problems with reading.'

He felt a bit stupid, sitting in a scholar's room, overflowing with books, in a university, even if it was only a dream one, confessing that he wasn't good at reading. But the Professor wasn't fazed. He picked up a volume from his desk and held it out to Matt.

'Have a try,' he said. 'Things are often different in Talia.'

Matt took the book reluctantly. His heart sank as

he opened it. Lines of fuzzy black type filled the pages; it was just the sort of thing he wouldn't be able to read.

And then something miraculous happened. The words somehow formed in his mind and he found he was reading, quite easily, a rather dull book about weapons. He stopped and looked up at the Professor, who was smiling encouragingly at him.

'You see,' said Constantin. 'In Talia you can read.'

Chapter 3

First Impressions

The alarm on his mobile phone screeched at Matt at the usual time, followed five minutes later by the even shriller sound of his alarm clock. Both phone and clock were on his desk across the room from his bed, the only arrangement that worked to get him up in the morning. He groaned under the duvet then flung it aside, staggered over to the source of the noise and pressed buttons till it stopped. He looked longingly at his bed, still warm and enticing. It seemed only minutes since he had fallen into that deep sleep.

And there was the book; just seeing it brought the whole dream back. Constantin had told him he was a Stravagante – a traveller between worlds – but what was even more amazing, he had said that Matt wasn't the only one to find his way to Talia from Barnsbury

Comp. That wasn't so extraordinary for a dream – after all, Matt had seen Georgia and Nick only yesterday – but Constantin had also mentioned Sky, the boy with dreadlocks, and another boy, who had died and lived again in Talia.

Matt shook the last shreds of sleep out of his head. Maybe he was wrong to think he wasn't good at Arts subjects? If he put this dream down on paper, it would make a great story for Creative Writing. The Professor had told him he could get back to his own world any time he wanted, just by falling asleep with the book in his hand while thinking of home. His 'talisman' was what Constantin called the book.

'Every Stravagante has one,' he had said. 'It is his or her most valued possession and must be guarded with their life. There are enemies in Talia who want to find out the secrets of stravagation.'

Matt picked up a book from his desk. It was a Maths textbook with little writing in it so he couldn't tell if his reading was any better. He turned instead to his childhood books on the shelf. He had always kept copies of the books his mother read to him as a kid, even if he struggled to read novels himself. Now he took out *Tom's Midnight Garden*, an old favourite, hoping to read it as fluently as he had the book in Talia.

But it was no different from before. The words still got themselves all snarled up like tangled fishing-line. That glorious feeling of extracting meaning from them without trying, like swimming underwater or flying, had disappeared.

But how could I have imagined something I've never experienced, thought Matt. I didn't think you could do that in dreams.

'Time to get up!' yelled his mum up the stairs and Matt hurried to get to the bathroom before Harry; understanding the dream would have to wait.

Alfredo bustled about the house organising a dinner that he thought worthy of the Duchessa and roping Marco in to help cook and serve it. But Luciano and Arianna would hardly have noticed if he had provided bread and cheese and a glass of ale.

They had gone out to walk about the city, Arianna with her fisherman's cap back on, and it felt like the day when they had first met.

'You have to be my guide now, Luciano,' she said. 'I have never been to Padavia.'

'I don't know it that well myself,' said Luciano, who had to stop himself from holding her hand. 'I've only been here two weeks. It's not the same as when you explained Bellezza to me.'

'Not so different,' said Arianna. 'Although I loved the city, I didn't know it as well then as I do now. I lived on Torrone, remember. Bellezza was for high days and holidays.'

'And now?'

She fetched a deep sigh.

'Much the same. It seems as if a duchessa's days are all special in some way. There are state occasions, or sitting in Senate or Council, or meeting ambassadors or listening to citizens' grievances. There's never time for just . . . being. Well, you know how it is. You've seen me wearing five sets of clothes a day. How do you think you will bear it when we are married?'

'I'll just have to enjoy watching you undress five times a day,' said Luciano and she punched his arm just as if she had been a real male friend.

'You know what I mean,' she said. 'How much time will we have together on our own to talk like this? And do you think we'd ever be able to roam the streets the way we did when you were my father's apprentice and I was an island girl visiting her aunt?'

'Is that why you have come to Padavia?' asked Luciano.

'I wanted to have one last birthday when I could just be me,' said Arianna pensively. 'It's really hard to be Duchessa all the time.'

'Come on then,' said Luciano. 'Let's make the most of it. I can show you the basilica. It's not quite as grand as the Maddalena in Bellezza, but it's pretty impressive.'

He led her into the many-domed cathedral and neither of them noticed that they were being watched by a rather bedraggled-looking figure, dressed in what had once been a handsome blue velvet suit.

*

Silvia was watching the Duchessa no less intently. There was something not quite right; Arianna would not meet her eyes. What was she up to? The banquet had been a muted affair because of the Duchessa's indisposition but now that the guests were gathered on the colonnaded balcony overlooking the sea, there was the usual excitement about Rodolfo's fireworks.

They were launched from a raft in the lagoon while

the company watched and for a while the Duchessa seemed like her normal animated self, clapping each firework and set piece. The customary winged rams flew across the sky in a shower of silver and purple stars, peacocks opened and closed their magnificent tails, two giant spotted cats leapt above the lagoon. At the same moment a groom brought the Duchessa's own two African cats up on to the balcony.

'There is definitely something not right,' said Silvia to herself. The Duchessa seemed nervous of the cats, patting them distractedly; she would normally have flung her arms round their necks and kissed their furry faces, even when dressed in her most formal clothes. Everyone knew how the young Duchessa loved her cats, although they had been given to her by her greatest enemy.

Silvia was supposed to be Rodolfo's second wife; just a handful of people knew that she was his only wife and the previous Duchessa, Arianna's mother. So in public she couldn't behave towards Arianna with anything more than the concern appropriate for a new stepmother. But she itched to get her on her own and put her to the test.

Rodolfo made his way back to the Ducal Palace, pleased with his display but worried about his daughter; perhaps it was just her illness but she really hadn't seemed herself this evening. He said as much to his wife, as soon as the guests had dispersed and Arianna had gone to bed.

'That's because she wasn't,' said Silvia tartly.

'Wasn't?'

'Herself. I had been suspicious ever since her maid told us about the sore throat yesterday, but when she was nervous of the great cats then I knew something was amiss. I made her look at me when she said goodnight.'

'And?'

'And what looked back at me were the brown eyes of the maid, not the violet ones of our daughter.'

'So,' said Rodolfo. 'She used a double. Did you not say anything?'

'What good would it have been to chastise the maid, who is probably terrified? Do you suppose the deception was her idea? No, we shall wait till Arianna returns.'

'And where do you think she will return from?'

'It does not take a magician to divine that, surely?' said Silvia, suddenly weary.

Rodolfo took her hand. 'She is with Luciano.' He felt as rejected as Silvia did. He had been reunited with his undreamt-of daughter for only two years and in all that time he had never been the most important man in her life. It still pained him to think of how he had missed her entire childhood, when she might have turned first to him for protection and love.

All he said was, 'She didn't see the fireworks.'

But Silvia squeezed his hand in sympathy for more than pyrotechnics.

'It's natural,' she said. 'But so very, very dangerous.'

*

Beatrice di Chimici was lonely in the vast palace in Giglia where she lived with her oldest brother Fabrizio and his wife. It was all so different from what had been planned. Before the weddings – and the murders that would for ever be linked with them – she had been going to live with her father Niccolò, the old Grand Duke. It would have been in the same great palace, taken from the Nucci as a penalty for planning the massacre, but her life would have been so much more vivid and rewarding. Ever since her father had been killed in the duel in the palace gardens, Princess Beatrice's life had felt drained of colour.

The new Grand Duke was very close to insanity. Along with the title, he had inherited only six months ago a vast empire of wealth and influence and a position as head of the most important family in Talia. But he was only twenty-three and the weight of his responsibilities was almost too much for him. Although he was so recently married, memories of his wedding day were blighted by the massacre that had included the murder of his brother Carlo, and by early next year he hoped to be a father. The di Chimici dynasty must carry on.

But Fabrizio was still in pain from the wounds he had sustained at the wedding. Carlo, who should have been living in the Ducal Palace across the river and bustling back and forth between the two homes along the special elevated corridor that Niccolò had built, was dead. And Gaetano seemed so far away, living in the old di Chimici palace, which had been home to all of them less than a year ago.

After the duel, Beatrice had wanted to go and live with Gaetano and his new wife Francesca in the old palace but Fabrizio wouldn't hear of it.

'I need you, Bice,' he had said. 'And so does Caterina.'

And Beatrice had always responded to her family's

needs. Her brother's plea carried more weight with her than if he had ordered her to stay with them. But ever since the terrible days after the wedding when she had nursed her two surviving brothers and Filippo Nucci as they recovered from their wounds, Beatrice had been restless.

All her life, she had been proud to be a di Chimici, a member of the most important and wealthy family in all Talia. She was a born princess and lived with the confidence and authority that her background brought with it. Fine clothes and jewels, the best to eat and drink that Giglia could afford, the obedience of servants and deference of citizens: all these had seemed to be hers by right.

But that had all changed in a few minutes in the Church of the Annunciation six months ago. It was all very well to know that a di Chimici cousin had killed a Nucci in Giglia a generation earlier. It was even possible for her sometimes to forget that young Davide Nucci had been stabbed and it was rumoured that her brother Carlo had wielded the dagger. But however much she might have tried to hide from the realities of bloody inter-family feuds, there was no escaping the truth in the Church of the Annunciation.

Carlo dead. Camillo Nucci dead. Fabrizio and Gaetano in mortal danger. Other Nucci and di Chimici dead or wounded. And all that before her eyes, in a nightmare of shouting and drawn weapons, swords flashing through the air, daggers stabbing. Beatrice thought she would never forget the sight of four brides in blood-soaked wedding finery.

And then the flood in the city and the slow nursing back to health of three young men, two she loved and one who was supposed to be her mortal enemy. That was when she had discovered that her feelings for the three were not so different. And as soon as he was well enough, Filippo Nucci had been exiled to Classe, forbidden ever to return to Giglia. She would never see him again.

She could no longer see herself or her family in the same light as before. Carlo had probably killed young Davide before the weddings and she was sure her father had committed or at least ordered murders. Hadn't he wanted to kill all the remaining Nucci and let Filippo die of his wounds? Those terrible scenes of six months before had taught Beatrice how fragile and vulnerable human flesh was; nothing was worth the deaths and wounds she had seen – not even the honour of the di Chimici. These ideas stayed with the Princess, haunting her dreams, and the magnificent new palace did nothing to dispel them.

Matt's day at school seemed as if it would never end. He was tired and confused and more impatient with his reading problems than he had been for years. He just wanted to leave them all behind him and move forward the way he had in his dream. He was distant with Ayesha at break and saw that he had hurt her. But it was as if he was moving in a bubble, like a hamster in a plastic ball, and couldn't reach out to her.

He looked curiously at the students Constantin had told him were Stravaganti – Sky, with the locks, Nick, the fencer, and Georgia, the girl with the stripey hair. The professor hadn't said anything about Alice, Sky's blonde girlfriend but she was probably one too. Matt caught himself thinking that what he had dreamed was real but that was ridiculous. Yet the four students were regarding him just as curiously.

At the end of school, he found them waiting for him at the gate.

'You OK, Matt?' asked Nick.

'You look tired,' said Georgia.

'Bad night?' added Sky.

'Whoa,' said Matt. 'What is this? The Sleep Police?' But he had the strangest feeling they knew exactly what had happened last night.

'Really,' said Georgia. 'Did you have . . . a sort of weird dream?'

They were all looking at him intently, even Alice. At that moment, Ayesha came out. Normally he would have walked her home but she hesitated when she saw him talking to a group of people she didn't know.

In that instant, Nick asked eagerly, 'Did you go to Talia?' and Matt knew he had to talk to them some more. He turned away from Ayesha and saw out of the corner of his eye that she was leaving, her head ducked down as if she was upset.

'Let's go and get a coffee,' he said.

They moved off towards Café@anytime, the only independent coffee shop in their bit of Islington. It was a popular hang-out with Barnsbury students. Ordering their drinks and finding a table big enough for five covered up what might have been an embarrassing silence. But once they were all served they couldn't avoid the subject that had brought them together.

'How did you know I dreamed about Talia?'

demanded Matt suddenly.

'Because it wasn't a dream,' said Nick. 'You didn't dream it – you really went there.'

'But how did you . . . ?' Matt stopped, seeing four pairs of eyes looking at him with identical anticipation. 'You've been there, haven't you, all of you?'

They all nodded but quiet Alice said, 'Only once. I went to prove to myself that was what the others were doing. I wouldn't have believed it if I hadn't seen it.'

'That book you bought from Mortimer is your talisman, isn't it?' asked Georgia. 'He told us after you'd gone that it came from the same place as mine.'

'Talia?' asked Matt.

'Originally, yes, but Mortimer doesn't know that. He thinks it came from an old woman's house near the school.'

'The one I live in now,' said Sky.

'Where did you go? What city?' asked Nick.

'Pad . . . something,' said Matt.

'Padavia,' said Georgia. 'That's where Luciano was going to university. Did you see him?'

Nick was looking at her strangely.

Matt shook his head. 'I *was* in a university. But the only person I met was called Professor Constantin.'

'Is he your Stravagante?' asked Sky.

'I guess so,' said Matt, slowly eating cappuccino foam off his spoon. 'He said he was *a* Stravagante – and he said I was one too.'

'Then you are,' said Nick. He looked upset.

'Who was yours?' asked Matt, not really believing that he was going along with all this.

Nick looked really unhappy now. 'I didn't have one of my own,' he said. 'I had to share Sky's. I'm not like the rest of you. I stravagated here *from* Talia and never went back – except as a visitor.'

Matt stared at him. 'You're Talian? Like an alien or something?'

'Not any more,' said Georgia firmly, putting her arm round Nick. 'He belongs here now.'

'But I am really Prince Falco di Chimici,' said Nick, straightening his back and looking every inch a noble. 'I was born in Giglia and my father was Grand Duke of all Tuschia.' Then he slumped. 'Until I killed him,' he said flatly.

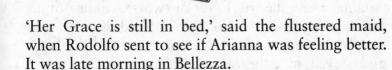

'Her Grace is still in bed,' said the flustered maid, when Rodolfo sent to see if Arianna was feeling better. It was late morning in Bellezza.

'Does that mean she is back from Padavia?' said Rodolfo. 'Or that she is still away and there is a bolster in her bed?'

He didn't seem angry but Barbara knew that he was often most dangerous when most quiet. He seldom raised his voice but she was nonetheless terrified of him. And what was she to do now, if he knew all about her mistress's absence? That must mean he knew it had been her at the banquet last night.

'Did you enjoy the fireworks?' he asked kindly and she burst into tears.

'Don't tease the girl, Rodolfo,' said his wife Silvia.

Barbara was, perhaps unwisely, not nearly so afraid of Signora Rossi and looked to her for guidance.

'You can tell us,' said Silvia. 'My husband has great powers of divination, as I'm sure you know. You cannot expect that he would not have seen through your little deception.'

This was not strictly speaking what had happened but it suited Silvia's purposes for the maid to be less nervous of her than of the Senator.

'Madama,' said the unhappy girl. 'I believe that Her Grace has just returned.'

'Then please tell her we will wait upon her in her parlour in half an hour,' said Rodolfo. 'And please attend on her yourself.'

*

Arianna knew she was in for the worst scolding of her life. It was worse than the time she had disobeyed the people she thought were her parents – and the law – and stayed in Bellezza overnight on the Forbidden Day. Then she had nearly lost her life. But the person who had saved her was her real mother, Silvia, who was now waiting for her explanation of why she had run away to Padavia, instead of attending her birthday celebrations.

But it had been worth it, however grave Rodolfo might look, whatever tongue-lashing Silvia might give her. She had been with Luciano and that was the most important thing. Arianna's cheeks were glowing and her eyes sparkling, in spite of the hideously early start she had made in Padavia, to get back in time to get the Bellezza ferry from the mainland. She entered her parlour, freshly dressed in green silk, with her head held high.

'Good day,' said Silvia icily. 'How is your throat today?'

'Quite recovered, thank you,' said Arianna more calmly than she felt. 'You may leave us, Barbara.'

'No,' said Rodolfo. 'She must stay.'

'Let us drop this charade,' said Silvia. 'You know, as we do, that the girl impersonated you at your birthday celebrations, while you were in Padavia with Luciano.'

Arianna sat down and indicated to the maid to take a seat too. Barbara perched awkwardly on the edge of a spindly chair; she was not used to sitting in the company of nobles.

'That is so,' Arianna said.

'That was an incredibly dangerous thing to do,' said Rodolfo.

'I know,' said Arianna. 'And stupid, foolish, selfish, careless – all the other things you are both going to say to me. But I had to go there. You can say whatever you like but you won't make me regret it.'

'Or stop you from doing it again,' said Rodolfo. 'So next time we must make sure that the deception is better planned.'

Chapter 4

Double Danger

Matt got through his homework as quickly as he could that night. He had tried to phone Ayesha about ten times but her mobile went straight to voicemail every time; he left only two messages.

It was hard to concentrate on Maths problems and web design with his love life in suspense and the thought hanging over him that he might stravagate again that night, without even knowing what that really meant.

He had decided that if the dream happened again, he would believe that it was real, that he really had travelled in time and space to another world, where Italy was just a bit different.

'Mum,' he asked casually when he'd finished the homework. 'Have we got an atlas?'

'Of course,' said Jan, surprised. 'It's in the dining room. Right-hand bookcase, bottom shelf.'

She always knew exactly where every single book was in the house. Matt found it straight away and spread the big atlas out on the dining table. There was a full, two-page spread of Italy, sticking its high-heeled and booted leg out into the Mediterranean. He pored over it, completely unsure where he'd been in the other Italy everyone called Talia. But there was only one place marked that began 'Pad' and that was Padua. It was on the mainland, near Venice.

'You don't do Geography,' said Harry accusingly from the doorway.

'I know I don't,' said Matt, stung. 'But there's no reason I shouldn't look at a map if I want, is there? It's a free country.'

Harry shrugged. 'That's debatable.'

Most of the time Matt and Harry got on reasonably well but every so often, when his little brother was being deliberately clever, Matt wanted to strangle him.

'Piss off,' he said now, turning back to his map.

'Italy?' said Harry, looking over his shoulder.

'Yeah, I'm thinking of taking Ayesha there next summer when the exams are over,' said Matt, rather pleased with this idea.

Harry looked at him as if he'd suggested a trip to the moon. 'But that's more than nine months away. How do you know you'll even be together by then?'

Now Matt thought he really would like to strangle his brother.

'Why shouldn't we be?' he said irritably. 'Do you know something I don't?'

'No,' said Harry. 'I was just *saying*.'

'Well don't. Don't say anything at all unless you've got something worth saying.'

Matt clapped the atlas shut and put it back on the shelf and went to his room in a foul mood. He went over to the computer and Googled 'Padua' just to take his mind off Ayesha. The Wikipedia entry told him that the city was called 'Padova' in Italian but the Latin name had been 'Patavia', which did sound a lot like Padavia. It was forty kilometres west of Venice.

The article was too long and hard for him to read it all but he noticed there was a link to another one about the University of Padua. He just about managed to read that it was founded in 1222 and was the second oldest university in Italy but there was too much text to scroll through to see if it had a Scriptorium. Matt would have searched under Scriptorium too, but he wasn't sure how to spell it and he still felt very tired from his disturbed night.

Arianna couldn't believe her ears. 'You're not angry?' she said.

'On the contrary,' said Rodolfo. 'I don't know when I was last angrier. But it is obvious that your need to be with Luciano is going to override every other consideration. So if you have to make these trips to Padavia, we must be sure that they are done as safely as possible.'

Silvia was as surprised as Arianna; she hadn't expected Rodolfo to be so understanding.

'First,' continued Rodolfo, 'we must establish that

Barbara here willingly impersonated you and would be prepared to do so again.'

He turned to the maid, who was very looking uncomfortable.

'Did my daughter explain the dangers to you?' he asked.

'There wasn't much need of that,' said Silvia. 'The last time she impersonated Arianna, she nearly died.'

Arianna suddenly felt guilt-stricken. 'It was Barbara who thought of the danger to me. She insisted that I take her young man Marco with me.'

Rodolfo strode to the door and summoned the footman who was on duty outside it.

'Are you Marco?' the women heard him ask. 'No? Then go and fetch him here immediately.'

'Please don't punish him,' said Barbara. 'He only did it because I asked him.'

'Punish him?' said Rodolfo, surprised. 'I intend to reward him, and you, for taking such good care of my daughter between you. If these deceptions are to continue, she will need a well-armed bodyguard to accompany her.'

Marco was shown into the room, still brushing the crumbs of his hasty late breakfast from his livery. He looked as nervous as his fiancée. A glance at the people in the room told him that their escapade had been discovered. He moved closer to Barbara.

'It's all right, Marco,' said Arianna. 'No one is angry with you for accompanying me to Padavia.'

'Indeed,' said Silvia. 'We are grateful to you for your protection of the Duchessa.'

'Did you go armed?' asked the Regent.

'Just a knife, my lord,' admitted Marco. 'But I am

useful with my fists too.'

'I am sure you know what happened in the Church of the Annunciation in Giglia,' said Rodolfo. 'When Barbara last wore a dress designed for the Duchessa.'

Marco said nothing but his hands clenched at his sides.

'The sort of people who would attack a woman for political reasons would not be deterred by fists and an ordinary knife,' said Rodolfo. 'The Duchessa herself had to kill an attacker in the church with her own Merlino-blade.'

'I know, my lord,' said Marco. 'I have heard Her Grace was very brave.'

There was a pause while all of them thought about that terrible day. Barbara was quite white and her hand went involuntarily to the wound in her breast.

'If Barbara is willing,' said Rodolfo, 'the Duchessa would like to travel in disguise to Padavia every few weeks.' He looked at Arianna and she gave him a little nod. 'I should like you to go with her, properly armed with your own Merlino-blade and a sword, both of which I shall furnish you with. But in the meantime, whenever your other duties allow, you must have lessons in how to use them. Is Guido Parola still in Bellezza?' he suddenly asked his wife.

'Yes,' said Silvia. 'He is not going to university in Fortezza until the New Year. He had some business with his brother to settle first here in the city.'

'Then send for him, if you will, my dear,' said Rodolfo. 'Impress upon him the need for secrecy and put young Marco in his hands for lessons in the use of weapons. In some ways it might be better to send one of the palace guards to Padavia with the Duchessa, but I would like to keep this secret known to as few people as possible.'

He paced the length of the small room.

'A duchessa is never more at risk than when she uses a substitute and her enemy knows it,' he said. 'It was in this very room that I saw Arianna's mother in a state of shock after Cavaliere Luciano saved her from an attempt on her life, while another woman posed as Duchessa.'

He did not say that the would-be assassin had been the same Guido Parola who would train Marco. Or that Arianna's mother was again in this room with him. Neither Barbara nor Marco knew that the previous Duchessa had survived the second attempt on her life and now lived as Rodolfo's second wife.

'But because we must not expose Barbara to any unnecessary risk,' he went on, 'I would also suggest that these impersonations never take place again on days when there are formal engagements. We don't want the palace too full of people at such times.'

'And these young people must be rewarded for their extra duties,' said Silvia.

'Indeed,' said Rodolfo. He went to a wooden chest on a table near the window and took out a velvet bag that chinked. He handed it to Barbara. 'This is for you both, for what you did yesterday. I believe you are soon to be married? Perhaps this will be useful towards your marriage expenses. There will be as much again for any further occasions when the Duchessa visits Padavia in disguise. But you must think carefully before you accept. Every such expedition puts you both in danger.'

When Matt found himself in the Scriptorium again, he was already in his Talian clothes. But he was in Constantin's 'studio' and on his own. Cautiously, he opened the door. Work in the Scriptorium was in full swing, with all the machines being used. Something about the quality of the light made him think it was earlier in the day than the last time, perhaps because he had fallen asleep so much earlier in his own world.

In spite of his disguise, Matt felt very exposed. He didn't know a soul in Padavia, except for the man called Constantin. He plucked up courage to ask one of the burly men operating a printing press if he knew where the Professor was.

'Lecturing,' said the man briefly. 'Won't be back for an hour or so.'

Matt wandered over to the main door; no one took the slightest notice of him. He pulled the dusty velvet hat over his forehead and pushed open the door to the street. And stepped out into the sixteenth century.

The streets were cobbled, the houses built close together, with lines of washing strung across the streets from one side to the other. The roofs were of terracotta tiles and the bright blue sky convinced him that he was indeed in a country well south of England.

There were no cars or buses but Matt could see there had been horses passing by and as he looked around him a fine-looking horse came trotting up. A young man about his own age swung lightly down from the saddle and tied the horse's reins to a wooden post – just like the cowboys in every Western Matt had seen.

But this was no cowboy. He wore elegant clothes and had long black curly hair tied back with a velvet ribbon. If Matt had met him in his own world, he would have thought he was a bit girly, but in Padavia, the horseman looked confident and at home. In spite of his easy grace and slight build, he seemed as if he could take care of himself. And he had a wicked-looking dagger in his belt.

Matt expected him to walk past and go about whatever his business was but, instead, he stopped and looked closely at him. Too late Matt realised he had forgotten about not having a shadow.

The newcomer grabbed his arm and pulled him back into the shade of a nearby building.

'Careful,' he said. 'You don't want just anyone to know you are a Stravagante.'

Matt had the strangest feeling that he knew this boy, at least by sight, but he couldn't think where he could have seen him before.

'Matteo?' said the boy. 'Matt? Professor Constantin asked me to look out for you.'

'But how did you . . . ?' Matt began, and then said, 'Oh I get it, the shadow thing. I thought for a minute we knew each other.'

'Not exactly – it's a bit complicated. I'm Luciano, sometimes called Cavaliere Crinamorte. I'm at university here, but my home is in Bellezza.'

Matt stared at him even harder.

'You're the one Constantin told me about – the boy from my school, who . . .'

'Died? Yes, that's me,' said Luciano. 'It's a long

story. Look, Constantin's tied up in a lecture. Why don't we go for a drink?'

He led Matt along the street and out into a square, carefully keeping to the shade. They stopped outside what looked like an ordinary house but it had a sign outside painted with the image of a black horse. Luciano ducked in under the lintel and Matt, who was several inches taller, had to stoop even more.

Inside was dark and a bit smoky from the log fire, even though it was broad daylight outside. No need to worry about shadows inside the Black Horse. Matt sat down at a crude wooden table and Luciano bought them tankards of a thin ale, which made him pull a face at first but which became more palatable with every mouthful.

'Be careful,' said Luciano, grinning. 'It's got more of a kick than you'd think.'

'It seems to be your job to tell me to be careful,' said Matt.

'That's right,' said Luciano. 'Mine and Constantin's. A new Stravagante is always a bit like a newborn foal in Talia. We old hands have to watch over you till you're up on your feet and not too wobbly.'

Even if Matt hadn't already decided to believe in Talia if he went back there a second time, meeting Luciano would have convinced him. He had remembered where he had seen him now. When Harry played trumpet in the school orchestra at Barnsbury, the family always went to hear his concerts. This Luciano had been a violinist and the son of one of Jan's best friends. Matt could just remember the school assembly when the Head had announced that Lucien Mulholland had died. It was about three years before.

'How old are you?' he suddenly asked.

'Nearly eighteen,' said Luciano. 'You?'

'Seventeen – just. But you've been here three years, haven't you? I thought you'd be older.'

'There was a lurch in time in your world about a year ago here,' said Luciano. 'It happened when Falco translated. You know who he is?'

'Nick Duke,' said Matt. 'He told me he killed his father.'

Luciano sighed. 'Actually, it was me. But there's a lot to tell you,' he said. 'I'd better get us another drink.

*

Enrico Poggi was in a sorry state. He hadn't had more than some casual work as an ostler over the last six months and his money had run out. He had only himself to blame, in a sense, since he had killed the golden goose when he gave Luciano the poisoned foil in the duel with Niccolò di Chimici. That act of revenge against his then employer had put paid to any more work for the di Chimici family.

So he had been drifting from city to city, avoiding ones where the di Chimici ruled. Padavia was one such independent city-state, though it had a close relationship with Bellezza. And Enrico still felt drawn to Bellezza, even though it would have been dangerous for him to go back there. Independent of the di Chimici it might be, but he had killed its ruler, the old Duchessa.

At least, he had been paid to do it and had believed he *had* done it – until six months ago, in the course of the duel, he had seen her alive and well. That was the moment he realised that the woman he had killed had been his own fiancée, Giuliana, who had been impersonating the Duchessa in her glass-lined audience chamber.

Enrico now had some very cheap lodgings in the south of Padavia, near the unhealthy great swamp that had drowned the old Reman amphitheatre. He had been idling through the city the day before when he had spotted Luciano going into the basilica with a peasant boy. A few enquiries told him that the black-haired Bellezzan was now studying at the University. But no one knew who the other boy was; he was a stranger in Padavia.

Luciano had been friends with peasants before – there were those two stable-boys in Remora, for instance – and this was probably another one of those. Enrico was tossing up whether to make himself known to the Bellezzan. On the debit side, Luciano would remember:

Enrico had kidnapped him in Bellezza.

He had killed the Duchessa, mother of Luciano's girlfriend, Arianna. (Or tried to.)

He had worked for the di Chimici and against the Stravaganti in Bellezza, Remora and Giglia.

He had kidnapped Luciano's friend Cesare in Remora.

He had stolen the flying horse.

He had helped Carlo di Chimici kill Davide Nucci in Giglia (though perhaps Luciano didn't know that?).

He had got hold of the poison to smear on the foils, in order for the Grand Duke to kill Luciano.

It was quite a list. On the other hand, on the plus

side was a really big favour. He had saved Luciano from being killed and enabled him to kill the Grand Duke. Would that count enough against his other crimes? Enrico was seriously thinking of throwing in his lot with the Stravaganti, even though he didn't know quite what they were or what they could do.

*

It was a lot for Matt to get his head round and it took many mugs of ale for Luciano to finish the explanations. By the time they left the Black Horse to find Constantin, Matt was as unsteady on his feet as the newborn foal Luciano had compared him to. The older boy seemed to hold his liquor better, in spite of his slighter frame. They stopped outside the Scriptorium and Luciano retrieved his horse.

'I've got lectures to go to myself now,' he said, 'but you can find me in the Refectory at lunchtime.'

'Pity I can't just text you,' said Matt.

'You have to forget all about the twenty-first century when you're in Talia,' said Luciano, smiling. 'You'll get used to the slower pace quite soon. But don't take it for granted. There are times when things can move quite fast in Talia too.' He shuddered, thinking of the bloody quarter of an hour in Giglia six months before.

He vaulted back up on to the horse and waved as he left. Matt let himself back into the Scriptorium, where he was relieved to see Constantin checking a printed page.

'Ah, Matteo,' he said, greeting him warmly. 'Everyone! This is Matteo Bosco, my new apprentice.

He knows nothing at all about printing, so we'll all have to teach him.'

There was a round of applause and Matt felt absurdly pleased. He had been a bit alarmed by Constantin's public announcement. He had so much trouble with getting letters round the right way that he didn't think he'd be very good at the reversed bits of movable type. Then he remembered that he had been able to read easily the last time he was in Talia.

The men had gone back to their work and Constantin clapped his arm round Matt's broad shoulders.

'Come this way,' he said. 'There's something I want to show you.'

He led Matt to the far end of the room and looked quickly round before putting his hand into a cupboard and pulling a switch. The cupboard swung open noiselessly and the two stepped through into a hidden room. There were no windows and the Professor had to light several candles before Matt could see anything. And then he was a bit disappointed. After the dramatic hidden entrance, all it contained was one more wooden printing press and the other paraphernalia, with no one working at it.

Professor Constantin looked at him expectantly.

'This,' he said proudly, 'is my Secret Scriptorium.'

Chapter 5

Spellbound

'Er,' said Matt. 'What's secret about it?'

'This is where I print the books that are not offic-
ially published by the University,' said Constantin.
'That one you are still holding, for example.'

Matt looked at his talisman.

'What is it?' he asked. 'Why is it a secret?'

'It's what I think you'd call a book of spells,' said
Constantin. 'And such things are dangerous in Talia at
present.'

I should never have listened to all those Harry
Potter tapes when I was a kid, thought Matt. Books of
spells – what next? Was Constantin going to pull out a
wand and reveal himself as a powerful wizard?

But he found himself unwinding the leather straps
round his book, curious to see if he could read it in

Padavia. The fuzzy black type stared back at him, still impenetrable.

'May I?' asked Constantin. He took the book, opened it at random and intoned:

'"*Remedium contra fascinum, sive oculum malum.*" That's old Talic for "Cure for the evil eye". Or rather the results of it.'

'What is it?' asked Matt.

'The cure? Oh, a vessel of water placed on the forehead of the victim. Pour in oil and if it forms into the shape of an eye, then he really has experienced the Jettatura – the evil eye. You can then, as it were, 'blind' the eye with grains of salt and that takes the curse off.'

'No,' said Matt, a bit thrown by the seriousness with which the Professor had given the explanation. 'What I meant was – what *is* the evil eye?'

'You don't have it in Anglia?' said Constantin, surprised. 'It's a kind of negative energy. Some people have the power to curse crops or animals or other people just by looking at them.'

'Cool!' said Matt. He found himself immediately thinking of Jago Jones.

'You approve?' said Constantin.

'Well, it could be useful, I suppose.'

'You can't make yourself have it, Matteo. You either have the power or you don't.'

'But how do you know if you've got it?'

'You find out by accident, usually, when you cast an envious – or even an admiring look – at something or someone and then crops die or people get sick. Then you have to choose.'

'Choose?'

'Whether you will learn the discipline to control it. Or whether you will use it to curse. Either way you have power.'

Matt was silent, thinking about different kinds of power. He knew he was supposed to think the better kind was not using the evil eye but he was still attracted by the thought of zapping people. One person.

'So is my book full of cures?'

'Yes. And curses. Blessings too, of course. Potions, incantations, enchantments, hexes, charms – spells, in fact.'

'So is there magic here in Talia?' asked Matt, feeling foolish as he did so.

'Some people call it that,' said Constantin. 'I think it's time I told you about the di Chimici.'

*

Grand Duke Fabrizio was getting nowhere in tracking down Luciano. He was pretty sure that he was not in Giglia. Fabrizio had sent soldiers to scour every palace, house, shop, bottega, church, farm and monastery in the city. No one knew anything of the young Bellezzan's whereabouts and in the end, Fabrizio had to accept that he had escaped.

The arrest warrant was valid throughout Tuschia, so he had sent messengers to Moresco, Fortezza and Remora, where other members of his family ruled. If Luciano had left the region, he would be arrested if he ever set foot back inside di Chimici territory in the north.

But that wasn't enough for Fabrizio. He also sent

spies to Bellezza to find out what they could there about the black-haired Cavaliere.

The only thing that had happened to make him take his mind off vengeance for his father's death was an unexpected visit from Caterina. She had come to him in his office in the Palazzo Ducale one day in early August. He was surprised when a footman announced the Grand Duchessa; she had not entered the palazzo since the celebrations in the week before their wedding. And why would she do so when she could talk to him at any time in their own palace?

It had taken his breath away to see her in this unaccustomed setting and to realise afresh how beautiful she was. It was a bright summer's day and she had been more simply dressed than befitted her rank but he couldn't regret it when he saw how blooming she looked – her hair a shining aureole and her face glowing like a country girl's. Only the expensive cut of her pale blue dress and the priceless necklace of pearls had marked her out as a ruler's wife.

'Rizio,' she said fondly, as soon as the footman had left. 'Must you stay indoors on such a day? Would you not like to walk back to the palace with me and stroll in the grounds? It seems hard to have gardens that people come from all over Talia to admire and yet never walk in them ourselves.'

'Did you walk here alone to see me?' he had asked, pulling her on to his lap and winding one of her gold curls round his finger.

'No,' she sighed. 'I had a guard with me. He's waiting outside. And we came across the corridor, not through the streets. I know you don't like me to go out on my own but I'd much rather walk with you than have a guard for company.'

'I'm glad you are being careful,' he said. 'No di Chimici is safe any more, not even in our own city.'

'So will you come?' she said, snuggling her head under his chin.

Fabrizio had inhaled the scent of her hair – honeysuckle and something muskier that reminded him of the pharmacy at Saint-Mary-among-the-Vines. He had more diplomatic and economic business left to do than he could bear to think of but he was also young and in love. What was the point of being Grand Duke if he couldn't sometimes ignore his duties and go for a walk in his own gardens with his lovely wife?

The guard walked at a discreet distance behind the couple as they had made their way back through Gabassi's corridor to the Nucci palace. And there, among the scented pines Caterina told him she was carrying a di Chimici heir.

Fabrizio had felt the pressure round his heart lift and his blood fizz like a bottle of prosecco. He lifted Caterina up and swung her around but very gently.

'Thank you,' he said. 'It will be a boy, won't it? Our little prince.'

'I hope so, if it will make you happy, Rizio,' she had replied. 'But if this one isn't a prince then we'll just have to make another. And princesses can be very nice too, don't you think?'

'Very – especially if they turn out as beautiful as their mother,' he said.

But Caterina prayed every night to have a son; she felt it was the only thing that would bring back the cousin she had married.

By the time Matt left for the Refectory, his head was whirling with more facts than he could cope with about Talia, the di Chimici family and a mysterious Doctor Dethridge who was due in Padavia in a few days. He felt relieved to see Luciano already sitting at a long wooden table with two pewter platters piled with bread, meat and tomatoes. He was reassured to see that Talian food was recognisable.

'How does this work?' he asked. 'Am I eating a second lunch in the middle of the night? I'm going to have to work out extra hard if I keep coming to Talia.'

Luciano shrugged. 'I don't know,' he said. 'But it's probably a good thing, because it gives you extra fuel and you will feel tired if you stravagate every night.'

He passed Matt a goblet of wine. 'You'd better drink this. The water isn't safe. You know that we are living over four hundred years behind your time here?'

'Constantin tried to explain it to me,' said Matt, sipping the wine cautiously and finding he rather liked it. He looked round at the other students all wearing black robes like Luciano. Many carried swords or daggers at their belts. 'It's a bit different from Barnsbury cafeteria, isn't it?'

'Not really. The biggest difference is that there are no female students.' Luciano smiled as if at a private thought. 'Apart from that, if you look past the clothes, they're just as loud and they talk about much the same things.'

'I don't get why I'm here,' said Matt suddenly. 'I mean it's cool, it's a good adventure. But why bring someone like me to a place that's all about learning and books and words? Constantin told me that Talians even call Padavia the City of Words. So why didn't the talisman choose someone – well, someone more into words and language?' Someone like Jago, he thought.

'It doesn't work like that,' said Luciano seriously. 'I was chosen because I was really ill. Georgia wasn't ill but she was miserable – being bullied by her stepbrother Russell. And Sky was just ground down by years of looking after his sick mother. The only thing we had in common – and I'm guessing we have in common with you too – is that we were all unhappy.'

There was an awkward silence. Then Matt decided he had nothing to lose. If everything he had been told was true, then this boy was dead in his own world and could not reveal Matt's secret.

'I'm dyslexic,' he said. 'Not just a mild case – severely dyslexic. I have to have computers and special programs just to do my schoolwork. And I have this really clever – and beautiful – girlfriend who's going to go to university and be a top lawyer. And . . . I'm terrified of losing her,' he finished simply.

'Well,' said Luciano. 'I can see why you're wondering about stravagating to a city where words are everything. But maybe that's exactly why. Maybe being here will cure you.'

'I did read a bit of one of Constantin's books quite easily,' said Matt. 'But it hasn't made it any better back home.'

'I had an illness,' said Luciano. 'One that never followed me here. Perhaps it's the same with dyslexia – though that isn't an illness, is it?'

Matt suddenly felt terrible. Luciano's problem had

been cancer and it had killed him in his own world. And here was Matt, strong and healthy in both worlds, whingeing because he was a poor reader and feared losing his girlfriend.

'No, not exactly,' he said. 'I'm sorry. It must seem a pretty lame reason for being unhappy compared with what you went through.'

'It's OK,' said Luciano. 'I don't think the reason matters. I think that the talismans just fall into the hands of people who are sad; it somehow makes them more receptive to what's needed here in Talia.'

'And what *is* that?'

'It's different every time,' said Luciano. 'But it's always somehow connected with the di Chimici.'

'Yeah, Constantin told me a bit about them,' said Matt. 'They've made some new laws about magic. God, I feel stupid even saying that.'

'I know,' said Luciano, grinning. 'I used to feel that. But the very fact that you're here means you've got to believe it. Still, I didn't know about the new laws. That must be why Constantin took your talisman to your world.'

Matt noticed he didn't say 'our world'.

'But there aren't any di Chimici in this city, are there?' he asked.

'No, not yet,' said Luciano. 'That's why my people thought I'd be safe here.' His hand moved involuntarily to his dagger.

*

The messenger in Giglian livery cantered into the city through the Western Gate and slowed only to ask directions to the Governor's house. His steaming horse took him to the great Palace of Justice that dominated a square in the centre of the city. But the Governor was not there.

Messer Antonio was the elected ruler of Padavia and went about his work as if he were a carpenter or baker. In fact in his private life before he went into politics he had been a blacksmith. He still lived in a modest house, which the di Chimici rulers of other city-states might have sneered at. The only difference between his old lifestyle and the new was that his present house was closer to the main square.

The Giglian messenger left his horse in the palace stables and set off on foot to find Messer Antonio. He passed an old Reman monument that looked like a tomb on legs and carried an inscription in old Talic. It was a strange city, he thought. Not many grand buildings and statues like his own Giglia but full of curiosities like this. He couldn't understand the Governor living in an ordinary house, though. The great Nucci palace, which the young Grand Duke inhabited, was much more his idea of a fitting home for a ruler.

Antonio was wrestling with laws on carriage taxes when the messenger was shown in. He looked up in relief, till he recognised the livery.

'Honoured sir,' began the envoy, sweeping off his plumed hat and bowing low. 'I bring greetings from His Grace the Grand Duke of all Tuschia.'

'Sit down man, do,' said Antonio testily. 'There's no need for all that flowery stuff. You come from Fabrizio di Chimici, I can see that. How about a cup of ale?'

The messenger, thrown off his script, sat on a plain

wooden stool and nodded. He had never been received so unceremoniously.

'What's afoot in your city, then, lad?' asked Antonio, when the ale had been brought.

'Er, my master is well and trusts that you are too?' he began hesitantly.

'Yes, yes, fine well,' said Antonio. 'As are my wife and daughters. And the Grand Duchess?'

'She expects an heir,' said the messenger, glad to get one of his pieces of information out.'

'Then let us drink a health to the Grand Duchess and her son if it so be,' said Antonio. 'I have had only girls myself but have never had cause to regret that. Is this what you rode here to tell me?'

'Not that alone,' said the messenger, relaxing under the influence of Antonio's strong ale. 'The Grand Duke is concerned that the young man from Bellezza who killed his father has not been found.'

Antonio's face turned to granite. 'Killed his father? I thought Niccolò di Chimici died in a duel? You make it sound like common murder.'

The messenger shifted uncomfortably. 'You might know that the young man, the Cavaliere Luciano Crinamorte as he is known, is no longer in Bellezza. Rumour in that city has it that he is here in Padavia.'

'And if rumour should be right?'

This was the difficult bit.

'My master asks that you agree to hand him over to his jurisdiction. That I . . . that he . . . that he come back to Giglia with me to stand trial.'

Antonio did nothing quickly. He supped his ale with as much deliberation and enjoyment as if he had been shoeing horses all morning.

'Well,' he said at last. 'I don't want to disoblige your master but he must know that his authority, great though it is in the Tuschian cities, does not extend to Padavia. Therefore no arrest warrant issued in Giglia has any weight here.'

'I believe, honoured sir, that the request was made more in the spirit of a favour between rulers than one made according to the law,' said the messenger. This was not going well.

'You know,' said Antonio confidentially, pouring more ale for the messenger. 'If we were sitting here discussing an ordinary murder – or assassination as it would have been – I would be sympathetic to the Grand Duke's request. But death in a duel is never subject to prosecution – unless, of course, one duellist played dirty.'

He looked the messenger in the eye and the poor man changed colour. It was common knowledge in Giglia that Grand Duke Niccolò had poisoned the foils. He said nothing.

'As it is,' said Antonio. 'I don't find that the Cavaliere has any charge to answer and it would be foolhardy for him to return to any Tuschian city while the new Grand Duke is so unreasonably angry with him.'

'So that is the answer I must take my master?' asked the messenger.

'Say to him that I rejoice in his good news and recommend him to look forward to the good fortune of a healthy child, not backward to the death of a father. And if the Cavaliere should find himself in my city, I will accord him all the welcome and protection that Padavia can afford.'

When Matt woke in his room after his second stravagation, he no longer doubted that he had become a traveller in time and space. For whatever reason, he was being transported to Talia every night and both of the people he had met there were in danger from the family called di Chimici. Luciano was basically on the run from a murder rap, though he hadn't in fact done anything wrong. And Professor Constantin was printing illicit material that would get him into serious trouble if it got outside Padavia and into di Chimici hands.

'The penalty for practising what they call magic is death,' Constantin had said. 'And what they call magic covers everything that the Stravaganti do.'

'Stravaganti?' said Matt. 'Including me?'

'Including you,' agreed Constantin.

It was all very well to feel unhappy in his own world about girlfriend problems or difficulties with schoolwork. But in his Talian life, which was clearly going to continue, it seemed that if he set foot outside the city, Matt was going to be as much a di Chimici target as Luciano.

He looked at his mobile phone and found a text message from Ayesha. He froze as he deciphered the dreaded words 'We need to talk.'

Chapter 6

University Students

When he got to the gates of Barnsbury Comp that morning, Matt found his best friend Chay waiting for him. He was relieved to see him. If they bumped into Ayesha, she would hardly dump him in front of someone else.

'What's up?' asked Chay. 'You look rubbish.'

'Cheers,' said Matt but the bathroom mirror had told him much the same thing. He had dark circles under his eyes like someone who hadn't slept. And in a sense that was true.

'Girlfriend trouble?' said Chay.

Matt looked up sharply. 'Has she said anything to you?'

Chay shifted uncomfortably and kicked at a little bit of gravel with his trainer. 'Might've,' he said, looking down.

'Come on,' said Matt. 'What did she say?'

'Just that you seem to have gone off her,' mumbled Chay. 'If you haven't, I think you need to tell her soon – before she gets in first and dumps you.'

Matt felt a weight lift off his heart. 'Of course I haven't gone off her! She's the best thing that ever happened to me. But I've got a lot of stuff going on. I'll tell her, don't worry.'

'What sort of stuff?' asked Chay. 'And what do those guys in the upper sixth have to do with it?'

Matt was absolutely stumped. How on earth could he tell Chay, who had been his best mate since junior school, that he'd found a book of spells that transported him to another world? And as he realised that there was no way to do it, his heart sank again. If he couldn't think of a cover story to tell Chay, then how could he explain it to Ayesha?

Guido Parola was a good teacher and he found Marco an eager pupil. There was a moment's embarrassment when they met for their first lesson and Marco recognised the red-haired assassin. When Guido had attempted to stab the previous Duchessa in her state mandola, Marco had been the mandolier in charge of the vessel.

But the old Duchessa, in reward for his service, had made Marco footman in the Ducal Palace and given him a handsome uniform and a bag of silver. In a few months he would be twenty-five and entitled to a generous mandolier's pension. Then he would marry his Barbara but meanwhile he must learn how to protect the young Duchessa and who better to teach him than a reformed assassin?

Reformed assassin! Guido was sick of the sound of those words but that was how his mistress, Silvia Rossi, Regent Rodolfo's wife, always referred to him and it was a punishment he had to bear. For he had indeed, tempted by money he sorely needed, agreed to kill the old Duchessa. And he was one of the small number of people who knew his mistress's secret – that she was the same Duchessa he had tried to kill and who had also survived the second assassination attempt that was supposed to have killed her.

Marco certainly didn't know that. He had never seen the old Duchessa without a mask or the Regent's wife with one. But he saw how Guido blushed when Signora Rossi referred to his criminal past.

'Guido is very handy with a dagger and a sword,' she said pleasantly. 'And those skills which would kill a ruler may also protect her. Teach Marco all you know, Guido, for my stepdaughter's life will be in his hands every time she travels to Padavia.'

She caught his eye as she said 'stepdaughter' and Guido nodded slightly; he knew how important Arianna's safety was to her real mother, standing before him.

'You mustn't mind Signora Rossi,' he told Marco, as soon as she had left them. 'It's just her way.'

'How long have you worked for her?' asked Marco.

'Oh, quite a while,' said Guido vaguely. He didn't tell the footman that Silvia had in fact released him from her service in the spring but he had needed to stay in Bellezza, to look after his dissolute brother, and hadn't quite been able to detach himself from the palace. But one day soon he would leave for Fortezza and begin his studies at the University there. He envied Luciano his life in Padavia.

'Well, let's get started,' he said. 'The most important thing to be prepared for is attack from behind.'

And he threw Marco to the floor, taking him completely off-guard.

*

Luciano was riding back home from the University when he heard another horse behind him. There was nothing unusual in that but he urged his own horse a little faster. The following rider speeded up to match him and Luciano felt the first chill of fear. He was caught between longing to get to the relative safety of his home and not wanting any pursuer to know where he lived. While he hesitated about which route to take, the other rider gained on him and a familiar voice called out, 'Luciano?'

Luciano pulled on the reins. 'Cesare?' he said. 'What on earth are you doing here? You frightened the life out of me!'

The two horses drew together, tossing their heads and taking in each other's scent, while the two young riders clasped arms. Cesare laughed at his friend's bemusement.

'I'm a student, like you,' he said. 'Just started.'

'But why?' asked Luciano rather bluntly.

'Do you think only cavalieri should be educated

then?' teased Cesare. 'I have the money to pay my fees and lodging – remember the silver Georgia gave me? – and my father thought I could do with having some of the rough edges knocked off me.'

'Of course,' said Luciano. 'I'm sorry. I didn't mean . . . But it's wonderful to see you! I'm just surprised they can spare you from home and the stables.'

'Well, the race is over for another year,' said Cesare. 'And I'm not doing a full degree. Just a year, to see how the other half lives.'

'Me too,' said Luciano. 'Look – come back home with me. We can have something to eat.'

'Fine,' said Cesare. 'I want to hear all you know about our friends,' he lowered his voice, 'from far away. Have you any news of Georgia and Falco?'

'He's not Falco any more,' said Luciano. 'Come back with me and we'll share our news.'

The two friends turned their horses towards the cathedral square.

'I'm glad to see you're keeping up the riding,' said Cesare.

'I don't get the chance in Bellezza,' said Luciano. 'And I was pretty sore after the ride here but Cara is a docile beast.' He patted his bay mare. 'Who's that you're riding? I don't recognise her.'

'No, Fiorella is new – since your time in Remora. She's Arcangelo's daughter.'

'Is she going to be a racehorse too?' asked Luciano, admiring the elegant lines of the chestnut.

'Maybe,' said Cesare. 'I bought her myself and when I get back home I'll train her up for the Stellata and see what she can do.'

His friend was used to the Remoran's modesty. He

was the best rider Luciano had ever known and as good a judge of a racehorse as many much older men in Talia. If Cesare thought Fiorella had a chance of competing in the Stellata race, she was probably a future winner.

'It's so good to see you again,' he said, giving the older boy another hug when they dismounted at Silvia's house. Luciano kept a groom but Cesare insisted on looking after his own mare and settling her with food and drink before going in to dine with Luciano.

'How do you like it in Padavia?' asked Luciano, as they ate Alfredo's rich bean soup.

'Well enough,' said Cesare. 'But I'm sharing a house with four other students. We pay a woman to cook for us but she's not as good as Alfredo.'

Luciano felt guilty about having a whole house to himself and several servants but he thrust the thought down. He had never expected to be rich in his old world and it was a bit awkward finding that he was quite wealthy in Bellezza and had to keep up the way of life of a future duke. Cesare lived in Remora with his father, the Horsemaster of the Ram, who was also a Stravagante, and a large family of young half-siblings. He wondered how long the silver that Georgia had given Cesare after she had won the Stellata would last.

'How is Georgia?' asked Cesare, echoing his thoughts. 'Have you heard anything about your old world lately?'

'Well,' said Luciano. 'I *hadn't* had any news for some time but a new Stravagante has just arrived in Padavia. He goes to the same school as Georgia and

Falco – though he's called Nick in their world. This one's called Matt, Matteo.

'But that's fantastic,' said Cesare, his broad, friendly face shining with pleasure. 'Can I meet him? He could tell us all about Georgia and take her a message!'

'He has met her, and Nick too,' admitted Luciano. 'But they weren't friends until Matt found his talisman. Now they've realised that he's a Stravagante like them.'

'And who is his Stravagante here in the city?' asked Cesare, quick to understand.

'It's Professor Constantin,' said Luciano, looking round him and lowering his voice, even though there was no one to overhear him. 'You know, the Rhetoric Professor. But keep that to yourself. Even in an independent city like Padavia it's best we don't speak about it publicly. The di Chimici are still on the warpath.'

Matt didn't see Ayesha till lunchtime. He got to the cafeteria late and there she was, sitting at their usual table. The smile she gave him when he put his tray down was just as radiant as usual but he thought her eyes looked tired, as if she had had no more sleep than him.

'Finally,' he said, as if he'd been looking for her all morning, instead of trying to avoid her. 'I got your text.'

'Good,' she said. 'Can we talk now?'

But just then a bunch of other sixth formers sat down at the table; Barnsbury's cafeteria wasn't exactly the best place for a heart to heart.

Matt smiled ruefully. 'Look,' he said. 'I'm sorry about yesterday. I've got some . . . well, some stuff going on.'

'With people in the year above?'

'Yeah. It's sort of to do with going to university,' he improvised. 'Getting advice and all that.'

'But that's great,' said Ayesha. 'There's no need to feel shy about it.' She didn't say anything about the fact that Sky was going to art college and Georgia and Alice were applying to read English and that these were unlikely subjects for Matt to be interested in. She was just glad that he was talking to her. And looking at her as if she were the most precious thing in the world. She squeezed his hand.

'Are we all right?' he dared to ask.

'Of course,' she said.

Matt grinned. 'I've got my first driving lesson tonight.'

'That's brilliant. I can't wait till you get your car.'

'Well I've got to beat you to it,' he said, aware that she would be seventeen by Christmas and able to have her own driving lessons. Jago, needless to say, had passed his test first time and had a red Audi that girls seemed to like. Matt was determined to get something less pretentious.

As though conjured up by this thought, Jago sauntered into the cafeteria, as if he owned it. He was surrounded by a group of friends, and among them was the boy with dreadlocks.

'Hey,' said Sky casually as he passed by the table. 'All right, Matt?'

'Fine,' said Matt. 'I was just telling Ayesha about how you and the others are helping me decide about uni. Ayesha, this is Sky,' he added.

'I know,' said Ayesha. 'You do Art, don't you?'

'And English and History,' offered Sky, wondering what exactly Matt had told her. 'But I'm going to study in the States for a while.'

'I could never afford that,' said Matt.

'My old man's paying,' said Sky.

'I don't think I can swing that one on Andy,' said Matt. 'Not on a singer's wages.' He mentally kicked himself for giving that away so easily but Sky just gave him a curious look.

'My dad's a singer too,' he said quietly. 'Georgia and Alice are trying for Cambridge,' he added, to change the subject.

'Is that what you want?' Ayesha asked Matt, surprised.

'Maybe,' he said. 'Not in English though, obviously. But they're pretty hot on IT there. I should think about it.'

Matt had no idea what he was saying. He just wanted to keep his girlfriend happy and not have to try to explain to her about Talia and magic and stravagation.

Luciano and Cesare talked late into the evening and consumed a lot of Bellezzan red wine from the stocks Alfredo had brought with him. The Remoran had heard some of what had passed in Giglia in the spring, but Luciano had to tell it all again in detail.

'And you really killed the Duke?' asked Cesare. 'Gaetano must have been a good teacher.'

'He was,' said Luciano. 'But that's not why.' He stopped, not wanting to talk about it. 'I'm going to enrol in the School of Fencing here,' he said. 'To keep up my practice. You should come with me.'

'I will,' said Cesare, awkwardly pulling his short sword out of its scabbard. 'I could do with some lessons or this will just be an ornament. But then you must enrol in the School of Riding with me. We don't want you to get rusty.'

'OK,' said Luciano. 'It's a deal. Fencing and Riding – that should be a bit livelier than studying Rhetoric!'

'But it can't be so bad if the teacher's a Stravagante,' said Cesare, slurring his words a little.

'We don't talk about that in class,' said Luciano uneasily. 'It's supposed to be a secret.'

*

In Giglia, Rinaldo di Chimici was having a conversation with his cousin that would have made Luciano even more uneasy if he'd known about it.

Rinaldo had risen through the ranks of churchmen at a dizzying rate and was now a cardinal in Remora, where his old boss and family member Ferdinando, was Pope. But Grand Duke Fabrizio had sent for him and Rinaldo had obeyed instantly; he always wanted to please the head of their family, whoever it was.

'The ruler of Padavia is stubborn,' said Fabrizio. 'He has recently refused to hand over the Bellezzan to me.'

'The Cavaliere?' asked Rinaldo. It seemed to him that wherever he went and whatever he did it was his fate to be involved with that black-haired boy.

'Indeed,' said Fabrizio. 'The Cavaliere Luciano Crinamorte, who is so popular and well-known in Bellezza. Though no one had heard of him till a few years ago. The young man who was with my brother Falco, when he took the poison that killed him and who later killed my father.'

'In a duel, cousin,' said Rinaldo hesitantly.

'In a duel, Eminence,' agreed Fabrizio. 'But whatever the rights and wrongs of that, you may know that my father, Grand Duke Niccolò, always believed that there was something suspicious in the way the Bellezzan befriended my brother and was present at his self-poisoning but then fled back to his city when Falco died.'

'I do remember,' said Rinaldo, wondering if he should tell his cousin now all he knew about Luciano and about how he used not to have a shadow. 'I was always surprised that Niccolò – may his soul rest in peace – let him go free in Remora.'

'Be that as it may,' said Fabrizio, 'Messer Antonio will not yield him up to my justice or even admit that he is in the city. But I have it on good intelligence that he has gone there to study.'

Rinaldo spread his hands. 'They have a fine university there, by all accounts.'

'So I am trying another tack,' continued the Grand Duke. 'You are aware of my new laws against the occult?'

'Yes,' said Rinaldo. 'And as a churchman I very much approve.'

'It is as a churchman that I want you to go to Padavia,' said Fabrizio. 'I have reason to believe that

Messer Antonio will look more favourably on my next request, to put these laws on his own statute. And if that request comes from a cardinal of the Reman Church and my kinsman, I think he will agree. And then, when the Bellezzan steps out of line, as I'm sure he will, we will have him.'

Matt's driving instructor was a kindly, grandfatherly type, called Brian. He was impressed by how much Matt knew already.

'My parents have been taking me out in Sainsbury's car park for practice,' he explained.

'Well, you haven't stalled or crashed the gears once,' said Brian, 'and that's very good for a first lesson. I'd like you to look in the mirror more though. Spend just a second or two longer assessing the situation before you give the signal.'

Story of my life, thought Matt. He still didn't know what he was thinking of, telling Ayesha that he was going to apply to do a Computing degree at Cambridge. It was only a matter of time before she told his parents. He thrust the idea to the back of his mind. He had to hurry to fit in his homework before bedtime now that he was having driving lessons as well.

He had to consider seriously whether or not to stravagate that night. He was already short of sleep and feeling knackered. But the strange things that were happening to him were becoming addictive. He still had no idea why he had been chosen to go there, why the talisman of the leather spell-book had chosen him, as Constantin put it, but he wanted to see Padavia again.

He was a bit in awe of Constantin – and of Luciano too – but he felt that the city held the key to a secret that had eluded him all his life.

Chapter 7

Against the Law

When Matt arrived in the studio, he was greeted heartily by Professor Constantin.

'Welcome, welcome,' he said, beaming. 'We are going to start teaching you the craft of printing today.'

Matt was surprised. 'I thought that was just a cover story,' he said.

'Well, if it is to be effective, you must know what we do in the Scriptorium and learn how to do it yourself. The men are already suspicious because you aren't related to any of them. There's a tradition in printing that sons follow fathers into the trade. I've told them you're an orphan and that your father was a printer in Bellezza. That's why I've taken you on.'

Great, thought Matt. They don't want me here and they've only got to start asking me questions to find out that story's full of holes. And as for spending all my time working with words . . . He remembered that the letters all had to be put together back to front and groaned.

Constantin clapped him on the back. 'Don't look so worried. It will be fine. I'll be teaching you myself when I've got the time. And you won't start by setting type. That's a very advanced skill. You'll begin by sweeping the floor and making ink, that sort of thing.'

So you read minds too, was Matt's reaction. But he followed the Professor into the Scriptorium and looked at the room with a fresh eye now that he knew he really had to work there.

There were five wooden presses, each one being operated by two men. They were all in action today, making the creaking sound that he had noticed before, which sounded a bit like an old sailing ship. Alongside each press, another man worked sitting on a high stool in front of a wooden case holding letters.

'Those are the compositori,' said Constantin. 'They really do have to have a way with words.'

Matt saw that they were working incredibly fast, rapidly picking metal letters out of the cases with their right hands and putting them into wooden sticks in their left. They were consulting sheets of paper, which were covered with loopy black handwriting – the original manuscripts he supposed.

'Yes,' continued Constantin under his breath. 'They are the aristocracy of the print room. What the others do is hard work – some of it dirty – and it requires precision and skill. The pressmen don't even need to be able to read. What they do is mechanical. The compositori have to be almost as learned as scholars.'

Around the sides of the room sheets of printed paper hung from ropes, like lines of washing. Matt could tell that they were there to let the ink dry. And at the far end of the long room two more men sat at either end of a long wooden table, reading through more sheets and making corrections with quill pens. He could tell by their clothes that they were even higher in the pecking order than the men with the sticks.

'My proofreaders,' said Constantin. 'They check the galleys for mistakes and if they find any, the compositore has to pick the wrong letters out of the forme and replace them.'

'Are they all working on the same book?' asked Matt.

'Oh good heavens, no. We have a different book on each press.'

'Five at a time? With all those loose sheets?' said Matt. 'Don't they get in a muddle?'

Constantin laughed. 'Sometimes. But not often. And they are all experienced men. There is my foreman, Biagio, to keep an eye on everything. That's him at the far end, with the curly moustache. And I am here myself as much time as I can spare every day.'

'What about the Secret Scriptorium,' whispered Matt, suddenly overwhelmed by how complicated the whole process seemed.

'Only Biagio knows anything about it,' said the Professor. 'I work there at night and he helps me. But of course I need paper and ink and other materials so he would know if it went missing from the print room.'

'Doesn't it take three people to run a press? The

two on the machine and the . . . the compositore?'

'That's where you come in.'

*

A carriage came rumbling across the cobbled streets of Padavia and pulled up outside an old house near the cathedral. The footman jumped down to help out a hearty-looking old man with white hair and hand down his luggage, and the passenger rapped on the front door.

He was almost knocked over by a much younger man with curly black hair who was coming out at the same time.

'Dottore!' said the young man. 'I didn't expect you so soon.'

'So I canne see,' said the visitor, clasping the young man in an affectionate hug. 'Ye seme to be fleeing away from me.'

'I'm going to be late for a lecture, but it doesn't matter. Not now you're here. They won't mind if I miss it.'

'Ah, how soone have ye bicome a sluggard!' said the old man but he smiled as he sent the footman round to the stables. 'My sonne,' he said proudly. 'The young Cavaliere.'

Doctor Dethridge's servant knew perfectly well who Luciano was; it was only a matter of weeks since the Cavaliere had left their home in Bellezza. And everyone in the city who had any dealings with the court knew how fond the old scientist was of his foster-son. The boy had come to Bellezza a few years ago as apprentice to Rodolfo Rossi, who was now the

Regent. The footman remembered now the rumours at the time that Luciano was a distant cousin of Rodolfo's, from Padavia. So it made sense that he had come back here for his further studies.

'Come in,' said Luciano. 'Have you breakfasted?'

'Aye,' said Dethridge. 'Indifferently well, at an inn on the way. But it wolde please me to sit down with ye for more refreshment.'

'I'll call Alfredo,' said Luciano. 'It's so good to see you! And how is Leonora?'

'My wife is right welle, thank ye, son. She has sent manye packages for ye, mayhap believing they have no vittles in this city.'

They were soon making a second breakfast, with Alfredo's cooking supplemented by Leonora's food parcels. The old servant was inclined to be offended until he saw that she had put in her own jars of pickled vegetables and tomatoes under oil.

'When are you giving your lecture?' asked Luciano, as they sat in the garden drinking milky coffee.

'The first one is tomorrow,' said Dethridge. 'Bot there sholde be six altogethire. Ye cannot describe the motion of the stars in shorter time.'

It had been a problem for Luciano, ever since he had translated to live permanently in Talia, that he couldn't reveal what his twenty-first century education had taught him about the physical world. He knew perfectly well that his foster-father would be lecturing on the way the sun and planets orbited the earth. Yet he could not share his own very scanty knowledge of the solar system with the Elizabethan.

Talia was still in 1579; Luciano had no idea when their equivalent of Galileo would turn up or if they had already had a Copernicus but he had always known instinctively that he couldn't just tell them that their view of the universe was wrong. He would have been hard-pressed to explain how it worked anyway.

For most of the time he could just ignore this sort of thing; it was hard enough becoming a sixteenth-century knight instead of a twenty-first century school student. But now his foster-father was going to give a series of lectures at the university Luciano attended, which would actually be full of errors.

'Ye are troubled by somme thinge?' asked Dethridge, sensitive as always to Luciano's mood.

'Not really,' said Luciano. 'It doesn't matter. But have you heard about the new Stravagante?'

'Yonge Mattheus?' said Dethridge. 'He is anothire from youre school thatte is builded on my olde laboratorie, is he not?'

'Barnsbury Comp, yes,' said Luciano, feeling a sudden pang of homesickness for the ugly buildings he would probably never see again. 'And you know who brought him?'

'My olde freende Constantine,' nodded Dethridge. 'He felte the neede for anothire Stravayger hire in the city.'

'How did he know?' asked Luciano. He had often wondered how the Talian Brotherhood knew when to send for someone else from his old world.

Dethridge shrugged. 'Mayhap the stones told him. Or the cardes. Al senior Stravaygers do their divinatiounes eche month. He scried that trouble was coming, I trow.'

'That's why you're really here, isn't it?' said Luciano, suddenly understanding. 'The lectures are just a front. You've come to give Constantin support. Something's going to happen.'

*

Cardinal di Chimici found Messer Antonio hard at work in the Palace of Justice. The Cardinal was shown into a great frescoed hall. At the far end was what looked like a sort of court, with tiered wooden benches full of people and an impressive judge's seat. Rinaldo guessed it was the Governor himself sitting in it. A wretched-looking man stood with bowed head before him. His trial was evidently coming to an end.

And justice was swift. Two constables took the condemned man over to a large circular stone on a raised plinth and started to strip him. Rinaldo trembled; he was squeamish about any sort of physical pain and he feared the man was about to be tortured or at least whipped. But to his astonishment the convicted man was merely made to sit in his canvas under-breeches on the stone. The people on the wooden benches jeered at him and he mumbled something Rinaldo couldn't hear. This exchange happened three times and then the man was roughly escorted out of the hall, clutching his clothes.

That seemed to conclude the proceedings and the people dispersed. A servant went across to Antonio and whispered in his ear and the Governor stood to welcome his guest.

'Eminence,' he greeted Rinaldo. 'You are welcome in Padavia.'

'Governor, I thank you,' said Rinaldo.

Antonio led him to his private office. Rinaldo was

surprised at the plain and untidy room after the opulence of the great hall. It was clear that the Governor was not a man accustomed to greatness, which made the Cardinal relax.

But the wine and cakes that were brought were as fine as any Rinaldo had tasted in Talia.

'I'm sorry you had to witness that,' said Antonio, taking a deep draught of the wine. 'I never enjoy that ritual, but it is our law.'

'Ah, what exactly had the man done?' asked Rinaldo.

'He was a debtor,' said Antonio grimly. 'Many of his creditors were there in the court and he had no means of settling what he owed them.'

'And what happens to him now?'

Antonio shrugged. 'He leaves the city, dressed only in what he stands up in and carrying no luggage. His house and any goods are now confiscated and the city sells them to pay his debts.'

'But he is free to go? He does not go to prison?'

'It is our tradition,' said Antonio. 'The public humiliation and renunciation of his goods are sufficient punishment for a proud Padavian.'

Rinaldo repressed a shudder. Born the younger son of a lesser branch of the great di Chimici family, he had always feared poverty. He could not get the picture of the man in his underwear out of his mind.

'But I expect his wife has salted away some small amount of money and goods,' Antonio was saying, 'and will follow him out of the city.'

Rinaldo felt a momentary regret. If he ever lost his cardinal's robes and hat, there would be no loyal woman waiting to help him start a new life.

'It seems a lenient punishment,' was all he said.

'Well, enough of debtors,' said Antonio. 'You said in your message that you had urgent business to discuss with me.'

Rinaldo was shocked by Antonio's bluntness. Brought up in courts and palaces, he had limited experience of bluff craftsmen like the Padavian Governor. His idea of a ruler was someone like his cousin Fabrizio or, in spite of his hatred for her, the old Duchessa of Bellezza. People with elaborate clothes and elegant manners who took care to hide their ruthlessness with expensive perfumes and flowery speeches. He wasn't used to someone of Antonio's directness and he wondered if there really was any more to him than there seemed.

The Cardinal took a parchment from his scrip and offered it to the Governor.

'You have perhaps heard of the new laws drawn up by my cousin, the Grand Duke of Tuschia?' he said.

'Which ones?' asked Antonio. 'I have heard that the Grand Duke has been most active in writing new laws since he inherited his father's title.'

'Grand Duke Fabrizio refers to the laws against magic,' said Rinaldo rather frostily.

Antonio looked serious.

'I hope you will agree,' continued Rinaldo, 'that the superstitious practices carried out in many of our cities and in the countryside are quite contrary to the teachings of the Church.'

As a matter of fact, Antonio did agree. He was a moderniser who had turned his back on the old goddess religion of the lagoon which had spread across Talia. Unlike many influential Talians who practised the two religions concurrently, Antonio loathed anything that smacked of the occult. Even the frescoes in his Hall of Justice annoyed him, with their astrological symbols and allegories.

'Go on,' he said, casting his gaze over the parchment.

'It is a list of interdictions,' said Rinaldo. 'They forbid citizens from taking part in any supernatural practices – using or purchasing spells, enchantments, hexes, or consulting practitioners of magical arts. Citizens must also not purchase, own or consult books containing such dangerous gibberish or, of course, print them.'

'Of course,' muttered Antonio.

'And anything hinting at goddess-worship is to be rooted out. It has undermined the authority of the True Church for far too long.'

'And the penalties?' asked Antonio, skimming through the parchment to the end.

'There can be only one penalty for heretical practices,' said Rinaldo. 'Death.'

*

Matt had passed an exhausting morning before he was allowed to escape to the University's Refectory for lunch. After being put under the care of Biagio, he had been set to making ink, a messy process involving mixing soot – lampblack, Biagio called it – with old linseed oil that had been boiling and reducing in a cauldron for five days. Matt guessed that this was the least popular job in the Scriptorium, given to the youngest or most recent member of the print room. It was hot, sticky and smelly work that left his hands and face covered in smuts.

He was desperate for a bottle of iced water but settled for a mug of cold ale, bought by Luciano. He was very relieved to find him in the Refectory, since he had no Talian money and was worried about how he would get any lunch.

'You can put anything you want on my battels bill,' said Luciano, when Matt had drained his first mug. 'I've told them to supply anything that Matteo Bosco asks for.'

'Cheers,' said Matt. 'That's me I suppose, though I can't get used to being called that.'

'As long as you are in Talia, yes,' said Luciano.

'Bizarre,' said Matt. 'But then the whole thing is, isn't it? How did you get to be so at home here? It's still freaking me out.'

'I've been here a long time,' said Luciano. 'Nearly two and a half years. But I was just like you when I first stravagated. Arianna had to teach me everything, and Rodolfo, of course.'

Matt had already heard about these important people during Luciano's long explanation in the Black Horse. They were now the co-rulers of Bellezza, the city that was like Venice.

'Constantin's got me making ink and learning all the printing stuff,' said Matt when he had polished off a huge platter of bread, cheese and meat. Luciano made him feel big and clumsy; in fact if he hadn't been one of his only friends in Talia, he would probably have hated him as much as he did Jago.

'I can tell,' said Luciano. 'You've got a big smudge of soot on your cheek. But that's good. It means you'll fit right in as a pressman.'

A young man with light brown hair and a friendly face came up and sat at their table.

'Cesare,' said Luciano. 'I want you to meet Matteo. He's the one I was telling you about.'

Cesare held out a suntanned hand and shook Matt's vigorously. 'You know Georgia, don't you?' he asked eagerly. 'How is she? And how is Fal— Nicholas?'

'I don't really know them,' said Matt, instinctively liking this open-faced boy. 'But they're both well. Georgia is choosing what university to go to.'

'Will you tell her that I'm at university here,' said Cesare proudly. 'Tell her I used the silver she gave me. I'd like her to know what I did with it.'

Matt had heard something of Georgia's adventures in Talia but it suddenly seemed much more real now that he had met someone else who knew her. He wondered what her relationship with Cesare had been. But whatever it was, it had come to an end now. She and Nicholas had told him they were not going back to Talia.

'There's another old friend here now, Cesare,' said Luciano. 'Doctor Dethridge has arrived. He's giving some lectures on Astronomy. You must meet him, Matt.'

'But isn't he the one who . . .' Matt lowered his voice, 'started the whole stravagating thing.'

'He is,' said Luciano. 'And what's more he's my foster-father. He and his wife Leonora took me on when I, you know, had to stay here.'

The other boys looked at him with sympathy. Cesare knew Luciano's story and laid a hand on his arm.

'A better father you couldn't wish for,' Cesare said simply.

Luciano thought of his real father, back in Islington, being a foster-father to Nick. Different from the old Elizabethan, but just as loving.

'No,' he said quietly, then pushed such thoughts to the back of his mind. It always unsettled him when a new Stravagante arrived from his old world. 'I feel a lot safer with him here, I can tell you.'

'What sort of person is he?' asked Matt.

'Well, he's older than my real dad,' said Luciano. 'He's in his late fifties but his hair is white. People age quicker here in Talia because life expectancy is shorter.'

'But he is not from Talia,' said Cesare quietly.

'He's still from more than four hundred years before Matt's time,' said Luciano. 'I don't know how long Elizabethans lived but I'm betting Doctor Dethridge would be considered old in his own time and place.'

'I don't think Shakespeare lived much longer than that,' said Matt, surprising both the others. Cesare had no idea who Shakespeare was.

'I didn't take you for a literary type,' said Luciano cautiously.

Matt laughed. 'I'm not. But my mum's an English teacher and she's always coming out with things like that.'

But what he thought was that Luciano had made a bad deal in swapping twenty-first century life expectancy for a curtailed existence in Talia. Then he remembered that the older boy hadn't had any choice and was glad he had kept his mouth shut.

'Anyway,' Luciano was saying. 'He's an alchemist – a natural philosopher, he calls it – but he's also a mathematician, an astronomer and a calendarist.'

'And a fine horseman,' added Cesare, before Matt could ask what a calendarist was. 'He helped me teach Luciano to ride in Remora.'

'One thing will strike you as odd about him, though,' said Luciano. 'Cesare and the others don't hear it but to all Stravaganti from the other world he sounds as if he's talking in old-fashioned English, Elizabethan English, in fact.'

'What, all forsooth and gadzooks?' asked Matt disbelievingly.

'It's not as bad as that,' said Luciano. 'You'll understand him fine.'

'I'd better get back to the Scriptorium,' sighed Matt, heaving himself off the bench. 'Mustn't let the real pressmen think I'm not one of them.'

Luciano and Cesare watched him go.

'He doesn't have any idea, does he?' said Cesare.

'None at all,' said Luciano. 'He's like a babe in arms.'

Chapter 8

A Date with Doctor Death

For the next week Matt needed all the stamina his rugby-playing and training gave him. By day he was working hard at school and by night he was a printer's 'devil'. Biagio told him apprentices were called that because of the black smudges that their faces got covered in while they were making ink. He was very relieved that the smuts never travelled back with him to his own world; it would have been really hard to explain to his mother why his bedclothes were full of soot.

So far he hadn't been back into the Secret Scriptorium. Constantin had told him that most of his work there happened at night and that was the one time Matt couldn't be there. He wondered if the Professor had forgotten about that when he brought him to Talia. But he had plenty to do during the time he was there and met Luciano and Cesare only at lunch or just before he had to stravagate home.

He was bursting with questions about what he was supposed to be doing in Padavia, more than he had time to ask when he was there and he hadn't met the famous Doctor Dethridge yet. So he sought out the others at Barnsbury more often. And that was problematic too, since Ayesha would only believe he needed to talk to them about university up to a certain point.

'I don't see how Nick can help,' she said. 'He's not even applying till the year after next.'

'No, but he's pretty bright,' said Matt.

'So am I,' she replied tartly, 'but you seem to be spending more time with him than with me.'

'You can't be jealous of Nick,' Matt said, giving her a kiss.

'Don't try and get round me,' said Ayesha, pushing him away.

'I don't go out of my way to see him,' lied Matt. 'But I do need to talk to Georgia and they're never apart.'

'They're a C.O.U.P.L.E.' she spelt out. 'Couples are supposed to spend time together. You should remember that.'

And she had flounced off tossing her black silky hair. Ayesha had never been prone to flouncing and hair-tossing in the past but it was becoming a habit lately.

Georgia, Nick and Sky were all eager to hear every detail of his visits to Talia and there was no way he could talk to them in front of Ayesha, or Chay, come to that. The day after his third stravagation was Saturday and he arranged to meet them again in Café@anytime.

'You saw Cesare?' Georgia had exclaimed and Nick was no less keen to hear about the Remoran. Although Sky said he had never met him, he listened almost as intently. Only Alice seemed bored; she was beginning to wish that she hadn't come.

'It's weird to think of him and Luciano being university students together,' said Georgia.

'I don't think either of them is studying for a full degree,' said Matt. 'They said something about doing a year each.'

Nick was nodding. 'That's right. You only do a degree in Talia if you want to teach. If you are a nobleman, you go to university for a year or so to, well, to cultivate your mind.'

'But Cesare's not a nobleman, is he?' asked Sky. 'I thought he was a stable-boy.'

'But not just any stable-boy,' said Georgia. 'He's the best horseman of his age in Remora and remember his father is a Stravagante.'

'He said to tell you he's using your silver for his fees,' said Matt. 'Whatever that means.'

Georgia and Nick looked at each other. Nick hadn't been there the day she had won the Stellata horse race but he knew about it and how Arianna had given her a bag of silver as a reward. Georgia hadn't been able to bring it back to her world – Stravaganti were forbidden to take anything between worlds, except talismans – and so she had given it to Cesare.

'I'm glad,' she said at last, with a sigh. 'I'd love to see him again.'

'Are you all definitely not going back?' Matt asked.

'I'm not,' said Sky, squeezing Alice's hand. 'I couldn't stand a year of doing A levels and stravagating at night. And after that I'm off to the States.'

Nick said nothing.

Georgia said, 'We wouldn't be in the same city as you anyway. My talisman takes me to Remora and Nick's to Giglia. I don't think we could get to Padavia and back within a day.'

'Why do you think I've been sent there?' asked Matt. 'You all seem to have had a reason to go to your cities and something dramatic to do. I don't understand why I just have to work in a dirty, noisy print room all day.'

'No one ever knows why they've been chosen to stravagate,' said Nick, even though he was the only one of them who hadn't been. 'And even when they think they know, they're often wrong.'

'You just have to hang in there and wait and see what happens,' said Georgia. 'And when it does,' she added, pulling a face, 'you may wish you were still making ink.'

William Dethridge was staying with Luciano while he gave his lectures at the University. He was enormously popular with the students and they came even if they were not studying Astronomy. Students of Law, Medicine and Theology all turned up, as well as the young men studying Rhetoric and Logic. By the second lecture, there were students standing at the back of the hall and queuing up outside to hear what he was saying.

'The fixed and the moving stars' was his subject.

Luciano waited for his foster-father after the lecture.

'You were brilliant,' he said, giving the Elizabethan a hug.

'Thanke ye,' said Dethridge, giving him a shrewd look. 'Yt was notte true, of course.'

'What!' said Luciano.

His foster-father took him by the arm and walked him to the Black Horse, buying two tankards of ale for them before saying any more.

'I've seene how ye looke at me,' said Dethridge. 'Whenne I talk about the universe. I'm notte a foole. Ye come from four hundrede yeres and more in the future. Yf thatte I thynke back to what was knowne four hundred yeres past and now, I onderstonde thatte ye moste know more than I do about the motioun of the planets.'

'I'm no astronomer,' said Luciano, stalling. 'Science wasn't my best subject at school.'

Dethridge fixed him with his blue stare.

'Do not dissemble with me, sonne,' he said. 'Ye knowe whatte I cannot – theories thatte have bene tested with instruments from youre twenty-first centurie. Yt most be knowne by eche and every childe thatte goes to school. But ye cannot tell mee.'

'Can I really not?' asked Luciano. 'Knowledge isn't like an object, is it? It's not like taking Talian gold back to our world or bringing medicine from our old world to this.'

'No,' agreed Dethridge, suddenly looking his age. 'Bot yt is still not allowed. Eche centurie moste discover the secrets of the universe for ytselfe.'

Luciano felt a sort of relief. He was so glad he didn't have to explain to his foster-father that men would walk on the moon in the twentieth century.

'Bot I shalle telle ye what I thynke,' said Dethridge. 'There's no need to saye yf I am righte or wronge.'

He lowered his voice. 'Yt has been a theorie for many years that we are notte the centre of the worlde. The grete starre thatte is our sunne is atte the myddel; every thynge else travels arounde yt. And the moone travels around us. Everything ordered in the grete dance of the spheres. Bot to saye yt or believe yt is a heresie thatte the Church wille not permit.'

Luciano looked at him astonished. Dethridge nodded.

'Constantine knows yt,' he said. 'Whatte do ye thinke he printes in thatte Secret Scriptorium of his?'

'I thought it was spells and things,' said Luciano.

'All secrets are the same,' said Dethridge. 'A secret is joste somme thynge that is not yet knowne to al. Bot the Chymists have set their face against lerning. Instede they want to fix al knowledge atte the poynte yt is now and controlle yt through the Talian Church. So Constantine moste do his werke hugger-mugger.'

'You're thinking about these new laws that Antonio has passed?' asked Luciano.

'Do ye knowe who was in this citee less thanne a weke ago?' asked Dethridge, without waiting for an answer. 'Thatte Ronald the Chymist.'

Luciano looked blank.

'Ye remembire thatte emissarie from Remora, who captured ye – Duke Nicholas's cozin?'

Luciano was surprised; they never talked about

what had led to his permanent translation to Talia but there was no doubt that Rinaldo di Chimici had been responsible, when he kidnapped him and kept him away from his talisman for so long.

'Rinaldo di Chimici was here?' he asked.

'Here, and talked Messer Antony into adopting the newe lawes the Grand Duke Fabrice has introduced in Tuschia,' said Dethridge.

'The laws against magic,' said Luciano slowly.

'On penaltee of dethe,' said Dethridge. 'Ye remembire thatte I have escaped thatte judgemente once bifore.'

They were both silent for a moment.

'So ye see,' he continued. 'Yt is beste for us if ye nevire telle me whatte ye knowe about the worlde from your olde lyfe. Yt wolde putte us bothe in daungere.'

*

The first Saturday that Matt had passed in Talia, the day after the Saturday in his own world, a lot of which he had spent sleeping, he was frustrated to discover that he still had to work in the Scriptorium; Talia obviously hadn't heard of weekends. Constantin explained to him that he would have Sundays free.

'Big deal,' murmured Matt.

'And all the major saints' days,' added Constantin. 'We have a lot in Talia. Next Tuesday, for example, is the Feast of Saint Luke the Evangelist and the Scriptorium will be closed.'

'Good,' said Matt. 'I'll get the day off.'

'But you will still stravagate?' asked Constantin.

And he did. He needed to know more about this strange world that only some chosen people could visit and to find out what on earth his task there could be. He had discovered that throughout Talia, Padavia was known as 'The City of Words', just as Bellezza was 'The City of Masks' and Remora, 'The City of Stars. But as far as he could tell, it should really be called 'City of Secrets'.

He spent that free Tuesday wandering the streets of the city with Luciano and Cesare, who had for once left their horses at home.

'I can't understand why you guys ride everywhere,' he said. 'It's not such a big city – you can walk to anywhere you need to go.'

'Luciano needs the practice,' said Cesare. 'They have no horses in Bellezza.'

'It's not like using an SUV to go to the local shop,' said Luciano, smiling.

Matt realised he had been thinking something like that.

'The horse needs the exercise as much as I need the practice,' Luciano went on. 'And a horse doesn't contribute to global warming – its fuel is organic.'

'I have no idea what you two are talking about,' said Cesare. 'What's an "essyuvee"? Is it another kind of animal?'

Matt laughed. 'You don't want to know.' He couldn't imagine what Cesare would make of life in twenty-first century London. He was finding it hard enough to adjust to the cobbled streets of Padavia where all the students carried daggers or arquebuses.

'Do you think it would be harder for a Talian to go to your world then?' asked Luciano, reading his thoughts. 'Falco seems to have adapted all right.'

'Yeah, I reckon it would,' said Matt. 'Life's just so much – louder. And faster. Anyway, Nick told me he was terrified of traffic when he first came.'

'I can't imagine what your world must be like,' said Cesare. 'Luciano has tried to explain it to me but it's just too different.'

'The basic things haven't changed though,' said Luciano. 'Love, death, that sort of thing. They're always the same.'

'That's why we've enrolled at the School of Fencing as well as the School of Riding,' said Cesare.

And Matt knew he wasn't talking about falling in love.

*

Messer Antonio was not the sort of man to be intimidated by nobles but he had listened more carefully to Cardinal di Chimici's embassy than to the earlier request to hand over Luciano to Giglian justice. And he had his reasons.

Although he was a good friend to Bellezza, he had long distrusted the goddess religion which had spread from the lagoon to most of Talia. Antonio was a man of reason and he disliked anything that hinted at superstition. The Church was a different matter. This was the late sixteenth century and a rationalist couldn't just come out and say he didn't believe in God. So Antonio had compromised and taken the line that the safest set of beliefs was that contained within the Talian Church.

Rinaldo had been speaking with the blessing of the

Pope, who was also a di Chimici, and Antonio had taken notice. He read through the Grand Duke's edicts against magic and all occult practices and, with a few minor modifications, had swiftly got them passed as Padavian laws.

And then he braced himself for his wife's reaction. Signora Giunta was a Bellezzan born and bred and though she went to church every Sunday, she also kept a little shrine to the goddess in her bedroom, decked with cheap gold trinkets, ribbons and flowers that were changed every day. In all their married life together, Antonio had not been able to persuade her that this was not seemly for the wife of the Governor of one of Talia's twelve powerful city-states.

The night that he signed the laws 'contra goetiam' (or 'against black magic'), Antonio went home with dread in his heart. As always, his four daughters ran to meet him and smother him with kisses. Giunta presided over a very good dinner table and when the children had gone to bed Antonio sighed as he lingered over his coffee, not wanting to dispel the feeling of well-being his food had given him.

'Giunta, my dear,' he said at last. 'There is something I must tell you. The Council today passed laws that will affect you.'

'Me?' said Giunta, puzzled, settling down with her lace-cushion, her fingers flying over the delicate work. 'How could your laws affect me?'

Antonio cleared his throat. 'They are laws against magic.'

'Magic? What has that got to do with me?' asked Giunta, her fingers stilling. 'Do you take me for a witch?'

But she was smiling and Antonio wished he didn't have to continue.

'It's serious, my dear,' he said. 'Magic is going to cover all superstitious and occult practices – including any observance of – well – of the old religion.'

There was a long silence. Giunta had resumed her lace-making but her full mouth was set in a determined line.

'You understand?'

'Oh yes, I understand,' said Giunta.

'Such practices will be punishable by death,' insisted Antonio. He didn't want there to be any misunderstanding between them.

'It will be interesting then, won't it?' said his wife.

'Interesting, my love?'

'Yes, if the lawgiver's wife is found to have an innocent statue of the Lady in their chamber. What would happen to her?'

Antonio was appalled. It had never crossed his mind that Giunta would simply not obey the laws, however much she resented them. If she was going to be so defiant, he had put her in terrible danger.

'Don't be ridiculous,' he said now, fear making his voice harsh. 'You of all people must be seen to obey the law. How would it look if I can't even count on obedience from my own wife?'

'So that is what you care about? Your reputation as a husband?'

Giunta sounded so contemptuous it made Antonio squirm. He tried to take her in his arms but she was as unresponsive as a plank of wood.

'No,' he said tenderly, though anger was taking the place of fear at the situation he had put them both in.

'What I care about is that if you are found out to be a practising goddess-worshipper, then you will die – horribly, by fire! And I could not bear to lose you.'

Giunta softened then and they sat together for a long time until the candles burnt down and they were in the dark.

Then he heard her say in a low voice, 'You haven't understood about the people of the Lady, Antonio. They have a higher law they must obey than that of any earthly city. I fear the consequences of your laws will be terrible – and not just for me.'

*

On Friday, Dethridge gave his third lecture. It was about what Luciano realised were eclipses of the moon, though he started by talking about 'nyghte blacknesse oute of sesoune' and about primitive beliefs that these sudden disappearances of the moon were caused by her being devoured by werewolves. 'Varcolaci' they were called and the red rim at the bottom of the moon was said to be her blood dripping from their mouths.

At the end there was a bit Luciano couldn't fully understand about how to calculate when such an eclipse might come again. When the group of students had finally dispersed, it was late afternoon and Matt emerged from the Scriptorium just as Luciano and Dethridge walked out of the colonnaded courtyard.

'Hey Matt!' called Luciano. 'Come and meet my father.'

Matt felt suddenly shy as the old man turned his piercing blue gaze on him. He was aware of his many smudges and smuts and wiped his hand on his breeches to make it clean enough to shake Dethridge's.

'Gretinges, Mattheus,' said Dethridge, and Matt saw straight away what Luciano had meant about his old-fashioned English. 'How do ye fare in Talie, yonge manne?'

'Very well,' said Matt politely. 'I'm sorry I couldn't come to your lectures but I am working in the Scriptorium.'

'Aye, with Professire Constantine. How do ye lyke werking with the presses?'

'Well, I haven't had much chance to work the press,' said Matt. 'The nearest I've got is spreading the ink on the print.'

They walked to where Luciano and Dethridge had tied up their horses. The two beasts were contentedly munching something in their nosebags, which the Stravaganti unhitched and slung on to their pommels.

'Come back with us,' said Luciano.

'I can't stay long,' said Matt. 'You know – the sunset rule.'

'I do,' said Luciano. 'Come for a bit. We'll just walk the horses. Or would you like to ride Cara?'

'No thanks,' said Matt, looking at the mare. She was a docile beast but still looked huge when viewed from up close. 'I'll walk.'

It was the first time he'd been to Luciano's lodgings and he looked around with amazement at all the luxurious carpets and hangings, while Dethridge took both horses round to the stables. 'He used to be an ostler, you know,' said Luciano. 'When we found him living in Montemurato.'

Alfredo brought them all red wine and Matt drank

deeply. When Dethridge got back from the stables, he quizzed Matt about his life in England and Matt did his best to satisfy him, stumbling a bit over the Elizabethan's language.

When he'd answered all his queries, Matt had some of his own. He'd heard about how all the stravagating had begun, with William Dethridge's accident. And Luciano had told him about how his foster-father had sometimes been discovered by people who thought he was dead when he was only stravagating. He was known as 'Doctor Death' by some.

'Do you mind if I ask you,' said Matt. 'How do you feel about England now? Do you feel like a real Talian? Or do you still feel English?'

Dethridge sighed. 'There is no holpe in thinking about the past,' he said. 'There was to be no going back for mee.' But he was looking at Luciano as he said it.

Chapter 9

New Allies

There was an impromptu concert in front of the cathedral. A group of gaily dressed, dark-skinned people with flutes, recorders, tambourines and fiddles had camped near the great bronze statue of a soldier on a horse. The centre of the city was filled with the alien sound of their music and singing.

Luciano saw them on his way to meet Matt at the Scriptorium and stopped to listen. He knew the look and sound of the Manoush. He scanned the group but there was no sign of Aurelio and Raffaella, the two he knew best.

One member of the group stood out from the rest. He was tall and lighter-skinned with rusty brown hair. Like all the Manoush, he wore it long, below his shoulders and some of it was plaited with coloured ribbons. As if aware of Luciano's gaze on him, the young man looked towards him and the Bellezzan found something in his grey eyes that attracted him.

The Manoush detached himself from the group and, tucking a flute into his belt, walked over to where Luciano stood watching them.

'Greetings,' he said, making a formal bow. 'I am seeking a Bellezzan named Crinamorte, a friend of my cousin Aurelio Vivoide. Can you help me?'

'I am he,' said Luciano, matching the Manoush's formal style.

The Manoush nodded. 'You look like his description.'

Luciano didn't object that Aurelio was blind and had never seen him; Raffaella could have described him to their cousin.

'I am Ludo Vivoide,' said the Manoush, bowing again. 'My people are here for the Day of the Dead.'

His tone was so matter-of-fact that it didn't seem sinister to Luciano but he still didn't know what he meant.

'Is that today?' he asked cautiously.

Ludo threw back his head and laughed, showing perfectly white teeth, the canines very pointed. Luciano was a little surprised – he had seen an awful lot of bad teeth since living permanently in Talia – but the Manoush's wide smile made him laugh too.

'I'm sorry,' he said. 'I really still don't know much about your festivals.'

'We are coming to the end of the old year,' said Ludo, serious again. 'We shall spend a week and a day preparing and then have the three-day festival in which we remember those departed from us. I think your Talian Church calls it the Feast of All Souls.'

Something stirred in Luciano's memory from what had happened in Bellezza the year before and light dawned.

'It's like Hallowe'en!' he said.

It was Ludo's turn to look puzzled. Luciano wondered what he'd make of pumpkin lanterns and trick-or-treating. He didn't think he'd like the sharp-toothed Manoush to play a trick on him.

'Don't worry about it,' he said quickly. 'It's . . . just another tradition from another place. Anyway, tell me about Aurelio, and Raffaella. Are they well? Are they coming here?'

'They were excellently well when I last saw them,' said Ludo. 'They were in Romula. I think they will celebrate the Day of the Dead there.'

'So it doesn't matter what city you are in?' asked Luciano, remembering how large numbers of the Manoush had converged on Remora in the middle of August the year before, to celebrate the Day of the Goddess.

'The year closes and opens in the same way wherever we are,' said Ludo simply. 'My cousin wanted me to give you his good wishes and,' he lowered his voice, 'a warning.'

Luciano shivered in the warm autumn sunlight. The Manoush saw more than most people and the blind Aurelio was the most perceptive of all of them.

'Are you free to talk now?' he asked Ludo. 'I was just going to see a friend. Someone that, like me, came to Talia from a long way away.'

He could tell from the sudden light in Ludo's clear grey eyes that he understood him.

'Another like you?' he asked. 'I would be honoured to meet him.'

*

Fabrizio di Chimici was delighted with the Cardinal's embassy to Padavia. He hadn't had such a success anywhere else in Talia. The other five independent city-states, Bellezza, Classe, Montemurato, Romula and Cittanuova, had all refused to introduce the laws against magic. With the six cities that were in di Chimici hands, Antonio's cooperation had ensured that just over half Talia was now vigilant against the kind of enchantments practised by the Stravaganti. And although he could not make Padavia yield Luciano up to Giglia, all the cities of Tuschia were closed to the Bellezzan.

What he felt he needed now was a new ally, a family member he could trust to carry out his wishes unquestioningly, without any sympathy towards the mysterious Brotherhood which so irked him. That ruled out his younger brother Gaetano, who was a friend of the Bellezzan Cavaliere's. Fabrizio loved his brother, but he could not understand why Gaetano refused to hate the young man who had killed their father and he could not trust him with the important business of revenge.

His sister Beatrice was also out of the question. She had been behaving very strangely ever since the weddings and the massacre at the Church of the Annunciation. Fabrizio sometimes wondered if she might be contemplating becoming a nun. But he couldn't spare her to a convent yet. He needed her to be a support to Caterina when the next di Chimici heir was born. The Grand Duchessa's pregnancy was just beginning to show – a tiny swelling under her waist that thrilled him when he placed his hand on it.

Rinaldo was already doing what he could, within the limitations of his role as a senior churchman. There was really only one di Chimici cousin Fabrizio could trust to help him – and that was Filippo of Bellona, Francesca's older brother. So he sent for him.

Filippo answered the summons readily. He was twenty-three years old, just a year younger than Fabrizio himself, with no title, no power and no wife; in fact with nothing to do but wait for his father, Jacopo the Younger, to die. He was vigorous, restless and ripe for a new purpose to his life.

The two cousins met in the Palazzo Ducale in the little room that had once been Beatrice's parlour, and was now a snug private study for the Grand Duke. It overlooked the River Argento and no one ever came here except by personal invitation.

They began with an exchange of courtesies about their families and Fabrizio told Filippo about Caterina's condition, which was not yet public knowledge. Filippo said that his parents were well and that he would be staying with his sister, Francesca, and her husband, Gaetano, in the old di Chimici palazzo on the Via Larga.

'I have not been there yet,' he said. 'I came straight here to see how I could be of help to you.'

Fabrizio was touched. This was what he wanted: a family member who was loyal and unquestioning. The cousins had all seen a lot of one another in the long childhood holidays they spent at Duke Niccolò's summer palace in Santa Fina. Being much of an age, Fabrizio, Carlo and Filippo had always been particularly close and Carlo's murder had left just the two of them.

'My father let the Nucci get away with exile from Giglia,' said Fabrizio. 'I would not have been so lenient.'

'I think Uncle Niccolò felt the same,' said Filippo. 'But Uncle Ferdinando overruled him, didn't he? Your father could hardly be seen to disobey the Pope.'

'Well,' sighed Fabrizio, 'the Church must be respected. I believe the Nucci are now living in Classe.' He curled his lip. 'What's left of them, that is.'

The Nucci, who had killed Carlo and wounded him and Gaetano, had lost two of their sons and had only one left. The parents were living quietly with him and their two daughters in the City of Ships, down the coast from Bellezza. Fabrizio expected no further trouble from Filippo Nucci.

'But there are other enemies we can do something about,' he continued. 'You remember what happened to Falco?'

'It was a tragedy,' said Filippo. As the youngest cousin, Falco, had been a great favourite with them all. First his body had been shattered in the accident with a horse and finally it appeared his mind had been affected and he had drunk poison. He was the only family member in di Chimici history to have taken his own life and he had been only thirteen.

'It was,' said Fabrizio. 'But perhaps not in the way that you think. My father believed that the friends he made in Remora knew something they did not reveal. In particular the one they call Luciano, who is now a

Cavaliere of Bellezza.'

'The one who duelled with your father?'

'The same one. He is the follower and friend of Senator Rossi, the Regent of Bellezza. And Father believed that both of them belonged to a secret order of scientists known as the Stravaganti.'

'I have not heard that name,' said Filippo.

'They are a secret order,' said Fabrizio. 'And I am certain they practise black arts of sorcery and enchantment.'

'Is that what made you pass the laws against magic?'

'My father told me that he saw Falco,' said Fabrizio quietly.

'Saw Falco? When?'

'At his own memorial race in Remora. He appeared on the flying horse. You remember it?'

'I heard about it,' said Filippo. 'I was not at the Stellata in Falco's honour, myself. But my father was and I remember he said that a young rider swooped over the campo on the winged horse. But it couldn't have been Falco. He had been dead a month.'

'Father swore it was an older Falco. It took him a long time to remember what he had seen, but before he died he believed that my little brother was taken to another place by the Stravaganti and cured of his ills. That they left a simulacrum of him here to die.'

'But why would they do such a thing?'

'That is one of the things I would like you to find out, cousin,' said Fabrizio.

*

When Matt came out of the Scriptorium for his short lunch break, he found Luciano waiting for him with a strange figure. He looked like a hippy from the sixties, with long hair, flowing clothes and Matt thought he also had ribbons in his hair. All that was missing were the flowers and bells. Matt immediately distrusted him. And then he noticed that the stranger was looking at him intently. He was suddenly conscious of his lack of shadow and took a step back under the colonnade.

'Hi, Matt,' said Luciano. 'This is Ludo. He's one of the Manoush.'

That meant nothing to Matt; in his talks with Luciano, Cesare and Dethridge, the word hadn't come up.

Luciano saw he was going to have to do some more explaining. He suggested they should all go to the Refectory, which was open even on a Saturday. It was far less busy than during the week and they easily found an empty table. The few students who were in the Refectory looked curiously at the Manoush, who stood out among their black robes like a jester at a funeral.

'There are many here who do not know the Manoush,' said Ludo composedly, looking at Matt.

'Would you like to explain a bit about your people?' said Luciano.

'We are wanderers, without land or city,' said Ludo. 'We follow the old religion and celebrate its festivals wherever we find ourselves in Europa. We are musicians and healers and good with animals.' He shrugged. 'Many people do not like us.'

Luciano suddenly thought of something. 'Are you

safe in Padavia? There are new laws in the city against magic.'

'We do not practise magic,' said Ludo.

'But the law covers everything that might be called superstition or occult practices,' said Luciano. 'And that includes following the old religion.'

'Are you sure?' asked Ludo sharply.

'Certain,' said Luciano. 'The laws were invented by Grand Duke Fabrizio, which means they are in effect in all the di Chimici cities too, and he persuaded the Governor to introduce them here. And the penalty is death.'

'Then seven cities will be closed to us,' said Ludo. 'The Manoush will not like that. We do not like boundaries and barriers.' He stood up, his food and drink untouched. 'I must go back and warn my people.'

'But didn't you say you had a warning for me too?' asked Luciano.

Ludo looked furtively round the Refectory.

'Aurelio says to be careful of the di Chimici.'

'Well, that's good of him, but I think I know that. They've already tried to get me expelled from here.'

'No, this is more. He says "Beware the heir", but he didn't say what that means.'

Matt was relieved to wake up in his own bed on Sunday. Not only would he have both Sunday and Monday off in Talia from the Scriptorium – Monday was the Feast of the Archangel Raphael apparently – but in his own world he had a whole week of half-term to look forward to. He yawned and stretched luxuriously and thought about going back to bed after a late breakfast. He hadn't set either of his alarms and it was already ten o'clock.

He wandered down to the kitchen in his bare feet and saw that his parents and Harry had finished their breakfast long ago. Their places had been tidied away and the dishwasher was stacked. He had no idea where they all were. He poured himself orange juice and a large bowl of cornflakes and switched on the kitchen TV.

He didn't want to think about printing, books, magic, laws and most of all he didn't want to think about stravagating. But his peace was soon disrupted. The doorbell rang and feet thumped down the staircase. He heard Harry's voice and soon his brother's tousled head poked round the kitchen door.

'Oh, you're up,' he said. 'There's people to see you.'

Matt groaned softly. 'Where are Mum and Dad?' he asked, wrapping his dressing gown tighter round him.

'Sainsbury's,' said Harry and disappeared.

Matt found Georgia and Nick standing sheepishly in the hall and waved them into the kitchen.

'I've only just woken up,' he complained. 'And I can't think till I've had some coffee. Do you want some?'

Georgia was sympathetic. 'You must be exhausted,' she said. 'I remember what it was like. Shall I make it?'

She busied herself with filter papers and cups while Matt finished his cereal. He looked longingly at the toaster but didn't really want to make any breakfast for the others.

'So,' said Georgia. 'How's it been going?'

'OK,' said Matt. 'I've met this new character.'

He hadn't really liked Ludo but he felt a sudden urge to know more about something or someone in Talia than these two did.

'He's a what-d'you-call-it . . . Manoush.'

'Ah,' said Georgia, as if she already knew about him. 'Was it Aurelio, the blind one?'

'No,' said Matt. 'It was a new one, one Luciano didn't know.'

At the mention of Luciano, he saw Nick's eyes swivel to Georgia with a look he couldn't interpret. But she had her back to them, filling the coffee machine with water and didn't notice.

'He's called Ludo something but he mentioned Aurelio,' said Matt.

'They're wonderful, the Manoush, aren't they, Nick?' said Georgia, looking nostalgic. 'So dark and mysterious.'

'This one wasn't dark,' said Matt. 'He was practically ginger.'

'Then he can't have been Manoush,' said Nick. It was the first remark he'd made since arriving and Matt suddenly felt really hacked off about the way these two treated him.

'Look,' he said. '*I'm* the one who met him and your precious Luciano TOLD me he was. And HE told me all about them. They seem to be some sort of Travellers or Gypsies. Ludo had to rush off and warn his mates about the laws against magic. Luciano seemed to think they'd get into trouble for worshipping the goddess or something.'

Nick had stood up, his fists clenched, but when

Matt said that the Manoush were in danger, he slumped back in his chair. When he had been Falco, he had loved the Zinti, as most Talians called them, and their music had been what led him to Luciano, Georgia and his new life in this world. Now he just felt helpless and frustrated that, if they were in danger, there was nothing he could do to save them.

'Do you want me to kill him?' asked Filippo matter-of-factly.

It did Fabrizio good to hear him offer so willingly but he replied, 'No. At least, not straight away. If my plan works, his blood won't be on di Chimici hands. What I want is for you to find out what you can about the Stravaganti and what it is that they can do. It might even mean befriending him.'

Filippo frowned. He would rather use force than subterfuge; it seemed more manly. But Fabrizio was his friend as well as his relation and, since Niccolò's death, the head of the family.

'If that is what you wish, cousin,' he said.

'I do. And if you can gain his confidence and trick him into performing any of their ungodly acts in front of you, then we can just hand him over to the Padavian authorities. Antonio might not have been willing to yield him to me but, if he's proved to have broken the new laws, he'll have to have him executed.'

Chapter 10

The People of the Goddess

The Manoush had gone underground. As soon as Ludo had brought them Luciano's news, the group had dispersed over the city, pulling long dark cloaks from their bags to cover their bright clothes and putting away their musical instruments. They pulled the ribbons out of their hair as they walked and wound it into tight buns or neat pony-tails. The transformation was almost magical in itself.

Most Manoush had friends in cities among the 'permanenti', as they called people who were not wanderers like themselves. It was not long before Ludo was knocking at the door of Messer Antonio's house near the main square. Fortunately for him, Antonio was not at home. It was Giunta, the Governor's wife, who was friend to the Manoush, and she opened the door herself.

In the past she would have welcomed him openly, entertaining as many of his friends as she could fit round her table. But since her husband's new laws – much as she disapproved of them – Giunta could not afford to be seen socialising with worshippers of the goddess.

As soon as she saw Ludo's unaccustomed sober clothes and his red-brown hair tied neatly back with a black ribbon, she realised he must know of the new danger.

'Come in, come in,' she welcomed him hastily. 'Are you on your own?'

'Just me this time,' he said with a rueful smile. 'We thought it would be easier to ask shelter with friends singly.'

Of course, both he and Giunta knew that shelter was the last thing he wanted. The Manoush always spent their nights under the stars, spreading their bedrolls in courtyards or fields, in most weathers, taking cover under trees or overhanging walls only in the worst of storms.

But in this new situation they would welcome hospitality and a place to hide if the authorities came after them. To do it in the house of the man who had published the very laws he would be breaking was typical of Ludo.

'Can you help me?' he asked Giunta. 'It will be dangerous.'

Her only answer was a contemptuous snort, which he rightly took to mean that her husband's laws were no concern of hers. She led him to a part of the house which was as much her domain as the study was Antonio's.

Beyond the kitchen and scullery, Giunta had a laundry room, which was the latest in sixteenth-century technology. A wood fire was always laid in readiness under a copper boiler and cupboards held clean linen for the household. Bunches of dried lavender hung from the low rafters and Ludo had to duck to avoid them. Outside was a little yard with a private well in the middle. The yard was strung with washing lines and held a wood-store, a chopping block and axe and a pile of logs.

Ludo's eyes lit up when he saw the wood.

'I could chop logs for you, Signora Giunta,' he said, taking off his dark cloak and hanging it over a line.

Giunta nodded. She pointed to a small wooden door that opened out of the yard into an alley.

'Come and go by this way,' she said. 'I will give you a key. You can sleep out here and take your meals in the laundry. You'll be quite safe. Only my laundry maid and myself come here and she won't give you away. She follows the Lady.' She paused and looked him shrewdly up and down. 'Only no trifling with her affections – Maria is a useful girl and I don't want to lose her.'

Ludo opened his eyes wide and pointed at his heart as if to say 'Would I?', but Giunta was not convinced. So good-looking a man, who never stayed long in one place, was bound to acquire a reputation and he was not as high-minded as his cousin Aurelio.

He took her hand and brushed it with his lips. 'You know you are the only woman for me, Signora,' he said.

*

The youngest stable boy in the Ducal Palace of Bellezza had the job of exercising Arianna's African spotted cats. His name was Mariotto and he loved the cats as if they were his own. Each day they had leather leashes fixed to their silver collars and walked sedately with him across the Piazzetta, to the amazement of all the citizens and the few tourists who were up early enough to see them.

Once away from the populous centre of the city and out in some of the swampy land that had not been built on, he let them run loose and stretch their long muscular legs for as long as they liked. There was little to hunt in the marshes, except a few waterfowl, and after about an hour, they would come back to him sniffing the canvas sack he had brought with him.

Then they would lie at his feet, gnawing on the hares or small wild pigs he had bought from a hunter, while Mariotto sat on a tussock of grass eating bread and cheese and feeling utterly content with his life.

After they had all slept in the sun for a bit, he would put their leashes back on and begin the slow walk home. Apart from another short walk in the evenings, with just a bone or two to gnaw on, this was their main exercise of the day.

Imagine his surprise when early one morning the masked Duchessa herself turned up at the stables at dawn, just as he was getting the cats ready. They heard her first and turned their elegant heads towards the sound.

'Florio, Lauro,' she cooed and they loped over to her, burying their muzzles in her hands. She had brought them tidbits of food from her own table.

'You shouldn't feed them till they've had their run,'

said Mariotto disapprovingly. He also disapproved of their names since 'Florio' was clearly a female, but the Duchessa had named them after a couple of male saints; he had no idea why.

Arianna was amused. She had become accustomed to the deference of servants over the two years since she had become Duchessa and it was refreshing to find one – even a rather small and grubby one – who was not overawed by her.

'You are quite right, Mariotto,' she said. 'We don't want them to get fat and lazy, do we? I'll help you make them run, though'

'You, milady?' he said dubiously.

'I am coming with you this morning.'

'But you can't,' he said bluntly.

'Can't, Mariotto?' said Arianna. 'Am I not your mistress and the ruler of your city? Are you sure "can't" is the word you are looking for?'

'But I have no weapons, milady,' he said, truly aghast at the thought of having her with him. 'How could I guard your safety?'

'I think two African hunting cats are weapons enough, don't you? No one would dare attack me while with them, Florio and Lauro would tear them apart.'

She threw on the plain cloak she had brought with her and looked at him expectantly.

Mariotto put the leashes on the cats, muttering under his breath.

The first day of half-term began with an early driving lesson for Matt. He was hopeful of passing his test first time and wanted to get in as many lessons and as much practice as he could. As his father was an opera singer it meant Andy was around till mid-afternoon. He got back every night after singing at the ENO, ate a very late supper and never got up early. So the second half of the morning was always a good time to get him to be an accompanying driver.

On this Monday after the driving lesson, pleased to know that he wouldn't have to spend all night working in the Scriptorium, Matt drove cautiously round the streets of Islington in the family car, while Andy complained about the soprano who was singing in the current production of *The Magic Flute*.

'Grade A bitch,' he said. 'Only told the conductor the chorus was too loud – took that corner a bit wide, Matt – too loud, I ask you! She's the Queen of the flipping Night, with a voice that'd break glass at fifty paces and suddenly *we're* too loud! I'm sure she was looking at me, too.'

'Well,' said Matt, 'you *do* have a loud voice.'

'Of course I do,' said Andy. 'I'm a flaming opera singer, aren't I? Not a fliggering horse-whisperer – watch your speed.'

'How do you think I'm doing?' asked Matt.

'What? Oh, fine, lad. You're doing really well. Hello, isn't that Ayesha? I DIDN'T SAY EMERGENCY STOP, DID I?'

But Matt had seen her too and she was with Jago. They weren't holding hands or anything but they were walking side by side in earnest conversation. A murderous rage welled up inside him and he wanted to mount the pavement and mow his rival down.

Andy, blissfully unaware, was winding down the

passenger window and waving. 'Hey, Yesh, how are you doing?'

Ayesha looked up and saw them. Why did she look so embarrassed? Jago just looked faintly bored and amused the way he always did; it made Matt want to smash his supercilious face in.

Matt started the engine and revved, making the car leap forward.

'Mirror, signal, manoeuvre, Matt,' said Andy, clutching the strap of his seat belt.

Matt watched the figures of his girlfriend and his enemy recede into the distance.

Luciano wondered what on earth Ludo had meant by Aurelio's warning, 'Beware the heir.' The obvious heir was Fabrizio, who had become Grand Duke after Niccolò. But then he wasn't the heir any more and, besides, Luciano was well aware he had to be careful of Fabrizio.

He thought of other di Chimici who might be described as heirs, but he didn't have much connection with any of them except Gaetano, who was now heir to the Principality of Remora. It should have been Carlo who would have inherited that most important city when their uncle the Pope died, but Carlo had been killed on his wedding day and Gaetano was next in line. Gaetano was Luciano's friend and he trusted him completely; he had no reason to doubt him.

The only other real 'heir' Luciano could think of was Filippo, Francesca's older brother. But what could Filippo di Chimici have to do with him?

He gave it up as a bad job and went to look for Cesare. What he needed was a good ride.

He found his Remoran friend already in the stables of his lodging house and pleased to see him.

'You heard about the Manoush?' Luciano asked, as soon as Cesare had saddled up and they had gone out through a gate in the city's northern wall.

'I heard they were here one minute and gone the next,' said Cesare.

'I think they're still here,' said Luciano. 'They're just keeping out of the way because of the new laws.'

'Right, yes, I see,' said Cesare. 'Goddess-worship.'

Luciano thought of something. 'You must have the new laws in Remora?'

'I suppose so,' said Cesare. 'They probably came in after I left.'

'But how is it going to work in the contrade? Won't people get into trouble for using all those zodiac symbols?'

Cesare looked startled. 'I don't know. I hadn't thought of that. But they can't outlaw all that from the City of Stars, can they? I mean, what would happen to the Stellata?'

*

When Matt arrived in the Scriptorium, the quiet and peace of the room with all its still presses did something to calm his inner rage. At first it appeared completely empty, the wooden presses seeming to hang lifeless from their ceiling struts.

He walked over to one of the machines and looked at the neat pile of printed sheets beside it. Again he found he could read without difficulty. It seemed to be a book about mythical beasts.

He was really enjoying reading about what a manticore was but after a moment the cupboard that concealed the door to the Secret Scriptorium swung open and Professor Constantin looked out.

His eyes lit up when he saw Matt.

'Ah, I thought I heard something,' he said. 'Come in.'

Matt hesitated. He had been going to find Luciano and Cesare but he was curious to see what might be going on inside the secret room.

Once in the inner room, he saw that Biagio was there too and, with an apron tied round his ample waist, was busy rubbing two leather ink balls on the ink-block. Above his head, several pages were already hanging up to dry.

'Matteo,' he said with relief. 'Come and take over. Then I can work the press.'

Trust me to arrive in time for the dirty work, thought Matt. Especially on my day off. But he rolled up his sleeves and took over the inking. As he fell into the familiar routine, he gradually felt the pressure of his anger falling away. The three of them worked together in virtual silence, Constantin as compositor, Biagio as puller and Matt as beater. They got a good rhythm going, Matt rolling the ink balls till they were well covered, then rocking them back and forth over the type that Constantin had set in the formes.

Biagio laid on the damp paper and turned the rounce – the handle that moved the carriage under the great press – then pulled the bar that brought the controlled weight down and literally pressed the paper against the type. Constantin also took on the task of removing the newly printed pages, peeling each one off the released carriage with a stick and hanging it up to dry.

By the time they stopped for lunch, there were an impressive number of these pages. Matt stretched until the muscles in his back and arms cracked.

'That was a good morning's work,' said Constantin. 'We shall take a break now.'

Matt looked up at the drying sheets, which he couldn't touch for fear of smudging them or getting ink on them from his hands.

'What book are we printing?' he asked.

He saw the swift look exchanged between Constantin and Biagio.

'It's a work of anatomy,' said Constantin. 'Of course the pictures are printed separately. Biagio and I have already done them on the rolling press – on Saint Luke's day. I'll show you.'

They left the inner room and stepped out into the main Scriptorium. The rolling press was at the other end from the proofreaders' table and Matt had never had much to do with it. It was less complicated than the letterpresses but it still took two men to operate it, inking the engraved copper plates and turning the handle to roll the paper through.

Constantin took him to a set of thin wooden drawers where already-printed illustrations were kept. He lifted out a heap of sheets containing maps and there, underneath, were pictures of a human body, showing the structure of the bones or the composition of the muscles. They didn't look exactly as they would in a modern textbook but to Matt's untrained eye, they still seemed pretty accurate.

'I don't understand,' he said. 'Why do you have to print this in secret? Aren't people supposed to know how their bodies work? It's hardly magic or superstition.'

Constantin put the sheets away.

'For many years,' he said, 'knowledge of the composition and working of the human body has been arrived at by guesswork, or by cutting up the bodies of horses and dogs.'

Matt wondered if sixteenth-century scholars knew that humans were related to chimpanzees and other apes. He didn't see how they could; how would a Talian have ever seen a chimp?

'You are right,' said Constantin, interpreting his expression correctly. 'A horse or dog does not function much like a man. But in Talia we have followed the pioneering work of the anatomist, Iohannis Armiger. We have taken his theories and descriptions of how the human body works for several hundred years. Until now.'

'And what now?' asked Matt.

Constantin lowered his voice.

'Before the laws against magic there were other laws, including one that said anatomists could dissect only the bodies of executed foreign criminals, both men and women.'

Matt shuddered.

'The problem is that there aren't enough of them. Medical students need many subjects to work on, male and female, old and young, those who have died by accident and those by murder, or any of a variety of sicknesses, babies both before and after birth – you understand that the law does not allow this.'

Matt had a vague idea that in his world you could leave your body to medical science but he had never really thought about it. He carried a donor card for organs but he was pretty sure it didn't mean his whole body could be dissected. The idea made him feel a bit sick. Constantin and Biagio were both watching him.

'I can see the idea troubles you,' said the Professor. 'Most people feel the same. And that is why we have the laws. But we also have here in the University of Padavia a very great scientist – an anatomist called Angelo Angeli. He has taken terrible risks to discover the truth about the human body and it is different from what Armiger believed.'

'You mean he cuts up bodies illegally?'

Constantin nodded. 'There are all sorts of poor people whose families cannot afford to bury them. A scoundrel called Gobbi has been putting them in touch with Professor Angeli. Money has changed hands. It's all against the law. But Angeli believes that if his book can be published it will mean that fewer dissections will have to be performed in future. And his discoveries will help everyone – doctors and the sick.'

'That's logical,' said Matt. 'But if it's so dangerous you have to print it in secret, how will students and doctors get hold of it?'

'We have an arrangement with the bookbinder,' said the Professor. 'The same one who works on our official publications.'

Matt knew the bookbinder, whose shop was at the end of the street in which the University stood. He hadn't thought about it before but all the secret books must have been bound somewhere, including the one that was his talisman.

'Isn't it terribly dangerous?'

'Very,' said Biagio. 'The more people who know about our work, the more danger there is. But Nando the bookbinder has as much at stake as we do.'

'How will people know when the book is ready?' asked Matt.

'We do it by word of mouth,' said Contantin. 'I will tell Angeli and he will tell his students individually. The ones he feels he can trust. He will keep a small stock of the books and the rest will be taken to a safe house, where they can be bought.'

To Matt it seemed incredible that something like the composition of the human skeleton would be treated in the same way as magic spells. Then he remembered that Luciano had warned him about keeping his knowledge of the solar system to himself. Now he thought he could understand why.

It seemed as if in Talia knowledge was under the control of a small number of people who wanted to keep it limited and strictly monitored. And Matt was pretty sure he could guess who those people were.

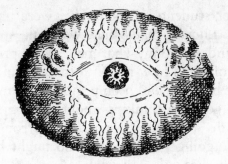

Chapter 11

The Evil Eye

The University was closed for Archangel Raphael's Day but Luciano and Cesare were waiting outside the Scriptorium when Matt came out.

'We guessed you were here,' said Cesare.

'Constantin has you working on your day off?' asked Luciano sympathetically.

'Yeah,' said Matt, yawning. 'And I'm starving.'

'The Refectory's closed,' said Cesare. 'But we can go to the inn.'

The Black Horse was rapidly becoming their local and had the advantage of being near the University and Scriptorium. It seemed that many other students felt the same. Today it was more crowded than usual so they had to share a table. Conversation about dangerous issues was impossible.

The other students at their table were particularly boisterous; Luciano said they were all students of Medicine and Anatomy. That made Matt prick up his ears. He wondered how many of them would soon be reading the book he had been printing that morning.

But that got him thinking about dissection and he looked with a ghoulish sort of horror at these cheerful, outgoing young men, who might have been cutting up bodies only yesterday.

'Do you get to do any Anatomy in your year here?' he asked Cesare and Luciano.

'No,' said Luciano. 'That's not considered part of a nobleman's education.'

'Should be,' said one of the medical students, who knew Luciano by sight. He tapped him on the chest. 'Everyone should know what goes on inside here.'

'I was just going to say,' said Luciano. 'That there are public dissections that anyone can go to. There's one at Christmas.'

'And some before that,' said the student. 'There's one quite soon. You should all come. Professor Angeli is an absolute demon at dissection.'

Matt wondered about whose body the Professor would be using for his demonstration; how could he know now which criminals would be executed in advance, particularly if they had to come from somewhere outside Padavia? But surely he wouldn't dare use an illegal corpse in a public demonstration?

*

Filippo di Chimici was already in Padavia. It had been difficult to explain to Francesca and Gaetano why he was leaving after only two nights in Giglia.

'Fabrizio has work for me to do in Padavia,' he had said, 'of a diplomatic nature.'

For Gaetano, who knew his family of old, the word 'diplomatic' had an ominous ring. He wondered if he should get word to Luciano.

But now Filippo had taken up residence in a grand palazzo near the cathedral. Though he didn't know it, he was staying only a few hundred yards from Luciano. It was his plan to attend some classes at the University and mingle with the students until he found his way to his quarry.

But it would be less pleasant going to the University than tracking down the Bellezzan. Filippo had already studied for two years at the University of Bellona, which claimed to be the oldest in Talia, and he felt nothing but contempt for the upstart institution in Padavia, even though both universities were over three hundred years old.

As soon as his servants had unpacked his luggage and provided him with lunch, Filippo went out to explore. He began with the cathedral, which was fuller than usual as it was a saint's day. Filippo was impressed in spite of himself, even though it was hard for a di Chimici to concede that any city not run by his family might contain sights worth seeing.

As Filippo wandered round the ornate interior, admiring the Tomb of the Saint and the many chapels decorated with fine frescoes, he didn't notice a shabby figure dodging between pillars and watching him.

Enrico prided himself on being a bit of an expert on the di Chimici. He had worked for three of them, helped one in a killing, been a little in love with another and had seen most of them at the fatal weddings in Giglia six months before. Besides, there was a strong family resemblance. The di Chimici were in the main a handsome family, though this Filippo of Bellona was a better specimen than his cousin Rinaldo, Enrico's first employer.

Filippo strolled round the cathedral as if he owned it, occasionally stopping to flick imaginary dust from his immaculate velvet cloak, and nodding his fine aristocratic head whenever he saw a painting or statue he approved of. Something about Filippo's bearing, as if he were one of the lords of the universe, made Enrico's blood simmer.

As the young Bellonan noble doubled back and passed him, Enrico shot him a look of pure, concentrated hatred. Ever since Enrico had realised that he had killed his own fiancée as a result of a di Chimici plot, he was now as much against the di Chimici as he had once been their loyal, if somewhat crooked servant. As he left through the main door, Filippo stumbled slightly, as if he had felt the force of Enrico's glower.

Outside the great cathedral two young men were lounging around near the statue of the bronze horseman. One was pointing out the finer points of the horse to his friend.

'Hang on,' said Luciano. 'That's one of the di Chimici, I'm sure.'

He had seen almost as many of them as Enrico had and, although he didn't know which one this was, he was as sure as the spy that this was a member of the family who were nearly all his enemies. His hand went involuntarily to the hilt of his sword.

Then he saw the spy himself slipping out of the cathedral and very casually beginning to tail the di Chimici.

'That's the rogue who kidnapped me in Bellezza,' he hissed, grabbing Cesare's arm. His friend was immediately alert.

'He kidnapped me too,' he said grimly. 'Remember? Stopped me from riding in my first Stellata.'

'We've both got scores to settle with him,' said Luciano. 'Let's follow.'

*

Matt went back to the secret room, pondering on dissecting dead bodies.

'Time to swap,' said Biagio, grinning through his curly moustache.

Matt was pleasantly surprised. So far he had always been the beater, if he hadn't been doing even more menial tasks like making ink or washing it off the type in the forme with hot lye and water, before the compositors redistributed the letters in their cassetini. Now, after washing all traces of his lunch off his hands, he took over the damping and laying of paper on the tympan of the press. It was delicate and precise work, fixing the paper exactly in place and laying over it the frisket – the thick paper template with cut-out shapes that made sure no ink got on the margins of the page to be printed.

They were printing the other side of the pages they had done in the morning and, to his surprise, Matt found that he was good at this work and enjoyed turning the rounce and pulling the bar. As with beating, he got into a rhythm with Biagio and Constantin and, at the end of their afternoon session, felt he had done a good day's work.

The candles were giving off their usual aroma of cooking fat, which made Matt feel a bit queasy after his lunch.

'Why do they smell like that?' he asked.

Biagio looked surprised; all candles in Talia smelt the same except for the expensive church ones. But Constantin answered, 'They are made from tallow – it's a kind of animal fat.'

I wonder if I could be a printer, Matt thought but almost immediately dismissed the idea. It must all be done by computers and photography in twenty-first century England and his experience in Talia would not help him. And who had ever heard of a dyslexic printer? he thought. But even that didn't diminish his sense of achievement as he stretched out on the floor in Constantin's studio, holding his spell-book and thinking of his own bed. He was asleep in minutes.

Matt woke late on the Tuesday, suddenly remembering that he was going to see Ayesha. She had said she'd come on his driving lesson with him. Brian didn't mind; she'd done it before. So she sat in the back seat, revising her History notes, while Matt practised his three-point turns in a cul-de-sac.

'Good,' said Brian. 'You're really getting the hang of that. 'It's doing you good having all these extra lessons and practising with your dad.'

He dropped them both outside Matt's house but

they didn't go back in. Instead they wandered aimlessly down to the High Street, Matt carrying Ayesha's bookbag. He wanted to ask her what she'd been doing with Jago the day before but couldn't quite bring himself to and in the end their conversation petered out. He couldn't tell her what he'd been doing and he was afraid of discovering what she had been up to.

Suddenly she stopped and held out her hand for her bag.

'We're not going anywhere, Matt,' she said.

He felt as if he'd just stepped off a cliff.

'You mean literally?' he said, trying to keep things light. 'We could go for coffee.'

'No,' she said sadly. 'I don't mean that. I mean that you don't talk to me any more. I don't know what you're thinking.'

That was true; he couldn't deny it. But it still hurt to hear her say it.

'I think we should take a break,' she said. 'Just to cool it for a while.'

'You mean you're dumping me,' said Matt bitterly. 'Don't dress it up in all that "it's not you, it's me" stuff.'

'I wasn't going to,' said Ayesha. 'It *is* you. Not me. You're the one that's changed. You're moody and irritable and jealous and suspicious. I saw the way you looked yesterday, in the car, when you saw me with Jago. I can't carry on like this. Sort out whatever it is that's bugging you and then let's see where we are after a few weeks.'

And she turned and walked away from him. When she got to the corner, he saw a red car take the turning and knew that this had been planned.

The worst of his imaginings was coming true.

If Filippo was unaware he was being followed, Enrico was even more so. His skills as a spy had been eroded by months of worry and hardship. While Filippo strolled along the street that led to the University, Enrico suddenly found himself grabbed from behind and bundled into an alley.

Luciano and Cesare had forgotten how bad he smelt! The spy ceased struggling as soon as he saw who they were and sagged alarmingly in their grasp. Now that they had got him, they were at a loss what to do with him. He was a pathetic figure, unshaven, dirty, with his clothes hanging loose on his scrawny frame.

Enrico held his hands up as if to say he gave in.

'Do what you like,' he said dejectedly. 'I don't suppose there's any chance of a meal first?'

The man's effrontery was staggering but they both felt rather sorry for the wretch.

Luciano didn't want to be seen with him in public and he didn't want Enrico to know where he lived. In the end, after whispered consultation, they frog-marched him to Cesare's lodgings.

The woman who cooked for Cesare and his four housemates was not best pleased to have to prepare extra food at an unexpected hour but she softened when she saw Luciano's silver and heard his polite words. While she was in the kitchen, Luciano and Cesare took Enrico out to the yard pump and stripped him.

To hear his howls, anyone would have thought he was enduring the worst of tortures. Indeed for Enrico, soap and water *were* torture. While he stood bedraggled and sneezing under the cold water, Cesare went up to his room and brought down a towel and some spare clothes for him to change into.

They were too big for Enrico and he was still shivering when they brought him into the kitchen where the cook put a steaming bowl of soup in front of him. He ate it swiftly, with big chunks of bread, bolting it like an animal, as if someone might snatch it from him before he could finish it.

And then he drank two more bowls, ate a chicken leg, downed three mugs of ale and finally burped long and luxuriously.

Sitting at the wooden table with his hair still damp from the swabbing, the scrawny spy looked – and smelt – halfway decent. But Luciano and Cesare were not deceived. They had both been kidnapped and held captive by this man. Cesare had missed only a horse race, albeit an important one. But Luciano had lost his old life; it was a consequence he lived with every day.

Still, he had to admit that he would probably have died in his old life anyway and his capture by Enrico had just made it happen sooner. Who knew whether he would have had the option of living in Talia if Enrico hadn't kidnapped him when he did?

'Well then, masters,' said Enrico. 'I feel better for that. And I'm ready to take my medicine. What are you going to do with me?'

'Never mind about that,' said Cesare gruffly. 'What about what you did to us?'

Enrico spread his hands. 'Only acting on orders,' he

said. 'But that's all over now.'

'What do you mean?' asked Luciano. 'You're a reformed character, are you?'

'Not especially,' said Enrico. 'But I've given up working for the di Chimici.'

'Why's that then?' asked Cesare.

Enrico spat in the fireplace. 'Because they are bad news,' he said.

'We could have told you that,' said Cesare.

'You accepted money from them to kill the Duchessa,' said Luciano sternly. 'That's worse than kidnapping either of us.'

'Yes but I didn't, did I?' said Enrico reasonably.

'Didn't what?'

'Kill the old Duchessa. I saw her with my own eyes, watching you and the Duke at the duel. And I heard that black monk with the long hair call out "Silvia!" That was her name, wasn't it? Silvia, the Duchessa of Bellezza.'

So Rodolfo was right, thought Luciano. He had told them after the duel that he thought it was Sky's calling out that had given the game away.

'And that was when I knew,' said Enrico. 'It was me that killed Giuliana. My own fiancée. She was acting as the Duchessa and I didn't know.'

'So you made sure I killed the Duke,' said Luciano.

'Yeah,' said Enrico. 'And you know what? I'd do it again. Or perhaps I'd just stab him myself. That's why I don't want anything more to do with the di Chimici.'

'But they couldn't have known that Silvia was going to use a double on that day,' said Cesare, who hadn't heard this part of the story before. 'You're both just as guilty of the death of the other woman as you would have been if the Duchessa had really died.'

'Do you think I don't know that?' demanded Enrico wearily. 'Perhaps I should just stab myself too?'

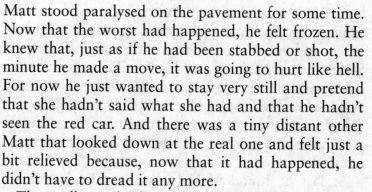

Matt stood paralysed on the pavement for some time. Now that the worst had happened, he felt frozen. He knew that, just as if he had been stabbed or shot, the minute he made a move, it was going to hurt like hell. For now he just wanted to stay very still and pretend that she hadn't said what she had and that he hadn't seen the red car. And there was a tiny distant other Matt that looked down at the real one and felt just a bit relieved because, now that it had happened, he didn't have to dread it any more.

The spell was broken when someone bumped into him on the pavement and said, 'Watch yourself, mate.'

Everything snapped back into focus. He could see and hear the traffic, smell the petrol fumes, mixed with coffee, incense, Indian spices and honey-scented candles coming from the shops around him. He forced his feet to walk back towards his house.

If he was honest with himself, he couldn't really blame Ayesha; he had been a lousy boyfriend ever since he had become a Stravagante. Maybe that happened to them all? He should ask Sky; Alice certainly didn't seem enamoured of the whole thing. And maybe that was why Georgia and Nick had given it up?

But the way he felt now, Matt didn't want to be honest about it. He wanted to blame someone other than himself and Jago Jones was the obvious choice.

He wished that he could really do magic. What was the use of being able to travel in time and space as part of a secret brotherhood, if he couldn't make Ayesha love him again? Or at least make Jago sorry to be alive?

Matt picked up speed and ran the rest of the way home. When he got there, he rushed upstairs to his room and rummaged in his desk. Somewhere he had Jago's address; he couldn't remember why any more. Something about meeting Harry after an orchestra rehearsal and fetching him home from the Jones's house after they'd picked him up, or something. He didn't trust his memory to find the house again without the address and it would be dreadful to make a mistake.

At last he found it. His heart was beating faster than usual but whether from running up the stairs or because of what he was about to do, he didn't know.

He took some deep breaths, then ran down the stairs again.

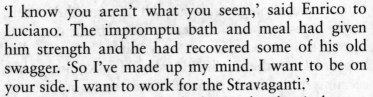

'I know you aren't what you seem,' said Enrico to Luciano. The impromptu bath and meal had given him strength and he had recovered some of his old swagger. 'So I've made up my mind. I want to be on your side. I want to work for the Stravaganti.'

Luciano and Cesare looked at each other in horror. The idea of this cold-blooded mercenary working for people like Rodolfo and Dethridge was not just ludicrous but alarming. Yet Luciano didn't want to turn him down straight out.

And an idea was forming in his brain. Perhaps Enrico could be useful to him after all?

Matt was out of breath when he arrived at Jago's house but he had plenty of time to get it back. After a quarter of an hour a fine drizzle started to fall. He sheltered in the doorway of a block of flats opposite. No longer warmed by rage and determination, he was shivery and miserable, like someone coming down with flu. He didn't even know if what he was planning would work. And he certainly knew it was wrong.

He pushed down all thought of what Constantin might say and instead ran through what he needed to know for his theory test in his head.

Matt lost track of the time; he seemed always to have been standing in the rain outside Jago's house waiting for him to come home. Several people had pushed past him to put their keys in the front door or buzz the entry-phone to the flats. Once, when a dog looked as if it was going to lift its leg against his jeans, he decided to move out into the rain and just get wet.

But eventually a red car pulled up across the road and parked outside the house. Matt didn't stop to think. He hunched his shoulders and ran across the road, rain slanting into his eyes.

Jago was just locking the car, pressing a remote control on his key. The car lights flashed once. Jago looked up startled as Matt loomed over him.

Then he smiled slowly. 'Hello, Woody,' he said. 'What can I do for you?'

Matt saw Jago's eyes widen as he realised that he

was going to hit him. But he was wrong. Matt fixed him with his gaze and put into the look everything he had ever felt about people like Jago. People who read and wrote effortlessly, who could talk about literature and write poetry and would probably leave university with first-class degrees and get jobs in journalism or the BBC.

If he was wrong and this didn't work, he was going to look really stupid. But it was working, just as he knew it would. He was putting the evil eye on his enemy.

Chapter 12

Consequences

'Don't forget Eva's coming to stay for a few days this week,' Matt's mother said at dinner.

Matt groaned inwardly. He didn't dislike his great-aunt but he had a horrible feeling that her vagueness concealed a shrewd mind and he worried that she might be able to tell just by looking at him what he had done.

Matt did not stravagate that night. He told himself it was because he had done it twelve nights in a row and was exhausted. But really he didn't want to see Constantin. And he didn't want Constantin to see him. He didn't want to look the Professor in the eye, or Luciano, or any other Stravagante; he was sure they would know what he had done.

So in a defiant mood he set the spell-book on his

desk and went to bed at ten and slept soundly for ten straight hours.

He woke refreshed in body but restless in his mind. There was a dull sense of doom hanging over him, made up of having really been dumped by Ayesha and of what he had tried to do to Jago. He hadn't hit him, hadn't touched him in any way. But he had tried with all his might to put the evil eye on him.

And Jago had staggered under the onslaught of his gaze. Making a dash for his front door, he had looked back at Matt, shaking, and said, 'You're mad, Wood. Do you know that? Stark raving. No wonder she wanted shot of you.'

Matt thought he would never forget those words. He had to shake his head to get the sound and image of Jago out of his mind; a part of him felt he was right.

There was no driving lesson that morning and he didn't feel like practising with Andy. Instead he phoned Chay and they went for a run, followed by a long training session in the gym. It was just what he needed; pushing himself to the limits of his physical endurance meant he didn't have to think.

They went for cold drinks, still out of breath and hot, even after their showers.

'All right, Matt?' asked Chay.

'Not really,' said Matt. He swallowed hard. 'Ayesha's called it off.'

'What? Oh, man. I told you to sort it out,' said Chay. 'I warned you.'

'I know,' said Matt. 'And I tried. But what chance have I got with Jago around?'

'He's always been around though, hasn't he?' said

Chay. 'They broke up long before you and Yesh became an item. So what's new?'

Matt shook his head.

'I reckon you're mad,' said Chay after a while.

'That's what he said,' said Matt.

'She likes you better than Jago,' said Chay. 'Otherwise she'd have gone back to him, not started with you.' Then he realised what Matt had said. 'You didn't go and see him, did you?'

'Yeah,' said Matt. 'Why?'

'Well, it was a dumb thing to do,' said Chay. 'Did you punch him out?'

'No, I'm not a Neanderthal,' said Matt. 'Even if I look like one.'

'Only . . .' Chay trailed off.

'What?'

'I heard he was in hospital.'

Luciano had a Rhetoric class with Constantin that morning and afterwards the Professor asked him to stay behind.

'Matteo didn't stravagate today,' he said quietly. 'I had to tell the pressmen that he was sick.'

'Perhaps he is,' said Luciano. 'But he seemed OK yesterday.'

'You don't know anything then?' asked Constantin. 'I thought he was all right too. We had a good day working in the Secret Scriptorium.'

'I don't like it,' said Luciano. 'It's always awful, not knowing what's going on in the other world.'

He was remembering the times that Georgia had

failed to turn up in Talia. The first time, it was because her stepbrother had stolen her talisman and she was away only a few days. But then he had taken it again and Georgia hadn't been able to stravagate for a long time. By the time she found the talisman and returned to Remora a whole year had passed in her world even though only a few weeks had gone by in Talia.

Matt hadn't any enemies, as far as Luciano knew. But suppose something had happened to his talisman – who knew when he might be back? The portal between the two worlds was notoriously unstable.

'You are worried,' said Constantin.

'Do you think I should stravagate myself and see what's happened to him?' asked Luciano.

'Leave it for a day or two,' said Constantin. 'I can cover for him in the Scriptorium till the end of the week.'

Luciano missed having lunch with Matt. He went back home and, to take his mind off Matt, Luciano told his foster-father about Enrico.

'And ye and yonge Caesar lette thatte scoundrel Henry goe?' Dethridge asked.

'We didn't know what else to do,' said Luciano. 'I suppose we could have reported him to the Governor but I don't have any evidence that he has committed crimes, except his own confession – and I don't know if he would repeat that in a court of law.'

'And ye saye he killed his owne betrothed?'

'I know that's not what he meant to do but you can't deny that Silvia is alive and someone died in the Glass Room. His Giuliana disappeared on the same day and Silvia told us she had used a double that day.'

'So do ye thinke he has reformed, like yonge Guy the assassin?'

'No, I don't think Enrico is anything like Guido Parola,' said Luciano. 'But he now wants to help us and though I can't see him as a friend of the Stravaganti, he might be useful in giving us information about the di Chimici. He's already told us that the one we saw in Padavia yesterday was Filippo of Bellona.'

'Whatte is Philip of Bellona doing so farre from home?' asked Dethridge.

'I don't know,' said Luciano. A vague feeling of unease surrounded that idea but he didn't examine it. He was still worrying about Matt.

*

Ever since the day Arianna had gone out early with Mariotto and the cats, she had been bringing her maid Barbara down to the stables to spend time with them. The poor girl was terribly afraid of any animal larger than a lapdog. She cringed when the cats came over to Arianna, sniffing her fingers and looking for treats. Arianna made the maid give them the fragments of meat she had brought for them.

Barbara would stand trembling, letting them lick her hands. But after a few days, when she saw that they were nicely behaved and would not bite her, she relaxed enough to stroke their heads, as Arianna encouraged her.

'There!' she said, pleased. 'Now you will not be so scared of them when you are pretending to be me and it will help convince people that you are indeed the

Duchessa of Bellezza.'

Mariotto sat in the corner of the stable, deeply disapproving. He barely understood what he overheard – how could the maid be the Duchessa? – but he knew it wasn't right to feed the cats without making them run. Florio was already putting on weight, he was sure.

Then one day, the Duchessa brought not only the maid, but the Regent, Rodolfo, and his wife. And there was a footman as well; suddenly the entire stables seemed full of finely-dressed people. Mariotto slipped out and watched through a knot-hole in the wall.

The maid stepped forward and put a hand out to the cats, who came easily to her and took the morsels she had brought for them.

'Very nice,' said the Regent's wife, moving over to stroke the cats herself. They responded to her confident touch and raised their whiskery muzzles to her face. 'You are almost as at ease with them as is the Duchessa. It will not give you away this time.'

'What do you mean, in hospital?' said Matt, suddenly horrified. 'What's wrong with him?'

Chay shrugged. 'Not sure.'

'And how do you know, anyway?'

'Ayesha phoned me.'

'Why would she do that?' said Matt.

'Well,' said Chay. 'She sort of wondered if you'd done anything to him. I told her not to be stupid.'

'She wasn't,' said Matt. 'I did sort of do something.'

'But you said you didn't touch him!'

'I didn't,' said Matt. 'But I did look at him.'

Chay laughed. 'Looked at him. What would that have done.'

'I don't know,' said Matt. 'I don't know what happened but I tried to hurt him. Have you heard of the evil eye? Oh, never mind. We'd better go to the hospital and see what we can find out.'

The Admissions Officer at Barts was a bit guarded about giving them any information. 'Family only,' she said.

'Can't you even tell us what ward he's in?' asked Chay.

'Intensive Care,' she said after hesitating. 'No visitors – only family.'

But she still wouldn't tell them what was wrong with him. The two boys left her office none the wiser.

'We could go up to Intensive Care,' suggested Chay. 'Maybe someone up there will tell us something?'

They took the lift in silence. Chay was seriously worried about Matt wittering on about the evil eye. And Matt was in a state of icy panic. He had wanted to hurt Jago, had hated him enough to wish the worst possible things on him. But even while he'd tried what Constantin called the 'Jettatura', he hadn't really believed that anything too serious would happen. 'You either have the power or you don't,' the Professor had said. And Matt hadn't known if he had the power. Now it seemed that he did.

The last thing he expected was to see Ayesha coming out of the Intensive Care Unit with Jago's parents. It gave him a horrible jolt to his stomach. Seeing her with them, as if she were a member of their family, just as she had so often been to places with Jan and Andy, brought home to Matt again what he had lost. And then he wondered for the first time what had happened to Jago's girlfriend Lucy.

Ayesha whispered something to Mr and Mrs Jones and they went into the lift, leaving her to talk to Matt and Chay. They looked drawn and exhausted.

Suddenly an image flashed into Matt's brain. This was where Luciano had died. He knew what had happened to him. And it was nothing like what had happened to Jago, but what Matt was seeing was a figure lying on a hospital bed hooked up to tubes and a mother and father agreeing to turn off the machines that were breathing for him.

He must have looked as ghastly as he felt, because Ayesha didn't yell at him. She took one look at his white face and marched them both off to the cafeteria.

'What happened?' she asked, when they were all sitting down with a murky cup of hospital coffee. She reached over and spooned two sugars into Matt's, even though she knew he didn't take it.

'That's really what we want to know,' said Chay. 'What's wrong with Jago?'

'They don't know,' said Ayesha wearily. 'At first his parents thought it was a sudden dose of flu. He's got a high temperature and he keeps shivering and then saying he's too hot.'

'Can't they give him something?' asked Chay.

'They are,' said Ayesha. 'But it's not working. They thought it might be meningitis and they've put him on strong antibiotics but he's still delirious. But before he went into the ICU, he mentioned your name, Matt.'

'What exactly did he say?' asked Matt.

'He said, "your ex is a nutter",' said Ayesha brutally. 'And I want to know what he meant.'

Enrico did not stay sweet-smelling for long but his wash and brush-up and his new clothes, not to mention a good square meal, had made a new man of him. And the Bellezzan had slipped him some silver too. The spy's lodgings on the far side of the swamp didn't cost much, so that he had enough money to keep himself in food for a few days and he was determined to earn more.

He had set himself to tailing Filippo of Bellona and now knew where he lived. Indeed the young di Chimici was now being followed from his home near the cathedral to the university building. Enrico watched while he went into the university offices and later came out with what looked like a list of some kind.

Enrico edged a little nearer and overheard Filippo asking for directions to a Rhetoric lecture by Professor Constantin; that made him prick up his ears. He knew that Luciano studied with that professor. There was no way that even a clean version of Enrico would be allowed into a university lecture room but he hung around outside chewing his nails until the students came out.

As he ducked behind a column in the courtyard, he saw that Filippo was deep in conversation with the young Bellezzan. He might have been worried if he could have heard their conversation.

'Do I have the honour of addressing the Cavaliere

Crinamorte?' Filippo had asked Luciano, as soon as Constantin's lecture was over. Luciano had recognised the di Chimici as soon as he entered the lecture hall and was intrigued that he had sought him out.

'At your service,' he said, making a formal bow.

Filippo bowed too, while Enrico watched this exchange of courtesies from behind his pillar.

'May I introduce myself? I am Filippo di Chimici, son of Prince Jacopo of Bellona. I come from Giglia where I have been staying with my sister Francesca and her husband Gaetano.'

At the mention of Gaetano, Luciano's suspicions were allayed. There had been a time when he and Duke Niccolò's third son seemed to be rivals for Arianna, but now that Gaetano was married to Francesca and Luciano engaged to marry Arianna, he felt nothing but affection for him.

'How are they,' he said cordially. 'I am very pleased to have recent news of them. I'm sure you understand that I can't visit them at present.'

'They are very well,' said Filippo. 'And Gaetano sends you his warmest good wishes,' he improvised. 'He says you became good friends in Remora.'

'We did,' said Luciano, pleased that Filippo wasn't taking up his allusion to the old Grand Duke's death. Perhaps this was another di Chimici he could be friends with? He certainly didn't look like Gaetano; Filippo was cast more in the mould of the older princes of the family's senior branch, tall and handsome, with finely-moulded features. Not like Gaetano, who could be thought ugly by those who didn't know him.

On impulse Luciano invited him to dine but Filippo

was insistent that the Bellezzan should be his guest.

Enrico watched the two young men leave the courtyard and slouched after them. All his instincts told him this was wrong.

Matt had thought that Ayesha was concerned about him but now he realised that she was in a cold fury. He had no idea what to say to her. It was one thing to admit what he'd done to Chay, who had no idea what he was talking about, but he had no intention of trying to describe the Jettatura to his girlfriend – his *ex*-girlfriend, as he must learn to think of her.

So he said nothing and stirred his coffee so hard it looked as if he might break the cup, while Chay babbled on.

'He didn't touch him, Yesh. I already asked him. He went round to see him but he didn't lay a finger on him.'

'And why did you go to his house, Matt?' said Ayesha intently.

'Even if he *had* hit him,' Chay was carrying on. 'It couldn't have given him meningitis, or whatever it is.'

'They don't think it's meningitis any more,' she said wearily, dropping her gaze from Matt's face at last. 'They're doing tests for tropical diseases now.'

'There you are then!' said Chay triumphantly. 'Matt couldn't have given him one of those, could he?'

'I don't know,' said Ayesha quietly. 'I don't know what Matt is capable of any more. He has been acting weirdly for days. Ever since his birthday.'

Matt still hadn't said anything.

'Maybe his new friends could tell me something,' said Ayesha. 'Anything that will help Jago.'

And she got up and left them.

William Dethridge was surprised by a knock on the door of the study in Silvia's old house. It was where Luciano wrote his essays and he felt most at home in its book-lined comfort.

'There's a man to see you, Dottore,' said Alfredo. 'One of the Zinti.'

'Showe him in,' said Dethridge. 'Yt semes we are notte to be joined by yonge Lucian for suppire. Maybe the Manoush wille sup with us in his stede.'

Ludo came in and bowed. He had been told by Aurelio that Luciano's foster-father was a very learned and distinguished man.

'Wel y-come, yonge manne,' said Dethridge, raising him up and clasping his hand.

'Greetings,' said Ludo. 'I am Ludovico Vivoide, known as Ludo. I think you have met my cousins Aurelio and Raffaella?'

'Aye, ladde, I ken them,' said Dethridge. 'And am ryghte gladde to mete anothire of their kin.'

'Is the Cavaliere at home?' asked Ludo.

'I have notte seene him since he lefte for his classe this aftire noone,' said Dethridge. 'Bot he is yonge. He moste notte fele thatte he needes to spend every even with an olde manne lyke me.'

Ludo frowned. 'Of course. But how would you know if he were in any danger?'

Dethridge looked up, worried.

'Nay, I wolde notte knowe. Bot I colde cast the stones,' he said at last. Looking at Ludo, he spread a black velvet cloth on the table and took a bag of polished glass stones from his pocket. On closer inspection it could be seen that each glass stone held a silver symbol of some kind inside it, but unlike Rodolfo's set, these were made of green rather than purple glass.

'See,' said Dethridge. 'I knowe notte yf ye use this method of descrying the future amonge your folke bot I always try yt whenne I am in doubte.'

'I have heard of this,' said Ludo, 'but among the Manoush we use cornstalks and see what pattern they fall into. Or the cards.'

They looked at the glass stones together.

The first contained a silver skull, the next a dagger. Then there was a crown, two fishes, a cat, a mask and a single eye.

'This reading likes me notte,' said Dethridge, now worried. 'I wille see what the cardes saye.'

He swept the stones back into his bag and took out a pack of Corteo cards.

Ludo settled down to watch, his chin in his hand.

Chapter 13

Tipping the Scales

Georgia couldn't have been more surprised to see Ayesha on her doorstep. The younger girl was looking haunted and anxious, her beauty masked by dark bruises under her eyes and her unwashed hair scraped back into a ponytail.

'Hi,' said Georgia. 'Come in. Are you OK?'

Ayesha stepped indoors as if sleepwalking. 'Not really,' she said. 'I've come to ask for your help.'

Georgia's mother and stepfather were both at work and Georgia had the house to herself. She took Ayesha into the kitchen and made her some tea. She had no doubt that the coming conversation was going to be difficult.

'What do you think I can do to help you?' she asked. 'What is it that's wrong anyway?'

'Do you know that Matt and I have broken up?' asked Ayesha.

Georgia felt a surge of relief. Perhaps this girl had simply come to her for some relationship advice. Though even that thought made Georgia smile; she was hardly qualified to be an agony aunt.

'No, I didn't know,' she said. 'I haven't seen Matt since Sunday. Sorry to hear it.'

'That's part of the problem,' said Ayesha. 'You saw him at the weekend and I didn't. He seems to spend more time with you and Nick than with me. And I was supposed to be his girlfriend.'

'Is that why you broke up?' asked Georgia, remembering a time when Alice had been jealous of her relationship with Sky, not knowing that they were both Stravaganti.

'That's part of it,' said Ayesha. 'And at first it wasn't exactly a break-up. I said we needed a cooling-off period. But it's much worse now. You know Jago?'

Of course Georgia did. Everyone in her year knew the star English student, and she and Alice were both a bit annoyed by all the attention he got. And she knew that he and Ayesha had once been an item. She realised that this was about more than a break-up.

'What about him?' she asked.

'He's in hospital,' said Ayesha. 'In Intensive Care. Matt got it into his head that I was, well, getting back together with Jago and he went round to see him.'

Georgia had a vision of an angry Matt looming over the slender Jago. She winced.

'No, not like that,' said Ayesha. 'At least, he swears he didn't hit him. But I think he did something worse.'

She hesitated. Now that she was here, she didn't

know how she was going to ask what she needed to know.

'He's been acting strangely ever since his birthday,' she said eventually. 'About the same time that he got friendly with you and the others.'

'In what way strangely?' asked Georgia, dreading what was coming.

'Look,' said Ayesha. 'Is he – are you – involved in some sort of cult?'

Is that what the Stravaganti are, thought Georgia. It was certainly how they might seem to an outsider – a secret brotherhood with more than human abilities. But Ayesha hadn't waited for an answer.

'I mean, it's your own business, of course,' she rushed on. 'But if Matt's put some sort of, well, spell on Jago, I need to know. The doctors can't cure him if they don't know what's wrong.' She dropped her head in her hands. 'I can't believe I'm even saying these things. But everyone's at their wits' end. And I'm scared that Jago is going to die.'

Now that she had said it, Ayesha started to cry. Georgia felt terrible. She grabbed a box of tissues from the counter then picked up the phone and dialled Nick's number.

'Is that a normal pattern?' Ludo asked Dethridge when he had finished laying out the thirteen Corteo cards.

Dethridge shook his head.

'There is notte sich a thynge with the arraye of cardes,' he said. 'Yt is different every tyme. Bot yt is an interestynge one.'

They leaned over the cards together. Starting at the middle left of the circle was the Book, one of the Major Arcana. The cards had been laid out face up and counter-sunwise, as was the traditional method. Next to the Book was a number card, the Ten of Salamanders, and then the Prince of Fishes. In the bottom position at the base of the circle was the card with the Moving Stars.

Both men studied the pattern intently.

'Do you take more notice of the Arcana?' asked Ludo, looking at the Scales, the Magician, the Lovers, Moon and Death, which were also part of the reading.

'Al wayes whenne the centre one is one of the Great Cardes, we think yt signifyeth some import,' said Dethridge, pointing to the Scales, which was the last card looking up at them from the centre of the array. 'And the thirteenth carde colours the humoure of the reading, as ye knowe.'

'So what do you think that means?' asked Ludo.

'Atte this tyme and in this place,' said Dethridge, 'I think it meaneth the law and justice.'

'The new laws?' said Ludo. 'Is that why Death is there opposite the Book?'

'I hope notte in the waye ye meane,' said Dethridge. 'He is a skeletone so mayhap is connected with the anatomistes here, rathire thanne the dethe penaltie.'

'And what is the Book?' asked Ludo. 'The first card is always important, isn't it?'

The Elizabethan nodded. 'I have an idea about thatte bot moste notte saye. I canne telle ye though thatte the Prince and Princess of Fyshes are yonge Lucian and the Duchess of Bellezza. They are the

169

lovires, who are also here.'

'But does it give you any idea if Luciano is in danger?' asked Ludo. 'My cousin Aurelio sent me with a warning to him.'

'I thynke notte,' said Dethridge. 'He is not close to the Deathe sygne and the sworde is notte here.'

'But the Death card is the thirteenth Arcanum, isn't it?' asked Ludo. 'And it's right there beside the thirteenth card, with the next being the Magician. I would read that as the death penalty for magic.'

'Mayhap,' said Dethridge, scooping the cards up quickly and wrapping them in a piece of black silk. 'And if thatte you are ryghte, we had best hide our means of divinatioun awaye.'

*

Luciano had a surprisingly good time with Filippo di Chimici. He was rapidly coming to the conclusion that Filippo really was 'one of the good ones', like Gaetano, Falco and Francesca. Filippo could be very charming when he put his mind to it and he plied Luciano with the best food and drink that di Chimici wealth could supply in Padavia.

But even though he had consumed a good deal of the Bellezzan red, which made him feel at home, Luciano kept his head. He did not know how much Gaetano had told his new brother-in-law about the Stravaganti and his years in Talia had taught him that it was dangerous to reveal anything about them.

'What do you think about the new laws against magic?' Filippo asked and Luciano immediately felt he must walk on eggshells with his reply.

'I don't really know much about it,' said Luciano untruthfully. 'I suppose it depends on the kind of magic. Some of it is obviously bad, like putting curses on people, but surely some is helpful? Spells to cure illnesses, for instance?'

'I agree with you,' said Filippo. 'The law can be a blunt instrument, and it doesn't distinguish between kinds of magic.'

'And I think it's a pity that it's all got mixed up with religion,' said Luciano. 'The goddess stuff, I don't know much about it but I don't see what the harm in it is.'

'Careful,' said Filippo. 'That's dangerous talk now, in this city and many others.' But he was smiling and Luciano still didn't feel any threat from him.

'I could do with some magic myself,' sighed Filippo.

'Why?'

'Well, my life is just coasting along. In a way I am waiting for my father to die and that is awful,' said Filippo, hastily crossing himself. 'I have no role in Bellona. My father makes all the decisions and he is not even teaching me how to be a good successor to him. And since Francesca went to Giglia there is no other young person to talk to about it. It might be different if I had a wife.'

'Do you not think of marrying then?' asked Luciano.

'I have thought of it,' said Filippo. 'But for one of our family it is important to have the approval of its head. That is my cousin Fabrizio now, of course, and he has had much on his mind. There is no one that I think of marrying at present.'

Luciano felt they were in dangerous waters with talk of the head of the family but was startled when

Filippo suddenly asked, 'And what about yourself? I heard a rumour about the young Duchessa of Bellezza?'

Luciano looked at Filippo's handsome and open face and decided that, if he knew already, it couldn't hurt to agree.

'Our engagement is a secret at present,' he said, aware that this was not only a di Chimici but a man five years older than him. 'But, yes, you are right. When my year at the University here is over, we shall be married.'

'Quite right to wait,' said Filippo pleasantly. 'I have spent time at the fine old University of Bellona myself. One cannot rush the education of a prince.'

Luciano suddenly felt very inferior. Although his marriage would make him a duke consort, he wasn't from a noble family in either world and he often felt a fake in Talia. For the first time he wondered who might have been his wife back in his old life. A picture of a girl with stripey hair crossed his mind before he suppressed it.

'Tell me about your family,' said Filippo. 'I think you know much about mine.'

This time Luciano was ready. He had a cover story that he was the orphaned son of Rodolfo's cousin in Padavia.

'Yet you are not the Regent's foster-son, I believe?'

'No. When Rodolfo saw how matters lay between his daughter and myself, the scientist Guglielmo Crinamorte and his wife Leonora offered to become my foster-parents.'

'Very proper,' said Filippo. 'I have heard something of this Dottore Crinamorte. Was he not originally from Anglia?'

'Indeed,' said Luciano. 'Though he has long made his life in Talia.'

Filippo felt that he had probed enough for their first meeting and turned the conversation to more general matters. When Luciano left the palazzo, slightly unsteady on his feet, he felt that he had made a new friend.

On his way home, though, a familiar scent assailed him and a much less reputable acquaintance fell into step beside him.

'Nice evening?' inquired Enrico.

'Very pleasant, thank you,' said Luciano, slightly annoyed.

'A word to the wise,' said Enrico, tapping the side of his nose. 'It doesn't do to get too pally with that lot.'

'Do you mean the di Chimici?' said Luciano. 'I know that many of them are not to be trusted but Gaetano is one of my best friends. And so was poor Falco.'

'And what did that lead to?' asked Enrico. 'Suicide on the one hand and a rash of murders on the other. All I'm saying is, be careful. And let me see what I can find out about this one.'

'All right,' said Luciano. It still felt strange to have Enrico working on his side but it couldn't do any harm to discover a bit more about the Bellonan.

'We've got to tell her something,' whispered Georgia as she let Nick in. 'She looks dreadful. And we've got to find out what Matt's been up to.'

'Hold on,' said Nick. 'Do you mean we've got to tell her about stravagation? Remember how that went down with Alice?'

They went into the kitchen, where Ayesha was still stirring her cold tea. She looked up with tired eyes.

'Oh, hi,' she said. 'You're Nick, aren't you? One of Matt's new friends.' Her face twisted so that suddenly she didn't look beautiful at all. 'Please tell me what's been going on.'

Nick was moved by her obvious distress but he still felt unsure. When they'd told Alice their secret six months ago, she hadn't believed them. Then she'd insisted on stravagating herself and he didn't think Matt would want Ayesha following him to Padavia.

'How much has Georgia told you?' he hedged.

'Nothing,' said Ayesha bitterly. 'No one will tell me anything and someone's going to die if you don't.'

Nick looked at Georgia, startled.

'Ayesha thinks that Matt has done something to Jago Jones,' she said. 'He's in Intensive Care and the doctors don't know what's wrong with him.'

There was enough in their histories about mysterious illnesses and unexplained deaths for Nick to realise how serious this was. But he couldn't understand what it could have to do with Matt's mission in Padavia – whatever that was.

'I don't see how what Matt's been doing could have affected this Jago,' he said. 'But we'll tell you if you like.'

He looked at Georgia, who nodded.

'Matt is a Stravagante and so are we – Sky too. You won't know what that means but it's a kind of traveller in time and space.'

'What? Like Doctor Who?' said Ayesha, looking angry. 'What do you take me for? I've been going out with him for three months and I KNOW him. He's a big, soft, dyslexic rugger player who's a great kisser and good with computers – not some alien Time Lord.'

'We were all just like you and everyone else till we were chosen,' said Georgia. 'At least, apart from Nick, but that's another story. There are these talismans that sort of seek out people of our age who are feeling miserable for some reason. And if we use them, we can get to Talia, which is like another kind of Italy only in the sixteenth century.'

'Was Matt miserable?' asked Nick.

Ayesha didn't answer straight away; they could see she was taking them more seriously now.

'It's true he doesn't have much self-confidence,' she said at last. 'And he was always so worried about whether I really liked him. He was always jealous of Jago – you know we used to go out?'

'Yes,' said Georgia. 'And then you and Matt quarrelled and you seem to be very caught up with Jago again.'

'But that was only yesterday,' said Ayesha. 'Yesterday! I can't believe how everything's changed in such a short time. But Matt was acting strangely before that and he's been hanging out with you guys for over a week. Are you telling me that this strav— thing has been going on all that time?'

'It must have been nearly two weeks ago,' said Nick. 'That was when we realised that Matt had a talisman. Georgia and I were there when he picked it up.'

'We're getting used to spotting them now,' said Georgia.

'But what has he been *doing* in this other place?' asked Ayesha. 'Have you been going there with him?'

'No,' said Georgia. 'We don't go there any more. Nor does Sky.'

'He's been working in a printer's,' said Nick.

'Why?' asked Ayesha. 'I mean, I can't believe any of this but a printer's is the last place I'd expect him to go. And what would that have to do with the state Jago's in?'

'That I don't know,' said Nick. 'You'd have to ask Matt.'

As if on cue, the doorbell rang and Georgia let in a wild-eyed Matt. He groaned when he saw Ayesha.

'Yesh . . .' he began but Nick interrupted him.

'She knows, Matt. We had to tell her.'

Matt turned his bloodshot eyes on Nick, appalled.

'But how come? I mean, how do you know what I did?'

'We only told her about stravagation,' said Georgia.

'Well?' asked Ayesha. 'What did you do exactly?'

When he got home, Luciano was surprised to find Ludo companionably drinking ale with his foster-father as if they had known each other all their lives. The rusty-haired Manoush had been playing on his flute and Dethridge had clearly enjoyed his visit.

'I'm sorry I wasn't home for supper,' said Luciano. 'But you don't seem to have lacked company.'

'Aye, never feare ladde,' said Dethridge. 'We have

been entertaining eche othire wondrous well. Bot where were ye?'

'I had dinner with Filippo di Chimici,' said Luciano. 'He's attending some classes at the University.'

Ludo looked at him with worry in his grey eyes. 'Were you careful? Remember my cousin's warning.'

Luciano felt a bit annoyed as well as rather drunk. Hadn't he been the model of discretion?

'Not all di Chimici are bad,' he said. 'And Filippo is Francesca's brother. We had a good time together.'

'And whatte did ye converse about?' asked Dethridge.

'All sorts of things,' said Luciano, uneasy under this cross-questioning. 'Our studies, Gaetano and Francesca, marriage.'

'Marriage?' said Ludo.

'Yes, he wishes he had a bride in prospect,' said Luciano. 'I think he's a bit lonely since his sister left home. He says he's got nothing to do until his father dies.'

That had come out worse than he meant.

'Beware the heir?' said Ludo softly.

'But he talked about a lot of other things too,' Luciano hurried on. 'The magic laws for one thing. He doesn't agree with them.'

'Interesting,' said Dethridge. 'In especial for thatte his cozin introduced them. But yonge Ludovic and I have bene talking about them too. I read the cardes in a spread of thirteen.'

'For me?' asked Luciano, who knew it wasn't the usual day in the month when his foster-father and Rodolfo did their divinations. He had been getting into the habit of doing them too but it was always at

New Moon and that had been a few days ago; Luciano had forgotten all about it this October.

'Aye,' said Dethridge. 'Just to ensure thatte ye were saufe.'

'And was I?' asked Luciano.

'Ludovic thynkes not,' said Dethridge.

'There was the Death card,' said Ludo. 'And yours. And many other things I could not understand. I am not an expert like Dottore Crinamorte but I am afraid for you.'

Chapter 14

Two Nights

Jan Wood and Vicky Mulholland took turns sitting with Celia Jones at her son's bedside. The three women had been friends since their children were at primary school and they had been part of the same babysitting circle. It was particularly hard for Vicky to be back in ICU, even though it was three years now since Lucien had died there.

She firmly pushed the memory down; Jago was not going to die. It was nothing like the situation with Lucien. Jago hadn't got cancer. But no one knew what was wrong with him and that was what was so devastating for Celia. When Vicky arrived to be with her that night, Matt's mother was doing her best to comfort their friend.

'At least he's no worse,' Jan was saying. 'The

doctors think he's stabilised. And the longer he's stable, the more tests they have time for.'

Celia looked ten years older than she had twenty-four hours ago. Vicky recognised the signs.

'Jan's right,' she said. 'You must stay positive.'

Jan fetched them both some coffee from the machine before heading for home. To her surprise, Ayesha was there. Jan hadn't known what was going on between Matt and his girlfriend but she did know that Ayesha hadn't been around much lately and she had seemed terribly concerned about Jago, more than just a friend would be.

Now she was in the kitchen helping Harry cook dinner. He was chattering on blithely about school orchestra, oblivious of the tension between Ayesha and Matt, which it took Jan only seconds to pick up.

Not for the first time, Jan wished her husband had a more ordinary job, one that meant he could eat dinner with his family; it was extraordinary how often quarrels broke out over a meal.

'Hi, Ayesha. Are you eating with us?' she said brightly. 'How's the food coming, Harry?'

'Fine, Mum,' said Harry. 'It's only heating up really. Yesh did the beans. And I put an extra potato in the oven because I thought she might stay.'

He beamed round at them. Thank God Harry hasn't started on girlfriends yet, thought Jan.

'Would you lay the table, Matt?' she said. 'We'll eat in the dining room.'

'I'll give him a hand,' said Ayesha.

Jan hoped they would sort out whatever it was soon.

That peasant boy is back, thought Enrico, who had taken to hanging round outside Luciano's lodgings. It hadn't taken him long to find out where the Bellezzan lived; his skills of detection had returned with his better fortune. Enrico knew the young Bellezzan didn't trust him any more than did the stable-boy from Remora did. But Enrico was fascinated by Luciano. The very fact that the Bellezzan hadn't hauled him off to the authorities counted in his favour. Yet Enrico had been part of a plot to kill him. Luciano must know by now that the foils had been tampered with at the duel. And that no one but Enrico could have smeared the poison on the Duke's blade. But the Bellezzan had given him food, clothes and some money and Enrico now owed him a debt.

The peasant boy wasn't alone this time; he was accompanied by an armed ruffian, no better dressed than himself, who was clearly keeping an eye out for the younger boy.

Funny, thought Enrico. How often did a peasant travel with an armed guard? The door of Luciano's house opened and the two were let in. At the same time a tall young man with red-brown hair and a black cloak slipped out. Enrico was torn for a moment but decided to follow the rusty-headed stranger.

Inside the house Luciano and Arianna were blissfully unaware of their new grubby guardian angel. Dethridge, who had been kept informed by Rodolfo, was not deceived by the masculine disguise and tactfully withdrew.

'Who was that leaving?' asked Arianna, when they had finally pulled apart, a little breathlessly. 'I thought he looked familiar.'

'Only because he's Manoush,' said Luciano. 'He's a new one – Ludo – and he brought me a message from Aurelio.'

'What message?'

'Oh, you know, the usual sort of thing – just to be careful of the di Chimici and beware of danger. But he's in worse danger than I am. You've heard about the new anti-magic laws being brought in here too?'

'Yes,' said Arianna. 'Antonio sent word.'

Looking at her in her coarse canvas breeches and homespun shirt, Luciano found it hard to remember that she was the elected ruler of Bellezza, who would have to be kept informed about Padavian laws, as the city was her near neighbour and ally.

'It would affect all the Manoush, wouldn't it?' she continued. 'All this clamping down on goddess-worship.' The fingers of her right hand began to curl but she unclenched them. The Duchessa had learned not to make the hand of fortune sign, common among the people of the lagoon.

'The whole reason they are here is to worship the goddess,' said Luciano. He went over to the window, whose shutters were open to the October night. 'It's half-moon tonight. In five days' time they begin to celebrate their Day of the Dead. However quietly they set about it, they'll be open to prosecution under the new laws.'

'What was Ludo doing here?' asked Arianna.

'I think he was trying to keep the Dottore company,' said Luciano. 'I've only just got back from dining with Filippo di Chimici.'

Arianna's eyebrows flew up under her fisherman's cap.

'It's OK,' said Luciano. 'I'm sure he's one of the good ones.'

'So you'll do it?' insisted Ayesha, as she and Matt clattered about his dining room with plates and cutlery.

'I said I would, didn't I?' he said. 'You can stay and watch me if you want.'

'All right,' said Ayesha. 'I will.'

Matt was surprised; he hadn't expected her to agree. Ever since the scene at Georgia's, when he had been forced to tell her about putting the evil eye on Jago, Matt had felt afraid of Ayesha. She hadn't screamed at him. In fact at first she had laughed and her contempt had been worse than her anger. She clearly hadn't thought him capable of doing something so powerful, even though she had made the connection between Jago's condition and Matt's new secret life.

But gradually he had realised that she hadn't underestimated him; if anything she had done the opposite. She had simply not believed that he could do anything so petty and mean.

They got through the meal somehow, with Harry chatting on cheerfully and Jan keeping a watchful eye on them. Then they pretended to watch a TV documentary about global warming, which was enough to account for their sombre mood. Even Harry's enthusiasm had been dampened down. When the phone rang, Jan was relieved to leave the room.

It was Vicky, who had left the ICU briefly to call with an update on Jago.

'No change,' said Jan, when she came off the phone. 'Are you going back to the hospital tonight, Ayesha,' she asked awkwardly. 'Or . . . ?'

'I'd like to stay here, if that's OK?' said Ayesha politely.

So they're back on, thought Jan. They don't seem very happy about it. Perhaps they'll stay up all night having what we used to call a 'deep-and-meaningful'. She suddenly felt old and wished that Andy was here to talk to about it. But it was no good worrying; she had to be up early to fetch her aunt from the station.

Matt didn't know where he stood with Ayesha any more. He felt shy undressing in front of her and getting into bed but he couldn't turn up in Padavia in more than his underwear because his robes would have to fit over it. She lay on top of the covers fully clothed, watching everything he did.

'Where's this talisman-thing, then?' she asked.

Matt brought the leather-bound book out from under his pillow. Ayesha took it in her hands and slowly unwound the brown leather strap from round it.

'How does it work?' she asked, impressed in spite of herself. 'You don't have to read it, do you?'

Matt winced. 'I can't,' he said. 'It's all in their version of Latin.'

'But you knew how to put that spell on Jago.'

'Professor Constantin told me about it.'

'What does he teach at this university of yours,

then?' she asked. 'Black magic?'

'He didn't teach me about it – I said he *told* me. And he didn't know I could do it. He warned me against trying, in fact. He's a teacher of Rhetoric – that's like sort of argument and logic.'

'I know what it is,' said Ayesha. 'We learn about it in Law. Barristers still have to know the basics – they haven't changed since Aristotle or someone.'

It was good to have her in his room again, on his bed, talking to him, even though she probably hated him now and was looking like shit. Is this what it is to love someone, Matt wondered. Not caring what they felt about you or how they looked? Just knowing them and wanting to be with them and wanting them to think well of you?

He wondered whether to tell her that the counter-spell for the Jettatura was in the book she held in her hands. If she had known Latin, she could probably have worked it out for herself and saved Jago without him. He couldn't remember enough about it himself – something about olive oil and salt. It sounded more like a recipe than a spell.

He had warned her that there wouldn't be anything much to see when he stravagated but in the end she was so exhausted that she fell asleep before him. He longed to put his arms round her but restrained himself. She wasn't here for sex or love; she was more like a UN inspector at a foreign election, wanting to see fair play.

If she had stayed awake, she would have heard his breath slowing but there would have been no other sign that the essence of him had slipped away to another world.

Enrico followed the rusty-headed man back to his lodgings, taking care not to be seen. Before they got there, the man met a group of friends and Enrico spotted bright colours and ribbons under their dark cloaks.

He nodded in the dark. Manoush. Funny how they always seemed to be around wherever the Bellezzan was. But then the group broke up again and the man continued on to the main square where the Palace of Justice stood. He dodged down a side road and Enrico followed him cautiously into an alley. The man unlocked a gate and disappeared.

Enrico walked back to the square counting houses and calculating which one's backyard now housed a Manoush.

Well, well, well, he said to himself, after checking twice. So Messer Antonio's house is giving shelter to a goddess-worshipper!

The spy filed this piece of information for future use; he didn't know yet what he could do with it but it was something to fall back on if the Bellezzan cast him off. For now he made his way back to the palazzo where the di Chimici was living. He had some serious infiltrating to do.

*

When Matt arrived in the Scriptorium, he felt as if he had been away for months. Several people asked him if he was feeling better and he nodded, not wanting to get drawn into difficult conversations; he had no idea what Constantin had told them and there was no sign of the Professor. Biagio soon had him knocking up ink balls and Matt forgot that he had ever been anywhere else.

But he shared a secret with Biagio ever since their session in the hidden press room, and the foreman treated him a little differently: nothing that the other men and apprentices would notice but there was a sense of shared danger that brought a form of friendship.

Every time he passed the new list of forbidden books that had to be posted up at the front of the Scriptorium, Matt read it and thought of how most of them were being printed on the secret press. And every time he felt the thrill of just being able to read the list. It was ironic that so many books were forbidden in the one place where he could have read them easily. But his work in Talia didn't give him much time to read anyway.

As the lunch break approached, Matt became anxious. He wanted to see Luciano and ask his advice but he needed to talk to Constantin too. He was going to have to confess what he had done and he wasn't looking forward to it.

The Refectory was full and it took him a while to see Luciano. He wasn't alone; a finely dressed, handsome young man, a bit older, was sitting drinking wine with him. Matt felt very aware of his shabby robes and inky hands.

'Ah, Bosco,' said Luciano with relief, as soon as he spotted him. But he didn't introduce him to his grand friend. 'Excuse me a moment, Filippo,' he said. 'I have an errand for this young man.'

And he took Matt out into the street.

'Sorry about that,' he said. 'I didn't want you to meet a di Chimici yet, even though I think Filippo is trustworthy. Where were you yesterday? Why didn't you come?'

He scrutinised Matt's face closely. 'Are you ill?'

'No,' said Matt. 'I . . . I've done something stupid. I really need to see the Professor.'

Luciano looked worried. 'I've got to go back to the di Chimici,' he said. He took some coins from a purse at his belt. 'Go to the Black Horse and get yourself some food. You'll find a boy there called Adamo. You can trust him – I can't say more now. I'll make sure Constantin comes to the Scriptorium this afternoon.'

Matt walked to the inn, feeling stranger than he usually did in Padavia. He couldn't shake off the memory that the real him was lying on his bed next to Ayesha all the time he was here. No sooner had he called for food and drink than a slender young man dressed as a peasant joined him at his table. But Matt thought, from his voice and his hands, that he wasn't quite what he seemed at first glance.

'I'm Adamo. Matteo Bosco?' asked the boy.

'That's me,' said Matt. 'At least in Talia.'

'You shouldn't tell strangers you aren't from Talia,' said the boy.

'Luciano said I could trust you,' said Matt. He didn't feel like playing games. He was desperate to get his interview with Constantin over and to get back to his world with a cure for Jago.

A woman brought his food and ale over and Matt spotted a tall man hovering round their table.

'Friend of yours?' he asked Adamo.

The boy leaned over to him and said in a whisper, 'He's my servant. And he is trained to run a sword through you if you offer me any insolence, so I'd be careful if I were you.'

Matt paused, a bite of food halfway to his mouth. 'Who are you?' he whispered back.

Adamo looked round the crowded inn before answering.

'The Duchessa of Bellezza,' she said quietly. 'Arianna Rossi. Luciano's future wife.'

The tall man was standing right behind her now and watching Matt intently. His right hand was under his cloak and he looked ready to move fast.

Matt continued to eat; at the moment it didn't feel safe to say anything. He had no idea why the Duchessa of Bellezza was sitting at his table and he was very keen not to antagonise her bodyguard. When Matt had finished his food, they left the inn together and Arianna walked beside him back to the University, while the tall man followed them.

'Luciano asked me to look out for you,' said Arianna. 'He knew that Filippo di Chimici would be around at lunchtime. He has been worried about you.'

'Yeah, I've got some problems back home,' said Matt, not knowing where to begin.

'I am sorry for that,' said Arianna. 'I hope it is not because of the task you are doing here. It would not be the first time.'

'Not exactly,' said Matt. 'But I didn't want to face Professor Constantin yesterday.'

'He is your Stravagante in Padavia, I believe,' said Arianna sympathetically and Matt found himself wondering what she would look like dressed as a woman. He thought she would be strikingly beautiful. It reminded him again of what he had lost with Ayesha.

'Matteo!' someone called and he saw Cesare riding up.

'Hi,' said Matt, wondering how he was going to introduce his companion.

Then he was thrown into total confusion by Arianna herself.

'Cesare!' she cried in a musical and very un-masculine voice. The Remoran looked astonished; he leapt from his horse and obviously didn't know whether to shake hands with the peasant boy or kneel at his feet. But she had remembered her disguise by then and managed a little bow to him.

'I am Adamo the peasant while I'm in Padavia,' she said quietly. 'And as such I must defer to Cesare Montalbano, the famous victor of the Stellata.'

In the ICU Vicky Mulholland was still sitting with Jago's mother, who had fallen into an exhausted doze in her chair. The boy was stable but still unconscious and Vicky was finding it harder and harder to stay positive for her friend. The nights were always the worst, she remembered. The lights of the ward dimmed, voices lowered and the blackness outside the window all made the hours pass more slowly and the hope that came with the dawn was often illusory.

Vicky thought back over the last three or four years. There had been the awful period of Lucien's first illness, his chemotherapy, which robbed him of his black curls, and then what now felt like a sort of reprieve when he had been well enough to come with her and David to Venice. It hadn't been long after that when they saw the hospital consultant and had been told that the brain tumour had returned.

But there had been something strange about Lucien's last weeks, something that the doctors in this hospital hadn't understood. He shouldn't have gone into a coma but he had and all his brain activity had ceased. The day she and David had stood and watched Lucien's breathing machine turned off had been the worst of her life. She could understand very well what Celia Jones was going through.

After the funeral of her son, Vicky had believed herself to be losing her reason. Not just mad with grief, which she recognised was part of what was happening to her, but genuinely, unpredictably mad. She had started to see Lucien in the streets of Islington. Of course David had said it was her imagination – until he saw him himself.

There hadn't been many such sightings and they didn't last long but the parents had to live with this secret; there was no question of telling anyone else.

And then, two years ago, the mystery that was Nicholas had landed on her doorstep, literally. A beautiful boy, with curly black hair, wounded in body and mind, needing a mother. Even though he was now a six foot plus fencing champion without even a trace of a limp, he was still the greatest single reason that she had survived Lucien's death. Vicky had never shaken off the notion that Nick was somehow Lucien's present to her.

It was ridiculous but no more so than seeing your dead son standing outside your house.

Vicky stretched her back muscles. She couldn't face another cup of hospital coffee. She wanted to go home, to look in on Nick as he slept in the room that had once been Lucien's and then to slip into bed beside her sleeping husband and take reassurance from him along with his warmth. But Celia needed her and she would stay.

When Matt got back to the Scriptorium, Biagio nodded at him.

'Master wants you,' he said. 'In the studio.'

With a feeling of dread Matt knocked at the studio door. It was a relief to find Luciano in there with Constantin even though it made the small room seem crowded.

To his surprise, the Professor clasped him warmly in his arms. Matt found himself looking down at his pink scalp, covered with his neatly cropped grey hair.

'Welcome back,' Constantin was saying. 'We were all worried about you.'

For one awful moment Matt felt he was going to cry. Neither of these two Stravaganti knew what he had done yet and he felt he had failed a test of character. Surely when he told them they would no longer care about him? And he wanted desperately for them to approve of him – even more than he wanted Ayesha to.

He swallowed. 'Professor, I need your help,' he said. 'You remember how we talked about the evil eye?

Well I did it. I put it on someone and now he's in danger. He might die. Can you please help me to take it off?'

There. It was done now.

Luciano and Constantin were looking at him gravely.

'Guilt is a terrible burden,' said Constantin and he reached out and put one hand on Matt's head. He closed his eyes and murmured a few words.

Matt felt a sensation like being in a bath while the water drains out. He was temporarily suspended between elements and when he came to himself again he felt clean and forgiven.

'Thanks,' he said, feeling that was inadequate. 'But does this mean that Jago's better now – because I'm sorry for what I did?'

'Unfortunately not,' said Constantin. 'You will have to use the counter-spell in your book. I can explain it to you again but it is too much for you to bear the burden alone. I will come back to your world with you.'

'No,' said Luciano. 'It is too dangerous for you, Professor. I will go with Matt.'

Chapter 15

A Face from the Past

The afternoon in Padavia dragged for Matt. He had
agreed to go to Luciano's house before stravagating
back to his world. He was enormously grateful that
the older boy was coming back with him. But he had
no idea how it was going to work. Lucien Mulholland
was dead; wasn't it crazy for him to risk being seen so
near to where he used to live?

At the end of their long working day, the pressmen
left the Scriptorium, rolling down their filthy sleeves
and talking loudly about the need to slake their
thirsts. Matt walked to Luciano's house near the
cathedral, feeling that he would need at least a pint of
ale before being ready to stravagate.

Alfredo let him in and took him into the elegant
dining room. It took Matt a while to adjust to the

candlelit scene. He recognised Luciano and Dethridge and Cesare, but also present was a beautiful young woman with chestnut-brown hair and violet eyes, in a low-cut dress of grey taffeta. It could only be the Duchessa with her disguise cast off; in fact he could also see the tall bodyguard a few paces behind the woman's chair.

Matt felt completely inadequate standing in the doorway in his printer's devil clothes. He had thought perhaps his mysterious trips to Talia had something to do with feeling out of place in his own life but he didn't feel as if he belonged here either. Maybe he would end up lost somewhere between Padavia and Islington and spend the rest of his days wandering in the void, with nothing to bind him to either world.

'There you are,' said Luciano warmly, and the feeling dissipated. 'Will you eat with us before we leave?'

'Can I have a wash first?' asked Matt.

'Of course. Alfredo will show you where,' said Luciano. 'I'd offer you a change of clothes but you're quite a bit taller than me – broader too.'

'That's OK,' said Matt. 'I probably need to stay in these clothes for when I come back.'

'You're right,' said Luciano, disconcerted by how much he had already forgotten about stravagating when you weren't a Talian.

When Matt came back, feeling a little less disreputable, he found a place laid for him between Luciano and Cesare, opposite the Duchessa.

'Welcome,' she said as he sat down. 'Refresh yourself – you work hard here in Talia, I think?'

Matt didn't need a second invitation. He ate and

drank heartily, noticing that Luciano himself took little. His host looked pale and tired. Matt saw how often Arianna looked towards him and realised that she was worried about the coming visit to his old world.

'We mustn't linger, Matt,' said Luciano, looking out of the window. 'The night is coming on and the morning will be wearing away in your world.'

Matt knew that Jan wouldn't come and knock on his door, not with Ayesha there. But he agreed; he was anxious to get this over with.

The two of them withdrew to Luciano's bedroom. The Bellezzan took a fine silver chain from out of a wooden box and pulled it over his head. Matt saw that he held a token of some sort, something like a frozen flower. They sat side by side on Luciano's lavishly draped bed.

'Tell me about your house,' said Luciano. 'If you tell me where it is and what your room looks like, I should end up there with you – if we're lucky.'

'Well it's not like this,' said Matt, looking round at his surroundings.

'I didn't always live like this,' said Luciano seriously. 'I was just another Barnsbury Comp kid like you.'

Matt was telling him random things about his house, when someone knocked softly on the door. It was Arianna. Her skirts swished as she came in, holding a candlestick, and she sat down on the other side of Luciano.

'You need to lie down,' she said. 'Both of you. I'll watch over you.'

Matt felt guilty for taking Luciano away from her;

they had told him about how rare her secret visits were. But it was nice to think she would be there, even if she couldn't really protect them.

She moved to an armchair beside the bed, setting her candle down on a low chest. The two boys stretched out under the sumptuous bedcovers. Matt immediately felt tiredness take over his body and shut his mind down. Luciano took longer, unwilling to close his eyes to the sight of Arianna sitting by his bed, wrapped in a soft red woollen shawl.

Georgia had been edgy ever since Ayesha's visit. It had been hard to concentrate on school work this term knowing that a new person was visiting Talia. And now something Matt had picked up on his stravagations was leaking into this world. Ever since the spring, she and Nick had been able to put their past behind them. For days at a time they could forget that Nick had been born in another world over four hundred years ago.

What she wanted now was to plan for the future. It was going to be hard enough going away to university and leaving Nick at school for two more years. She didn't know if their relationship would survive the separation. That was hard enough for ordinary couples who didn't go to the same place, let alone ones with such a big age gap. Though people were much more understanding when it was the boy who was older.

What would help them get through, Georgia was certain, was their shared past. She had enabled the old

Falco to become Nicholas, to mend his body and find a new family. She had seen him pretend to drink poison in Remora, had watched while he flew the winged horse at the Stellata and seen his di Chimici father die in his arms.

For his part, he knew all about how her stepbrother had bullied her and how she had been hopelessly in love with Luciano, who was devoted to Arianna. She had chosen Nicholas over Luciano, the ordinary everyday world over Talia and didn't want to have to think about her choices ever again. She remembered how restless Nick had been when Sky was visiting his home city of Giglia and how he had begun to regret his decision to translate permanently away from his old life.

Georgia dreaded that all this new activity in Talia would set Nick off again. All that stuff about the evil eye had definitely meant something to him. Georgia felt sorry for Ayesha too; she couldn't believe what she was being told. Like Alice and Sky, Georgia thought. Alice never mentioned Talia and stravagation; it was as if she was trying to forget it had ever happened. And Sky played along with it.

But even Sky had been intrigued by having a new Stravagante in the school. It was coming back to all of them. Georgia had even caught herself wondering if Merla the flying horse could take her from Remora to Padavia and back in a day. It would be lovely to see Cesare again. She had trained herself not to think that about Luciano.

In the end, she just couldn't wait to hear what had happened in Talia. She dragged on a jacket and set off for Matt's house. On the way, after some thought, she rang Nick's mobile.

There must have been some small difference in Matt's breathing or something because as soon as he found himself back in his own bed, Ayesha opened her eyes. There was a tiny moment when she smiled at him automatically and it was like any other morning waking up next to her. Then realisation returned and she sat up abruptly.

'Well?' she asked. 'Have you got the cure?'

Matt nodded. He was still holding the leather spell-book but now he knew what the '*remedium contra fascinum*' was. He wasn't looking forward to applying it though.

'It's in here,' he said.

Ayesha looked doubtful. He had been holding that same book the night before.

'It's OK,' said Matt. 'I know what I have to do.'

'If you say so,' said Ayesha uncertainly. Then she seemed to make up her mind to trust him. She shook her head as if scattering all doubt from her mind. 'Can I use your shower?' she asked briskly. 'I feel really skanky.'

Matt gave her a towel from the airing cupboard. The house was strangely silent. Andy would still be in bed but Jan and Harry must be out somewhere. Matt waited anxiously in his room; would Luciano turn up there or at his own old home, which was the other possibility?

Ayesha's little scream told Matt that he had dozed off. She had come back from the bathroom fully dressed with her long black hair all wet about her shoulders, expecting to find just him, and there was an older boy sitting on the chair by the desk. Luciano was wearing a plain white shirt and black trousers but he couldn't fake a pair of trainers and his buckled shoes looked outlandish.

'Who are you?' Ayesha was demanding. 'Matt, who's this?'

'I'm Luciano,' said the boy simply, his voice a bit husky as if he hadn't used it much lately. He looked round the room with interest. 'You described it well, Matt. I feel as if I recognise it.'

'This is seriously weird,' said Ayesha, sitting down on the edge of the bed. 'You're from that other place, aren't you?'

'I am now,' said Luciano. 'But I used to be like you.'

The doorbell rang. Matt didn't want to leave them alone together but there was an iron rule in their house that Andy Wood's morning sleep was not to be disturbed. He went down and found Georgia and Nick on his doorstep.

'Checking up on me?' he said ruefully.

'Just couldn't keep away,' said Nick. 'Did it go OK?'

'Have you got the counter-spell?' asked Georgia.

By then they were outside Matt's bedroom.

'Better than that,' said Matt. 'I brought reinforcements.'

'Luciano!' said Georgia. In an instant she had flung her arms around him. Nick piled in after her and the three hugged one another.

'It's good to see you,' said Nick. But Matt noticed that he glanced towards Georgia the way he hadn't when Cesare was under discussion.

'So, he's legit,' said Ayesha, who was brushing her hair to calm herself.

'More than that,' said Georgia, feeling annoyed at Ayesha's coolness. The girl had no idea what Luciano had been through in either world. And even if Georgia loved Nick best now, Luciano would always be a hero to her.

'Can't you lend him some clothes, Matt?' said Ayesha. 'If he comes to the hospital looking like that, everyone will be suspicious.'

'We've been through this already in Talia,' said Luciano. 'We're different sizes. Even Nick's taller than me now!'

'Are you coming to the hospital?' asked Georgia. She felt a surge of hope; Luciano was here and everything was going to be all right.

'Matt's got the counter-spell,' said Luciano. 'But he needs help. The more the merrier.' He looked round at all of them.

'Let's have breakfast first,' said Matt. He was suddenly starving.

Filippo di Chimici had brought several servants with him to Padavia and Enrico had soon chummed up with one particularly friendly footman. They had found a shared interest in horses and Strega, and Giuseppe was perfectly willing to talk about his master over a few glasses of their favourite drink.

'Staying with Prince Gaetano his brother-in-law in Giglia, wasn't he?' said Enrico.

'For all the time he was there,' said Giuseppe.

'Not there long then?'

'Couple of nights,' said Giuseppe. 'He spent more time at the Nucci palace.'

'Oh, with his cousin?'

'The Grand Duke,' said Giuseppe. 'He was the one who sent for him.'

'Sent for him?'

'I delivered the letter, didn't I?' said Giuseppe. 'Family crest and brought by a servant in the Grand Duke's livery. Next thing we knew we were all packing up and heading for Giglia. But we were hardly unpacked in the Palazzo di Chimici before we set off here again.'

'Interesting,' said Enrico. 'Another drink?'

He was using up Luciano's silver fast but it would be worth it.

Five hungry teenagers were filling the kitchen when Andy Wood came down to breakfast: Matt, Ayesha ('so they're back on again') and three that Andy didn't know – two strikingly handsome youths with black curls (one of whom was rather strangely dressed) and a girl with tiger-striped hair. They all jumped guiltily when he came in.

'Don't mind me,' he said. 'Just let me at the coffee.'

Matt introduced Georgia and Nick but the other young man seemed to have gone. Ayesha made his coffee for him. Andy noted that they had left him some bacon and tomato and set to with the frying pan. He wondered if he had hallucinated the second black-haired boy.

But Matt was acting very strangely, taking an unopened bottle of olive oil from the cupboard and a carton of sea salt and a shallow mixing-bowl.

'What is this?' asked Andy. 'Are you and Yesh setting up a cookery school?'

Matt was saved from answering by the return of Jan and Harry. But he was disconcerted to see that they were accompanied by his great-aunt Eva. He had completely forgotten she was coming to stay for a few days and knew it would make it difficult to get away.

The kitchen was ridiculously full now. Georgia was asking if she could wash up the breakfast things, and Jan, a bit disconcerted by the impromptu morning party, was politely saying she needn't worry and everything could go in the dishwasher.

Matt allowed himself to be embraced by Eva and then said, 'Sorry, but I promised we'd go to the hospital to see Jago.'

'That's good of you,' said Jan. 'I'm sure Celia would appreciate a break. And I can't go myself. But I doubt they'll let all of you in. Are you two close friends of Jago?' she asked Georgia and Nick.

'No,' said Nick. 'Georgia and I won't go in. We'll just wait outside.'

Both the Wood parents were relieved when Matt and his friends left and they were back down to a manageable four. But they didn't see the young people being joined by the second black-haired boy in the front garden and Andy had already forgotten he had ever been there.

'That was a close thing,' said Matt to Luciano, giving him a slice of toast. 'My mum would have recognised you.'

'I recognised her,' said Luciano. 'She used to teach me English.' His expression was unreadable. 'We'd better get along to the hospital.'

He attracted some odd glances on the bus but people soon looked away.

'It's like *Star Wars*,' whispered Ayesha. 'It's as if he had some sort of Jedi powers.'

'Well, I hope the Force is with us this morning,' said Luciano.

Ayesha was embarrassed; she hadn't meant him to hear.

'How is this going to work?' asked Nick. 'I mean, Matt knows the spell and he's got his ingredients but I don't see them just letting even him and Ayesha walk into ICU and start messing around with salad dressing or whatever it is.'

'I think that's where I come in,' said Luciano. 'We'll have to play it by ear but I think it will be up to me to create a diversion.'

*

Staff Nurse Stella Watkins had worked on ICU a long time but the case of Jago Jones was not like any she had seen before. He wasn't any worse but he wasn't getting any better either. She was always worried about unexplained illness on the ward. There had been talk of tropical disease but so far no doctor had recommended an isolation cubicle. Yet Staff Nurse Watkins couldn't help visualising some unknown sickness infecting the unit and endangering all her other patients.

It distressed her to see Jago's mother in such a state

of despair too. Stella Watkins had seen many grieving parents over her years in ICU – that Mrs Mulholland was one she remembered well – but there had been some ecstatically happy and relieved ones too. She prayed that Jago's mother would be one of these.

But there was no sign of it yet. Nurse Watkins bustled round Jago's bed, taking his temperature, pulse and blood pressure. 'No change,' she mouthed at Mrs Mulholland, who was a bit more awake than Mrs Jones. Then, softly, 'Isn't it about time his mum got off home and let someone else sit with him for a while?'

And then the Asian girl came in. She was stunningly good-looking and Nurse Watkins had seen her before; she thought she was probably young Jago's girl. She was just what was needed at the moment, anyway: a fresh young person, looking well-rested and positive. She could sit with Jago or at least keep Mrs Jones company if she refused to leave.

'There now, Mrs Mulholland,' she said brightly. 'You take a break and let the young one take over.'

'Thank you,' said Vicky. She was deathly tired and very stiff from dozing all night in a hospital chair. 'I will pop home for a bit if that's all right, Celia?'

Celia Jones nodded, still groggy from her own uncomfortable night.

'You go, Vicky. I'll be all right. Ayesha will sit with me.'

Ayesha was wondering how on earth to get Jago's mother to leave so that she could let Matt in to do what he had to, when she heard a scream from the hall.

'That's Vicky,' said Celia and both she and Nurse

205

Watkins left Jago's cubicle.

Ayesha ran into the corridor and, deliberately ignoring what was happening at the other end, dragged Matt into the cubicle.

'Quick,' she said. 'We probably don't have much time. I don't know how long your Luciano can distract them.'

Matt rummaged in his plastic bag. Now that it had come to it, he felt foolish balancing the mixing bowl on Jago's forehead; it didn't help that Ayesha was looking sceptical. He poured some water into the bowl from the carafe on Jago's bedside table then added a little olive oil from the bottle.

Outside there was still some commotion going on.

'What now?' asked Ayesha. 'Don't you have to chant or something?'

'Now we wait,' said Matt. 'It shouldn't take more than a few moments.'

And it didn't. Forming in the water was the unmistakable greeny-yellow outline of an open eye.

'Like *Big Brother*,' said Ayesha, fascinated.

'More like Sauron in Mordor,' said Matt, excited in spite of the danger. 'It's the evil eye, all right.'

He struggled with the canister of salt, trying to get it to the setting where only a sprinkling would come out, then cast it at the oily 'eye'. Immediately the pattern on the surface broke up.

'Is that it?' said Ayesha, in an agony of anticipation. 'We've got to get rid of this stuff. Mrs Jones and the nurse will be back any minute.'

'Wait,' said Matt.

There was a change in Jago's shallow breathing. He started to move his head.

'Quick – take it off!' said Ayesha, rushing to catch the bowl before it spilled water, oil and salt all over the bed.

Jago's eyes opened. 'Ayesha?' he said croakily. Then he saw Matt and suddenly looked scared.

They just had time to push the bowl and carrier bag under the bed before Nurse Watkins came in.

'Who's this?' she asked sharply then, sniffing, 'What's that funny smell?'

'Oh nurse,' said Ayesha. 'Jago's just woken up. Isn't it wonderful?'

Staff Nurse Watkins was as white as her own plastic apron. What she had seen in the corridor was something her mind could not encompass. So she dealt with something she could understand and bleeped the duty doctor.

'Go and tell his mother. You, young man,' she said to Matt. 'You shouldn't be here anyway. Go and tell Mrs Jones that her son is awake.'

Matt walked out in the corridor feeling ridiculously happy. He had probably lost Ayesha but Jago wasn't going to die. He felt as he had when Constantin had placed his hand on his head and taken away the guilt.

Outside he found Luciano and Celia Jones and a woman he knew to be Mrs Mulholland. All at once, he understood what had happened. It was Vicky Mulholland that looked on the verge of fainting and Jago's mother who was comforting her. Luciano was stroking the hair of the woman Matt now realised was his mother.

'Look after her,' he told Matt and disappeared into Jago's cubicle.

Nurse Watkins scarcely registered that Luciano had

come into the cubicle before he had taken her hand, looked into her eyes and murmured something under his breath.

'I . . . I must go and find the doctor,' said Nurse Watkins, brushing a hand across her forehead, and left Luciano and Ayesha alone with Jago. The sick boy looked terrified at the sight of Luciano; he was a year older than Ayesha and he knew what he was seeing. He remembered Lucien Mulholland. But Luciano put his hand on Jago's brow and said more words to him and the boy relaxed.

'Now we must take Matt's stuff and leave quickly,' warned Luciano.

Ayesha grabbed the bowl. 'I'll tip this away in the visitor's loo,' she said practically.

Luciano pulled the bag out from under the bed and they both went out into the corridor. Ayesha sped off in the other direction while Luciano went to Jago's mother.

'Mrs Jones,' he said, 'your son is well again,' and he passed his hand in front of her eyes.

Celia Jones hurried into the cubicle without a second look at her friend. That left Matt and Luciano with Vicky and they were soon joined by Ayesha with the empty bowl.

'Are you all right?' she asked Vicky, still not knowing who she was.

'Oh yes,' said Vicky Mulholland, smiling. 'I couldn't possibly be better.'

Chapter 16

When is it Right to Kill a Man?

At the hospital entrance, Nick and Georgia were astonished to see Luciano walking out with Vicky, with Matt and Ayesha trailing behind. Vicky was keeping herself upright and steady as she walked in silence to the car park, but it was costing her an effort. Nick and Georgia fell in beside Matt and Ayesha and spoke in whispers.

'Did it work?' asked Nick.

'Yes,' said Matt. 'At least he's come out of the coma. I think he'll be all right. But it was pretty hairy.'

'What about, you know, Luciano's mother?' asked Georgia. 'Didn't she freak out when she saw him?'

'Yes, but that helped a lot. Luciano said he was going to create a diversion but I don't think even he dreamed of bumping into his mother.'

'Mine too, now,' said Nick.

'What do you mean, his mum?' said Ayesha. She was completely in the dark about what was going on. 'How can that Talian be Mrs Mulholland's son?' Then she remembered something and her hand flew to her mouth. 'You don't mean . . . not the one that died?'

There was just time for Matt to nod and then they were at Vicky's Renault.

'I haven't got room for you all,' she said brightly, fumbling in her bag for her keys.

'That's all right, Mrs Mulholland,' said Matt. 'I'll walk Ayesha home.'

Without any consultation, Nick and Georgia got in the back and Luciano sat next to his mother. It was over two years since he had been in a car.

'What happened to the Peugeot?' he asked Vicky.

She turned in her seat, the keys still dangling in the lock.

'Can I touch you?' she asked quietly.

In answer Luciano reached over and hugged her. Vicky clung on to him tightly and the others heard her sobbing. Georgia reached out to Nick; this must be very peculiar for him.

'How are you here?' said Vicky at last, as Luciano got tissues out of the glove compartment and handed them to her. 'You seem much more real than the other times.'

'I'm getting better at it,' he said.

'You sound as if you have a sore throat,' she said, concerned.

'I'm quite well,' said Luciano. 'You don't need to worry about me.'

Vicky gave a bitter laugh and blew her nose.

Nick couldn't restrain himself any longer. 'Are you all right, Vicky?' he said, reaching awkwardly forward to touch her.

'Oh, Nick,' she said. 'I don't know. It's wonderful to see Lucien again but so weird. I think I must be dreaming.' She switched the engine on.

'Are you OK to drive?' asked Georgia.

'I will be as long as no one says anything,' said Vicky. 'I just want to get home and call David.'

Barbara had, as predicted, managed much better this time. For a start there was no state dinner to worry about. She had dined with Rodolfo and Silvia alone, apart from the servants, and the Regent and his wife were kindness itself, introducing no topic that could trip her up. But it was still disconcerting to be waited on and she could not relax.

It was a relief when a groom brought the great cats into the salon. Barbara was used to them now and they to her. They were ready to be stroked and looked expectantly for morsels saved from her plate. It did not strike them as unusual that the maid sat where the mistress should; they cared only that she smelled familiar and was in the habit of giving them food.

When the cats had been taken away, Rodolfo dismissed the servants and Barbara immediately felt better. It was nice just to be sitting down, something maids didn't do very often. And the dress was lovely. She smoothed the embroidered green silk of the skirt between her fingers; milady had such lovely things.

'I wonder how Arianna is getting on,' said Silvia,

sipping the digestivo the servants had brought.

'At least she will be well protected,' said Rodolfo. 'Parola tells me your fiancé has been an apt pupil, Barbara.'

'Thank you, sir,' said Barbara. She had also been wondering what was going on in Padavia. She would be glad when the Cavaliere had finished his studies and was safely back in Bellezza. 'I think that Marco has enjoyed the lessons.'

There was knock at the door and a footman brought a message to Rodolfo on a salver.

While the servant waited for a reply, Rodolfo read it out loud.

'His Eminence Cardinal di Chimici desires to wait upon us, my dear,' he said to Barbara. The girl sat up straight.

'Now, sir . . . Father?'

'If convenient,' said Rodolfo. 'If you are unwell, I can put him off. But a cardinal of the Reman Church should, of course, be received with all honour and respect.'

It was clear what he wanted her to do. Barbara nodded.

'Very well,' said Rodolfo to the footman. 'Please show His Eminence to the red drawing-room and bring further refreshment for us all there.'

When the footman had gone, Silvia said, 'I think I should absent myself from this audience.'

'No,' said Rodolfo. 'I think you should be there. We have to face the di Chimici as man and wife at some point.' He glanced towards the girl in the green silk dress. 'Will you be all right, my dear? You don't have to say much beyond a greeting. I can speak for you.'

'I shall do my best, sir,' said Barbara.

'But you must remember to call me "Father",' said Rodolfo kindly.

'I shall try, sir,' said the maid.

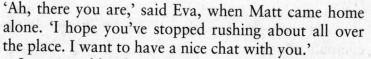

'Ah, there you are,' said Eva, when Matt came home alone. 'I hope you've stopped rushing about all over the place. I want to have a nice chat with you.'

Jan popped her head round the door. 'Oh Matt, I've just had a call from Celia at the hospital. She said that Jago might be coming home as early as this afternoon! But you know he's better, don't you? Celia said you'd visited him this morning. That was good of you.'

'He's a good boy,' said Eva comfortably.

You don't know how wrong you are, thought Matt, but there was nothing he could do but smile. 'That's great,' he said, feeling that his face was going to crack and fall off.

'Where's Ayesha?' asked Jan.

'I took her home,' said Matt.

'Oh what a shame,' said Eva. 'I was looking forward to meeting her properly. I thought she looked a lovely girl.'

Matt said nothing. He wasn't going to tell his great-aunt, in front of his mother, what the situation was between him and Ayesha. He wasn't even sure he knew what it was himself. Yesh had been acting very strangely on the way home. Realising who Luciano was seemed to have flipped her over the edge. He'd left her at her house, telling her mother she was overtired and needed to lie down.

'Now tell me all about your university plans,' said Eva. 'Jan tells me you're thinking of Cambridge.'

Matt groaned inwardly. He wondered who had told Jan but she had tactfully withdrawn.

'Which college?' Eva was asking.

'Queens',' said Matt at random, remembering one that Georgia had mentioned.

'Oh, very good,' said Eva. 'Just down the road from my old college, Newnham. Are they good for computers?'

'Yes,' said Matt, secure that Eva was so language and literature-focused that she wouldn't be able to contradict him. 'But I thought you were at Pembroke?'

Eva laughed. 'I *taught* at Pembroke before I got the job at Sussex, but that was a men's college when I was an undergraduate. Newnham was where I got my degree – women only.'

It sounded like something out of the Ark to Matt. 'I don't suppose I'll get in, though,' he said hastily. 'It's very hard.'

'Well, at least you won't have to sit an exam,' said Eva. 'They'll go on your A level results and an interview.'

'I haven't even done my AS yet,' Matt reminded her. 'I don't have to decide until next year.'

'It's good to start thinking about it now though,' said Eva. 'Maybe if you haven't spent my birthday present yet, you could get a book about the application process?'

Matt felt guilty; he hadn't thanked her. He never did. Writing was hard for him but he could have phoned. He decided on a whim to tell her the truth.

'I got this,' he said, pulling the Talian spell-book

from his jeans pocket. He never went anywhere without it now.

Eva seemed fascinated. She took the book from him and unwound the leather straps almost reverently.

'How extraordinary,' she said. 'A strange book for a dyslexic to choose.'

Matt froze. Usually Eva was rather vague about what was going on but she seemed pin-sharp today. But if she knew, *really* knew, about his condition, why did she persist in sending him book tokens?

'It spoke to me,' he said in the end.

'I can understand that,' said his great-aunt. 'Books have been speaking to me all my life. But it's unusual for you, isn't it? Oh, I know you think I'm a gaga old woman who can't remember what my great-nephews are like. But that isn't so. I just kept sending you the tokens in the hope that one day you'd find the right book. The one that spoke to you. I didn't think it would be a Renaissance book of spells though.'

'You know what it is?' said Matt.

'I know what it looks like,' said Eva. 'A Latin spellbook from some time in the sixteenth century. I'd like to know where you got such a valuable book for twenty pounds. In fact I'd like to go there myself.'

*

The scene at Luciano's old house was uncanny for all of them. He hadn't managed ever to get inside it in his previous stravagations, let alone speak to his mother, or hug her. Nick felt completely superfluous. Usurped, even though he was the usurper, the one who now slept in Luciano's old bed. As soon as Vicky had called her husband and told him to come home immediately, Georgia dragged Nick off to the kitchen to make coffee; she was as at home in his house as in her own.

'You've got to give them some time alone,' she insisted. 'Don't look so miserable. He'll be gone in a few hours – you're her son now.'

But it wasn't as easy as she was pretending. She had been so used to Nick being jealous of Luciano on her account that it was hard to accept his new set of feelings about another woman, even though that woman was his foster-mother.

In the living room, Vicky was bombarding Luciano with questions. Where was he living? Was he really well? Had he sent Nicholas to them? And, worst of all, was he ever coming back permanently?

'It wasn't me, Mum,' said Luciano. 'It was Georgia who arranged for Nick to live here.'

'Georgia?' said Vicky, utterly flummoxed. 'But how is that possible?'

Luciano spread his hands in a gesture that unconsciously echoed one of his master Rodolfo's. 'How is any of it possible? You can ask Nick and Georgia the details. It must have been killing them these last two years not being able to say anything to you.'

'Two years?' said Vicky. 'It's been three, Lucien. A lot of this I don't understand but don't expect me to believe I haven't been grieving every day of three years and more.'

'That's something else Georgia and Nick will have to explain,' he said. 'I'm going to have to go soon. It's night in my world and I have a big day at university tomorrow. I've got to give a sort of speech.'

'You're at university?' asked Vicky. 'Oh, don't go yet. Wait for David. It would be too cruel if you disappeared before he got here. There's so much to ask you.'

'OK,' said Luciano. 'But, Mum, can we phone up for pizza?'

Rinaldo di Chimici was enjoying himself. He knew that the Regent's supposed second wife was the old Duchessa – he had recognised her at the duel in Giglia – and he was determined to let her know that he knew it. Of the new young Duchessa, he took hardly any notice at all, even though his embassy was to her.

'I used to be Ambassador here, ma'am,' he said. 'From Remora. That was before I entered the Church, of course.'

'Indeed,' said Silvia, uncomfortable in spite of Rodolfo's reassuring presence.

'Yes,' he continued. 'Unfortunately, I was here at the time of the late Duchessa's unfortunate demise.'

'And what brings you here this time?' asked Rodolfo, anxious to change the subject.

'Ah yes,' said the Cardinal. 'My visit.'

After his unexpected success in Padavia, Rinaldo had taken it upon himself to visit all the independent city-states to see if he could get them to put the anti-magic laws on their statute books. His motives were twofold: if he succeeded, he would be high in the Grand Duke's regard, but he also wanted to take on the task because he thought it was right.

He had always distrusted the goddess-religion, even

though he knew that some older di Chimici practised it alongside the official observances of the Reman Church. And now that he had entered that Church himself, with his eye on the highest prize within it, he embraced with zeal the mission to wipe out all superstition and supernatural beliefs that were outside the official faith.

He didn't have much hope of succeeding in Bellezza but he wanted to start there just to see the Regent's so-called second wife with his own eyes; he had a score to settle with her.

'I'm sure it has not escaped your attention,' he said to the young Duchessa, suppressing a desire to call her 'my dear', 'that your near neighbour and ally, Padavia, has adopted the new laws introduced by my cousin, the Grand Duke?'

The girl looked at him like a sheep and it was her father that answered.

'Messer Antonio has informed us of his new laws, of course,' said Rodolfo. He gave Barbara a tiny frown, as if to say 'leave this to me'.

'Naturally, the Grand Duke would be very pleased if Bellezza saw fit to follow her neighbour's wise decision,' said Rinaldo.

'Naturally,' said Rodolfo.

'May I take it then that you will consider his request?'

'It seems that Your Eminence's role in the Church benefits from your past experience here as Ambassador,' said Rodolfo. 'We will, of course, "consider" any request from a fellow head of state. My daughter will ask her Senate and we will convey their answer to you in Remora. But enough of business – will you take some brandy?'

Rinaldo did not stay long. He was mollified that the Regent hadn't dismissed his request out of hand and intrigued to discover how little power the new Duchessa seemed to exercise. 'A mere puppet,' he would tell Fabrizio, 'manipulated by her parents, if indeed her parents they really be. I saw her make that primitive hand of fortune sign those low-class lagooners use. Perhaps that midwife witness lied? In any event, she is no threat to us. Take away the Regent and she would need a new puppet-master. Forget about any violence towards the Duchessa of Bellezza. It is the father we need to eliminate.'

The Cardinal rode back to Padavia, well-pleased with his visit. Even if the Regent persuaded the Senate to block the anti-magic laws, if his new plan succeeded, Arianna, the Duchessa of Bellezza, would soon be without her lover or her father and then Bellezza would fall into di Chimici hands like a ripe plum.

*

'You turn up here after three years, won't tell us anything and then say you've got to get back to write an essay?' Luciano's father had said when he got in, sounding almost angry. But he had clutched his head and started to cry, so that Luciano could not feel anything other than sympathy.

But he did have to get back, much as he wanted to stay. Luciano was behind with his studies. With all the worry over Matt, Arianna's visit and his developing friendship with Filippo, he hadn't been giving his university work enough time. And he had been neglecting his riding and fencing too. He was ashamed at how often Cesare had been to their training sessions without him.

So he had left from his old house to return to Padavia as soon as he'd had a pizza and a shower. When he got back, Arianna was fast asleep in the chair beside the bed. He covered her gently with a quilt and, groaning, went to his little study and stayed up the rest of the Talian night writing his 'Disquisitio' for Professor Constantin's class.

It had been more than usually difficult to concentrate. Seeing his old home and his parents had been more than unsettling. Of course he had known that he was running a risk in offering to accompany Matt, but he hadn't expected to run into his mother in ICU. That had actually been a wonderful bonus, being able to talk to her and to convince her that he was well and living another life.

But two things had been unbearably painful: one, the hope that Vicky still held that he would come back to them, the other seeing Nicholas, the old Falco, so settled into his place. He had even had to stravagate back by lying on Nick's bed, which had been his own not much more than two years ago.

David had asked all the awkward questions, even more than Vicky, and in the end Luciano had been longing to get away. Now his body was still tingling from the hot shower and the warm fluffy towel and he could still taste the pizza; it had been so good.

When is it right to kill a man? Luciano forced himself to focus on the subject. In a few hours he would have to give his oration, making all the right gestures, using all the approved metaphors and similes and laying down a convincing case in favour of the proposition. All the Rhetoric students had to do it. Even the Professors had to take part in public 'Disputationes' once a term, to demonstrate their continued skills and provide a model for their students.

Luciano had missed two of Constantin's lessons. He could have followed the practice of the richest students in Padavia and sent a servant to take notes for him but that felt like cheating.

So he slaved over his paper as the candles guttered, marshalling his arguments and dreading the dawn.

In the end, Matt took Eva to Mortimer Goldsmith's antiques shop. She was delighted with it and hit it off with Mortimer immediately. They soon unearthed the Cambridge connection – 'my great-nephew is applying to Queens', you know' – and then they were away.

'I was a Trinity man myself,' said Mortimer. 'But my late wife was at Newnham. Perhaps you knew her?'

Amazingly it appeared that Eva had known, slightly, the woman that Mortimer later married; she had been in her last year when Eva came up to Cambridge. Matt soon felt like a spare wheel. He could have just left them to it and they would have chatted all afternoon.

He leafed through some more old books in Mortimer's shop but there was nothing like his spell-book and they were no easier for him to read than anything else. It was giving him a headache trying to decipher them.

Mortimer decided to close the shop up for lunch and suggested that Eva and Matt should join him for a bite at a nearby café.

'That's OK,' said Matt. 'You go ahead. I expect you have lots to talk about. I ought to see Chay. Will you be OK to get back afterwards, Eva?'

'Don't worry about that,' said Mr Goldsmith. 'I shall, of course, walk Mrs Holbrook back to your house.' He raised his hat gallantly as Matt left the shop.

Eva seems to have made a hit there, thought Matt. If only his own love life was so easy. Ayesha had been so shocked by realising who Luciano was that he hadn't been able to ask her if she had forgiven him for what he had done to Jago. And he didn't know yet if Jago would really be all right.

Matt called Chay on his mobile and arranged to meet him in the park. It wasn't long before he saw his friend jogging towards him. He felt a surge of affection for Chay who knew nothing of spells and magic and Talia and was just a regular bloke, who went to the gym and had been his mate for years.

'Hey, Chay,' he said, stepping out to greet him.

'Hey, man,' said Chay, giving him a big grin and a high five. 'What's up?'

'Well,' said Matt, falling into a slow jog beside him. 'Jago's better.'

Chay stopped. 'That's fantastic! Do you mean he's out of Intensive Care?'

'Even better,' said Matt. 'He's leaving hospital later today.'

'So what was wrong with him?' asked Chay, resuming their training pace.

'I don't think they ever knew,' said Matt. 'He just opened his eyes and the doctors said he was OK.'

'So it wasn't anything you did to him?' asked Chay. 'I never thought it was, you know.'

'No,' lied Matt. 'It wasn't anything to do with me.'

The class was full and Luciano saw to his unease that Filippo de Chimici was in the front row. He believed Filippo was his friend and some of the things he was going to say were going to be hard to get out with him there. Constantin had a slate on which he was going to award marks for arguments, how they were arranged, expression, memory of facts and delivery.

He would ask the class what they thought before coming up with a final mark.

Luciano cleared his throat nervously and began:

'When is it right to kill a man? Any honourable person's first reaction to this question will be a horrified "Never!" but a moment's thought will tell us that there are occasions when it might be the lesser of two evils. For example, if you saw someone about to stab a child, you would act without thinking to save that child, even if it meant killing the attacker. I shall list the cases where it is appropriate, even desirable to kill another human being.' And then he delivered a fine *coup de théâtre*. 'As someone who himself has killed a man, I feel I am in a unique position to tackle this topic.'

He certainly had his audience's attention now.

Luciano moved steadily through the arguments about defending the weaker and more vulnerable, through coming to the aid of one's comrade-in-arms, fighting to defend one's country in time of attack, protecting one's family, property and finally oneself.

'I have been present at a massacre,' he said, 'when many peaceable people had to take up arms to defend themselves against the murderous assault of armed men upon a ceremony in a church – consecrated and hallowed ground.' He paused to let this sink in.

'And I have been challenged to a duel to the death by someone I believed myself not to have wronged. I took part to defend my honour and in the course of the duel killed a man who was older than me, a more experienced fencer and a person of great personal wealth and position and influence.'

Filippo's eyes glittered as Luciano reached his concluding arguments.

'It was not my intention to kill him but his wound proved fatal. There is no doubt that, had I not struck him, he would have killed me. That was his intention and his wish. In the circumstances I did the only thing I could. It does not mean that I am proud to have done it. On the contrary, I regret it deeply. But it was a case when it was right, as in the other cases I have set out, to kill a man.'

Luciano went back to his seat and the class erupted in applause. Constantin nodded his approval. Luciano's speech had not followed all the classical rules of Rhetoric but it had made a powerful impact on his audience, which was one of the main purposes of teaching the discipline. He would get a high mark.

Filippo di Chimici was applauding along with the

others. But he was not smiling in congratulation. Luciano did not realise that by admitting in public to killing a di Chimici, even while not naming him, he had appeared to boast of it in front of a family member and that was an insult that could not be pardoned. In that moment Luciano's fate was sealed.

Chapter 17

An Anatomy Lesson

Luciano came out of the Rhetoric class dazed by lack of sleep and surrounded by fellow students who wanted to clap him on the back and buy him a drink. He was relieved to discover that one of them was Cesare, who took him in hand and led him to the Refectory, managing to lose several of their followers on the way there. He organised food and drink for both of them, and for Enrico, who had a habit of turning up when free refreshments were likely.

'Drink up,' said Cesare to Luciano. 'You've earned it. That was brilliant. I don't think I'll ever be able to stand up in front of a roomful of people and declaim like that.'

'Was that what you did, signore?' asked Enrico. 'And what were you declaiming about then?'

'Killing people,' said Luciano. 'You should have been there. You could have given your professional opinion.'

'Now then,' said Enrico. 'There's no call to be personal. Was he there? Filippo?'

'In the front row,' said Luciano.

'And was he impressed?' asked Enrico innocently. 'I mean if you were talking about killing people, you must have mentioned his uncle, seeing as how you haven't killed a lot of people.'

'He clapped,' said Luciano, beginning to feel uncomfortable. 'I don't see what you're getting at.'

'Only that the di Chimici don't like people boasting about how they put their relatives away,' said Enrico. 'Especially in public.'

'I wasn't boasting,' said Luciano irritably. 'I just said it was the right thing to do.'

There was a sharp hiss as Enrico breathed in through his teeth. 'Oh dear,' he said. 'Oh dear, oh dear.'

But Luciano was getting tired of this and wanted to be back at home with Arianna. He started to get up but then saw the boy 'Adamo' coming in, followed by the tall companion who was never far from his side. Immediately Luciano was on his guard.

'Congratulations,' said Adamo gruffly. 'Marco and I sneaked in at the back. You did a great job.'

'Enrico Poggi,' said the spy, standing up and bowing. 'At your service.'

'Adamo, um, Cesarini,' said the boy, randomly seeking inspiration from seeing Cesare. 'And this is Marco.'

Enrico offered to get chairs for them but Adamo

shook his head and said, 'No, thank you. We have to get back home. I just came to say goodbye and to congratulate you, Signor Luciano.'

And Luciano had to watch his love walk away without embracing her or knowing when he would next see her. He had wasted all their time together, first with stravagating and then writing his speech. He wondered if pizza and a shower had been worth it, even though he had seen his parents. But that was a mixed blessing in itself.

While Luciano had been dazzling the Rhetoric class, Matt was fast asleep. He hadn't meant not to stravagate but the book had fallen out of his hand just as he was losing consciousness. He struggled to reopen his eyes, desperately aware that there was something he needed to do but it was no good. He was just too exhausted by the strain of all the business at the hospital.

He didn't wake up until Jan knocked on his door, saying 'Driving lesson in half an hour.'

'Your concentration is a bit off this morning,' Brian remarked, after Matt had been slow to get away at a green traffic light and messed up a perfectly easy reverse around a corner.

He can say that again, thought Matt. His mind was in Talia, wondering what excuse Constantin had made for him this time and whether the other pressmen would be against him on his return.

'I wouldn't worry,' Brian was saying. 'We all get off days when we're learning any new skill. The important thing is not to do it when you're a qualified driver.'

Matt was grateful. It seemed as if he had good men looking out for him in both worlds. After the lesson, he was at a loose end and found himself mooching past their favourite café. He looked in and saw Sky, for once without Alice, reading one of the newspapers. The dreadlocked boy looked up and, on an impulse, Matt went in.

He didn't know this Stravagante as well as he did Nick and Georgia and this was a chance to talk to him on his own. The other two were so caught up in each other and some underlying stuff about Luciano that they could be hard work.

Sky greeted him warmly. 'Last day of freedom,' he said when Matt brought his cup over to his table.

'What? Oh yeah, half-term. But we've still got the weekend.'

'We have every weekend,' said Sky. 'Today is the last day of our week off.'

Matt looked down at the paper Sky had been reading. There was a picture in it of the veteran rock star, Rainbow Warrior. He looked familiar and something clicked in Matt's brain. 'Is he your dad?' he asked.

'So you can see the resemblance,' said Sky. 'Yeah, he's my dad and time was I'd have to read the newspaper if I wanted to know what he was doing. But it's OK now. He's got a big UK tour coming up. I'm going to see him on Sunday.'

'Is it him you're going to stay with in the States next year?'

Sky nodded. 'Him and his wife. She's OK, actually.'

'It must be cool being a famous singer's son,' said

Matt. 'Mine sings chorus at the opera – how uncool is that?'

'I expect it's OK if your dad's a nice man,' said Sky. 'It took me a while to find out that mine wasn't so bad. In fact it was going to Talia that did it.'

'So it does something for you, this stravagation, does it?' said Matt. 'I thought it was supposed to be the other way round. Not that I've been any help there yet. More of a nuisance, really,' he said, thinking about how Constantin and Luciano had got him out of the mess he'd made.

'It changes people,' said Sky. 'Makes their lives better. Look at Georgia. She says she was a miserable, lonely kid being bullied by her stepbrother before she went to Remora and now she's confident and happy and going out with Nick.'

'It wasn't exactly a happy experience for Luciano, was it?' said Matt, lowering his voice. 'He died, for God's sake.'

'He thinks he would have done that anyway,' said Sky. 'And you've got to admit being a Knight of Bellezza beats lying six feet under.'

'But he's doing that too, isn't he?' said Matt. He shivered, as if someone had walked over his own grave. He wondered if it was a premonition of winter.

Just then, two girls walked into the café. One was Alice, who gave Sky a radiant smile; the other was Lucy, the girl who had being going out with Jago. Matt supposed she was history now, but she didn't seem upset. On the contrary, she seemed on top of the world.

'Hi, you two,' said Alice, slipping into a seat at their table and giving Sky a kiss, while the other girl queued to give their order.

'Lucy seems happy,' said Sky.

'She's just been with Jago,' said Alice. 'He's much better but still needs to sleep a lot so I asked her if she'd like to join us for coffee.'

'Are she and Jago still on then?' asked Matt in a whisper.

Alice looked surprised. 'Why shouldn't they be? She came back early from her trip to Paris with her parents as soon as she heard he was ill. Of course she missed all the drama at the hospital but I expect she's glad about that. They seem pretty devoted to me.'

Suddenly the day felt brighter and warmer to Matt. He made his excuses, waving to Lucy, and left the others in the café. He was going to see Ayesha.

Angelo Angeli was giving one of two public dissections that Frida, but Ludo the Manoush was not in the Anatomy Theatre. His people had a deep respect for the remains of fallen companions and elaborate rituals for their disposal. At this time more than any other, leading up to the Day of the Dead, what was going on under Professor Angeli's knife would have seemed a sacrilege.

Ludo's hiding-place at the back of Antonio's house had not been discovered but he spent as little time there as possible, not wanting to put Giunta more at risk than necessary. When he could, he met up with others of his kind and roamed the city. They couldn't wait to get away from Padavia. It was like a prison to them. Not to be able to play or sing or wear bright clothes made them feel like caged birds. But they would stay until the 3rd of November when the three days of their Festival of the Dead would be over. And then they would leave this city and not return unless it repealed the laws that forbade the worship of their Lady.

And they would have to be careful how they celebrated their festival. They usually carried out their rituals at night or in the early morning anyway, for it was then that the moon, believed to be a form of the goddess, would watch over them. So, with luck no Padavian citizens would see them carrying out what would now be illegal acts.

Ludo was restless; he wished that he had never come to this city. From the day he had met Luciano, he had lived in semi-hiding, like a shadow of his real self. He respected the young Bellezzan, who Aurelio had told him came from another world, and he knew that the young printer was also one of the same kind, though not the horse-boy of Remora.

But Ludo could not forget two things. One was the reading of the Corteo Cards that he had seen Dottore Crinamorte lay out, with the figures of Death, the Scales and the Magician all close together. The other was having seen Filippo di Chimici. For Ludo had a secret of his own, one that he had not shared with Luciano: he was only half-Manoush.

Ever since he was small, his mother had told him that his father had not been of their people. Ludo had not felt the lack of him; the way in which the Manoush lived meant that there were always older men around. And he was especially attached to his older cousin, Aurelio. But he was curious about the other half of himself, that made him look different from his fellows, the only redhead in a tribe marked out by its glossy black hair and dark skin.

But it wasn't till his mother had been dying a few months ago that she admitted to him that his father had been of noble birth. 'The highest in the land,' she said. 'If you ever fall on hard times, if the Manoush should ever fail you, the di Chimici will take you in.'

She had died before he could find out any more. He had no idea which branch of the family he might belong to. And since his mother's death he had made no attempt to find out. She had given him a signet ring bearing a crest but he kept it in a bag close to his chest and never looked at it.

He had seen Filippo of Bellona several times now and was fascinated by him. He had stared at the young noble, studying his features to see if they could be brothers. And it did not seem impossible; there was a resemblance. But he didn't know if his own mother had ever been in Bellona and since the Manoush wandered the earth and had visited every city-state in Talia, no one branch of the di Chimici was more likely than another to house his unknown father.

Ludo had fantasised about every di Chimici he knew of, including the late Grand Duke. But he knew this was a dangerous path to follow. He was Manoush and must remain so. He dragged his mind back to the array of cards; there had been something else significant, which the Dottore had not wanted to reveal. The Book. On a whim, Ludo turned his steps towards the Scriptorium.

*

When Matt arrived on Friday morning, his second Friday in a row, as he thought of it, Constantin had taken him to one side and told him that the pressmen thought he had been sent to collect a new supply of paper the day before.

'But what happened, really?' he asked. 'Why didn't you come? Were you unable to reverse the evil eye?'

Matt cursed himself for being a thoughtless bastard. He had forgotten Constantin didn't know what had happened with Jago and must still have been worrying. 'I'm really sorry,' he said. 'I was so tired I just fell asleep without stravagating. But you haven't seen Luciano then?'

'No, I expect he thought you would tell me yesterday,' said Constantin. 'Tell me what happened.'

Matt gave him a short version of the events at the hospital. The Professor sighed with relief. He patted Matt on the shoulder.

'Well done,' he said. 'We must talk again about the control of this power but I have to go to the Anatomy Theatre now.'

'It's OK,' said Matt. 'I've learned my lesson.'

Then Constantin had left for the dissection and, to his surprise, Biagio had called Matt over to be a beater on one of the presses. One of the pressmen was genuinely sick and Matt was to fill his place.

It meant a hard day's work ahead of him, with the tallow candles lit in the early afternoon, and Matt was glad he had managed a good sleep the night before. Still, it was better than making ink and washing type. And he was still feeling happy from his visit to Ayesha. She hadn't said she would take him back or that she had forgiven him but she was much kinder and softer than she had been towards him for days and he had begun to feel hope. At least she wasn't going out with Jago.

In the middle of the morning, the rusty-haired Manoush had walked in. Matt had been taking a break to drink watered wine, while his puller damped more paper and the compositor took the pages they had printed to the proofreaders for checking.

Biagio was talking to Ludo and Matt nodded to show that he knew him. But he was surprised to see him here; he somehow hadn't expected the Manoush to go in for reading much.

Ludo had entered the Scriptorium passing the list of forbidden books that all printers now had to have posted up in their workplace. He asked Biagio what kinds of book they were still allowed to produce.

'Many kinds, sir,' said the foreman. 'Works on duelling, history, music, fortifications, poetry, mathematics, maps . . .'

Ludo seemed so interested in their work, that Biagio showed him books in all stages of production.

'Do you make the loose sheets into books here too?' asked Ludo.

'No,' said Biagio. 'Nando the bookbinder does that. His shop is just three doors down on Salt Street.'

Matt was eavesdropping; he had wondered about this himself. He knew, as Ludo didn't, that this Nando must also bind the forbidden books that were printed in the Secret Scriptorium.

*

Doctor Dethridge was taking Luciano to see the

anatomy demonstrations. Matt had told them something about the book he had helped to print in the Secret Scriptorium and so they weren't surprised to see Professor Constantin in the theatre too.

The Anatomy Theatre in Padavia had been open only a year and its fame had spread throughout Europa. Universities in many other countries were copying its remarkable design. Six tiers of seats for spectators rose up in a funnel from the central dissecting table and it could accommodate up to three hundred students at a time.

Still there was not a spare seat to be had when Professor Angeli entered the theatre. His dissections were famous; not only medical students attended them but students from the other schools and even members of the public came to watch him work. Students got in for free but spectators from outside the University had to pay two soldi each.

The bodies for dissection were prepared in a room on the ground floor below and Luciano remembered what Matt had said. The Professor was supposed to use only the corpses of executed criminals, and those must be from another city, not Padavia.

The dissecting table was lowered by an ingenious mechanism, through a trap door into the room below. Then it returned, raised to the surface by the same feat of engineering, with the cadaver strapped to it. In this way, the body did not have to be carried in past the students and could, at the end of the demonstration, also be tidied away in a seemly fashion.

There was total silence in the theatre except for the clanking of the machinery as the table with the corpse rose into view. Luciano was surprised to see that it was that of a young well-nourished man. He had been expecting someone older and more battle-scarred. But he had to admit that he still wasn't sure which crimes were punishable by death in the cities near Padavia.

Why, this dead man might be from Bellezza, might have been condemned to death by Arianna's Senate and the warrant signed by her own hand! It made him shiver.

'Observe the arrangement of the muscles in the arm,' Professor Angeli was saying, calmly lifting away the skin of the man's left arm and exposing his biceps as if he were carving a roast chicken.

Luciano swallowed. He could see the smaller table containing all Angeli's dissection instruments; it looked like the equipment for a torture chamber. Luciano tried to remind himself that even in a modern autopsy room in his old world there would be things going on that might be sickening to watch.

He could tell by looking at the faces around him which spectators were medical students and which not. The medics were all absorbed, intent on watching what Angeli was doing and listening to his commentary. The rest had a greenish tinge to their faces and tended to find things of interest on the ceiling to look at. Some held handkerchiefs to their mouths. There wasn't a woman among them.

As Angeli cut into the breastbone and turned back two large flaps of skin to show the muscles of the chest, someone made a dash for the exit. Luciano thought from the glimpse he caught of the disappearing back that it might have been Enrico.

After the dissection was over, Dethridge took Luciano down the theatre stairs to where Professor Angeli was wiping his instruments. The mechanism was lowering the table, now fouled with blood and organs, through the trap door.

The two men shook hands; they knew each other slightly and Angeli had been to Dethridge's Astronomy lectures. Luciano hoped very much that he would be let off shaking the Anatomy professor's hand when he was introduced. He could see that his foster-father now had blood on his.

'Whatte an ingenious machine ye have installed,' said Dethridge, looking with interest at the descending table taking the gory remains away.

'Come and see the other end of the operation,' said Angeli.

He signalled to an assistant to finish cleaning the instruments, pulled off his bloody apron and led them to the floor below. The table had just reached the ground. A servant was waiting to remove the cadaver and its detached portions into a plain deal coffin, while a second held a bucket and cloths to clean the table. When these grisly tasks had been performed and the body taken away, Professor Angeli showed them a lever on the side of the table.

To Luciano's surprise, the whole top flipped over, revealing another dissecting surface, complete with straps. Tied to it was a large dead dog. Luciano thought he would be sick.

'Ah,' said Dethridge. 'For substitutioun?'

'We cannot always get the criminal bodies,' said

Angeli. 'And then I take what I can get. But I always have an animal here, in order to make a quick exchange, just in case the authorities turn up.'

'And is this one an executed criminal?' asked Dethridge in a whisper.

'No,' replied Angeli equally quietly. 'I couldn't get one. And I need the bodies to be fresh. This man died last night.'

Luciano looked at the dog. And at Professor Angeli.

'Please excuse me,' he said. 'I think I need some fresh air.'

Chapter 18

The Watcher Watched

Rinaldo di Chimici's messenger was beginning to feel weary. He had ridden from Bellezza to Giglia with letters for the Grand Duke and now, as soon as he had taken some refreshment, would be off to Padavia. His master had told him he was going straight to the City of Words from Bellezza and the messenger couldn't understand why. They had been there only a few weeks before and he didn't see what Church business took his master there again.

But one good thing was that the Cardinal would be staying in the Bishop's palace, which was very comfortable. The Bishop of Padavia was Chancellor of the University and lived in a very grand style; even the servants benefited from it.

Of course the messenger couldn't read, in common

with most of the people the di Chimici employed in this role. And even if he had been able to, he wouldn't have dared break the seal on his master's letters.

He might have wondered why young Fabrizio di Chimici's eyes lit up at his cousin's letter but the doings of nobles were as far out of his sphere above him as the scurrying of ants on the road under his horse's hooves was beneath him. The messenger was just happy to work for such great men and have such a good horse to ride and fine livery to wear.

And he was glad not to be going back to Bellezza. What kind of city banned horses? He had been made to leave his fine beast on the mainland when the Cardinal took the ferry over to the lagoon city. And he knew that his master felt the same way. Of all the cities in Talia, this was the only one where horses were not allowed. Why, he had even heard that there were people within the City of Masks who had never seen a horse, let alone ridden one!

The letter he was bearing from the Grand Duke to the Cardinal needed the utmost secrecy; Fabrizio di Chimici had impressed upon him that he was not to hand it over to anyone but his cousin himself. In it the young Grand Duke authorised the planning of an assassination in Bellezza and the stepping up of a devious plot to kill another man in Padavia.

'Take this letter too,' he had told the messenger, giving him extra silver. 'It is for another of my family, Filippo of Bellona, who is also staying in Padavia. It will be easy for you to find out where he is lodging and I should like the Cardinal to be in touch with him.'

Filippo di Chimici would need no urging from

Fabrizio to do everything in his power to entrap Luciano. He had sat seething during the Bellezzan's 'disquisitio'. True, his uncle hadn't been named but many people in Padavia knew about the duel already and, after the speech, many more would ask Luciano for the details.

The di Chimici took their family honour very seriously and to hear the black-haired youth justify killing his uncle had been a purgatory for Filippo. Since that day he had employed his own spies, to keep watch on the Bellezzan and bring news if he did anything, however small, that could have been seen to infringe the anti-magic laws.

But this was not enough for Filippo; he wanted to do something to provoke Luciano. He had tried to win his confidence and friendship and the Bellezzan had been responsive, but only up to a point. On the subject of the Stravaganti he had refused to be drawn.

'To my cousin, the heir apparent of Bellona, Prince Filippo di Chimici, greetings,' began Fabrizio's letter. After many flowery phrases commending himself and his Grand Duchess and expressing his wishes for Filippo's good health, in the manner of the time, he got down to business.

'It is imperative that we discover the secrets behind the Brotherhood of which we have spoken. There is some mystery involving travel to another world and it is vital that we discover the mechanism by which this is effected. There must be some spell or enchantment which they use. Study the Bellezzan, observe his companions. There must be something we can use to get him into trouble with the Padavian authorities. And if there is no other way, then take him captive and search him. It has been done before. Our cousin Rinaldo will be in the city by the time this reaches you. Join forces with him; there are things he knows about the Cavaliere.'

*

Ever since stravagating to his old world with Matt, Luciano had been restless. In the end, he decided to get in touch with his old master and personal Stravagante, Rodolfo. In his palazzo next to the Ducal Palace of Bellezza, Rodolfo had a set of mirrors, which he kept trained on various places in Talia, in order to keep in touch with other Stravaganti. Each member of the Brotherhood had a big cheval glass in their home and a hand-mirror when travelling so that they could communicate with one another, but no one had more looking-glasses than Rodolfo.

Luciano hadn't used his hand-mirror to reach Rodolfo since coming to Padavia, except once, so that the older Stravagante could see he had arrived safely – a bit like sending his parents a text message. Now, although they wouldn't be able to hear each other, he wanted to see Rodolfo's face.

He took out the ebony-backed mirror and concentrated. At first there was nothing to see but his own face – like phoning a number and hearing it ring without being answered. But Stravaganti were very well attuned to one another's wavelengths and it wasn't long before another face became superimposed on Luciano's reflection.

It was a wise face, lined by cares to look older than its owner, and framed by once-dark hair that was now nearly all silver. And it looked concerned. Without hearing the words, Luciano felt them forming in his mind.

Luciano! Are you well? Is anything wrong?

No, master, Luciano thought back, *I just wanted to see you.*

The face in the mirror relaxed into a smile and Luciano could see beyond the lines to the handsome young mandolier who had melted the heart of the last Duchessa of Bellezza.

It is good to see you, too, Luciano. Arianna tells me your studies are going well.

She heard my rhetorical speech. I'm glad I didn't know she was there.

She said you stayed up late to write it . . . after you had stravagated.

You know about that? I had to, to help Matt – Matteo – the new Stravagante.

And did you?

Yes. He'd got himself into trouble, using a hex he'd learned about here. But he's put it right now. Constantin was going to go but if he'd been found out in Padavia it might have led to a search of his Scriptorium. Then they might have found the secret printing press.

I see. And how did you find the stravagation?

Rodolfo always knew what was troubling Luciano; it was a relief really.

I saw my parents, Luciano spoke-thought.

That must have been unsettling. Did you speak?

Yes, and touched and hugged. And they were upset, particularly my dad. I think perhaps I've been cruel to them.

And to yourself.

Well, I got a pizza and a shower out of it.

Pizza? Did it have a sheep's stomach on it?

Luciano laughed and saw Rodolfo's lips curve back at him. They were both remembering their first conversation when Luciano had turned up in Talia over two years ago and tried to explain twenty-first century life to Rodolfo. Luciano said then that you could get anything put on top of a pizza, even haggis.

No, it had anchovies and chilli peppers and olives and artichokes.

It sounds delicious. But it has made you sad.

It was a statement not a question.

It has unsettled me, master.

Luciano felt the long pause in Rodolfo's thoughts, at least the ones he could read.

It is a privilege to be able to return. Not a right. The dead do not return.

Only ghosts, master.

You are not a ghost but a living and vigorous young man. One who will soon be my son under the law. But you could turn into something no better than a ghost.

Master?

You, like young Falco, can live in only one world, Luciano. He made his choice and it was for your old world. You had no choice and this is the only world for you now. You cannot dip back into your old life for the food and luxuries you miss in this. And you can't just visit your parents whenever you feel like it. It would drive you mad.

That is what is happening.

Then I am sorry you went back with Matteo. Shall

I come to you in Padavia?

Luciano was touched. Rodolfo would not hesitate to put aside the demands of a being Regent of an important city-state to come and comfort his old apprentice.

No, it's fine. I'm fine. The Dottore is still with me here. But I didn't want to tell him. He has his own sadnesses about his old life.

To tell him of yours will not add to his. Remember, you are both Stravaganti. He will understand.

*

After a second day of covering for the sick beater, who had been injured in a tavern brawl, Matt found himself spending Sunday in Constantin's Secret Scriptorium. The Professor looked more troubled than Matt had ever seen him. He kept glancing at the door of the secret room and in the end propped it open so that he could see into the larger room, though Matt couldn't see how this would make things safer.

'We have three more clear days,' said Constantin.

'How come?' asked Matt.

'Well, tomorrow is All Hallows' Eve, then we have All Saints' Day followed by All Souls' Day. The Scriptorium will be closed for three days, so we can work in here.'

Matt wondered how Biagio explained to his family why he never took a day off. Perhaps he didn't have one? He hoped Constantin was giving the foreman lots of extra money.

'Are ordinary people allowed to celebrate that?' he asked. 'I thought it was just the Manoush?'

'It is a three day festival of the Church,' said Constantin. 'There will be special services in all the churches and in the basilica. But the Manoush, if they celebrate at all, will do it in a different fashion.'

It had been only a week since the Manoush had come to Padavia and Matt had first met Ludo. During that time, he had seen him a few more times, looking far less colourful. Matt liked him a lot better dressed in black and without the ribbons. He wondered, as he worked, what risks the Manoush would be taking on the next day. And what had brought Ludo to the Scriptorium two days before.

When Matt left the Scriptorium for a short lunch break, he walked instinctively towards the Black Horse. And didn't notice a figure slipping after him. But that spy also didn't notice the man following him, who was wrapped in a black cloak and had reddish-brown hair. And Ludo was unaware that he was being followed by Enrico, who had somewhere found a feathered, and somewhat battered hat in his favourite blue.

*

'Pregnant!' said Arianna. 'How can he be?'

'Because he's a she, Your Grace,' said Mariotto, who was standing in the Duchessa's parlour, looking very awkward in his stable-boys' clothes. 'I did try to tell you before. Florio is a female. I always said it was a daft name for a girl, saving Your Grace.'

Arianna laughed. 'Quite right. So you did. She must be renamed Flora. So that was why she was putting on weight – nothing to do with my table morsels?'

'Seems not, milady,' said Mariotto sulkily.

'But this is splendid news,' said Arianna. 'When do you think she will have her babies? And how many? I wonder if it is like kittens.' She loved the idea of a whole litter of baby African spotted cats.

'I don't know, milady,' said Mariotto. 'Little cats take nine weeks but it stands to reason that a bigger cat will take longer. And we don't know when she got pregnant. We are working in the dark here. Perhaps Your Grace could find an expert on African cats?'

'Perhaps I could. I shall look into it immediately.' Arianna was already wondering what Rodolfo would say if she said she'd like to keep all the babies.

As Mariotto was leaving, he bowed to make way for the Regent, who was coming to see his daughter.

'You look happy,' he said, smiling at Arianna.

'My African cats are going to have African kittens,' said Arianna. 'I never realised they were a pair like that.'

'Are you ignorant of what Luciano tells me are called "the facts of life" in his world?' asked Rodolfo.

'No,' said Arianna. 'I think I am just very stupid. When did you speak to Luciano?'

'About that, a long time ago,' said Rodolfo. 'You must allow a father to be discreet about his conversations with a future son-in-law.' He was smiling, but Arianna had come to know him very well over the last two years.

'But you have spoken to him,' she persisted, going to the heart of the matter.

'In a sense,' said Rodolfo. 'He used the mirror to contact me.'

'And how is he?' asked Arianna. 'I had to leave him

in a public place. And I was worried about him. He looked so tired and strained.'

'I think strained is right,' said Rodolfo. 'You know that he saw his parents and his old home?'

'No,' said Arianna, shocked. 'He worked all the rest of that night and said very little about his stravagation when I woke in the morning. Only that the counter-spell was successful and the boy Matteo cursed was well again. I was thinking more about the new Stravagante and how he must be feeling.' She looked stricken.

'I wonder if it was a good idea to send him to Padavia,' said Rodolfo.

'Matteo?'

'No, Luciano,' said Rodolfo. 'I don't feel easy not having him under my eye here.'

'Perhaps you should disguise yourself and go and visit him,' said Arianna ruefully. 'You might be more use than me.'

Rodolfo came and kissed her on the forehead.

'Don't castigate yourself,' he said. 'But perhaps that is not a bad idea.'

*

In Padavia, the game of cat and mouse continued, although there was more than one mouse. Matt returned to the Secret Scriptorium, still unconscious of his several followers. Filippo's spy loitered in Salt Street, waiting for him to come out again. He idled past the bookbinder's, looking in at his windows to pass the time. At the end of a very long afternoon, by which time he was jaw-achingly bored, he saw Biagio and Constantin coming out of the Scriptorium.

The spy made a note to tell his master that they had been working on a Sunday. That wasn't exactly against the law but it was unusual. He thought it would be only a matter of minutes before the printer's devil came out again. But time passed and there was still no sign of his quarry.

Eventually he went to the only window that gave on to the street and risked peering in. At first he thought he was looking at a heap of clothes but then saw that the boy was lying on the floor in a room that looked like the boss's office.

Sleeping at work, thought the spy. But then something stranger happened. The boy was there one minute and gone the next. The spy thought perhaps he had just imagined the apprentice lying on the floor; the window was quite dirty. But the clothes were gone as well. The boy had just disappeared. And then he remembered another detail: he had been holding in his hand a book very like the ones the spy had seen that afternoon in the shop of Nando the bookbinder.

*

Ludo was sure that Matteo, whom he knew to be a Stravagante like Luciano, was under surveillance but he didn't know whose man was spying on the boy. He had lingered in Salt Street himself but been disconcerted towards dusk to feel a hand on his shoulder. A rather unpleasant smell assailed his nose and a short man in a blue hat smiled ingratiatingly at him.

'Time to pool our resources, don't you think?' he said.

'I don't know what you mean,' said Ludo.

'Let me spell it out for you,' said Enrico. 'You're spying on him, he's spying on young Matteo and I'm spying on you.' He finished with a self-satisfied air.

'Why?' said Ludo, startled. 'Why are you spying on me? Who are you working for?'

'The young Cavaliere,' said Enrico promptly. 'Luciano What's-his-name. I think you and I are on the same side. Mind, you should get a bit better at spotting a tail if you and your mates are going to have your festival-thing tomorrow.'

Ludo was stung by the remark but found it hard to think of Luciano employing this unsavoury man.

'What do you mean about pooling our resources?' he asked cautiously.

'Well,' said Enrico, 'do you know who that is spying on young Matteo? Because I do. And maybe there's something you know that I don't. Pooling resources, see?'

Ludo would have preferred to check with Luciano first but he wanted Enrico's information.

'Very well,' he said. 'I fear that there will soon be a prosecution under the anti-magic laws, resulting in death by burning. And I suspect that a book or books will be involved. That is why I am watching Matteo in the Scriptorium.'

'Interesting,' said Enrico, though he didn't really know what to do with this information. Still, he filed it for future use. 'Well, that not very clever spy is one Giuseppe, a servant of Filippo of Bellona.'

'Really?' said Ludo. 'So he spies on Luciano's friend?'

'And on the Cavaliere himself,' added Enrico. 'The question is, why?'

Going back to school on Monday was tough. The weekly routine always seemed like more of a grind after a week off. And everyone was a bit scratchy, thinking about how they should have done more work at home instead of just relaxing. The weeks till the Christmas holidays stretched out endlessly and it would be November the next day, the month that put the final nail in the coffin of summer.

The one bright spot was that it was also Hallowe'en and there was going to be a party. The house where Sky lived backed on to the garden of a much larger house, which was virtually next door to the school. And the student who lived there was a sixth former named Chrissie. She was a high-flyer, who got staggering exam results and was expected to go to Oxford. In return, her parents took a relaxed attitude to her enjoyment of hard-partying.

When she told them she wanted a Hallowe'en party, they laid down a few house rules and then arranged to go out for the evening. Chrissie was a popular member of the sixth form and issued a general invitation to everyone in their common room. That was in addition to all the people she had personally invited during half-term.

'You'd better come, Sky,' she said. 'There'll be such a racket, you'll feel as if you're there anyway. Bring Alice.'

'Thanks,' said Sky. 'You haven't left us long to get costumes together.'

'It's not a kids' party,' said Chrissie. 'You don't have to do much.'

Matt had also been invited and wondered if he dared ask Ayesha to go with him; she was definitely going. Jago hadn't come back to school and there was a rumour his parents were taking him to convalesce in the Caribbean.

'Jammy bugger!' said Chay. But Matt didn't begrudge it to Jago. He was just pleased there was no chance of his showing up at the party.

Chapter 19

A Hallowe'en Party

The Manoush were up early on the thirty-first. For them it was the last day of the old year and the vigil on the eve of their Day of the Dead. The last day of the old and the first day of the new year were both associated with the people who had gone before them into the world beyond this one and it was a solemn ceremony of chanting and prayers, sober enough not to disturb even the most zealous of anti-magic law officers.

They were alert to passers-by though, just in case any were informers. Enrico was watching from a dark doorway but he was no threat; Ludo had told his friends about the spy, who seemed to want to help them.

They were back where Luciano had first seen them,

camped outside the cathedral. But as the sun rose, they cast back their dark cloaks and let their colourful clothes show as they lifted their arms in greeting to their goddess's consort.

For the Manoush, the sun was an intercessor, and an old friend, one they could implore to take care of the souls of the departed and speak for them to the queen of heaven herself. This was just the beginning of their rituals; the main part would happen in the evening and would be much more dangerous for them.

Since All Hallows' Eve was also a festival of the Talian Church, there would be late worshippers still straggling through the square when the Manoush came to celebrate their twilight rites. And those would be far more noticeable. But for now there was no one to hinder them.

As their ceremonies concluded and the group broke up, Ludo fell into step beside Enrico – but not too close. They walked up the street of the Saint and along Salt Street very near to where they had met the night before.

'Look, there's a light in the studio,' said Enrico. 'It's early for the professor to be about.'

They moved closer and looked cautiously through the mullioned window.

'It is the boy, Matteo,' said Ludo. 'Surely he doesn't usually arrive this early?'

It was true but Matt had made a bad mistake. He had been to the gym with Chay after school and rushed to shower on getting home. In the end, he had eaten supper in his dressing gown before getting changed to go to the party. He hadn't exactly asked Ayesha to go with him but she'd said she would see him there, looking very serious, so he didn't want to be late.

But he lay on his bed for a few minutes before getting dressed and it had felt very comfortable. He stretched and felt all his overworked muscles relax. His right arm was thrust under his pillow, his hand resting lightly on the spell-book, as he dropped into a deep and refreshing sleep.

And he woke with a start, to find himself in the studio before dawn broke over Padavia. He was so confused about where he was and why he was there that he had lit one of Constantin's candles.

Ever since then he had been trying to get back to sleep, clutching the talisman and concentrating hard on his room at home. But his anxiety about what Ayesha would think if he didn't show up at the party kept him wide awake. And now he could hear tapping on the studio window.

Matt looked up and saw Ludo, the Manoush, unexpectedly accompanied by Enrico, the spy and assassin that Luciano seemed to have forgiven. He sighed. If he couldn't get to sleep, he might as well say hello to them. He opened the window, since the Scriptorium door was locked from the outside.

'We saw the light,' said Ludo. 'And wondered if there was anything wrong.'

'Yeah,' said Matt, looking warily at Enrico. 'I shouldn't be here. It's sort of accidental.'

'Can't you get out?' asked Enrico.

'Well, I could get out the window, I suppose,' said Matt.

'We'll help,' said Ludo, offering him a hand. 'Why don't we see if Luciano will give us breakfast?'

'Hey, Ayesha,' said Sky. 'You look great.'

Ayesha made a very plausible if rather too attractive witch, with her long hair loose and wearing green eyeshadow and a shimmering black dress. She was casting anxious glances round Chrissie's living room.

'Hey, Sky,' she said distractedly. 'Have you seen Matt?'

'Not yet,' said Sky. 'I heard him saying he was going to the gym after school – with Chay.'

'Oh, right,' said Ayesha.

'Look, there's Chay over there,' said Sky. 'He's the one under the sheet.'

Ayesha drifted over to a very unconvincing ghost, who was drinking beer through a straw and a hole in his sheet.

'Chay, is that you?' she asked.

'Mmn,' mumbled the ghost, then detached itself from the straw. 'Hi, Yesh. All right?'

'Fine,' said Ayesha. 'Chay, have you seen Matt?'

'Not since the gym,' said Chay.

'But he is coming?'

'Oh, yes. He just went home for a shower and a quick meal.'

Ayesha looked at her watch.

'Don't worry,' said Chay. 'He'll be here. Come on, let's find you a drink.'

Luciano was still fast asleep when Alfredo knocked at his bedroom door.

'You have visitors, signore,' said the old servant. 'And they want breakfast.'

Luciano hurried into his clothes, still only half awake. He took the stairs two at a time and found a strange collection of people in his dining room. Whoever he had been expecting, they made an odd combination: the Manoush, the spy and the Stravagante.

'Hi, Matt,' he said. 'Why are you here so early?'

The sky outside his windows was still only pearly grey.

'Mistake,' said Matt. 'I fell asleep in the early evening and must have touched the book.'

'We thought,' said Enrico, 'that breakfast might help him to get back to sleep?'

'I just couldn't get back off in the studio,' admitted Matt.

'It's always hard when you're stressed,' said Luciano. 'You need to be really relaxed to stravagate. But it gets easier with practice, so you can even do it in an emergency. Still, let's fill you up with breakfast and make you sleepy.'

Ludo was just as interested in the food as Enrico; he had been up for most of the night. In spite of the early hour, it was quite a merry occasion. But as soon as his stomach was full, Enrico reverted to his role as spy. He stood at the window, watching as the city woke up.

Then dodged back behind the shutters.

'We're being watched,' he hissed.

'By Giuseppe?' asked Ludo.

'No,' said Enrico. 'I don't know this one. I don't

think it's Matteo he is spying on. We weren't followed from the Scriptorium, I'm sure.'

'Well, if it's not Matteo they're waiting for,' said Ludo. 'It's probably me.'

'You think it's an informer for the Governor?' said Luciano.

'Well, it could be,' said Ludo. 'We did celebrate our ritual outside the cathedral. Someone might have seen us.'

He pulled a dark tunic out of his bag and put it on over his colourful shirt and took the blue and green ribbons out of his hair. Raking through the red-brown locks with his fingers, he tied his mane back with a plain black ribbon.

'Will you still go ahead tonight?' asked Luciano.

'We have to,' said Ludo, simply. 'It is what we came to do. To let the old year move from the present to the past. And help tomorrow be today.'

'But it'll happen all the same, whether you and the other Manoush have your ceremony or not,' said Enrico reasonably.

'It does seem a huge risk to take,' said Luciano. 'You could all be arrested.'

'We might have to move the ritual to another place in the city,' conceded Ludo. 'I have no desire to die for the goddess, but we are her people and she will protect us.'

Matt thought a good sword might be more useful, but the Manoush always went unarmed.

'Do you want to stay here?' asked Luciano. 'I have no classes today. The University is closed for the festival.'

'No,' said Ludo. 'Thank you but I'd have to leave eventually. The important thing is that the spy, whoever he is working for, shouldn't follow me back to where I'm staying.'

No one asked where that was; only Enrico knew that Ludo was sheltering in the Governor's house where he could be discovered at any minute.

Alfredo came in with a note on a silver plate.

'Messenger brought this,' he said, handing it to Luciano.

Enrico was back at the window in an instant but the watcher had gone.

'It's from Filippo,' said Luciano. 'He wants me to meet him at his palazzo.'

'Do notte goe,' said a voice from the doorway. William Dethridge came in wrapped in a voluminous green velvet dressing gown. He was wearing a long nightcap and all the young men in the room might have laughed if it hadn't been for the deadly seriousness in his voice.

*

Cesare was out early, riding Fiorella. He was taking advantage of the University's being closed for the Festival of All Souls to give the mare some proper exercise. They were in the south of the city, where the great oval swamp lay, covering the old Reman amphitheatre. A gallop round the outside made a great racetrack and Cesare gave the horse her head.

At the end of several circuits he slowed her down, her sides heaving, and walked her slowly back to the north of the city as the sun climbed into the sky dispersing the layer of pearly grey cloud. As he walked the horse back to his lodgings, enjoying the clear morning air, he spotted a familiar figure striding through the streets. But it couldn't be? Why would the Regent of Bellezza be in Padavia? Surely Luciano would have mentioned it?

Cesare reined in the horse and called quietly, 'Senator?'

'Cesare!' said Rodolfo, smiling up at the Remoran. 'Well met.'

Cesare swung down lightly from the horse.

'I'm very pleased to see you, sir,' he said, bowing.

Rodolfo clasped him warmly in his arms. 'Paolo told me you were studying here,' he said. 'And I hoped I'd meet you.'

'Have you come to see Luciano?' asked Cesare. 'Or is this a state visit?'

'Entirely private,' said Rodolfo, looking round him. 'Secret, you might say.'

He was not in disguise but it was true he didn't look like a visiting head of state, even a substitute one. He was wearing his usual black velvet, but not grand clothes. In fact, his cloak looked a little threadbare.

As Cesare watched him, he suddenly thought that Rodolfo didn't look much like himself at all. He wasn't sure now that he would have recognised the Regent if he hadn't seen him from behind.

Rodolfo smiled. 'Does that work?'

Cesare nodded, surprised. 'I don't know what you did but I wouldn't have known you.'

'That's the idea,' said Rodolfo. 'It's nothing more than a temporary glamour – quite easy to cast.'

'I'd better come with you to make sure Luciano knows you, then,' said Cesare. 'Would you like to ride my horse?'

'No, I'll walk beside you,' said Rodolfo. 'I know the way. My wife used to live there.'

*

'Why not?' asked Luciano. 'Filippo means me no harm, I'm sure.'

'Then why is he having you followed?' said Enrico. 'You and your friend Matteo?'

'I have made my divinatiouns again,' said Dethridge. 'And yt is notte goode. Worse, I have dreamed of capture and of dethe – I saw a bodie of a yonge manne on a slabbe and sharp knives.'

Luciano did not like the sound of this. Other people's dreams might be shrugged off as just that but this was William Dethridge, the man who had started the whole process of stravagation; he was no ordinary dreamer.

'But what can I do?' he said. 'Filippo will be insulted if I ignore his message.'

'Lette someone goe in your stede,' said Dethridge. 'One of these yonge menne hire canne wear your clothes. Yf he is taken on the way or whenne he gets there, he canne say hee is bot a messengire from ye. I wolde goe myselfe bot no one could mis-take me for ye.'

Luciano looked dubiously at Ludo and Matt. Ludo was much too tall and his hair too noticeable. Matt was of a much heavier build. Enrico was out of the question.

'It would be too dangerous for the Manoush. He's not really supposed to be in the city at all – he's a goddess-worshipper.'

The others knew Luciano was right and Matt had a

262

sinking feeling that he knew what he was going to have to do.

A loud knock at the door made them all jump. Alfredo came in beaming, leading Cesare and a stranger in black velvet. There was something familiar to Luciano about his gait though.

'Signori,' said the servant. 'We are honoured.'

'I have never been able to deceive Alfredo,' said the stranger. He passed a hand over his face and was immediately recognisable.

Enrico shrank inconspicuously into a corner but neither Ludo nor Matt knew why Luciano and Dethridge looked so delighted, clasping the newcomer in their arms.

'It's Rodolfo,' explained Luciano. 'My . . . the Regent of Bellezza, Arianna's father.'

The introductions were made and Luciano was relieved to have Rodolfo's opinion on the decision they had reached.

'I agree,' said the Regent. 'It is too dangerous for Ludo. It may be dangerous for Matteo too but if he is willing to do it I can help with the disguise.'

Matt groaned inwardly, thinking of Ayesha waiting for him at the party. But if he went soon, he'd be able to stravagate back in time; even though it was a school night, there was no doubt the party would go on at least till midnight.

'OK,' he said. 'What do I have to do?'

He and Luciano swapped clothes, which was uncomfortable until Rodolfo passed his hand over both of them. After the transformation it wasn't exactly that Matt and Luciano looked like each other; it was more that each could have been mistaken for

265

the other at a distance, because of their clothes.

'You'd be surprised,' said Rodolfo, 'how often people see what they expect to see and don't really look closely.'

'You'll have to ride Cara,' said Luciano.

'No way,' said Matt, startled. 'I can't ride. I've never even been on a horse.' He felt strangely vulnerable in his new slighter shape, even though it made him realise that Luciano was tougher than he looked.

'That's all right,' said Cesare. 'I'll go with you. It's easy – we won't go faster than a walk and I'll be there to grab the reins if anything happens. That is if no one minds?'

'Good idea,' said Rodolfo. 'You can at least ride as far as the palazzo.'

'And where shall I go?' asked Luciano, feeling that he'd like to go and flex his new muscles threateningly at someone.

'I think you should go to the Scriptorium and wait for Constantin,' said Rodolfo. 'Explain what Matteo is doing and that he might be late.'

He turned to Matt. 'The glamour will wear off as soon as you are in the palazzo. Just tell Filippo that Luciano is unable to come and then get out as quickly as you can. Go to the Scriptorium or come straight here.'

He scrutinised the boy's altered face. 'They don't know you are a Stravagante. Just be sure to keep your talisman hidden and stay out of the sun.'

Rodolfo looked at Enrico as he said it, as if challenging the spy to keep this information secret.

Cesare fetched the two horses from the stable, saddled and bridled, while Ludo left through the garden. The Manoush wasn't sure if the man Enrico had seen watching the house earlier was looking for him or not, but he had no intention of leading anyone to Giunta's back yard.

Rodolfo was going to stay and have breakfast with Dethridge and wait for news. Luciano left first, with Enrico by his side, surprised at how much he welcomed his company.

Then Matt and Cesare rode out of the side gate. Cesare had got Matt mounted in the courtyard and he found, to his surprise, that he didn't feel too awkward or uncomfortable; maybe looking more like Luciano had given him some of the Bellezzan's skill as well. Or maybe Cara was just a very docile and gentle ride.

For a while, Luciano and Enrico were in sight and Matt was relieved to see how different Luciano looked, even from behind.

'He's good, isn't he?' said Cesare, following Matt's gaze.

'Rodolfo? Yeah, but he's a bit terrifying,' said Matt. 'The old doctor is much more sort of friendly-seeming.'

'True,' said Cesare. 'But Rodolfo is a good friend too. You just need to get to know him.'

It wasn't far to Filippo's palazzo and, though they were both nervous, nothing happened on the way. Matt's heart was thumping loudly in his ears as he walked Cara into the courtyard of the palazzo. He and Cesare parted outside the stables, Cesare heading back to his lodgings. 'Good luck,' he whispered.

Liveried servants came forward to take Matt's horse and, though he dismounted awkwardly, no one showed any surprise. A grander servant led him into an ante-room, where he waited nervously, and then two footmen opened the double doors into Filippo di Chimici's salon.

Matt walked forward tentatively. He recognised the grand noble that Luciano had been having lunch with in the Refectory but there was also another man, one he didn't know. And this man, who wore scarlet robes and an alarming wide-brimmed red hat, was looking at him with disapproval.

'I thought you announced the Cavaliere Crinamorte,' he rebuked a servant. 'This is no such person.'

Matt realised that what Rodolfo called the 'glamour' had worn off. Luciano's clothes were feeling uncomfortably tight. He stepped forward.

'I regret any misunderstanding, sir,' said Matt to Filippo di Chimici. 'The Cavaliere sent me with his apologies. He is unable to attend you this morning.' He bowed and began to retreat.

'Just a moment,' said Filippo haughtily. He turned to the man in red. 'I've seen this fellow before. He does errands for the Bellezzan.'

The sun, which had been so slow to clear the sky earlier that morning, had at last broken through the cloud and was streaming through the tall salon windows. Too late, Matt realised he had forgotten Rodolfo's advice. The man in the red robes had got up and was pointing excitedly at the place where Matt's shadow should have been. He turned and made a dash for the doors but the two footmen were standing in front of them.

'Seize him!' called the Cardinal. He turned to Filippo. 'We have missed the prey but caught its cub. I think we have found ourselves a young Stravagante.'

The Hallowe'en party was in full swing and getting quite raucous. Chrissie's parents hadn't stipulated a finish time; they were staying over with the friends where they had gone to dinner. Chrissie was an only child and she had convinced them that she had worked so hard all through half-term that it didn't matter staying up late on one school night.

Witches, wizards, ghosts, ghouls and skeletons were all dancing on the lawn while loudspeakers blared out of the French windows. None of the costumes was very professional but everyone had made some effort. Chrissie floated around in a long dress of smoky-grey chiffon rags and white make-up and her boyfriend, Byron, was a Black Goth, so hadn't needed to dress any differently to look spooky.

Everyone was having a good time apart from Ayesha. Matt hadn't showed up and Jago wasn't there. Chay, who was a good mate, had eventually got tired of her gloomy mood and sloped off to dance with a girl in a tight, red catsuit, who claimed to be a devil.

Nick and Georgia were slow dancing and Sky and Alice were in a clinch under a tree, not even bothering with the music. Ayesha wondered whether to cut her losses and go home. She suddenly thought what the party would look like to someone who had no idea about Hallowe'en: a Martian or something like that. It would be completely incomprehensible – a terrifying scene of spectral figures dancing in the flickering shadows from the flames of a small bonfire – a vision of hell.

At Silvia's house Rodolfo and Dethridge waited anxiously for news of Matt and Luciano. By lunchtime neither young man had returned and the two older Stravaganti set out for the Scriptorium.

Constantin confirmed their fears; Matt had not turned up to work in the Secret Scriptorium. At first he thought he had, but it was only Luciano under the glamour, which had worn off almost immediately. Constantin was so worried about the young Stravagante that he sent Biagio home and locked the secret room. Luciano had also been worried about Matt, and Constantin feared he might have gone to Filippo's palazzo in search of his friend.

Dethridge was all for following him straight there but Rodolfo restrained him. 'If Filippo has taken Matteo prisoner, he will not admit it. And he will know that we suspect his friendship towards Luciano. It is, after all, possible that Matteo has just stravagated back. Didn't Ludo say that he had arrived early in the city by mistake? I suggest we find Cesare and ask what happened at the palazzo first.'

So the two men went to Cesare's lodgings, where he was glad to be rescued from an essay he was struggling to write.

'No, nothing bad happened,' he said. 'The grooms took Luciano's horse and a footman showed Matt in through the main door. After that, I couldn't see him any more and I came back here.'

'Was there anything unusual at all about the palazzo or the stables,' asked Rodolfo. 'Think hard,

Cesare. Any little detail might give us a clue.'

'Well,' said Cesare. 'There *was* a carriage I didn't recognise and some servants in a different livery polishing it. It was rather gaudy, red and gold and it had a strange crest on it.'

'Whatte creste, ladde?' asked Dethridge. 'Thinke hard.'

'Well, it had a sort of flat red hat on top of a sort of family coat of arms, which I couldn't see,' said Cesare. 'And dangling from the hat on each side were lots of scarlet tassels.'

Dethridge and Rodolfo exchanged glances.

'The Cardinal?' said Rodolfo.

'Ronald the Chymist,' said Dethridge, and pulled a face as if there were something very nasty-tasting in his mouth.

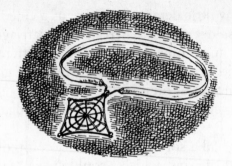

Chapter 20

Brave New World

The two footmen bound Matt's hands and dragged him to a small room up several flights of stairs. He was locked in and left to fume for about ten minutes. It had all been so civilised he hadn't even shouted for help; it would have seemed out of place. No more violence had been used than was necessary to restrain him and compel him into this room and even now he couldn't believe that anyone was really going to hurt him.

Matt was obviously in some sort of store room, not much in use.

His legs weren't bound and he walked to the small window which had a view only of an internal courtyard, with washing hanging on lines across it. It wouldn't do any good to shout from here even if he could get the window open.

He wondered whether Luciano would have met the same fate if he had come himself. He was pretty sure that the di Chimici already knew that the Bellezzan was a Stravagante, even though he now had a shadow. Matt cursed his own stupidity again for standing in the sunlight.

A key moved in the lock and Filippo came in, accompanied by the man in red, who had taken off his hat. A burly servant followed them.

'Strip him,' said the man in red, not bothering to look at Matt.

The servant had to untie his hands before he could pull off Matt's jacket and shirt but there was no point in trying to escape. Matt just stood there, feeling humiliated but not yet too scared. Then the servant pulled off his velvet breeches and all three men stared at his underwear.

Matt had been wearing just a singlet and boxers when he lay down on his bed after dinner in his own world – it seemed like an age ago. There was nothing in the least special about them but of course to sixteenth-century Talians they must look as outlandish as a futuristic silver jumpsuit.

'Search the clothes,' said the man in red. 'Take all his possessions.'

There was nothing but a lace-edged handkerchief with a crest embroidered in one corner, a velvet pouch with drawstrings, filled with silver, a sharp-edged dagger which had been in Luciano's leather belt, and the talisman – the only thing that really belonged to Matt.

'How does this help us, Rinaldo?' asked Filippo.

The man in red ignored everything but the book. He took it from the servant and unwound the leather straps.

'The Bellezzan had a book,' he said. 'It is the key to their mystery, I'm sure. And our informant said this boy was holding a book like this when he disappeared. But this is not like the one the Bellezzan had. That had handwritten pages. This is a printed book.'

Suddenly Matt realised that he had multiple problems. If this Rinaldo and Filippo kept the book, he wouldn't be able to get back home. And Luciano had warned him of the consequences if he stayed in Talia beyond one of the nights of his own world. It would be much worse than missing Ayesha at a party. He thrust that thought to the back of his mind. Luciano had been very ill, with cancer, and Matt was in the best of health. Maybe he could last two nights? But he'd still need the talisman in the end or he'd be stuck in Talia for ever. This was too terrifying to contemplate.

But more pressing was the realisation that his talisman was also a forbidden book. True, it had been printed before the new anti-magic laws but it had been produced in Constantin's Secret Scriptorium because he had known it was dangerous material even then. And these two di Chimici could shop Matt to the Governor and have him executed for possessing it.

And did it have Constantin's mark on it? Matt hadn't checked but he knew that all the other books in both press rooms bore the watermark of the wolf's head that was Constantin's symbol. What if it was traced back to him and the Scriptorium searched? Would the secret press be discovered?

Matt now felt surrounded by the prospect of imminent death and not just his own but that of those dear to him in the city. His only hope was that a lot of people knew where he was and several of them were Stravaganti; surely Rodolfo would rescue him?

*

Luciano had left Constantin's Scriptorium without any clear idea of what to do next. He couldn't go to Filippo's, in case his invitation had been genuine; the di Chimici would be very surprised to see him, just after a messenger had arrived to say he wasn't coming. He had no idea where Ludo was and he needed something to keep his mind off what might be happening to Matt.

In the end, he took Enrico to the School of Fencing, which was open in spite of the religious festival, and had a good work-out with the spy.

Forty-five minutes of vigorous exercise did not improve Enrico's personal smell and Luciano thought again that life in Talia would be much improved by the invention of the shower. But he was impressed by the spy's skill and dexterity. For someone who had not been brought up as a nobleman, he shared a lot of their accomplishments. Luciano wondered briefly if he could dance but had to smile at the thought. What woman would want to whirl around the dance floor in Enrico's arms? And yet the man had once had a fiancée.

They went to slake their thirst at a tavern and then Luciano decided that it was now possible to show up at Filippo's palazzo. He left Enrico on watch outside and knocked at the impressive great door. He felt horribly aware that he was still wearing Matt's Talian clothes, which were rather shabby and now too big for him. The footman who answered the door eyed him superciliously.

'The Cavaliere Crinamorte of Bellezza to see Prince Filippo of Bellona,' Luciano said firmly, squashing Matt's floppy hat in his hand and running his fingers through his black curls, in the hope that Filippo wouldn't care too much what he looked like.

'Wait here,' said the footman curtly and walked away into the depths of the house. Luciano supposed the servant hadn't been on duty before at any of the times he had visited Filippo and hadn't recognised him. But he realised, with shame, that he wouldn't himself know whether he had seen this man before. How quickly he had adapted to a life where servants were just anonymous givers of service, whose own lives and concerns remained unknown.

But it was a different footman who came to collect him and they did recognise each other. This one was more polite and ushered Luciano into the green salon, where a rather flustered Filippo came forward to greet him. Luciano saw his eyes flicker briefly over the printer's devil outfit but the heir of Bellona was too well-bred to remark upon it.

'You got my message earlier?' Luciano asked.

'Oh yes, thank you,' said Filippo. 'Your . . . er . . . messenger said you were busy.'

'He's not still here, is he?' asked Luciano and saw a guilty look pass over Filippo's face. In that moment he knew that his companions had been right. Filippo di Chimici was not a true friend.

'No, he left as soon as he had delivered your message,' said Filippo and Luciano knew he was lying. But he could hardly ask to search the palazzo.

An agonising quarter of an hour passed for both of them, with Filippo having to think of a reason for asking Luciano to call, and Luciano having to pretend that he didn't know Matt was being held prisoner somewhere in the building. They parted on terms of forced cordiality, both eager to get away.

Luciano made his way out to the stables and immediately recognised Rinaldo di Chimici's carriage. It made him even more fearful for Matt's safety. Cara was happily munching hay, which confirmed that Matt was still in the palazzo somewhere. Filippo hadn't thought about the horse and the stable-man just assumed that Luciano had been with his master a long time. He looked the same as the young man who had brought the horse in and the stable-man took no notice of clothes.

Luciano walked his mare back to Silvia's house. He had signalled to Enrico to stay put at the palazzo and the spy had settled in for a long watch. Luciano's thoughts were in a whirl. What would have happened if he had gone to Filippo himself instead of Matt? Would he now be held captive? Luciano had a horror of that, ever since Enrico had kidnapped him in Bellezza. And Rinaldo was behind it then, just as he was now.

*

Matt was exhausted. He was tied to a chair and the man he now knew to be Rinaldo di Chimici had been questioning him for what felt like hours. What did he know about Luciano Crinamorte and Rodolfo Rossi? Were they both members of the Brotherhood called Stravaganti? What about the Dottore? And Matt himself? Was he a Stravagante? And what did the Stravaganti do? How did they travel to the other world and was Falco di Chimici there? How did the book work? Why did some Stravaganti have no shadows?

It went on and on. Feeling like a soldier who would reveal no more than his name and number, Matt insisted that he was Matteo Bosco, a Bellezzan orphan whose father had been a printer, and who was now working for Professor Constantin in the Scriptorium. He knew nothing about stravagation or shadows but he did know Luciano Crinamorte. They had something in common as orphans. Falco di Chimici he had never met. (That was sort of true.)

'And what was your father's name?' asked Rinaldo suddenly.

Matt was flummoxed. 'Andy . . . Andrea Bosco,' he said.

'We shall send to Bellezza to check if such a person has ever existed,' said Rinaldo.

At that moment, Filippo came back into the room.

Matt thought he heard him whisper Luciano's name. He felt sure that the Bellezzan had come to look for him and his heart lifted.

'He has told me nothing we did not know,' said Rinaldo. 'You try.'

He threw the precious book to Filippo, who took a chair and sat opposite Matt.

'Send for some wine, Rinaldo,' he said. 'The boy looks worn out.'

Ah, thought Matt, good cop. He knew he mustn't relax.

Rinaldo went to summon a footman and Matt wondered why he hadn't just sent the burly servant. He soon found out.

Filippo was turning the spell-book in his hands. He longed to find out the secrets of stravagation. If he could, he would rise even higher in the favour of the Grand Duke.

'Matteo,' he began. 'Tell us about this book. Why do you carry it? It must be precious to you, especially since I think you know it is illegal to own such a book now?'

Matt tried to keep all emotion out of his face. He said nothing.

'It must contain wonderful secrets,' continued Filippo. 'But both my cousin, the Cardinal, and I have looked in vain for any reference to stravagation. There are many spells and we imagine that one of them must hold the key to your travel to another world.'

Good, thought Matt. They still believe I'm Talian, in spite of my underwear.

'It is unfortunate that you will not tell us about it,' said Filippo pleasantly. 'Ah, good. Here are the refreshments. Let me give you some wine.'

Matt should have seen it coming. The footman was dismissed and Filippo poured three glasses of a ruby-red liquid. He and Rinaldo drank thirstily and Matt felt himself licking his parched lips; he couldn't help it.

Then Filippo took the third glass and hurled the contents in Matt's face. Tied up as he was, there was nothing he could do about it. He shook his head to get the drops out of his eyes as Rinaldo and Filippo laughed at him.

Then the blow. Out of nowhere, Filippo slapped him hard across the face twice – a classic one-two. Matt could no more resist it than he could the wine. His head snapped back and forth and he wondered how much worse it was going to get.

Filippo was massaging his right hand with his left.

'You,' he said to the servant. 'Take over.'

Think about something else, Matt told himself. He hadn't been in many fights in his life and never in a situation where he couldn't defend himself. He braced himself for the blows and concentrated on Ayesha. She was beautiful and she would be waiting for him at Chrissie's party. He tried to imagine her in that garden, surrounded by friends all dressed up for Hallowe'en, but looking out only for him.

The Cardinal was squeamish about what was going on but Filippo was enjoying the violence. He was clutching the book and screaming at Matt.

'You will tell us what we want to know! Tell us about the other world! You, hit him again!'

And then something unexpected happened.

Somehow in the midst of all the hitting and yelling and pushing his face into Matt's, just as Matt thought he might be going to faint, Filippo got in the way of one of the servant's blows. He fell to the ground clutching the book, out cold.

Ayesha had almost reached the point of giving up and going home when something inexplicable happened.

She was in the garden, drinking beer and feeling sorry for herself when suddenly a man seemed to appear out of nowhere in front of her. He was very handsome and in fancy dress but not like a Hallowe'en figure. He wore a ruffled white silk shirt, black velvet trousers and an embroidered purple satin waistcoat. In fact, he looked like a New Romantic, with priceless jewels on his fingers.

And he was clearly terrified. He looked at Ayesha and the other party guests, the skeletons and ghouls and witches dancing round the bonfire, as if he were in a madhouse and expected the occupants to attack him.

'Hello,' she said, feeling sure that this apparition had something to do with Matt.

But the man was incapable of saying anything. And then she saw what he was holding.

'What are you doing with Matt's book?' she asked sharply. She moved to take it from him, forgetting that she was wearing long, pointed false black nails. The man flinched. Then her spiderweb necklace swung forward and the man's eyes rolled up inside his head leaving just the whites showing, briefly, before he vanished, still holding the book.

Luciano rode straight home from Filippo's palazzo and found the three other Stravaganti waiting for him with Cesare. He quickly told them what had happened.

'Enrico's still watching Filippo's place,' he said. 'But we've got to get Matt out of there. I saw Rinaldo's coach in the stables and you know what happened when he kidnapped me.'

He was very pale, reliving his own agony of more than two years ago. He didn't know what would happen to Matt if he was unable to stravagate home but he wasn't prepared to take any chances, after what had happened to him. And Matt had gone to the palazzo on his behalf.

'I wish I'd never agreed to the substitution plan,' he said, furiously tugging his hair.

Rodolfo came and laid a hand on his shoulder.

'We must plan his rescue carefully,' he said. 'We must save not only Matt but his talisman or he won't be able to get home.'

*

Rinaldo was kneeling over the prostrate Filippo and the servant, appalled by what he had done, dashed out of the door, leaving it open behind him. Matt saw his chance and took it.

His arms were bound to the chair behind him but his legs were free and he stood up and stumbled out of the room. Down one flight of stairs, fearing any minute that he would trip and tumble to the bottom, he heaved himself round and smashed the spindly chair to firewood against the banister. The rope fell in coils round his feet but his wrists were still bound. And he could hear Rinaldo shouting from the floor above, raising the alarm.

I've got to get out, he thought, shaking drops of blood and wine off his face. They'll kill me if they catch me.

It was easier getting down the rest of the stairs now that he wasn't encumbered by the chair but it was still difficult to keep his balance with his wrists bound. He could hear footsteps running up the stairs towards him, so pushed at doors along the corridor until he found one that yielded when he barged it.

It was a bed-chamber, not large by di Chimici standards but still three times the size of Matt's own room at home. He had no idea whose room it was but he had three aims: to stay hidden, to untie his wrists and to find some clothes before he was arrested for indecent exposure.

He could hear his pursuers going up the stairs to the top floor amid lots of shouting. He decided that it was safe to explore the room. The bed was high and elaborate, with brass knobs at the corners. With great effort and after lots of tries, Matt managed to lower his wrists over the bedpost and work the rope until the knots gave way. It was excruciatingly painful, since the bonds were quite tight.

Just the freedom of getting out of his bonds filled him with relief, even though he was still inside the di Chimici palace, with no clothes, his talisman taken and with his face throbbing and bloody. A search of the bedroom showed it held no clothes; it didn't seem to be currently occupied.

Cautiously, Matt opened the door, whose flimsy lock he had broken, and peered down the corridor. Now that he had the use of his hands, he could turn doorknobs and soon found an even grander bed-chamber.

Result! he thought. This room was obviously being used. There were no wardrobes – Talians didn't seem to go in for them – but there was a deep wooden chest, which proved to be full of clothes. Matt found breeches and a shirt, ridiculously ruffled and embroidered. No shoes or hat and he drew the line at what looked like a pair of men's tights, but at least he was decent now, even if the sixteenth-century clothes were a bit tight on his twenty-first century frame.

Again he peered out. He heard Rinaldo's high voice ordering the servants to search every room of the palazzo.

'And one of you go straight to the stables, in case he's already got there. He won't be able to ride, though – his arms are tied.'

Sorry, Cara, thought Matt. You'll have to be collected later. He waited behind the door until the footsteps of the man deputed to go to the stables had passed him on the stairs, rubbing his wrists and feeling his face stiffen. He would soon be a mass of bruises.

Then he ran down the stairs as lightly as he could, every sense alert for the sound of pursuit but the servants were obviously searching the rooms on the floor above. He got within sight of the front door before spotting the footman who had remained on duty there. It was the same one who had been snooty to Luciano but Matt didn't know that. He just hated him for being there between him and the door. Matt froze on the stairs and hid behind the thick newel post at the bottom.

It would not be long before the searchers reached this floor. Not stopping to think, Matt waited till the man was looking away, then reached him in three strides and caught him round the throat from behind. He put his other hand over the man's mouth to stop him from calling out, turned him round and, saying, 'Sorry, mate,' hit him hard.

The footman crumpled and Matt felt really bad. He knew just exactly how much that had hurt. Then he noticed that the man had quite big feet. Quickly he slipped off the footman's shoes and buckled them on to his own feet; they weren't too bad a fit.

Then he wrenched open the door and raced towards the cathedral square.

*

'There now,' said Rinaldo. 'You'll be all right in a minute. Have some wine. You were only unconscious for a few seconds.

Filippo struggled into a sitting position, supported by the Cardinal's arm. He looked wildly into his cousin's face.

'I did it,' he said. 'I went there.'

'You're delirious,' said Rinaldo. 'You didn't go anywhere. You were knocked out and only for a few moments, as I said.'

'You don't understand,' said Filippo impatiently, holding out the book. 'There was a beautiful witch. Beautiful, but terrible. She was draped in spiders.'

Rinaldo shook his head. Filippo was babbling, clearly having had a nightmare in the brief period for which he had been knocked out.

'It was the other world, I tell you,' said Filippo. 'And it is a dreadful place, full of spirits and magicians.'

'A dream, Filippo,' said Rinaldo. 'That's all it was. That stupid servant of yours . . .'

'Where's the boy?' asked Filippo, trying to stand.

'I'm afraid he got out,' said Rinaldo. 'But don't worry. The palazzo is being searched. We'll soon have him again.'

'It was the other world,' insisted Filippo, feeling dizzy. 'The world of the Stravaganti. The beautiful sorceress recognised the book. She asked me why I had it. "Matt's book", she called it.'

'Really?' said Rinaldo, excited now. 'You think you have found the secret? How did you do it?'

'I don't know,' said Filippo, trying to shake the fuzziness out of his head. 'Perhaps you have to hold a book while someone hits you?'

The Cardinal felt so frustrated he would have been happy to oblige any time.

Chapter 21

The Day of the Dead

Matt's arrival at Silvia's house caused a sensation. He found four Stravaganti and Cesare planning his rescue but their conference broke up abruptly when they saw him.

'Matt!' cried Luciano. 'Your face! What have those bastards done to you?'

'Given me a pretty thorough working over,' said Matt, grimacing. It hurt to talk. His lips were swollen and bleeding and both eyes beginning to close up. He was going to have the most almighty pair of shiners by the end of the day and he just hoped they wouldn't be visible in his own world. If he could even get to his world.

'I didn't tell them anything,' he said, trying hard not to let his voice crack. 'But they've got the talisman.'

Rodolfo sent Alfredo to bring warm water and cloths to bathe Matt's wounds.

'How did you get away?' asked Luciano.

'The servant who was beating me up missed and knocked Filippo out,' said Matt. It made him want to smile but he couldn't without his face hurting. 'So I legged it out of there. Had to steal some clothes, though. And I . . . I had to hit the footman to get out the front door.'

'Good,' said Luciano, clenching his fists. 'I felt like hitting him myself, the stuck-up sod.'

'But how am I going to get back?' said Matt. 'It must be the middle of the night by now and my parents will know I didn't come back from the party. And if they ask anyone who was there, they'll know I never went to it.' Panic was rising in his throat. 'And if they go into my room, won't they find me unconscious?'

'Nay, ladde,' said Dethridge, putting his hand on Matt's arm. 'Lette us deal first with the first thinges. Alfred here moste bathe thy woundes. Thenne truste us thatte we shall get ye home.'

Matt didn't know how they would do it. But for the first time since he had been captured, he suddenly felt sure that they would.

As it happened, Matt's parents were not worrying about him. While his body lay apparently sleeping on top of his bed in his underwear, Jan had gone to bed assuming that he was at the party as planned and that she just hadn't heard him call out goodbye. When

Andy got in from the opera house and had his usual late night meal and drank pints of mineral water and orange juice, he had found a note from Jan saying, 'Don't lock up, Matt at Hallowe'en party.'

So he had left the front door unbolted and gone to bed.

Ayesha was quite another matter. She knew what she had seen at the party and was desperate to find out what it meant. As soon as Filippo had vanished, she looked desperately round the figures flickering in the firelight, looking for the ones she knew to be Stravaganti.

Alice was not best pleased when she found them.

'Can't we have one night out without talking about stravagation and Talia and . . . and weird stuff?' she protested when Ayesha dragged Sky, Nick and Georgia off to the kitchen, outside the immediate range of the loudspeakers. There was still a heavy thudding underlining Ayesha's frantic attempts to explain what she had seen.

'Who could it have been?' Georgia asked Nick, ignoring Alice.

Ayesha stared at Nick. 'He didn't look totally unlike you,' she said. 'Older, early twenties, I'd say. But he had the same sort of nose and cheekbones. Only he was wearing fancy clothes.' She lowered her voice. 'A bit like, you know, that Lucien when he came here.'

'Definitely Talian then,' said Sky.

'And probably a di Chimici,' said Georgia. 'You're sure it was Matt's book he was holding?'

'Absolutely,' said Ayesha. 'I couldn't mistake it.'

'Of course it was a di Chimici,' said Nick. 'Who else

but a member of my family would steal someone's talisman and try to use it to get here? It must have been one of my cousins. Or maybe my brother Fabrizio.'

'The thing is,' said Ayesha. 'Whoever it might be, it looks as if he succeeded, at least for a few moments.'

'And whoever it is has got Matt's talisman,' said Georgia. 'That means he can't get back.'

Nick looked stricken. 'We've got to help him,' he said.

'But how can we?' asked Sky. 'My talisman and Nick's take us to Giglia,' he explained to Ayesha. 'And Georgia's takes her to Remora. We couldn't get to Padavia and back before nightfall.'

Ayesha looked blank.

'He means daybreak,' said Georgia. 'Night and day are reversed between there and here.'

'So there's nothing we can do?' said Ayesha in despair.

'I'm sure the Stravaganti in Padavia are all working to get him back,' said Georgia.

'And there *is* something we can do,' said Nick. 'We can go round to his and look after that end of things.'

'Don't be daft,' said Sky. 'How can we get in? His parents will be in bed and, even if they aren't, how can we just show up and say, "I think your son might be lying comatose in his room and we'd like to look after him till he regains consciousness"? They'd go spare.'

'I've got a key,' said Ayesha, taking her key-ring out of her black sequinned bag.

Enrico eyed Matt's face with an almost professional air.

'You look horrible,' he said.

'You're no oil painting yourself!' said Matt, wincing. 'At least I've been beaten up.'

Alfredo had done his best with hot water, warm cloths and a tincture of arnica. But if anything, Matt looked worse: the arnica turned a sort of orangey-purple on his skin, mottling his face with a second layer of bruises.

Enrico had followed him back from Filippo's, guessing correctly that Luciano wouldn't need him to stay there any more.

As soon as Alfredo had finished ministering to Matt, he busied himself providing lunch for everyone, never happier than when the house was full of unexpected guests.

An argument was raging among the Stravaganti about how to get Matt home.

'I must go and get him another talisman,' said Constantin, white-lipped. 'One from his world.'

'But it will be the middle of the night there,' said Luciano. 'You'd be completely disoriented. And what are you going to find as a talisman at that hour? A takeaway kebab? Let me go. I know people there. There are three Stravaganti who would give me something, let alone my parents.'

'And I'll goe with ye,' said Dethridge. 'I am tired of staying here, keping out of the waye of daungere.'

'I wouldn't say you were doing that,' said

Constantin. 'No Stravagante is beyond danger in this city, at this time.'

'You are all forgetting something,' said Rodolfo. 'This is not a case like Luciano's where a new talisman from the other world can take Matt back. His body is still in both worlds. He can't get back without the spell-book.'

There was a horrified silence. It was broken by Enrico.

'Then I'm your man,' he said cheerfully. 'I'll steal it for you.'

He held up a hand to still the chorus of protests.

'Which of you here has ever stolen anything?' he asked.

There was silence.

'I thought not. Look, I know Rinaldo di Chimici; he'd let me into his place and I bet Filippo would too if the Cardinal's still there.'

'Let me help,' said Cesare. 'I can't stravagate but I can do anything that would help at this end.'

Rodolfo was looking hard at Enrico. 'I don't know how it is that that you have gained Luciano's confidence,' he said. 'But I don't forget that you tried to kill my wife. Why should we trust you?'

'But I didn't, did I?' said Enrico. 'It was *my* wife I killed – at least the woman who was going to be my wife. And I got rid of the Duke. Where would the young Cavaliere be today if I hadn't switched the foils?'

No one felt very comfortable with this view of the situation. Both Cesare and Luciano had been captured by this man and most of them knew what he was capable of.

'I'm not claiming to be a reformed character,' said Enrico, looking round at them. 'As I told the Cavaliere, it's just that I don't want to work for the di Chimici any more. That's when my troubles began, spying for that Rinaldo. His Eminence, as he is now.'

'I think perhaps we have to trust him,' said Constantin. 'He's our only chance of getting the talisman back.'

'Agreed,' said Rodolfo reluctantly. He turned to Enrico. 'But if you betray us, I shall search you out wherever you are and you will regret it.'

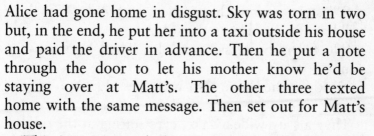

Alice had gone home in disgust. Sky was torn in two but, in the end, he put her into a taxi outside his house and paid the driver in advance. Then he put a note through the door to let his mother know he'd be staying over at Matt's. The other three texted home with the same message. Then set out for Matt's house.

'This is crazy,' said Sky. 'Even with your key, how can so many of us get in without their hearing us?'

'It'll be all right, as long as we get into his room,' said Ayesha. 'We can say in the morning that he let us crash after the party.'

'Well, that will work if he wakes up,' said Georgia.

Still, it was a tense time, unlocking the front door and crowding into the entrance hall.

'We'd better throw the bolts,' whispered Ayesha. 'Or his mum will notice in the morning and think he stayed out.'

They crept up the stairs, trying to sound like one

teenager instead of four. But the weirdest thing was letting themselves into Matt's room. He was there, but not there.

His body lay on top of the bed, on his stomach, arms under the pillow, breathing regularly and looking like any other sleeping boy. Ayesha couldn't help rushing over and hugging him. He stirred in his sleep and put one arm round her but his eyes stayed closed.

Matt had a sofa-bed in his room and they opened it up as quietly as they could. Ayesha disentangled herself from Matt's embrace and he rolled back on to his front. She found them a duvet and some pillows from a deep drawer under Matt's bed.

'I'll sleep next to him,' she whispered. 'You three will have to manage on the sofa.'

'No funny business,' said Sky. 'Shall I go between you?'

Nick punched him. 'No way,' he said. 'You're next to me.'

They all lay wide-awake, eyes staring at the ceiling. But gradually, lulled by the sound of Matt's steady breathing and exhausted by worry, they fell into a troubled sleep.

In Padavia, the Stravaganti had come up with a plan. Constantin was going back to Salt Street with Enrico to pick up a substitute book from Nando's. It wouldn't be exactly the same inside, but it should be enough to fool the di Chimici, if Enrico could exchange it for the original. Cesare went with them, determined to do something to help Matt.

But after they left, a grimmer plan was being discussed.

'If Enrico fails,' said Rodolfo, making sure that the Stravaganti were out of Matt's earshot. 'We all know what will happen. I think we had better go ahead with the plan to bring back another talisman – just in case.'

'Ryghte,' said Dethridge. 'I am ready.'

'Take care of Luciano,' said Rodolfo, looking at his old apprentice. 'And Luciano, you look out for the Dottore. It might be difficult for you both seeing your old home.'

Without telling Matt what they were doing, Luciano and his foster-father went to lie down on Luciano's bed. Holding their talismans – Luciano's white rose and Dethridge's copper vessel – they concentrated their minds on where Dethridge used to live. Luciano thought it would be easier to find his way to Matt's home from there and he hoped to bring a talisman from as near to the Woods' house as possible.

'There's a school there now,' he reminded the Dottore. 'Not like a school in your time. It's a big glass and concrete building – think of a big palazzo made mainly of windows.'

*

'Enrico Poggi?' said the Cardinal. 'What the dev— I mean what on earth can he want? I didn't even know he was in the city.'

'Isn't that the wretch who caused my uncle's death?' asked Filippo indignantly.

'Yes, but we must be consistent about this,' said Rinaldo. 'We want to avenge that death on the Cavaliere, not this insignificant criminal.'

'So shall we agree to see him?' asked Filippo.

'It is possible that he might even be able to help us,' said Rinaldo. 'He has been useful in his time.'

'Show him in, then,' Filippo told the footman, 'and get that eye of yours seen to. You look like a ruffian.'

The footman went away, seething. It was not his fault he had been attacked.

The di Chimici cousins were mortified that they had let the Stravagante called Matteo escape. But they were still excited by Filippo's glimpse of the other world. They felt that they were on the verge of discovering the secrets of stravagation and they still had the book, which was the key to the whole mystery.

'Your Highness, Your Eminence,' said Enrico, entering the room bowing, his blue hat in his hand.

But his eyes were darting everywhere and he soon spotted the talisman on the table between the cousins; Constantin had given him its near twin.

'What impudence brings you here?' asked Rinaldo haughtily. There had been a time when he feared this ruthless agent of his but since the duel, he felt as if he had the upper hand.

'Only wishing to help, Eminence,' said Enrico humbly. 'I have some information I thought you might be willing to pay for.'

Rinaldo sighed. 'It's always money with you, isn't it? Well, tell us what you know and we'll decide what it's worth to us.'

Enrico had thought long and hard about what information to give the di Chimici. He didn't want to endanger any of the Stravaganti but he had to offer them something, to justify his visit. He had toyed with the idea of telling them about Ludo the Manoush being sheltered in Governor Antonio's house, which was an interesting nugget, but had decided against it. Ludo seemed to be pretty thick with the Stravaganti and Enrico had nothing against the Governor.

'Well,' he said. 'Someone's breaking the law in this city, on a regular basis.'

'Many, I should think,' said Filippo.

'Someone high up,' said Enrico. 'A professor at the University.'

Rinaldo and Filippo exchanged looks.

'Go on,' said the Cardinal.

At that moment, there was a commotion in the street outside. Enrico was the only one who didn't go over to the window. He had arranged carefully with Cesare to let off some Reman candles at precisely this moment. Rodolfo had supplied them and Cesare had used his tinderbox to spark them off. In the moment it took the di Chimici to look out of the window and for Cesare's voice to be heard apologising, 'Sorry, Sorry. They're for tomorrow. They've gone off too soon,' Enrico had silently swooped on the table and switched the leather books.

As the cousins turned back to the room, he was putting the fake back, untying the thongs around it.

'What are you doing with that?' asked Rinaldo sharply.

'Nothing,' said Enrico, easily. 'I just wondered if it had anything to do with the Professor I was telling you about. The rumour is, he's been publishing forbidden material.'

'Magic?' asked Filippo eagerly.

'No,' said Enrico. 'Medical stuff. He's a professor of Anatomy – Angeli's the name. And the word is that not all the corpses he cuts up are criminals, the way they should be.'

'Well, this is a book of spells and other such pagan rubbish, not medicine,' said Rinaldo irritably. 'Now if you knew anything about that, you might be useful.'

Enrico shrugged and put the book down. 'Sorry,' he said. 'Not my kind of thing, all that hocus-pocus. I'll be off then, shall I?'

'You are lucky that we don't have you arrested,' said Rinaldo. 'I think my cousin Fabrizio would be very interested to interview you about what happened at the duel.' Then he seemed to think again and tossed the spy a few silver coins. 'All information is valuable, I suppose. But don't come back unless you know something about the Cavaliere Luciano, the Stravaganti or people breaking the anti-magic laws.'

Dethridge was clutching tight on to Luciano's arm as soon as they arrived. The old man was trembling.

'They have lit a bone-fire,' was all he managed to say.

Luciano took a moment or two to orient himself. He could see the outline of the school and realised that they were behind Sky's house.

'This must be the garden of the house where they were having the party,' he said. 'Don't worry about the bonfire, Dottore. They lit it for the party. Lots of people will be building fires this week for November the fifth. Do you remember what I told you about Guy Fawkes?'

Gradually, he led his foster-father away from the school and towards Matt's house. He was glad he had warned him about bonfires, because they saw several more waiting to be lit in people's back gardens. The alchemist had been condemned to death by burning in his old life and that was why he had fled to Talia.

But it felt so weird to be with Dethridge in their old world!

'I don't suppose you can recognise any of it?' he asked.

Dethridge shook his head. 'There are so many houses,' he said.

Luciano hadn't worked out what to do when they got there. But he knew from his earlier visit which room was Matt's; it had a dormer window on the second floor.

'Come on, Dottore,' he said. 'Let's concentrate and see if we can find out anything.'

All that happened was that a head stuck itself out of the window.

'Who's there?' a voice whispered. 'Luciano?'

'It's Falco,' said Luciano, relieved. 'Only we must call him Nick, here. They must have come to look after Matt while he is out of his body.'

'They?' asked Dethridge.

'Where Nick is, there is bound to be Georgia,' said Luciano, smiling.

A movement at the door and there indeed was Georgia, beckoning them in. Her eyes widened when she saw Dethridge. But this was no time for exuberant reunions. The two Talians followed her cautiously up to Matt's room, which was now looking a bit overcrowded.

Ayesha sat up in alarm when Luciano and the Elizabethan came in.

'It's all right,' hissed Georgia. 'This is Doctor Dethridge, the first Stravagante. Though I don't know why he's here.'

Luciano didn't want to explain in front of Ayesha why they had come. To let her know that there was a possibility Matt might be stranded in the other world and die in this one.

'We came back because Matt's been robbed of his talisman in Talia,' he said.

'We figured that out,' said Sky. 'Is he all right?'

'He is now,' said Luciano. He went over and looked at the figure sleeping on the bed. It did him good to see Matt's face unblemished. He lifted the pillow and revealed Matt's left hand holding the book.

'What's to stop us taking this one, Dottore?' he asked. 'Just in case Enrico doesn't succeed?'

'Enrico!' said Georgia. 'You haven't got *him* doing anything, have you?'

'Naye, ladde,' said Dethridge, laying a hand on Luciano's arm. 'Ye canne notte take it. We canne notte have two manifestatiounes of the same thynge existing in the same worlde at the same tyme. Do ye not thinke Maister Rudolphe wolde have done that for ye, if sich a thynge were possible?'

'Why does he talk like that?' whispered Ayesha.

'He's an Elizabethan,' said Sky.

And then Matt stretched and sat up.

Ayesha gave a little scream and was immediately shushed.

'Blimey,' said Matt. 'Has the party moved here?'

He reached out for Ayesha and she curled up against him. He smiled at her but looked shocked to see the Talians.

'What are you doing here?' he demanded.

All day, Ludo and his kin had kept a low profile. Hurried conferences and messages passed between them had led to a change in setting for their evening rites. They agreed that the square outside the cathedral was too dangerous and instead arranged to gather near the swamp. The advantage was that the sky would be clearer to them there, unobscured by buildings with towers and the moon was only three days off the full. They would be able to see this embodiment of their goddess and she would show them any would-be pursuers.

When night fell, they gathered at the appointed place, their dark cloaks pulled round their colourful clothes. But as the ritual wore on and their chanting and dancing grew more energetic, cloaks were cast off, hair shaken loose and instruments pulled out of bags. And as their sober clothes fell from them, the Manoush reverted to type and gave themselves up wholeheartedly to their intercessions for the dead.

They called to the spirits of those they had lost, summoning them by name to come back from their wanderings. Unlike people who spent their lives in one place, the Manoush had no graves to visit; their dead were burned where they fell and their ashes given to the wind. They had nowhere to bring flowers or candles so the rituals around the Day of the Dead were all about the spirits of their lost ones, calling them to join them in celebrating the start of a new year, just as the dead had started a new chapter of their lives.

The sound of chanting and wailing was bound to draw attention to the Manoush and it was not long before the city watch discovered them. Ropes were brought and the worshippers, still pleading with the goddess, were taken away to the Palace of Justice.

They left without a struggle and the swamp returned to silence and heavy cloud hid the moon, like a thick veil drawn over a grieving face. If the spirits of the Manoush dead had come as summoned, they were now on their own.

Morning had broken over Islington and the sun rose on many school students who had stayed late at the Hallowe'en party and wished they hadn't. In Matt's house, Jan and Harry were up first as usual, while Andy slept and dreamed of playing rugby with a huge soprano.

Matt came downstairs cautiously feeling his face. It didn't hurt and he'd checked in the bathroom mirror that his bruises didn't show but it was as if he was wearing a mask and knew that underneath was a screaming mess of pain.

'Hi, darling,' said Jan. 'You look rough. Coffee?'

'Mm,' said Matt. 'Please.'

'Good party?'

He made a noncommittal noise then said, 'A few guys came back to sleep. Is that OK?'

'Of course. Do you think they'll want breakfast? I bet you'll all need an early night tonight.'

'If we could just give them cereal and coffee, that'd be fine,' said Matt.

He suddenly felt so glad to be home that he put his arms round Jan and gave her a kiss.

'Good Lord,' she said. 'You're in a good mood! Do I take it that you and Ayesha are back together?'

'Maybe,' said Matt and grinned, glad that his face didn't hurt too much to do it.

There were about thirty Manoush filling the gaol in the Palace of Justice. They had to be kept together in two cells, though Antonio would have preferred it if they'd had no opportunity to confer with one another.

He was not best pleased at being got out of bed just after midnight and told that were some two and a half dozen new prisoners detained under the anti-magic laws. He had not expected to have to invoke the death penalty so soon or for so many people.

But he didn't understand why the brightly dressed and wild-eyed people, men and women, were so distraught. Almost all were weeping and some were howling like animals in pain.

'What's the matter with them?' Antonio asked the gaoler. It was true that they were all liable to be sentenced to death, the Governor realised uncomfortably, but he hadn't expected this reaction.

'They do not sleep indoors,' said a familiar voice. And there was his wife, wrapped in a vast shawl, who had followed him, unnoticed, from their house. 'You know nothing about the Manoush,' said Giunta icily. 'It is like putting a wild animal in a cage, to separate them from the stars at night.'

Chapter 22

Death by Burning

Rodolfo had told Matt not to stravagate the next night and he was glad of another day before he had to face the pain of his injuries back in Talia. School was bad enough. There didn't seem to be a single sixth former without a hangover and some had called in sick.

'Thank goodness Guy Fawkes' Night is on a Saturday this year,' said Jan Wood in the staffroom. 'Or we'd have all this to go through again. It's like teaching eighteen bowls of cold porridge.'

Her son, of course, was one of the few who were not the worse for drinking too much at the party, for the simple reason that he had not been there. But somehow everyone assumed that he had, including Chay, and thought that was why he looked a bit rough.

Matt didn't correct them. What could he say? I was really in another world, getting a vicious beating, and I might have died if it hadn't been for my friends there?

He shuddered whenever he thought of it. He had never been so pleased to see anyone as when Enrico had come back to Luciano's house and pulled the book out of his jerkin. He had just been so glad to hold it in his hands, like a lifebelt.

'Thanks, mate,' was all he could say. 'You've saved my life.'

Rodolfo had made him stravagate home straight away so he didn't see if Enrico got any kind of reward.

And what a homecoming! His room full of friends, Ayesha kissing him as if she meant never to stop and, inexplicably, Luciano and his Elizabethan foster-father standing in the middle of the room silently cheering. He was glad they had stravagated back almost immediately. Four extra Barnsbury students to find breakfast for was just about OK; Jan had coped with more than that in the past. But two sixteenth-century Talians, one of them talking like Shakespeare, would have been a bit much to explain.

Ayesha joined him for lunch just as usual and it was enough just to look at her, smiling across at him. But she wanted it put into words.

'You gave me such a fright last night,' she began. 'Promise me you won't do anything like that again.'

'I can't promise not to go to Talia,' said Matt. 'I don't know if what I went there to do is done yet. But

I can promise to try not to be captured again. I'll be extra careful.'

'You said you were pretending to be Luciano when you were taken prisoner,' said Ayesha. 'Maybe that's what you were supposed to do. Sort of take the bullet for him. Not that they hurt you, of course.'

Matt hadn't told her what the di Chimici servant had done. There was no point. She'd only worry and there was nothing to see in this world. He wondered whether it would have shown if they'd broken his nose. And what would have happened if they'd killed him?

'But the main thing is you're here and we're OK, aren't we?' Ayesha was asking.

'We are as far as I'm concerned,' said Matt. 'Have you forgiven me for what I did to Jago?'

'Well, it was incredibly stupid,' said Ayesha. 'But it doesn't seem to have done any lasting harm. And now that you've explained about stravagation I can understand about why you wanted to be with the others so much.'

'You see why I couldn't tell you before?' asked Matt.

'I wouldn't have believed you,' said Ayesha. 'Not if I hadn't seen what happened to Jago and then you bringing Lucien here. I still don't understand most of it but I do believe that's what's happening to you.'

'You don't fancy a quick trip to Talia, like Alice?' Matt asked.

Ayesha shook her head. 'No. I've talked to her about that and she said it was horrible. She had to wear pantomime clothes and there was this scary big sculptor lady who terrified her and everyone was carrying knives and swords. And she said that Sky and Nick both got stabbed.'

Matt made a mental note to ask them why their wounds had come back to this world with them when his hadn't. He wasn't as confident as Ayesha that his mission in Talia had been fulfilled. But he was happy just to be able to hold her hands over the table and know that they were back together.

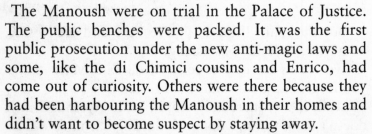

The Manoush were on trial in the Palace of Justice. The public benches were packed. It was the first public prosecution under the new anti-magic laws and some, like the di Chimici cousins and Enrico, had come out of curiosity. Others were there because they had been harbouring the Manoush in their homes and didn't want to become suspect by staying away.

Messer Antonio was extremely ill at ease with the whole process. Of course he didn't approve of goddess-worship; it was anathema to him. But it had rattled him seeing the distress of the Manoush in his city's prison. It wasn't just their hatred of sleeping indoors; they had seemed genuinely to believe that the New Year could not begin properly without their rituals being completed.

One of their number, a man called Ottavio Camlo, seemed to be a sort of spokesman. He was about Antonio's own age, his grizzled hair worn long and tied back by a black ribbon. He had explained to the Governor that, if they were prevented from celebrating the Day of the Dead in the way their traditions demanded, there was a danger that spirits summoned up on the night the Manoush were arrested would continue to walk the streets. The fact that he was in imminent danger of losing his life seemed to bother him less than this possibility.

The guards who had arrested the Manoush were the prime witnesses to their impious acts. But they were hardly needed. The group of travellers did not deny that they were goddess-worshippers; they would have scorned to.

'Do you plead guilty to an act of pagan worship and ceremony in Padavia last night?' asked Antonio.

'We were indeed performing our annual ceremony to welcome the Day of the Dead,' said Ottavio, speaking for the whole group. 'We see no guilt in that. It is our religion.'

'Well,' said Antonio, not wanting to be impressed. 'It is not the religion of this city-state. And the laws of Padavia clearly declare it illegal to practise it here. There are notices in all the public places. The Zinti can read, can't they?'

Ottavio looked straight ahead. 'The Manoush read the notices,' he said.

'Then the verdict of this court must be Guilty,' said Antonio. 'You knew the law and yet you went ahead and broke it.'

'We respect the law,' said Ottavio. 'But we cannot put law above religion. We have a greater duty, to the goddess.'

There was a buzz of agreement from the other prisoners.

It was just as Giunta had warned him that terrible night when he told her about the new laws; these goddess-worshippers were brave, there was no doubt about that. But it chilled him to think what he must now do.

There was no way out for Antonio, no tiny chink in the law through which the travellers could escape and move to another city, whose laws were less strict.

'It is therefore my solemn and disagreeable duty to pass the most severe sentence on you and all your people arrested last night,' said Antonio. 'It is this court's verdict that the prisoners be taken from this place and held in captivity two more nights until the legitimate church festival of All Saints is concluded. Then on Thursday they must suffer the full penalty of the law and be subject to death by burning.'

Before he went to bed that night, Jan called Matt to the phone. It was his great-aunt Eva.

'Hello, Matt,' she said. 'How are you?'

'Fine,' he said. 'Well, actually, I'm pretty tired. Going to have an early night.'

'I won't keep you,' said Eva. 'I just wanted to tell you something. I've been thinking about it ever since I got back. My father had the same problem as you.'

'Needed an early night?' said Matt. He didn't really feel like a profound conversation.

'He had problems with reading and writing. It wasn't called dyslexia in his day and I think he suffered terribly at school from teachers who thought he wasn't very bright.'

'I know how he felt.'

'The thing is, Matt, he was one of the most

intelligent people I have ever known. He worked hard all his life and he valued education. He was so proud when I got into Cambridge. He really wanted me and your grandfather to have a better life than he had. But reading and writing were a mystery to him.'

'Well, thanks for telling me,' said Matt. He had been told by one of his ed psychs that dyslexia was hereditary. But this was the first time he'd heard of any family member with reading problems; he'd thought till now that they were all brainy bookish types on Jan's side and all musical or arty ones on Andy's.

'Why haven't you mentioned it before?' he asked.

'I think I've been rather a foolish old woman,' said Eva. 'I've been putting my head in the sand like the proverbial ostrich. I didn't really want to accept that you were the same as my dad. I hoped you would grow out of it in time. But Jan really put me right on my last visit. I understand now that you have to have all the extra help you can get. And if you do go to Cambridge, or any other university and there's anything I can do to help with computers or extra tuition, please ask me first. I've got far more money than I need.'

'Thanks, Eva,' said Matt. But her acceptance of his dyslexia meant more to him even than the offer of money. He wouldn't have to pretend with her any more.

'That's all right,' said Eva. 'And thank you for introducing me to that delightful Mr Goldsmith. He's coming to visit me in Brighton in a few weeks. I think I really do need to get rid of some of my books.'

Go, Eva, thought Matt, as he staggered up to bed.

For the second day running, Constantin did no work in his Secret Scriptorium. Feeling was running high in the city and it was just too dangerous. Those in favour of the anti-magic laws were in a fever of spying and informing on fellow-citizens. Those who thought the laws unnecessarily repressive were scandalised by the verdict on the Manoush.

As soon as their sentence had been given, a tall red-haired prisoner had jumped up and condemned the court for being willing to kill them all indiscriminately. 'Let the men among us burn but release our women and children,' he demanded.

The word was that the Governor was ashamed in the face of such bravery but stood firm on his verdict.

It had never been expected that the first prosecution and execution would involve such a large number. Even if they were burned in groups, a great quantity of fires would have to be built. The whole of the Piazza dei Fiori was filled with men and brushwood preparing for the grisly task.

Constantin saw it on his way to visit the anatomist, Angelo Angeli. He stopped, filled with disgust at what human beings were capable of doing to one another. In the next square preparations were going on for the evening's festivities celebrating the Church's Festival of the Dead. There would be feasting and drinking and fireworks as soon as the evening services were over.

So close, thought Constantin, to the place of

execution and so unmindful of what would happen there in two days' time. He had lived long enough to accept life and death as inextricably woven into the pattern of the world but such callous indifference to the fate of fellow human beings shocked him.

Professor Angeli had rooms off the market square. He was delighted to see Constantin. He poured wine for them both and rubbed his hands in anticipation.

'Have you come about the book?' he asked as soon as it was decent to do so.

Constantin took a volume from his canvas satchel.

'Here it is Angeli – the *Teoria Anatomica* – I have brought you one copy. Nando has the rest hidden, ready for sale.'

The Professor put on his reading-glasses, the very latest invention.

'But this is quite wonderful,' he said, greedily turning the pages. 'The engravings are magnificent!'

Constantin inclined his head and drank deeply from the wine glass.

'You seem downcast,' said Angeli. 'Is it always so when you have completed the production of a great work?'

'It is not that,' said Constantin. 'It is the coming deaths of nearly thirty people old and young, for practising their religion.'

'I heard about that,' said Angeli. 'It is a terrible thing. But they did break the law.'

'Which they believed to be wrong,' said Constantin. 'Ah well, you will have plenty of opportunity on Thursday to observe the effect of fire on human bodies.'

'Do not say so,' said Angeli. 'It will not be an occasion for rejoicing.'

*

'We can't just let them die!' said Luciano, pacing up and down the room. 'They've done nothing wrong. And these are Aurelio and Raffaella's people. Ludo is my friend.'

'I have no intention of letting them die,' said Rodolfo. 'The only question is, how best to save them? There is no loophole in the law – it is very clearly worded and they broke it.'

'Whatte aboute an appeal for clemencie?' asked Dethridge. 'The Governour seems a decent manne. Mayhap we could appeal to his sense of honour? Atte least for the femayles and childer?'

'I think that Antonio is deeply regretting passing those laws,' said Rodolfo. 'But he has very little room to manoeuvre.'

'I have escaped the fyre myselfe,' said Dethridge. 'And I shalle notte stand aside and watch othires suffer yt.'

'That's it!' said Luciano. 'You escaped to Talia, using your talisman. We must get talismans for all the Manoush, so that they can do a . . . a sort of mass stravagation to my old world.'

'And then what?' asked Rodolfo, but not unkindly. 'Who will look after thirty such travellers in your old world and give them food and work? Do you come from such a civilisation that all of them would be made welcome and kindly treated? And could they survive, taken from the rest of their people?'

Luciano saw all the problems, collecting thirty talismans for a start, then explaining to two and a half dozen terrified people about stravagating to the world of the twenty-first century. He had a flashback memory of Eastern European women with toddlers begging on the Tube, carrying little bits of cardboard with a few words giving their history written on them.

What could the Manoush write? They would be the most displaced persons ever in the history of London. And although it would be true that their lives would be in danger if they were sent home, how could they ever explain that to the authorities?

'Well, perhaps not. But then what are we to do?' he asked Rodolfo.

'I wolde helpe him collect the talismans,' said Dethridge eagerly. 'Yt wolde not be so badde to goe agayne. I have seene whatte yt is lyke, now.'

'I think we must have a different plan,' said Rodolfo. 'If the Manoush are to be taken away, it must be to somewhere nearer here.'

'Where?' asked Luciano.

'Bellezza,' said Rodolfo. 'If only there were a Stravagante there now. But we are all here.'

'My wife is there,' said Dethridge. 'I have taught her how to use the mirror.'

'And my wife is there too,' said Rodolfo. 'Leonora can go to her for help.'

'I'm sure Arianna would want to help,' said Luciano. 'But we've got to rescue them first.'

Dethridge was counting on his fingers. 'I have yt!' he said. 'The execution will be in two days' time. Yf we have enough of our friends to unbind them, I canne warrant thatte we wille be able to do yt. There wille be a riske, of course, bot yt canne be done.'

*

Rinaldo was flushed and excited at the success of the trial, as he saw it. He had sent his long-suffering messenger with a letter to Fabrizio in Giglia, telling him that around thirty 'pagans' were to suffer the full force of the new laws. Laws that he, Cardinal di Chimici, had influenced the city's Governor to adopt.

He could still not report any success in getting Luciano to incriminate himself by committing magical acts. And he doubted whether he should say anything about Filippo's unintentional short trip to the other world.

The two cousins had experimented with holding the book and hitting each other but with no result except one black eye (the Cardinal) and one split lip (Filippo). They gave up their experiments by mutual agreement, glaring at each other.

The servants gossiped among themselves about how the two noble cousins had clearly been in a fight – and one of them a churchman. It was a matter of great satisfaction to the footman that Matt had attacked.

The di Chimici were no nearer to discovering how stravagation worked but Filippo was definite that he had been transported to another world and that it was connected to the book. Neither man had any idea that the original book had been switched by Enrico.

But Rinaldo had decided to investigate what the spy had told him about Professor Angeli. He paid a visit to the Anatomy Theatre, which was not in use over the three-day holiday, and looked at the room which held the bodies before dissection and examined the mechanism by which the table rose up into the theatre.

The porter who showed him around, a man called Gobbi, explained that the corpses for dissection were those of recently executed criminals, though they must be those born outside the city.

'What if there are no executions when the Professor wants to demonstrate to his students?' asked the Cardinal.

'Well, then he would postpone the demonstration till there were some, Eminence,' said the porter. 'Or use an animal.'

Rinaldo was getting nowhere; he decided to see what the power of silver could discover.

On Wednesday, two days after Chrissie's party, Matt sought out the other Stravaganti in a corner of the common room.

'You're looking better,' said Georgia.

'I feel it,' said Matt. 'I got a good night's sleep last night, instead of stravagating. How about you guys? Have you recovered from Monday?'

'Yeah,' said Nick. 'More or less, except that Alice still isn't talking to Sky.'

Sky glared at him.

Matt noticed that the fair-haired girl wasn't sitting with them. She was usually so quiet that he didn't notice whether she was there or not. But now he could see that she was over the other side of the room, having a heart-to-heart with Lucy. She wasn't Matt's type at all but he could see that Sky was a bit upset.

'Sorry,' he said. 'I seem to have caused a lot of trouble.'

'You couldn't help getting caught,' said Georgia. 'Can you tell us more about it now?'

Ayesha had orchestra practice, so Matt was able to tell them the whole story, not leaving out the beating this time.

'That's awful!' said Georgia. 'But you went in Luciano's place?'

'Maybe that's what you were sent to Padavia for?' said Sky. 'My mission turned out to be about saving his life in Giglia, though it wasn't by any act of bravery.'

'I don't know,' said Matt. 'I'm going back tonight to find out. The thing is, I wonder why my bruises don't show here in this world? Alice told Ayesha that you two got stabbed in Giglia and your wounds came back here with you.'

Sky and Nick exchanged glances, their animosity of a few moments ago forgotten as they remembered how they had fought on the same side in the Church of the Annunciation and both received sword cuts. Surreptitiously they both rolled up their sleeves to show Matt their scars. Sky's was much more noticeable against his dark skin.

'I don't know why you left your injuries in Talia and we didn't,' said Sky. 'Maybe it's because our wounds were deep and Brother Sulien had to stitch them?'

All three of them peered at Matt's face.

'I can sort of feel them,' he said. 'I mean I know

they're there but they don't really hurt and there's nothing to see.'

'My cousins are brutes,' was all Nick said. 'I never liked Rinaldo but I thought better of Filippo.'

'I think he's acting on orders from above,' said Matt. 'No offence, Nick, but I think your big brother's behind it.'

Georgia put her arm round Nick. 'You can't help your family,' she said quietly. 'Remember how nice Gaetano and Francesca are? And Fabrizio and Filippo are their brothers.'

Matt remembered something else. 'It must have been Filippo who stravagated to the party,' he said. 'He was holding the book while that thug was hitting me and his face got in the way. Filippo was knocked out but only for a few seconds.'

'Do you think they know what that means then?' asked Georgia. 'Do the di Chimici know that all you need is a talisman and losing consciousness while thinking of the other world?'

'I don't know,' said Matt. 'But they haven't got a talisman any more.' He drew the book from his jacket pocket. 'This is the real thing.'

Fabrizio read his cousin's letter eagerly.

'Thirty goddess-worshippers!' he said. 'They will have to burn them two or three to a pyre!'

He felt that the tide was beginning to turn in his favour. That the whole uncontrollable mass of magic and superstition, which it was his duty to stamp out, had received a significant blow.

And surely now was the time to strike to get rid of the young Bellezzan? He and his family had been too restrained so far.

The Grand Duke took up his pen to write to Filippo and sent the messenger for refreshment.

'The Duchessa of Bellezza must find herself a new lover,' he muttered. 'The Cavaliere Luciano Crinamorte's days are numbered.'

Chapter 23

The Condemned

When Matt arrived in the studio the next morning, he was still wearing the clothes he had stolen from the di Chimici palace. Worse, his face throbbed with all the aches and bruising he had been shielded from in his own world.

There was no sign of Constantin. The presses in the Scriptorium were still and there was no sound from the secret room. Matt knocked on the cupboard that hid the secret door but here was no answer from inside. He went back into the studio, wondering what to do next. It was the third day of the Church's Festival of the Dead and so the Scriptorium was enjoying its last day of rest. So he couldn't understand why Constantin wasn't working in the secret room, taking advantage of the holiday.

He tried the door of the Scriptorium but it was locked from the outside. Matt had only two choices: stravagate back home or climb out the window of the studio as he had done the last time he was here. Curiosity dictated his decision.

As soon as he was out on the street, Matt wasn't sure he had done the right thing. He had lost his hat at Filippo's and passers-by stared curiously at his short hair. Then they did a double take at the sight of his face. Matt thought he must look pretty bad.

He wanted to keep out of Filippo and Rinaldo's way and the University was shut; in the end, he went to Cesare's lodgings, in the hope of finding the Remoran and getting hold of the news. The streets were strangely silent, with hardly anyone about.

Matt walked through the market square, which was still without its stalls and traders. There seemed to have been a big party there the night before; people were picking up litter and putting it in canvas sacks. He saw the burnt-out ends of rockets and Reman candles scattered on the ground and there was the smell of gunpowder in the air.

Feels as if Padavia itself is hung-over, he thought.

What he saw in the next square pulled him up short. He stared unbelievingly at the ten huge bonfires which had been built there. Rising starkly out of each were three wooden stakes and it didn't take much imagination to guess their purpose. Each pile of brushwood had a long ladder propped against the side.

Matt hurried to Cesare's and rapped on the door. The woman who answered it was one he had seen on a few other occasions but she didn't seem to recognise him; in fact she shrank back and tried to close the door.

'It's all right, signora,' said Matt. 'I am looking for my friend, Cesare Montalbano. I have been here before.'

She opened the door wider and peered at his face.

'You have been in a fight, I see,' she said. 'And seem to have come off worse.'

'You should see the other bloke,' said Matt trying to smile but it ended in a wince and a groan.

'We don't want any of your student vendettas here,' she said.

'I promise I am Cesare's friend,' said Matt. 'And there is no one else with me or behind me. Is he in?'

The woman let him in rather grudgingly and Matt went up to Cesare's room.

'Dia, you look terrible,' said Cesare.

'Do I really look that bad?' asked Matt. 'I haven't seen myself in a mirror yet.'

Cesare gestured to a glass propped up on a chest in his room. Matt bent down and inspected the damage. His eyelids were no longer swollen and his lip had gone down a lot too, but he had a rainbow of bruises around his eyes and along his jaw.

'I see what you mean,' he said. 'There's nothing to see in my world, you know. My face is completely normal. I suppose I should be glad they didn't break my nose or knock a tooth out. That might have been difficult to repair during stravagation.'

'Have you heard what's happened?' asked Cesare.

'I haven't spoken to anyone,' said Matt. 'Constantin isn't at the Scriptorium and the streets are deserted. What's going on?'

'The Manoush are in prison,' said Cesare. 'They were arrested the night before last and tried yesterday and –'

'Don't tell me,' said Matt, horrified. 'I saw the bonfires on the way here.'

'You've guessed it,' said Cesare. 'All of them condemned to burn. All those who celebrated their Day of the Dead.'

'So what are we going to do about it?'

'Rodolfo and Dethridge have a plan. We had a meeting about it last night. But it's a risk. I don't know that it will succeed.'

*

Luciano had been busy with the other Stravaganti, making arrangements in Bellezza through means of the mirrors. It wasn't easy, because the women were not as expert at think-speaking and sometimes Rodolfo wrote important instructions backwards and held them up to the glass.

And it had been frustrating seeing Arianna without being able to touch her or kiss her.

'She seems to be trying to tell me about kittens,' Luciano said to Rodolfo. 'Big spotty kittens is what I'm getting. She seems very excited about it.'

Rodolfo laughed. 'We are trying to organise a dangerous escape plan for thirty people and Arianna wants to tell you about her cats! It is the one called Florio and it turns out to be a female. Expecting babies. Arianna is thrilled.'

'Then I must be too,' said Luciano, smiling. 'Perhaps she will have a whole collection of them to be her bodyguard? It's not a bad idea.'

'Well, they won't be born in time to help protect the Manoush,' said Rodolfo. 'I wish my daughter would concentrate.'

'Ye sholde be gladde she has some thynge to be light of herte aboute,' said Dethridge. 'I am happye that she is not livinge as we be, in the shadowe of the stake.'

'You are quite right, Dottore,' said Rodolfo. 'And wise as always. I would not want her or our wives to live in a city where it is possible to burn men, women and children, just because they follow their religion.'

'You forget,' said Luciano. 'Arianna knows as well as any of us, except the Dottore, what it is to be condemned to death by burning. If she had not been shown to be your daughter and Silvia's, she would have been executed for being in Bellezza on the forbidden day.'

'You both instruct me,' said Rodolfo. 'My master and my apprentice. I am justly rebuked.'

'Your daughter's tender heart has room for the Manoush as well as for her cats,' said Constantin. 'But I am glad she has not had to see them in prison. They are a terrible sight.'

At that moment, Cesare arrived with Matt; they had come by a circuitous route avoiding both the Piazza dei Fiori and Filippo's palazzo.

Everyone's attention was diverted by Matt's face. Luciano felt a sharp thought penetrate his mind.

Who is that thug? He looks terrifying!

He was glad that Arianna could only think the thought and not speak it aloud.

It's Matteo, the new Stravagante, he thought-spoke. *You've met him. He was beaten up by the di Chimici.*

'I just heard about the Manoush,' said Matt. 'Sorry I wasn't here. What can I do?'

'You can both go and visit them in prison,' said Rodolfo. 'But we'll have to find Matteo a hat to cover his hair. And perhaps it should have a broad brim to conceal his face.'

*

Filippo was sure that the di Chimici were close to finding the secret of stravagation. He was in favour of imprisoning Luciano and finding his talisman, then torturing him till he told them what they wanted.

Rinaldo preferred a more direct course of action. Fabrizio wanted the Bellezzan dead and Rinaldo wanted to be the one to feel the Grand Duke's gratitude. He might be a cardinal, but he was a complete hypocrite: he had no qualms about ordering another man's death, if it would benefit him. But as a human being and a squeamish one, he was reluctant to wield the knife himself.

Yet he could not forget that both his attempts to hire assassins to do his dirty work for him in the past had ended in failure. So he had devised a method of dispatching the Cavaliere that was both ingenious and, he thought, impossible to trace back to him or his family. And he would enjoy watching him die, in spite of his qualms about physical violence.

But what the Cardinal did not know was that Enrico, his former spy, had been following him as he went about making his arrangements.

Enrico did not know exactly what was being plotted but he had a pretty good idea about the main plan and it made him feel sick. He was on his way now to Silvia's house to tell the Stravaganti and warn Luciano.

*

Cesare and Matt went to the prison to see the Manoush. Their task was to let them know about the rescue but it was difficult with the guards listening.

Ludo was in one cell and Ottavio in the other; by tacit consent they had become the two leaders of the group. Cesare went to talk to Ottavio, leaving Matt to communicate with Ludo.

'I'm so sorry about what happened,' said Matt. 'I didn't know till this morning.'

'You look as if you have had troubles of your own,' said Ludo.

Luciano had lent Matt one of his hats, his favourite elaborate plumed and purple number which made Matt feel more conspicuous than his bruises did. He had taken it off as soon as he had been let into the prison.

'True,' he said. 'A bit of a brush with the di Chimici. But at least we've convinced Luciano that Filippo is not on his side.'

'I'm glad,' said Ludo.

Matt was just amazed that this Manoush could care so much about other people when he was doomed to die a horrible death the next day. Matt was a bit ashamed to remember that he had once not liked Ludo much.

The guards seemed to have lost interest in the prisoners. They were quiet throughout the day; it was only first thing in the morning and at nightfall that they became difficult. Matt leaned closer to Ludo and whispered to him.

'There's a plan to rescue you tomorrow. You must watch Doctor Dethridge for the signal. Then all the Stravaganti, and Cesare and Enrico, will release you. We may get one or two others to help, like Biagio the printer. As soon as you are outside the city walls, head for Bellezza. All right? Is there anyone in the city you can trust to bring your people's belongings to them at the city gate?'

Ludo clasped hands with him through the bars. It was only the fierceness of his grip that made Matt realise that Ludo was indeed scared of dying and putting on a brave show to keep his people's spirits up.

'I thank you,' he said. 'For my people and myself. And if you can get a message to Giunta, the Governor's wife, I'm sure she will organise the gathering of our belongings. But if the goddess does not look favourably on us and the plan fails, I want you to promise me something.'

'Anything,' said Matt recklessly.

'Take this ring,' said Ludo, pulling a small bag from a thong round his neck. 'No, don't look at it now. It belongs to my father. I don't know who he was but he was a member of the di Chimici family. I am ashamed of that now. But I used to be proud of it. If I perish in the flames tomorrow, find him for me and tell him that his son died bravely.'

The guards came to usher them out at just that moment and Matt could do no more than close his hand over the little bag and nod his assent. 'I'm sure what you ask won't be necessary,' he said, putting all the meaning into the neutral words that he could.

But it was a heavy burden he took out of the prison. He couldn't even take the bag with the ring back home with him. He had been told very firmly about the rules that Stravaganti mustn't take anything between worlds but their talismans. He would ask Luciano what to do. Perhaps he or one of the other Stravaganti would know what to do with it.

*

Giunta had refused to share Antonio's bed ever since the passing of the anti-magic laws. Or rather she had turfed him out of his own chamber.

'You would surely not want carnal knowledge of a pagan?' she had said. 'A goddess-worshipper and sympathiser with the heathens? No, as long as this city sets its face against the Lady, then I must set my face against you.'

It made the Governor acutely miserable and short-tempered with his staff. But his domestic discomfort was as nothing compared with the open strife that followed the arrest and condemnation of the Manoush.

'Women and children!' Giunta spat at him after the trial. 'You would burn not only the men but the weakest of the tribe, just for following their religion?'

'It is the law, woman,' said Antonio. 'What would you have me do? It is the parents who are to blame for leading their children into such known danger.'

'I would have you repeal the laws,' said Giunta. 'They weren't your idea to begin with. And why should you dance to the tune of a Grand Duke in Tuschia? Is Padavia not an independent city-state? Classe and Bellezza are our nearest allies and they have both resisted introducing the di Chimici laws.'

'You know we have always disagreed about goddess-worship,' said Antonio.

'I'm not talking about our personal opinions,' said Giunta. 'I'm talking about what's right for the city. Will you follow our tradition of learning and liberality that has existed for three hundred and fifty years or will you be under the thumb of a family that thinks they have the right to determine what is known and believed? Because if so, Padavia might as well give in and become another di Chimici principality.'

*

As well as planning for the reception of the rescued Manoush, Arianna had also made a formal plea to her ally, Governor Antonio, to show clemency and reprieve the travelling people from their death. Swiftly his reply had come, stubbornly sticking to the letter of the law. There was nothing left to be done except hope that the plan of the Stravaganti in Padavia would succeed.

'You can trust Rodolfo,' said Silvia.

'I wish that it was already Thursday and the whole thing over,' said Arianna. 'I can't bear the waiting.'

'Don't wish your life away, Arianna,' said Silvia. 'Not even one day of it.'

'I can't help it,' said Arianna. 'I wish Luciano would leave Padavia. The city is much more dangerous than we thought when he enrolled at the University. And I'm just stuck here unable to protect him.'

'Well, apart from the times you've visited him there,' said Silvia tartly. 'And he's got three Stravaganti to look after him.'

'All men,' said Arianna. 'Why aren't there more women Stravaganti? Giuditta Miele is as scary as any of them but it's always called "the Brotherhood". It's not fair. It's just like your rotten old rule about mandoliers.'

'Which you overturned the minute you were crowned, I might remind you,' said Silvia. 'Do I detect a new ambition burning in your breast?'

'Oh, don't be so maddening!' said Arianna. 'Why shouldn't I train to be a Stravagante? I'm as brave and as clever as Luciano, as loyal as Georgia and Sky . . .'

'And as wise and controlled as Rodolfo?' asked Silvia.

All she got in reply was an infuriated snort from her daughter.

*

When Matt returned to Silvia's house, Luciano was no longer there. He had gone to the School of Riding, determined to catch up with his practice, while Cesare was occupied. He had said he needed something to keep his mind off tomorrow's execution.

So Matt had to ask Rodolfo what to do with Ludo's ring. He told him the whole of the Manoush's whispered story.

'I will keep it for him,' said Rodolfo, taking the little bag and putting it in a pocket. 'We won't look at it unless the worst happens. If our rescue plan is a success, we shall give it back without looking at its crest. This is Ludo's secret, not ours.'

Matt was very relieved to hand it on to someone else. But now he felt at a bit of a loose end. No one seemed to need him very much in Talia and he wondered again if his role was over. Everyone was caught up in the plan to rescue the Manoush and Matt didn't really know if they were expecting him to take part. The execution was scheduled for after dark, so he would have to have a cover story at home since it involved staying in Padavia past waking up time in his own world.

He was just thinking about stravagating home early, when Enrico arrived, out of breath.

'Greetings, masters all,' he said, his small eyes glittering. 'Bruises coming on nicely, Signor Matteo! Where's the Cavaliere? I have important information for him.'

Matt was looking forward to being back home where people didn't comment on his face all the time.

'He's at the riding school,' he said curtly.

Enrico's mood changed immediately to alarm.

'On his own?' he asked.

'Why, what is it?' asked Rodolfo. 'What have you found out?'

'I think I know what the Cardinal is planning to do,' said Enrico. 'And it isn't pretty. Luciano shouldn't go anywhere without a bodyguard.'

'Then what are we waiting for?' asked Matt. 'Signor Rodolfo, shouldn't we get to the riding school?'

'Yes, immediately,' said Rodolfo, looking extremely worried.

Matt didn't need any more encouragement; he was desperate for action.

'Come on, Cesare,' he said. 'Enrico can tell us what he knows on the way.'

*

Luciano was learning to ride bareback. It was something that Cesare did easily; the Stellata was ridden without saddles. And Georgia, when she had stravagated to Remora, had learned to do it almost as well.

But Luciano had never even sat on a horse before he visited the City of Stars; they were banned in Bellezza and horses had never been part of his old life in Islington. Since the Stellata though, he had overcome his old fears and developed a real love of riding. It was so much more exciting than sitting in a carriage, with someone else in control of the reins.

And bareback was best of all. He wasn't very good yet at hanging on with his knees and still letting the horse know what direction he wanted her to move in. But Cara was a sweet-natured and sensitive animal and responded well to pressure on the reins. Still, the aim was to be able to ride well even without a bridle so he knew he mustn't rely on his hands.

After an hour in the ring, Luciano and his mare were losing concentration and the instructor called time.

But, as he turned Cara's head for home, he realised that he hadn't thought about the Manoush or the di Chimici once in the last hour. It was a rest his brain had needed but it meant he wasn't ready for what happened next.

It was beginning to get dark as he neared home and

the shadows were gathering in the streets off the cathedral square. He didn't see the two men until they jumped on him, one grabbing Cara's reins, the other pulling him off the horse's back. Then his arms were held and his mouth gagged before he could reach his Merlino-blade and fight back.

Before Enrico, Matt and Cesare set out to look for Luciano, his horse had already returned, riderless, to her stable.

Chapter 24

The Table Turned

When Matt saw Cara coming into the stable, he knew immediately what it meant.

'We're too late,' he said.

Cesare ran back into the house to alert the others and then they all scoured the streets between Silvia's house and the School of Riding for any clues as to when and where Luciano had been taken.

The instructor was still at the school and told them when Luciano had left.

'So he must have been nearly home,' said Rodolfo.

'Look,' said Matt. 'I've got to stravagate, or there'll be trouble. I'm really sorry. I hate leaving you all with no idea about what's happened to Luciano.'

'Yes, you must go,' said Rodolfo distractedly. 'We will keep searching. And you will come back tomorrow? We need you in the Piazza dei Fiori. Even more if, goddess forbid, Luciano isn't back by then.'

'I will go with you back to the Scriptorium,' said Constantin. 'I don't think any of us should go anywhere alone at present.'

Matt was touched. He strongly suspected that, if they were attacked, he would be the one protecting the Professor rather than the other way round. But it was good of him to offer.

Cesare and Rodolfo, Enrico and Dethridge, split into pairs and went back over the ground to Silvia's house, asking everyone they met if they had seen a young black-haired man pulled from his horse. But no one had seen anything or, if they had, they were not saying.

'I'll have to tell Arianna,' said Rodolfo. He was not looking forward to it.

*

Luciano himself was completely unaware of the alarm his disappearance had caused. He was heavily drugged, a state that wasn't entirely unpleasant. No one was hitting him, nothing hurt, and his only problem was that he felt terribly thirsty.

Faces swam in and out of his vision. One was wearing a big red hat and he knew that meant something bad but he couldn't remember what that was. Hands searched his clothing, taking his possessions, but even that didn't worry him.

The thing he prized most wasn't with him. Just at the moment he couldn't remember what it was but he knew it was very important and he was glad that it was safely in a box at his home.

Home. He tried to picture it but the image in his mind was very blurry. Was there a silver mask on the wall? Or maybe a mirror? Mirrors were important, he knew that. In fact he thought he would say it out loud.

The face with the red hat came back and said, 'You've given him too much.'

This struck Luciano as very funny. Too much what?

'No,' he heard himself saying. 'Not enough.'

Or was that someone else?

Someone put a cup to his lips. Wonderful, thought Luciano. And then the world went black.

*

'What is he saying?' said Arianna. 'Luciano is missing? Silvia come and look. I can't make out what Rodolfo means.'

Her mother joined her at Rodolfo's mirrors. His tired, careworn face was looking out at them and sending thought-messages. But the two women were so disturbed by the impact of the first one that in the end Rodolfo had to resort to mirror-writing:

Luciano has been taken. We are all looking for him. You must not worry. I will tell you as soon as there is any news.

'Not worry?' said Arianna. 'How can he say that? I mean write it? Tell him I'm coming to Padavia. Write it backwards. I haven't got time to send it as a thought message. I must find Barbara and Marco.'

And she whirled out of the room before Silvia could reason with her. Rodolfo looked back at his wife with

335

an expression of mixed exasperation and admiration.

You're no help at all, Silvia thought back at him. *You think everything she does is wonderful!*

Matt had hardly been able to get through the school day for worrying about what had happened to Luciano. Enrico's hints about the Bellezzan's fate were quite enough to keep his mind off his classes. The spy had been quite sure that Rinaldo di Chimici had raised the stakes and was now determined to kill Luciano. And he believed that the Cardinal had chosen that day because the city would be so caught up in the coming execution of the Manoush that they would have no attention to spare for one missing youth, no matter how well-connected.

At lunchtime the Stravaganti bought sandwiches in the cafeteria and took them out on to the freezing cold football pitch. Matt had told them there was something important to discuss and, although Ayesha was with them, there was still no sign of Alice.

As soon as he told them that Luciano was missing, the others were equally horrified.

'I can't bear it,' said Georgia. 'After all he's been through! Why couldn't the di Chimici just let him be? He won that duel fairly, which is more than Duke Niccolò would have done, if Enrico hadn't switched the foils.'

'You forget,' said Nick, white-faced. 'We didn't play fair either. It was because he saw me that my father was distracted and Luciano had the chance to wound him.'

It was hard for Matt to remember that Nick had been a di Chimici himself; he was such a twenty-first century person now. But there was still something of the aristocrat about him. It was a sort of confidence that Matt completely lacked. Nick was good-looking and clever and excelled at his sport of choice. He had the girlfriend he wanted and a loving foster-family but there was also something indefinable and extra about him, a sort of glamour that Matt associated with celebrities.

Then he had a strange thought: Nick actually looked rather like Luciano. The Bellezzan could have been his brother – maybe that's why he had been chosen to stravagate to Talia in the first place? And to end up living there as a nobleman? It made Matt feel even more inferior.

But then he looked at Georgia's stripey hair and tattoo and at Sky's long dreads and chestnut skin and realised that, although they were both pretty special-looking, no one would ever mistake either of them for a member of Talia's ruling family. Besides, if the talismans worked that way, his would have chosen Jago.

'What can we do?' asked Sky. 'I was at the duel too, remember, and I've already seen one di Chimici trying to kill Luciano. And we stopped it because we were there, all of us.'

'There's nothing,' said Matt. 'Even those of us who *were* there couldn't do anything. I'm going to stravagate back as soon as I can tonight. It's terrible not knowing what's going on.'

'But what would this cardinal actually do?' asked Ayesha. 'He wouldn't really harm Lucien, would he? I mean they let you get away, didn't they?'

Matt exchanged glances with the others. They realised that his girlfriend had been given a censored account of his captivity. And that she had no idea just what a dangerous place Talia was.

'This cardinal,' said Nick, 'is my cousin Rinaldo. Two years ago he wasn't even a priest and now he's in line to be the next Pope, when our uncle dies. I don't doubt that if Uncle Ferdinando lives too long for his convenience, Rinaldo will find a way to help him out of this world. And if he'd do that to a member of his family, what chance would an enemy have?'

Professor Angeli's anatomy demonstration was on Thursday this week. Doctor Dethridge was not intending to go again; he was too preoccupied with the disappearance of his foster-son and the coming execution of the Manoush.

But the theatre was as packed as in the previous week. And, unknown to the authorities, many of his actual students now owned copies of Angeli's *Teoria Anatomica*, in which the Professor's discoveries were outlined.

Among the spectators who had paid their soldi at the door were Rinaldo and Filippo di Chimici, in a prime position in the front row. Rinaldo had a scented handkerchief ready to hold to his nose; he knew he would find this demonstration difficult to watch.

No one ever knew what type of cadaver would be used for the dissection; it was rumoured that Angeli himself often didn't know till the table rose up. He didn't make the arrangements himself but relied on Girolamo Gobbi.

But although they did not know whether the corpse would be old or young, male or female, the spectators in the Anatomy Theatre did know what type of dissection it would be; last week's was musculature. Today's would be the structure of the heart.

There was a special frisson in the theatre, knowing that Professor Angeli would soon be plunging his hands into a person's body and taking the very core of his or her physical being out of the once-living shell. There was more anticipation for the demonstration than usual because of it, and students and members of the public alike craned their necks over the wooden railings.

Professor Angeli was standing by his table of instruments, his sleeves rolled up and a canvas apron over his clothes, when the machinery that operated the table could be heard clanking underneath the theatre.

At last it rose into view. There was a collective sigh. The cadaver strapped to the table, naked but for a loincloth was young and male and exceptionally good to look at. It was Luciano.

*

Constantin was distraught about Luciano's disappearance; Rodolfo had specifically asked him to look after the boy and he had failed to protect him. Coupled with the earlier attack on the Stravagante he was responsible for, it seemed to the Professor that he had been a poor guardian. Now it appeared that a scruffy and smelly spy was better at finding out what had happened.

When Matt arrived in the Scriptorium, he was surprised to find Enrico waiting for him.

'I'm sending young Matteo on an errand with this man,' Constantin told Biagio. But Matt had the impression that it was more for the benefit of the other pressmen, who were looking distinctly grumpy after their three-day holiday. 'He did two days' cover for Giovanni last week,' added the Professor, nodding towards the beater, who was back but with a bandage round his head.

Matt couldn't wait to get outside with the spy and pump him for what he knew.

'Don't forget your hat,' said Enrico meaningfully and Matt had to go back into the studio and retrieve Luciano's ridiculous purple number with the pressmen looking at him. He got a few whistles on the way out.

'What's happened?' he demanded as soon as they were out in the courtyard. 'Have you found Luciano?'

'No,' said Enrico grimly. 'But I'm pretty sure I know where he is. And if I'm right, we've got no time to lose.'

But instead of going out on to the street he dragged Matt up the stairs of the colonnaded court, towards the Anatomy Theatre, explaining as he went.

*

Luciano was dreaming that he was going to die. He recognised that it was not his own dream but Doctor Dethridge's – the one he had the night before Matt was captured. Only Luciano was the young man lying on the slab and the knives were being sharpened for him. Unlike Dethridge, Luciano had a twenty-first century knowledge of Aztec sacrifices and he became certain that his heart was going to be cut out of his living body.

A knife was coming closer and closer to his chest and he tried with all his might to wake up. This was the worst nightmare he had ever had. His body felt paralysed. He couldn't open his eyes. But he could hear voices, whispering, like waves on a shore. And he felt sure that there was a bright light somewhere above him. He could sense it, red through his eyelids.

And then there was a voice he recognised.

It was Matt saying, 'Fooled you, again! You thought it was the Cavaliere, didn't you? But it was Matteo, my servant. See, we used the glamour again. We look like each other – I've even got the bruises your servant gave him – but I'm wearing my own hat!'

The whispers rose to a roar of shouting and accusation.

The Cardinal's voice and Filippo's.

Matt again, in a louder voice. 'The di Chimici believe they have given Cavaliere Crinamorte's body for dissection but it is not him. I am the Cavaliere, under a spell to deceive the Cardinal and his thugs. The poor creature on the table is my servant Matteo, disguised to look like me.'

That's not right, thought Luciano through the fog of sleep. I *am* the Cavaliere. I remember when Arianna gave me the ribbon. It was blue. I did pretend to be Matt once but not now. I wish this dream would be over.

Was that Enrico speaking now?

'And either way, Cavaliere or servant, that's not a condemned criminal on the table, is it?'

A terrible jolt passed through Luciano's brain. Perhaps this wasn't actually a dream? With every atom of strength he had left to fight the doped haze he was in, he tried to move his right arm.

There were screams in the space outside his head.

'It's not even dead,' cried a voice. 'Its arm moved. I saw it.'

And then Luciano seemed to topple into a vortex, spinning and falling slowly into a new kind of darkness where everything was quiet.

*

Matt and Enrico ran down the stairs outside the Anatomy Theatre, leaving the demonstration in upheaval. They found the room where the bodies were prepared and, as they pushed their way in, Gobbi rushed out.

'Leave him,' said Matt, hurrying to the table, which had swung over, sending a wretched dog's corpse to rise up to the theatre, and leaving an inanimate Luciano hanging from the straps on this side. Gobbi had effected the switch over that had been planned if anyone discovered the Professor was not operating on a criminal's corpse.

'Quick,' said Matt. 'We've got to unstrap him before the table goes up again. Angeli operates it from up there.'

They worked at the buckles and Luciano collapsed to the floor, just as the table started to rise up again.

He was still not able to open his eyes but felt

himself being carried and smelled something pungent that seemed familiar.

'Enrico?' he croaked.

'That's me, signore,' said the spy, desperate to get as far away from the Anatomy Theatre as possible. Matt was taking more of Luciano's weight but they made a clumsy, shambling trio.

As they came out into the Great Court Enrico heard footsteps and signalled for Matt to stop. They took cover behind a statue of one of the founders of the University. As they watched the main entrance, two members of the city guard came running in and headed up the stone stairs to the Anatomy Theatre.

'I hope Professor Angeli doesn't get into any trouble,' said Matt.

'Nah,' said Enrico. 'He'll be all right. It's a dog, isn't it? And no sign of any other corpse. The Cardinal though, that's another matter. I don't reckon the students will let him or Filippo off lightly. It's one thing to buy stiffs off poor folk that can't afford to bury them. But it's quite another to go drugging and poisoning respectable young students like our Cavaliere here and then try and get them cut up while they're still alive!'

I'm alive, thought Luciano. Stripped and drugged – poisoned he said. And not able to see anything yet. But my heart is still in my body. I can feel it beating.

*

Arianna had set out as soon as she had been able to, after explaining to Barbara and Marco that she must go to Padavia earlier than planned. She was in an agony of impatience; everything took so long to organise. Clothes for Barbara, a change of duty for Marco – the Duchessa herself was in her boy's clothes long before everyone else was ready.

The journey to Padavia had never seemed so long: first the mandola to the top of the islands, then the ferry to the mainland and then waiting for the public coach. Arianna longed just to go to the Ducal stables and commandeer her own state carriage and urge the horses to the City of Words herself. But it would have been madness to blow her disguise.

When we have found Luciano, she told herself, willing herself to stay positive, *I can be useful about the Manoush. Rodolfo said we needed more people to release them when the Dottore's plan comes off.*

The coach stopped near the Piazza dei Fiori and Arianna had to stuff her fist in her mouth when she saw the bonfires. She had banned the practice of execution by burning in her own city; it had always seemed a barbaric punishment to her, even before her own imprisonment and trial.

Rapidly, she turned her back on the square and marched, with Marco following behind her, towards the cathedral. But their way took them past the entrance to the University. Arianna stopped and clutched Marco's arm. She had seen two people she recognised carrying the naked body of a black-haired young man into the Scriptorium.

*

Constantin was looking through some proofreaders' corrections when there was a hammering at the Scriptorium door.

Enrico and Matt fell into the room carrying Luciano's body.

'It's all right,' puffed Matt. 'Not dead. Drugged.'

Constantin signalled urgently to the proofreaders to clear the papers off their long table so that Luciano could be put on it. While this was going on, two more people burst into the Scriptorium, a young peasant boy and his older companion. To the astonishment of the pressmen, the boy rushed over to the inert body and started keening in a high voice. All work on the machines had stopped and Biagio automatically locked the door.

Matteo the apprentice turned to the boy and grabbed him by the arms. 'He's not dead,' he said again. 'Not dead. Adamo, do you hear me? He's been drugged, poisoned, but he'll be better when it wears off.'

'He could probably do with a drink,' said Enrico, wiping his brow. 'I know I could.'

'Adamo' stopped wailing. 'Do you swear to me, Matteo?' said the boy, deadly serious and gripping his hands. 'Do you swear on what you hold most dear that this is not Luciano's corpse?'

And Luciano, hearing her voice, opened his eyes at last.

'Arianna?' he said.

'What did I tell you?' said Matt. 'He's going to be all right.'

Chapter 25

The Moon in Hiding

All the men in the Scriptorium had stopped work. The printers were variously engaged in fetching clothes for the half-dead boy who had appeared in their midst, and ale for his rescuers. Constantin ordered enough for all the pressmen, from the youngest beater to the proofreaders and then went into his studio to contact Rodolfo through a hand-mirror.

Luciano was still half-paralysed by the powerful drug he had been given but he was propped up against the wall behind the proofreaders' table, wrapped in Constantin's university gown and soon some colour returned to his face. He was able to sip a little of the ale when it came.

After her initial display of grief, Arianna had given up all pretence of being male and pulled her cap off.

Constantin, coming back out of his studio, assured her that the pressmen were all loyal and would keep her secret.

'Gentlemen,' he said, raising his tankard. 'I give you Her Grace, the Duchessa of Bellezza, visiting us in disguise.'

The pressmen drank deep and a holiday mood began to spread. It was not often that such interesting incidents enlivened their day in the Scriptorium. And there was still the mass burning to look forward to at nightfall.

Matt put the ridiculous purple hat on Luciano's head, where it looked very well. He was beginning to feel a little drunk; the adrenalin of the rescue made a heady mix with the strong ale.

'Can you tell us what happened?' he asked.

'I can't remember,' said Luciano, his voice sounding rusty and his throat still very dry. 'I was coming back on Cara and then two men jumped me. I don't think I'd be able to recognise them again. Is Cara all right?'

'Fine,' said Matt. 'She just walked home.'

'Then I was gagged and blindfolded and taken somewhere that smelled of incense.'

'Bishop's palace, I reckon,' said Enrico. 'That just proves it was the Cardinal – he's staying there.'

'They took the gag off and made me drink something,' said Luciano, 'and then it's all a blank till I woke up on Professor Angeli's dissecting table.' He shuddered.

'Dissecting table?' said Arianna. She knew nothing about the Anatomy Theatre and wasted no time thinking about it. 'How do you feel now?' she asked.

'Lucky to be alive,' said Luciano. He gave her a shaky smile.

'I think they really meant to do it this time,' said Enrico. 'Rinaldo must have employed some professionals.'

'What day is it?' asked Luciano. He could have been missing for an afternoon or a week, for all he knew.

'Thursday,' said Matt.

'Then I must snap out of it,' whispered Luciano, trying to shake the fog out of his head. 'We've got to save the Manoush.'

*

William Dethridge had been on edge all morning. Repeatedly, he looked at the sky, frowning if any small wisp of cloud appeared. He licked his finger and held it up to the breeze, then returned to his room and repeatedly shook the stones or dealt out the cards.

When Rodolfo got Constantin's message through the hand-mirrors, he called the Doctor down and they left for the Scriptorium, with Dethridge on Cara. Both men were filled with unspoken relief. Ever since Luciano's last capture, which had resulted in such a cataclysmic change to the boy's life, they had both felt under an enormous obligation to keep him safe and well.

So it was inexpressibly cheering to find Luciano, dressed in a rather random collection of clothes, sitting cross-legged on the proofreaders' table. And to see Arianna sitting next to him, in her boy's disguise but without a hat, her legs dangling over the edge of the table.

There was a definite air of celebration in the

Scriptorium, with the pressmen standing around drinking ale and toasting the recovered youth, who had been brought in looking like a corpse and come back to life under their eyes. They were also intrigued by the disguised Duchessa and a bit overawed, but not as much as they would have been if they had seen her dressed as the ruler of her city.

'Thank the goddess you are all right!' said Rodolfo. 'Was it the di Chimici again?'

'Rinaldo,' said Luciano. 'At least, so Enrico and Matt tell me.'

And then his rescuers had to tell the story again. It was gradually dawning on Arianna how close the anatomy professor had come to killing Luciano. The drug he had been given had suppressed all his physical functions, reducing even his breathing to such a shallow level that the short-sighted Angeli would certainly have plunged his scalpel into Luciano's chest if Matt hadn't come in at that point and raised the alarm.

'The only question now,' said Luciano. 'Is how long it takes for the drug to wear off. I still don't think I can walk yet.'

'I have your horse,' said Rodolfo. 'We will get you home and then you must go to bed and sleep.'

'I feel as if I have been asleep for centuries,' said Luciano. 'What I want now is to be up and doing.'

'Bot ye will be fitte for noughte until ye have slepte naturally and lette the poyson dissolve oute of your veines,' said Dethridge.

'You must rest,' said Rodolfo. 'You will not be present in the Piazza dei Fiori tonight unless you are fully recovered.'

Matt realised that the pressmen thought he meant that Luciano might miss the spectacle. He recoiled from their bloodthirstiness and was more determined than ever that the Stravaganti would succeed in rescuing the Manoush from the flames.

'Time to get back to work,' said Constantin and the pressmen put down their tankards and returned to their beating and pulling, their compositing and proofreading.

Rodolfo and Matt took Luciano's weight between them and half dragged, half carried him out to where Cara was tethered, and hauled him on to her back. Although he had no strength in his legs, Luciano managed to stay upright while the others walked beside him back to the house.

But when they got there, he made no further protest about going to bed. Arianna went up to sit with him but he was asleep within minutes and she came down to join the other conspirators.

*

Antonio was not looking forward to the mass burning. He was a humane man but not a very imaginative one; he saw things in black and white. He had adopted the di Chimici's anti-magic laws, they had been posted clearly in every square and public meeting-place of the city, the Manoush had disobeyed them and were thus subject to the most extreme penalty of the law. It was that simple. Why, the travelling people had not even claimed to be innocent; they had put up no defence at all!

Something deep in Antonio's mind respected them

for that. He abhorred their religion, with its pagan devotion to the moon goddess and her solar consort. But he was impressed by the manner in which they stuck by it. In some way, they had as great a sense of their duty as he had of his; the difference being, of course, that they were wrong.

His willingness to persecute the wrongdoers in the matter of religion versus superstition had received a severe blow from the bitter denunciations of his wife. Now that her worst predictions had come to pass, Giunta was now threatening to leave him, to take their young daughters and move back to Romula, where she came from. It was another city-state independent of the di Chimici and had not adopted the laws as Antonio had been persuaded to introduce. There, she said, she could practise the goddess religion, without fear of persecution.

But he would be disgraced and his children brought up as heathens! And nothing would be worse than being without the wife he loved. Yet he knew she would be safer in a city that was more tolerant of her religion. His mind was in turmoil.

Antonio could not wait for the execution of the Manoush to be over. Even the young Duchessa of Bellezza had written to ask him to reprieve them. There were moments when he felt completely alone, with nothing to support him but his own convictions. And yet he knew he was not a monster.

*

As the evening drew in, the Manoush became very quiet. They had been defeated in their attempts to celebrate their festival of the New Year and as far as they were concerned, were still accompanied by the ghosts of their dead. These spirits had been summoned but not allowed to return to the world beyond death because of the breaking off of the rituals.

In a way, this was a comfort to the Manoush. The spirits of their dead would accompany them on their painful last journey; in fact they had come to see their own impending death as a necessary sacrifice to compensate for the interruption in their ceremonies.

Only Ludo did not share in this view. He shrank from the spirits, who might have included his mother, who had died only a few months ago; he was not ready to join her in the afterlife. Ludo was terrified of the coming ordeal. But he would not show it. The children did not yet understand what was going to happen to them and he was determined that their terror should not begin any earlier than it had to because of his cowardice.

These three days in the prison had taught him a lot about himself and some of it was that he was not as Manoush as he wished to be. More than ever he wanted to be like his people, steadfast for the goddess and reconciled to their fate. Ludo just couldn't accept that his life was about to end, without his ever having known about the other half of himself, the half that had noble blood in his veins.

He dared not hope that Matt's plan would work. The most he allowed himself to wish for was that he would not be shamed in his death, would not scream and beg for mercy but allow himself to be martyred in as dignified a manner as was possible. For this he prayed fervently to the goddess or any other deity that would listen.

*

People had been gathering in the Piazza dei Fiori since mid-afternoon. Ordinary citizens, making sure they had a good position from which to see the burnings. There were food-sellers wandering amid the crowd with trays of frittata slices and fried seafood dipped in batter. The inns near the piazza were doing a good trade in mugs of ale and tankards of spiced wine.

At one end of the piazza a rough platform had been built on which the Governor would stand and read out the indictment of the criminals before sitting to watch their death. To either side of him would sit the Bishop of Padavia and Cardinal di Chimici as upholders of the true faith of the Church of Talia.

As the time grew nearer, young men in university gowns joined the mob. Some were medical students, interested to see the effect of fire on a living body. But most were just curious to be at an execution. There had not been a burning in Padavia for several years and now there were so many condemned.

Minstrels wandered through the square playing lutes and recorders and a few jugglers caught small coins when they had demonstrated their skills.

Half an hour before the execution was due to start, a more sober group of people entered the piazza. Rodolfo in his accustomed black had not sought to change his appearance but his daughter was still in her boy's disguise, with Marco close beside her. William Dethridge and Professor Constantin were with them.

Not far behind came Matt and Cesare, still half supporting Luciano between them.

He had insisted on coming, even though his legs still felt like overcooked pasta. Enrico was there too, surprisingly matey with Biagio from the Scriptorium. Every single member of the group was equipped with a sharp Merlino-blade; all except Luciano, Enrico, Arianna and Marco were strangers to the weapon. But they didn't have to get into a dagger fight. If William Dethridge was right, all they would have to do was cut the prisoners' bonds at the right time.

A roar from the crowd greeted the Manoush as they were at last led out into the square. The children had picked up something of the atmosphere and began to cry as they were bound to the stakes along with their parents and friends. Ludo looked straight ahead, unable to focus on the mob and see from what quarter help might come. He did not register the ten rescuers, five of them Stravaganti.

And yet there was a fine view for all who had come to see the burning. It was the night of full moon and the square was illuminated as much by her round white face as by the cressets and braziers burning at each corner.

When every single prisoner had been tied to one of the stakes, Messer Antonio mounted the platform with the two churchmen. Nervously he scanned the crowd to see if Giunta were there. He very much did not want her to be.

A herald stood on the platform and blew three long notes on his trumpet. Antonio stepped forward and read from a parchment the list of names.

'All of the prisoners so named have admitted to

taking part in a ceremony of pagan worship of the Old Religion,' he said.

A low chanting began among the prisoners. The women started it and the men took it up, even the children joining in as Antonio struggled to complete his indictment.

'They have all been tried before the court of this city and condemned to death by burning,' he continued.

The chanting grew louder.

'And so it is my unpleasant duty to instruct the guards to set the flames to the pyres. Unless there is anything that any of the Manoush wish to say. Any recantation of their heathen beliefs?'

Antonio could scarcely be heard above the sound of the goddess's people chanting now. William Dethridge was looking intently at the sky but had as yet given no signal to his followers.

But another voice rose above the singing.

'The Manoush may have no last words, but I should like to speak for them.'

It was Professor Constantin. Antonio knew him as a learned teacher at the University. And it was true that there was a Padavian tradition of letting the condemned or a representative speak a farewell. The Governor nodded and Constantin climbed the steps to the stage, accompanied by a slight young man who trod cautiously, like an invalid.

There was a sharp intake of breath from the Cardinal. But the Manoush had fallen silent.

'It is my job at the University,' began Constantin. 'To teach the art of Rhetoric. Every year young men come to me to learn the art of persuasion and advocacy through the power of words. And yet today

I stand before you as one bereft of the power of speech. What is about to happen here is an affront to the dignity of all human beings – both the executed and the executors.

'Have we not come further than this in the centuries since our beloved city was founded by the Remans or in the three hundred and fifty years since our university was instituted? You see before you some thirty souls, men, women and children, who are about to be sent to their deaths in the cruellest way possible.

'And what is their crime? To do something that was not against the law a month ago and may not be again in another month.'

Antonio looked as if he was about to protest but Constantin continued.

'They were practising their religion,' he said. 'Oh, I know it is not the same as the religion of most of us here – though I suspect there are some others in the city who follow the goddess – but it is just that: their religion. They are believers, just as we all are. They have their ceremonies and their rites – all harmless, all representing no threat or offence to any citizen of Padavia.

'This young man here,' he said, 'is one of my students. Recently he delivered a speech on a set subject – When is it Right to Kill a Man? He had given the matter a lot of thought. And I'd like to ask him to repeat his conclusions for everyone gathered here. Tell the people, Luciano, what good reasons you listed for when the taking of another human life is right.'

As Luciano stepped forward to speak, the other members of their group began to file unobtrusively through the crowd, positioning themselves each as close as possible to one of the as yet unlit bonfires, leaving the two nearest the stage for Luciano and Constantin.

'Thank you, Magister,' said Luciano. 'I began by citing the example of seeing a man about to stab a child. Which of us, I asked would not kill the attacker to save the child? And yet, today you are about to witness the deaths of half a dozen children and will do nothing to stop it.

'To defend the weaker, to save one's comrade, to liberate one's country or one's city from a tyrant. To fight in time of war. To protect one's family or one's home. In extreme cases to save one's own life.

'But I ask you, citizens, whose family or home is threatened by the Manoush? Does their religious celebration harm a single one of us? Do they bring war or tyranny within the city walls? Is any one of them a threat to any one of us? And yet we would have them burn?'

Luciano addressed the crowd but his eyes were fixed firmly on William Dethridge, who gave him a very slight nod and held up one hand with the fingers spread, as if to say 'five minutes more'.

'Today I was nearly killed myself,' Luciano went on. He had the full attention of the crowd. And particularly of the two di Chimici cousins, one on the platform behind him, the other in the piazza. Neither of them was sure whether this was indeed the Cavaliere or the boy Matteo under a glamour, such as the Stravaganti had effected twice before, or so the di Chimici believed.

'Such an experience makes one dwell on the nature

357

of life and death,' said Luciano. 'The body is a fragile thing and yet it contains something even more important – the soul.'

There was a sighing in the piazza like a hundred little gusts of wind. It made the flames of the torches flicker on this still night.

'It is a terrible thing to take another life,' said Luciano. 'But even greater than the harm we would do to these bodies bound here before us, is the loss of some thirty souls, doomed to join their fellow-departed without any ceremony. It is enough to anger the dead.'

The sighs were louder now and it seemed to every person in the square that they could see shadowy forms, creatures made of mist and moonshine, congregating around each bonfire.

'And to anger the goddess that these people worship,' said Luciano quietly. 'Are we all so sure that our own faith is the only true one? Look at the moon, the embodiment of the Lady they worship. See, doesn't she look angry? Are those not tears of blood forming on her face?'

There was not a person in the square now except the rescue party, who were not looking at the sky. A redness was creeping over the face of the moon. And a darkness. As they watched the moon's face was being slowly engulfed.

'This is madness!' shouted Rinaldo, jumping to his feet. 'The Professor and his student have spoken for too long. Light the fires!'

The guards looked uncertain. But Messer Antonio, white-faced, gave the signal. The guards approached with torches, reluctant to get near the misty shapes that sighed round each pyre. The Manoush were quite silent, now, even the children, though whether comforted by the shades of their ancestors or terrified by them, no one knew. Ludo's heart was beating so loudly in his ears he did not know that the entire crowd was silent, holding its breath.

Then one guard ran forward and thrust his torch into the brushwood. Flames leapt up as all the others followed suit.

A woman's voice howled from the crowd.

'Shame on you! Can't you see that the moon is grieving for her people? Fetch water!'

At that moment the entire face of the moon was covered and the square plunged in darkness save for the flames. All was confusion. The citizens of Padavia, whether swayed by rhetoric or influenced by the loss of the moon, had changed their minds. Some ran to get buckets of water, others snatched torches from the guards and headed towards the platform, though with what aim it was not clear.

Only the Stravaganti and their followers had a clear plan of action. Constantin helped Luciano off the stage in the dark and they made for the nearest bonfires. Every rescuer had three Manoush to release. Among Matt's was Ludo.

The young Stravagante looked at the red-haired traveller as he pulled him and two women away from the bonfire.

'Quick, follow me,' he said. 'There are horses and carts waiting for you outside the city wall. You will be taken to Bellezza. You will be safe there.'

In the square people were running about aimlessly, terrified by the disappearance of the moon.

'Yt woll laste at leaste an houre,' Dethridge had told the rescuers. 'Plentye of time to gette all the Manoushe out of the citye.'

At the Western Gate, sympathisers were waiting with the bundles the Manoush had left at their houses; Giunta had organised that well. But before Matt and the others had reached the walls, another cry went up.

'Fire! Fire! The city is on fire!'

Matt heard a groan in the darkness. It was Rodolfo.

'Stravaganti! To me! To me! Arianna and Cesare, if you can hear me, take the Manoush to the gate with the others. All Stravaganti to me – we must save the city from the flames!'

'You go,' Ludo told Matt. 'I will help the others.'

Matt took out a small velvet bag and gave it to the Manoush. 'Here,' he said. 'I won't need to tell your father what you said, now, whoever he may be. But it would have been true. You faced death bravely.'

He clapped Ludo on the shoulder then plunged back into the city.

*

Flames were licking at the edges of wooden buildings. There was so much that was combustible about the city. Rodolfo led the others to the cathedral square where the wide open space in front was so far free of fire.

'Don't they have a fire brigade or something?' Matt asked Luciano. They were both panting and had black smudges on their faces. 'You look like as much of a printer's devil as I do,' said Matt.

'There is a fire team,' said Constantin, 'financed by

the city. But the University has taken the money for equipment and spent it on salaries for professors. I'm afraid that Padavia will burn if we don't do something.'

He turned his face away, frightened for his books and manuscripts and his wooden presses. He did not want the other Stravaganti to see the tears on his face. After all, the Manoush had been saved and that was the most important thing.

'But we can do something,' said Rodolfo. 'Is there not a swamp in the south of the city?'

'Yes,' said Luciano. 'Enrico lodges near there.'

'That is indeed the nearest water supply,' said Constantin. 'But without enough firemen, no chain of buckets could reach the centre. The University will soon be in flames.'

'To the swamp, then,' said Rodolfo.

They sprinted as fast as they could. Luciano, still not recovered from the di Chimicis' poison, was by now running on adrenalin alone. He didn't know how much more he had to give.

In the south of the city, the oval swamp lay still under the obscured moon. It was an unhealthy place, full of biting insects and noxious smells. The five Stravaganti stopped at its northern edge.

'Now,' said Rodolfo. 'Unless you have a better idea, Dottore, I propose we lift this rotten marsh and lay it over the centre of the city like a wet handkerchief.'

'My owne thoughte exactly!' said the Doctor.

Matt felt hysterical with exhaustion.

'That's fine then,' he said. 'We'll just do that, shall we? Shouldn't be much of a problem.'

Constantin put an arm on his shoulder.

'Now you will see what the power of thought can do,' he said. 'What the Stravaganti are capable of. What you are capable of.'

Rodolfo made them all stand in a line on the edge of the swamp, the two younger ones each flanked by the older Stravaganti.

'Concentrate!' said Rodolfo. 'Lock minds.'

Matt felt a jolt through his head that felt like being struck by lightning.

'Now,' said Rodolfo. 'We don't want the city to burn. We don't want it to die instead of the Manoush. Our friends are safe. Now we must save Padavia. Think of the swamp.'

Matt's mind filled with the image of the green, rank-smelling oval.

'There is enough water and weed here to smother the fire,' said Rodolfo. 'Think of it. Slimy green sludge coating the flames, cutting off the air that feeds them. Now, everyone at once, take the swamp and put it where it's needed.'

Matt felt panic rising in his throat as he visualised the wet green mass rising, rising from its quiet bed and moving above him. What if his concentration should fail and the swamp fall on them? They would all be drowned. But the Stravaganti had linked arms, without his being aware of it, and being between Constantin and Dethridge gave him courage.

He was caught up in something much bigger than himself now and couldn't have stopped if he wanted to. Slowly, he felt the mass of water move towards the fire.

*

The citizens of Padavia were rushing around in panic. As soon as they had realised that the city was on fire, they had abandoned the Manoush and the bonfires. It was doubtful that they even knew the prisoners had been rescued. Some ran uselessly to wells to fetch buckets of water but the fire had taken hold on some wooden buildings near the market and was already beyond suppression by such small-scale efforts.

Other householders had decided to flee and were leaving their houses with bags and bundles. But the city was still dark, the moon's face hidden from its people, so that citizens blundered into one another, set off in the wrong direction, lost one another in the choking smoke and darkness.

Biagio the printer had run to the Scriptorium, aware of the damage to all the papers and books, secret and public, that the fire could do. He had rescued his Manoush and put them into the hands of the disguised Duchessa of Bellezza but nothing would persuade him to leave his city while it burned.

There was no sign of the Professor and Biagio didn't know what to do for the best. He pulled out a key to the Scriptorium and was about to go in, willing to die alongside the wooden presses rather than abandon his post.

But then he sensed a strange new smell on the air. Above the fiery reek coming from the smouldering buildings about to burst into flames, came a dank, stifling stench like the very worst of open drains or swampy marshland. Biagio stared up at the sky and rubbed his eyes.

He couldn't see anything because of the hidden moon but he sensed an even darker shadow crossing her face – an impossibly large oval shape moving slowly across the heavens. And the smell was coming from that shape. It seemed to hover in the air for a few moments before rushing down towards the centre of the city like a black cloud of swamp gas.

Other citizens had noticed it now and stood staring up at the sky. Neither they nor Biagio understood what they were seeing; some were inclined to think it was the end of the world and to lay down their bundles and themselves in the cobbled streets and give themselves up to their fate.

But Biagio realised that whatever was coming presented a new danger and flung open the door to the Scriptorium, calling everyone on Salt Street to take cover. Soon the silent presses were surrounded by a crowd of babbling hysterical Padavians. As Biagio slammed the door shut, a weight of water and weed fell on the city, pouring past the window like a slimy green rain.

The streets were awash with foul-smelling water, reeds and the occasional startled fish. Padavians ran in all directions, seeking shelter from the water in buildings they had shunned a short time before, when they were afraid of being trapped by fire.

The five Stravaganti had walked slowly in a line from the site of the swamp to the centre of the city, carrying the weight of water above and before them until Rodolfo, at one end of the line, gave the order to lower the swamp over the heart of the fire.

Matt felt the intolerable strain of lowering the swamp slowly enough to avoid drowning the citizens but he was aware of their not holding it firmly enough. It seemed to slip from their minds and land on the burning city with a sound like a magnified sigh. And then the whole of Padavia steamed and hissed like a giant bonfire in a thunderstorm.

*

Arianna paused at the gate to look back over the city. At first she could see nothing. The moon was still dark and there were no torches burning. That was right: there were no flames of any kind. It was as if the whole city had been snuffed out by a blanket.

'The fire's gone out,' she said to Ludo, who had come to stand beside her.

'They've done it then,' he said. 'Saved the city as well as us.'

'You must get away,' said Arianna. 'Get all your people into the carts.'

'Aren't you coming with us?' asked Ludo.

'Of course,' said Arianna.

And she turned away from the gate. It had never been harder but she knew that her duty was to get the Manoush back to Bellezza. Yet every nerve screamed to her to run back to Luciano and the others, to check that they were all safe.

'I'm sure they're all right,' said a familiar voice at her shoulder. It was Cesare.

As he came to stand by her, the moon slowly began appear again.

And by the time they were on the road to the coast, she had come out of the red shadow and was shining down on her people, clear and silver, with all stain of blood and fire wiped from her face.

Epilogue: *New Beginnings*

The Manoush stayed in Bellezza till Christmas. They had a festival around that time too. A lot had changed since the first night of their rescue, when they had all congregated in the courtyard of the Ducal Palace to complete their rites for the Day of the Dead. It was Ottavio who convinced them that this was the right thing to do and it was true that, by daybreak, the Manoush were all sleeping peacefully on their bedrolls and the shadowy shapes that had travelled with them from Padavia were no more to be seen.

'We can't keep them all here,' Silvia told Arianna. 'How are petitioners to get through the courtyard? Or Senators and Councillors to come into the palace?'

'I don't think they will stay,' said Arianna, who was looking down on the sleeping travellers from the stone gallery on the first floor. 'They needed a refuge after their ordeal in Padavia and somewhere to carry out their rituals but I think now that they will make their own arrangements in this city as they do in any other.'

She thought that she would never forget that night journey under the full moon. Getting the Manoush to understand that they must all travel by water to the lagoon city and then ferrying them to the Piazzetta in the fleet of mandolas that Silvia had waiting for them. And all the time not knowing if Luciano and her father and their other friends had escaped the fire.

Cesare had been wonderful and, surprisingly, so had Enrico the spy. Biagio was the only one of the rescuers, apart from the Stravaganti, who had not travelled with them. Once the Manoush had been loaded into the carts, the pressman had hurried back to the Scriptorium, as anxious as Constantin about the presses and all the printed paper.

Just before dawn, Arianna had arrived, filthy and weary in her room, but before she woke Barbara to change places with her, she had run to Rodolfo's mirrors. And there they were, Rodolfo, Luciano and William Dethridge, all waiting up to send her the thought message she needed:

City saved. No one harmed.

But she did not understand the next one: *Padavia a bit wet and smelly.*

She thought back as hard as she could: *Manoush all safe too.*

The two older Stravaganti disappeared out of the mirror and she was left looking at Luciano's face. It was much easier to think-speak to just one person.

You look exhausted. Go to bed. I love you.

They sent the same message.

Before Christmas there was a wedding in Bellezza. Not in the great silver-domed basilica but a quieter affair, in the Duchessa's private chapel. The bride wore a silver brocade dress that now had a white lace bodice where once there had been a bloodstained tear. In her hair, at her throat and ears glinted diamonds and amethysts, worth all the money her family had earned for generations. These were presents from her mistress the Duchessa, who had also promised the couple one of the four spotted African cubs who had been born to the newly named Flora the week before.

Barbara's father had died some years earlier, so Rodolfo walked her up the short aisle to where Marco waited for her. She had no bridesmaids, but Luciano and Arianna stood as witnesses to the marriage and signed their names on the marriage certificate: Arianna Maddalena Rossi, Duchessa of Bellezza and Luciano Davide Crinamorte, Cavaliere of Bellezza.

'Us next,' whispered Arianna as she handed the pen to him.

At the party which followed a whole band of Manoush played flutes and harps and tambourines. They would not forget that Marco had been one of the rescuers who had led them out of captivity in Padavia. He and all their other saviours were honorary Manoush, as far as they were concerned.

The tall flute-player with the rusty-brown hair was particularly energetic, playing jigs and galliards with vigorous abandon. Chief among the dancers was Doctor Dethridge, twirling his wife Leonora round the palace ballroom with the enthusiasm of a man a third his age. But Luciano and Arianna were not far behind them.

'It's so good to have you home,' said Arianna. 'Must you go back to Padavia?'

'Well, I'm not a fully-fledged aristocrat yet,' said Luciano smiling down on her. 'My Rhetoric might be all right but apparently my Grammar and Logic still need a lot of work.'

'How much Grammar and Logic do you need to be my Duke Consort?' asked the young Duchessa.

'Oh, I don't know,' said Luciano. 'Two terms' worth, they think.'

'So we can't get married till the summer?'

'It will be nicer then, won't it?' said Luciano. 'Why don't we do it just after your next Marriage with the Sea?'

'Then we'll be like my parents,' said Arianna.

'I can think of worse role models,' said Luciano, watching Silvia and Rodolfo lead a stately pavane, while Ludo took a break to drink some wine. He was surrounded, as usual by a gaggle of girls, some Manoush, some not, who seemed to find him irresistible.

'Let's announce it, anyway,' said Luciano, suddenly tired of all the secrecy. 'I want all the world to know.'

The week before Christmas Matt passed his driving test, first time. Triumphantly he brandished his IOU at Jan and Andy as soon as he got back.

'Ouch,' said Andy. 'Right before Christmas.'

'It can be my present,' said Matt.

'But we've already got you one,' said Jan.

'What did you say in the Golden Dragon?' asked Matt. 'You said "On your eighteenth birthday or when you pass your test, whichever is sooner." That sounds pretty conclusive to me. And I have witnesses.'

'Hey, that's not fair,' objected Harry. 'Can I have an extra Christmas present worth hundreds of pounds?'

'You can have a car when you pass your test, like Matt,' said Andy. 'Or maybe we'll insure you to drive his.'

'No way am I sharing a car with Harry,' said Matt. 'I'll be at university by the time he passes, anyway.'

'Stop teasing him, Andy,' said Jan.

'Come on then,' said Andy and took them round the corner to where he had parked a second-hand silver Toyota two days before. 'I knew you'd pass,' he told Matt, handing him the keys.

It was a car Matt had shown Andy on the forecourt of the local garage the week before and he couldn't believe his luck.

'Can I drive it now?' he asked. 'Am I insured?'

'Yes,' said Jan. 'At a premium you wouldn't believe, with a huge excess, so just go carefully.'

'I'm only going to Yesh's,' said Matt. 'I haven't told her I've passed yet.'

He climbed in and put on the seat belt. The car started first time and he pulled out like a star pupil. His parents and brother waved him off and he waved back at them in the rear-view mirror.

'Both hands on the wheel!' shouted Jan.

'Yeah, yeah,' muttered Matt. He felt great.

He had hardly thought about Talia for the last few weeks and hadn't been there for over a month but he suddenly thought of Luciano stranded there for ever. He would never drive round to see his girlfriend and take her out for a pizza, even though he did live in a sort of Italy.

Poor sod, thought Matt. And at that moment he wouldn't have changed places with anyone in the world.

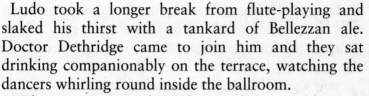

Ludo took a longer break from flute-playing and slaked his thirst with a tankard of Bellezzan ale. Doctor Dethridge came to join him and they sat drinking companionably on the terrace, watching the dancers whirling round inside the ballroom.

'The Lovers,' said Ludo, smiling, nodding at Luciano spinning Arianna around.

'Aye,' said Dethridge. 'The Prince of Fishes that is to bee. Skilled in debate. And his Princesse – courageous and headstrong. They make a fine paire.'

'You saw that in your reading the night that Luciano had dinner with Prince Filippo?' asked Ludo.

Dethridge drank deep. 'There were two wayes to divine the meaninge of that arraye,' he said. 'The Boke with the Scales and the Dethe carde so close to the Magician and the Salamandires mayde me fear its meaning was dethe by burning as the penaltie justice would deal out for the use of magycke or the printinge of the secret bokes.'

'So that could have been me or Matteo or even

Luciano if the Governor had found out he was a Stravagante,' said Ludo.

'Aye, yt coulde have bene ony of us,' said Dethridge. 'Myself, or Professire Constantine or even Maistre Rudolphe.'

'But in the end it was me,' said the Manoush. 'Me and my people, just for following our religion.' He shuddered in the cold night air, remembering how close he had come to losing his life in the flames of the Padavian bonfires.

'Bot there was anothire way to rede it whenne the tyme came,' said the Doctor. 'The Dethe carde was a skeleton and I beganne to thynke it was the Anatomie that was meant and thatte whenne yonge Lucian escaped the knife he wolde overcome the verdicte of the courts with his fine powers of argument.'

'You weren't sure though?' asked Ludo.

'Nay, bot there was anothire carde next to the Boke – remembire?' said Dethridge, his eyes twinkling. 'Yt was the Moone and yt reminded me thatte I had bene explaining to the studentes how to reckon the tyme of an eclipse. Some werke with my chartes and tables and I knew the moon would hide hirself thatte nyghte.'

'Thank goddess for your learning, master,' said Ludo, standing up and making the Elizabethan a deep bow.

Doctor Dethridge raised him up and clapped him on the shoulder.

'Backe to the danse,' he said. 'Yt is notte a nyghte for darke thoghtes.'

Ludo followed him back into the ballroom but it took several dances for him to shake off his sombre mood.

A week after Christmas, on New Year's Day a state visitor came to Bellezza. Messer Antonio, the Governor of Padavia, wanted to see the Duchessa and her parents. He was one of the few people who knew that Silvia, the previous Duchessa had not died in the Glass Room two and half years before but was living privately as the wife of the Regent.

'Antonio,' said Silvia, when he was shown in. 'It is a pleasure to see you.'

Her daughter, the Duchessa, was altogether frostier and more formal. The last time she had seen this man he was standing on a wooden platform reading the names of thirty prisoners condemned to a horrible death.

That was what he had come about.

'The Cavaliere's speech before the burning made a deep impression on me,' he said, looking at Luciano, who was standing by the Duchessa's chair. 'I have decided to follow your recent example here, Your Grace, and remove Death by Burning from the statute as a means of applying the most extreme penalty. There will be no more public fires in Padavia.'

'I am glad to hear it,' said Arianna. Her silver mask glittered with diamonds.

'And I . . . Well, I have held a special Senate and we have agreed to remove the recent anti-magic laws from the statute book,' he continued.

'And no doubt your wife is pleased about that,' said Arianna, more kindly.

'I think I saw one of the condemned Manoush in

the courtyard,' said Messer Antonio. 'The tall red-haired one with the flute.'

'They are frequent visitors at my court,' said Arianna. 'And the music of the Manoush is always welcome here.'

'And will be again in Padavia,' said Antonio. 'I admit I was wrong.'

'What made you change your mind?' asked Rodolfo.

'What happened that night,' said Antonio. 'I knew I was wrong when the Cavaliere spoke and the Cardinal ordered the fires set.'

'But you gave the signal,' said Arianna. 'You can't blame the Cardinal.'

'I was stubborn and stupid,' said Antonio. 'But what happened next is what really changed my mind. I don't like magic but I had to admit that it took a miracle to save my city from the fire that night. And it was not my church and the Cardinal's that delivered it. What people witnessed in Padavia was beyond laws and decrees – beyond the natural order – but without it I would be governor of a heap of ashes.'

He looked at Luciano and Rodolfo. 'I want to offer both the Regent and the Cavaliere the freedom of the city of Padavia,' he said, drawing out from his bag two large silver ceremonial keys. 'And if you can tell me the whereabouts of the others who helped you to douse the flames on that night I would extend the same privilege to them.'

'Well,' said Luciano, looking at Rodolfo. 'One lives in your city himself. He is no other than my teacher, Professor Constantin. He comes from outside Talia but now lives as a citizen of Padavia.'

'I have been told as much,' said Antonio. 'I will visit him on my return and see what further honours he will accept.'

'I think,' said Luciano, 'that he would settle for having a proper team of fire-watchers in the city.'

'And another of our number is the Cavaliere's foster-father,' said Rodolfo. 'Dottore Crinamorte, although a citizen of Bellezza, also came to lecture at your university.'

'Ah, yes, the famous Astronomer,' said Antonio. 'I should be glad to meet him. But my informants tell me there was a fifth who wrought the miracle on that night, a young man who worked as Constantin's apprentice. Yet he has not been seen in the Scriptorium since. There is a rumour among the pressmen that he perished on the night of the fire.'

'That is what Constantin allowed them to think,' said Luciano. 'Once his role in Padavia was over. But Matteo is alive. He lives in another place.'

'And he is coming here tonight!' said Arianna. 'He and Constantin. I am sending the ducal carriage to bring them to the ferry. We are having a special party here in the palace. I hope you will join us?'

*

In Giglia the bells were ringing for more than the New Year. In the early hours of the morning, a little ahead of her time, the Grand Duchessa had given birth to an heir – Prince Falco Niccolò Carlo di Chimici.

Fabrizio thought his heart would burst with joy and pride as the tiny swaddled prince was put into his arms. 'You will be my heir,' he whispered into the flushed ear of the baby – Grand Duke Falco the First of Tuschia.'

'That's an awfully big title for such a little boy,' said Caterina fondly from where she lay propped up on a heap of pillows in their four-poster bed.

'You have made me so happy,' said Fabrizio to his young wife.

'I'm glad,' said Caterina. 'And so glad I could give you the son you wanted.'

'Did you suffer terribly my darling? It seemed to take an awfully long time.'

'Not too much, Rizio,' lied the Grand Duchessa. 'It is always supposed to be hard with the first one. Our next will be easier.'

'You are already thinking of the next?' asked Fabrizio.

'Well,' said Caterina, blushing. 'As soon as I am well enough to have you back in my bed. I hope we shall have lots of children.'

Fabrizio lay the little prince back in his absurdly elaborate cradle and took his wife very gently in his arms.

'I should like to watch over you both tonight,' he said. 'I can sleep in the chair. And when you really are well again, we shall indeed make more babies. We shall fill all of Talia with our children. And one day there will be one ruling in Bellezza and another in Padavia and the other independent cities too.'

'We must leave somewhere for Gaetano and Francesca's children too,' said Caterina, stroking her handsome young husband's hair.

'Perhaps,' said Fabrizio. 'Now, if you will excuse me

for a short time. I must send messengers out all over Talia with the good news.'

*

Matt and Constantin were on their way to Bellezza as Antonio was having his audience with the Duchessa.

It hadn't been difficult for Matt to stay after dark. It was easy enough to provide a cover story at home for why he was not going to be there in the morning. His body would lie in Ayesha's room where he had left it, safe till he got back with his talisman.

This was his first visit to Bellezza but it was quite a short distance from Padavia, which he now thought of as 'his' city. It would be good to see Cesare and Ludo again, who were bound to be there for Luciano and Arianna's betrothal feast.

Betrothal! They were only a year older than him and Ayesha but Matt couldn't imagine getting engaged, at least not for ages yet.

'Talia makes you grow up quicker,' Luciano had told him. 'If you and your girlfriend lived here, you'd be in a hurry to get on with it too.'

Matt tried to imagine it. Living in Padavia all the time. Listening to music played on lutes and recorders, instead of on electric guitars and keyboards. Drinking ale and wine instead of water and lager. Going to inns instead of coffee bars.

And riding in carriages instead of fast cars. On the other hand there was no pollution from cars or even from city lights. He thought he would never forget the sight of the full moon over Padavia on the night of the burnings, just before the total eclipse.

377

But his time in Talia had taught him something even more important. He now knew that he could do things. OK, the reading and writing were still a problem and he doubted that he'd ever be as fluent in his own world as he was in Talia. But once you have rescued not just one person from a horrible death but thirty, and then gone on to save a whole city, taking a bit of stick about being dyslexic didn't seem like much of a problem.

Something that used to feel like a boulder he had to bear the weight of every day had somehow dwindled to a pebble he could keep in his pocket.

'What are you thinking?' asked Constantin, as they set off across the lagoon to Bellezza.

'That they've got plenty of water to hand if their city ever catches fire,' laughed Matt.

'Goddess forbid they will ever need it,' said Constantin.

'I expect she *will* forbid it,' said Matt. 'They've got three Stravaganti to defend it after all.'

'And in time perhaps more,' said Constantin. 'It is as well. They will need as many as they can get. Your job might be done here but there will always be a need for more Stravaganti in Talia, as long as there are di Chimici.'

Historical Note

Of all the Talian cities I have written about so far, Padavia is the most different from its Italian counterpart. Padua is a fine city, full of wonders, but they are not grouped together in an obvious centre as they are in other cities in the Stravaganza sequence.

It does indeed have an ancient university, founded in 1222 and yielding only to Bologna as the oldest university in Italy (which is why Filippo di Chimici, Prince of Bellona, is a bit sniffy about the University of Padavia). In Padua, the main university building is the Palazzo del Bo', which used to be a tavern of that name, meaning 'at the sign of the ox'. I have changed it to 'Montone', meaning 'ram'. In the Italian city, alas, it does not have a Scriptorium attached.

But it *does* have the most famous anatomical theatre in Europe, built in the 1590s, just a bit later than the one in Padavia. And the medical school there was home to great anatomists like Fallopius. Galileo Galilei taught astronomy there a bit later than the date of Matt's stravagations and Doctor Dethridge's astronomy lectures.

The cathedral or basilica referred to in the book is equivalent to the great domed Basilica del Santo, outside which stands Donatello's bronze equestrian statue of the 'Gattamelata', or 'Honey-cat', a famous fifteenth-century mercenary soldier.

The city is referred to in an old saying as having 'a saint without a name, a café without walls and a meadow without grass'. The saint without a name is Anthony, whose very ornate tomb is in the basilica. The café without doors is Pedrocchi's (because it remained permanently open from 1831–1916), which dates from a later period than the stories of the Stravaganti. The meadow without grass is the Prato della Valle in the south of the city. This is a vast oval open space which was once the site of a Roman amphitheatre, later a swamp and later still the place where the 'Battles of Love' were held, which were highly stylised festivals involving decorated floats and exotic costumes. Now it is an elegant address, with huge balconied apartments overlooking the Prato – a cool arrangement of fountains, statues and walkways but no grass. It is near here that Enrico had his lodgings in Padavia, when the area was still a swamp.

Padua is half an hour by train from Venice and that great lagoon city was its dominant partner and then controlling authority in the Renaissance. But even Venice has no jewel to compare with the Arena Chapel in Padua, frescoed throughout by Giotto. Unfortunately, Matt had no time to visit its equivalent in Padavia. But any modern reader following his journey should not fail to do so.

The 'Jettatura' or 'evil eye' has a long history in Italy and is believed to exist still as a power in many areas, particularly rural ones. The cure that Matt employs is a traditional one.

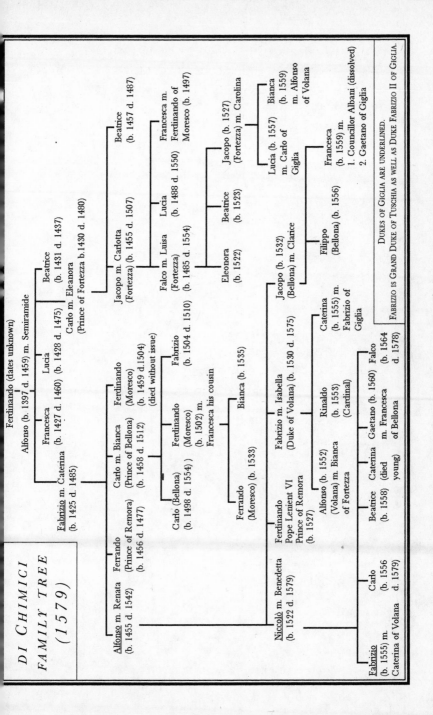

DI CHIMICI
FAMILY TREE
(1579)

Ferdinando (dates unknown) m. Semiramide
Alfonso (b. 1397 d. 1459)

Francesca (b. 1427 d. 1460)   Lucia (b. 1428 d. 1475)   Beatrice (b. 1431 d. 1437)
Carlo m. Eleanora (Prince of Fortezza b.1430 d. 1480)

Fabrizio m. Caterina (b. 1425 d. 1485)

Alfonso m. Renata (b. 1455 d. 1542)   Ferrando (Prince of Remora) (b. 1456 d. 1477)   Carlo m. Bianca (Prince of Bellona) (b. 1458 d. 1512)   Ferdinando (Moresco) (b. 1459 d.1504) (died without issue)

Beatrice (b. 1457 d. 1487)

Jacopo m. Carlotta (Fortezza) (b. 1455 d. 1507)

Francesca m. Ferdinando of Moresco (b. 1497)

Falco m. Luisa (Fortezza) (b. 1485 d. 1554)   Lucia (b. 1488 d. 1550)

Fabrizio (b. 1504 d. 1510)   Ferdinando (Moresco) (b. 1502) m. Francesca his cousin   Carlo (Bellona) (b. 1498 d. 1554)

Eleonora (b. 1522)   Beatrice (b. 1523)   Jacopo (b. 1527) (Fortezza) m. Carolina

Lucia (b. 1557) m. Carlo of Giglia   Bianca (b. 1559) m. Alfonso of Volana

Ferrando (Moresco) (b. 1533)   Bianca (b. 1535)

Jacopo (b. 1532) (Bellona) m. Clarice

Filippo (Bellona) (b. 1556)

Francesca (b. 1559) m.
1. Councillor Albani (dissolved)
2. Gaetano of Giglia

Ferdinando Pope Lenient VI Prince of Remora (b. 1527)

Fabrizio m. Isabella (Duke of Volana) (b. 1530 d. 1575)

Caterina (b. 1555) m. Fabrizio of Giglia

Alfonso (b. 1552)   Caterina (died young)   Rinaldo (b. 1553) (Cardinal)   Beatrice (b. 1558)   Gaetano (b. 1560) m. Francesca of Bellona   Falco (b. 1564 d. 1578)

Alfonso (Volana) m. Bianca of Fortezza

Niccolò m. Benedetta (b. 1522 d. 1579)

Carlo (b. 1556)

Fabrizio (b. 1555) m. Caterina of Volana

DUKES OF GIGLIA ARE UNDERLINED.

FABRIZIO IS GRAND DUKE OF TUSCHIA AS WELL AS DUKE FABRIZIO II OF GIGLIA.

MARY HOFFMAN

is a best-selling author and book critic. Her love for Italy and Italian history has infused her Stravaganza series, which has earned glowing reviews. Mary bought 'Matt's spellbook' in the shop of Medici-Riccardi palace in Florence. It is exactly as described in *City of Secrets* – apart from not having any spells! And she had a wonderful weekend in Antwerp visiting the Plantin-Moretus Museum and seeing a wooden printing press at work.

Mary is also the author of *The Falconer's Knot* and *Troubadour*. She has three grown daughters and lives with her husband in a big old converted barn in West Oxfordshire, England. She blogs at The Book Maven (bookmavenmary.blogspot.com).

www.maryhoffman.co.uk
www.stravaganza.co.uk

STRAVAGANZA

City of Ships

MARY HOFFMAN

Isabel has never quite measured up to her twin brother, Charlie.
But in Classe, a city she stravagates to, she can be herself without
anyone comparing her to him. And with the fierce Gate people
threatening to attack both Classe and the city of Bellezza, Isabel
is called on to help save the cities.

Chapter 1

Imaginary Twin

Isabel was feeling sick. She always did on results day. Not because she did badly; her results were usually quite respectable. But because Charlie always did better.

It wasn't his fault that he was brilliant at school subjects any more than it was his fault that he excelled at all sports and could play any wind instrument. Or that he was attractive to girls and got on well with teachers. It wasn't even their parents' fault that Isabel felt less favoured; they had always been scrupulously fair in their treatment of the twins.

Charlie was Isabel's twin brother and she had to love him. She *did* love him. But twins were supposed to have this almost magical closeness and Isabel didn't feel that at all. How she felt was jealous.

Her brother was the older by ten minutes and had been heavier at birth by a pound, which put Isabel in an incubator for a couple of days and left Charlie to breastfeed direct, while Isabel had to drink expressed milk. What a little thing to determine the course of the next sixteen, nearly seventeen, years! But it did. That accident of birth was something Isabel felt she had never caught up with: Charlie would always be older, stronger, in some way just more satisfactory than she was.

So she had invented a different twin for herself. Charlotte was a female version of Charlie but with the crucial difference that she had been born ten minutes *after* Isabel. This gave Isabel the chance to feel just a tiny bit superior and she knew that the imaginary Charlotte was a bit jealous of her. That made her feel special. If there was any magical twin-type closeness, it was with Charlotte rather than Charlie.

'Hurry up, Bel!' called Charlie from outside the bathroom door. 'I need to brush my teeth.'

She wasn't going to be sick after all, even though she had felt too nauseated to eat any breakfast. Isabel, let Charlie in and he flashed her a look of concern. 'You OK? You're looking a bit washed out.'

'Thanks for nothing,' said Isabel, then realised she was being unreasonably touchy. 'Really, I'm fine. Just a bit Monday-morningish.'

'Tell me about it!' said Charlie indistinctly through his toothpaste. 'It's the mocks results today, isn't it?'

'Yeah,' said Isabel, and ran downstairs two at a time, trying to show how little she cared.

They didn't walk to school together; that would have been taking twin-ness too far.

Isabel set off a regulation five minutes before Charlie but he always reached Barnsbury comp before her, even though he picked up several mates on the way. Sometimes Isabel thought she could remember the sight of Charlie's heels as his kicked his way out of the womb before her with a cheery wave and a 'See ya!'

Isabel's friends Laura and Ayesha usually waited for her at the school gates. They were there now, Laura looking nervous and Ayesha pretending to. Ayesha always got spectacular results.

'Hey, Bel,' they greeted her. And then Ayesha's boyfriend, Matt, came up and Isabel fell into step behind them with Laura.

Neither Isabel or Laura had a boyfriend but they didn't begrudge Ayesha hers, even though he was undeniably fit. Yesh was just so beautiful it was obvious she wouldn't be single. *Unlike us*, thought Isabel.

Laura was pretty in a thin, neurotic sort of way, with big eyes and dark brown curly hair. Isabel could have been pretty too. She had naturally blonde hair and dark brown eyes, but what was in Charlie a striking combination was in his sister easily over-looked. It had something to do with the way she did herself down, walking round with her shoulders hunched and her eyes on the ground, as if braced for bad news. She did her best not to be noticed and as a result she never was. The only person she felt more attractive than was Charlotte – and she wasn't real.

'Are you worried?' Laura asked, chewing the edge of her fingernail.

'Is the Pope a Catholic?' said Isabel. 'I can't wait for

today to be over. At least I'll know the worst.'

'You don't do so badly, do you?'

'Just not as well as Charlie,' said Isabel quietly.

Laura shot her a look. Isabel pulled herself together; she didn't talk about how she really felt about Charlie. Mostly she went along with how great it was to have a charismatic twin brother, and she knew Laura had a little bit of a thing for him.

'Take no notice of me,' Isabel said. 'It's probably just PMT.'

They walked into their first lesson and Isabel braced herself; at least she would do better than Charlotte.

The Captain of the *Silver Lady* was deeply embarrassed. Not only had he lost the most expensive silks in Flavia's cargo, but he had a horrible suspicion about the pirate who had relieved him of the goods.

'Describe him to me,' said the merchant, surprisingly calmly, pouring them two cups of Bellezzan red wine.

'Signora, he looked just like every other pirate I've had the misfortune to encounter,' said the Captain after he had drained his cup. 'Unkempt, rascally . . . but I must admit he was polite.'

'And he took just the silk?'

'He took the silk and then asked whose ship it was, Signora,' said the Captain uncomfortably.

Flavia sighed. 'And what did he say when you told him?'

'He . . . He smiled, Signora. And then he said something strange – "It's a new ship. She should have told me." Could it be . . . ?' he hesitated. 'Could it be that you know this brigand?'

Flavia did not answer. She weighed out the amount of silver due to the Captain for his entire cargo.

'But I have not brought it all safely into harbour,' he protested.

'No matter,' she said. 'I think the silk will find its way to me.'

The Captain did not wait for her to change her mind.

'Oh, well done, both of you!' said the twins' mother enthusiastically, when she got in from work.

Their father was equally encouraging and ordered an Indian takeaway to celebrate. Homework was abandoned and beer opened even though it was a school night.

Isabel painted a smile on her face and kept it from peeling off all evening, until she went to bed and let her face gratefully droop into its real expression. Their parents were always so *fair*! She couldn't blame her problems on them. Or on Charlie, who – damn him – was actually a really nice brother.

It's all my fault, she thought. *I'm rubbish. If I'd been an only child, without comparisons, my results would have been genuinely good. It's just that Charlie's are always better. Everything about him is better. And I'm a rat for even thinking what it would have been like if he hadn't been born!*

The curry and beer sat heavily on her stomach as she tried to find a comfortable position and get to sleep. She fell back into her usual habit of imagining Charlotte.

'Oh, Bel, I wish I'd got your averages! A levels will be a doddle for you.'

Then suddenly the thought of what she was doing nauseated Isabel.

Give it a rest, she told herself. *It's pathetic that you can't cope without an imaginary sister. What about your Art result?*

It was true that her Related Study work on mosaics, which had been assessed as part of the mocks, had got a stunning Charlie-type grade. Isabel was so glad that Charlie didn't do Art; it was the one area where she felt she had an edge on him and she couldn't have borne it if he had chosen it for A level.

Flavia was at the mosaic-maker's in the Via Bellezza. Fausto Ventura was the busiest mosaicist in Classe. His bottega employed a dozen people who were always busy cutting stone and coloured glass into tesserae. Others applied them to the designs and fitted them on walls and floors throughout the city. But only Fausto drew up the designs. His unique visions covered almost every surface in modern Classe – every new church or villa.

And he was Flavia's friend. Not just because she imported most of the coloured glass and silver 'smalti' from Bellezza used in his workshop, but because she loved art and had a good eye for mosaics. She spent her considerable wealth on adorning the walls and floors of her house with his work and he often visited her there, reminding himself of the peacocks and lilies, leopards and dolphins he had created from chips of marble, glass and the silver smalti that were the Classe's trademark.

But today she had come to visit him, and Fausto could see she was perturbed. He invited her into his private studio at the back of the bottega where he worked on his elaborate designs.

'What is it?' he asked.

Flavia hesitated then took the plunge. 'I have lost some of my cargo to pirates,' she said. 'The *Silver Lady* came back but lacking some of her silks.'

Fausto spread his hands in the universal gesture of pity mixed with resignation. 'It happens,' he said. 'Is the loss of money very great?'

'It is not so much that,' said Flavia. 'Although they were very fine silks. But my ships are subject to dangers on all sides now. I have heard a disturbing rumour that the Gate people have placed their own men on pirate ships along our coast.'

'So first they sell you the silk and then they rob it back off you before it even reaches Classe?' said Fausto. 'Twice the profit for them, or more, depending on how many merchants they can steal from in this way.'

'Perhaps,' said Flavia. 'Although I don't think it was the Gate people who took my silk this time. But that's not what really worries me.'

Fausto had known Flavia a long time and he was sure there was something more to the silk story than she was revealing, but he was prepared to let her tell him in her own time.

'I have heard from Rodolfo in Bellezza,' continued

Flavia. 'His daughter has been told that the Gate people are amassing a war fleet. She's coming here soon to talk to Duke Germano about an alliance between our cities.'

'Well, that's good, surely?' said Fausto. 'Germano is sure to say yes. We have always been on good terms with Bellezza.'

'Indeed,' said Flavia. 'And who are we both on bad terms with?'

'You mean besides the Gate people?'

'Someone much closer to home than them.'

'The di Chimici.'

It wasn't a question. Classe was one of the few city-states that remained independent in the north of Talia. Fabrizo di Chimici, the young Duke of Giglia, was now Grand Duke of Tuschia, and his family ruled in half the great cities of the peninsula. But there were fierce pockets of resistance to the family's empire-building schemes, and here in the north-east Classe, Padavia and Bellezza made natural allies against the powerful di Chimici.

Two elected duchies, with Duke Germano and Duchessa Arianna at their head, plus Antonio, the elected Governor of Padavia, had held out against all attempts to compromise their independence – from threats to marriage proposals, from diplomacy to assassinations. There was a natural free spirit among the people of these three cities that resisted any attempt to bring them into the di Chimici fold.

And they were linked by more than a spirit of independence. Classe and Bellezza were both on the sea and both maintained a fleet of ships to defend their coasts; Padavia was inland and did not need ships but relied heavily on the other two cities to protect its trade routes. Antonio was willing to pay some of his city's dues to help with the upkeep of the two fleets.

'What exactly do you think they're up to?' asked Fausto, taking Flavia's silence for agreement.

'I think the di Chimici might have forged an alliance with the Gate people,' said Flavia slowly. 'Rodolfo thinks so too. He hasn't told the young Duchessa of his suspicions yet but I know he fears the worse.'

'But wouldn't it be madness to combine with Talia's fiercest enemies?' asked Fausto.

'Some say the young Grand Duke *is* mad,' said Flavia. 'Whether it's true, I don't know. But if he has really done it, then those of us living on this coast are in terrible danger.'

'It's all very well for Fabrizio di Chimici, sitting safe inland in Giglia,' said Fausto, agitated himself now. He had a vision of fierce sea-warriors from the east overrunning Classe and destroying its great buildings full of mosaics.

'Those who lie down with dogs will rise with fleas,' said Flavia bitterly. 'He will pay a heavy price, but not before we do.'

'So what can we do?' asked Fausto. 'Is there anything the Brotherhood can do to stop them?'

Fausto knew that his friend was a member of a powerful and clandestine society of people who had secret gifts. She did not talk about it much but he was aware that she had a special way of communicating with the Regent of Bellezza and others in Talia who were also members of that small band known as Stravaganti.

'We can certainly try,' said Flavia. 'And, as you know, we have allies far beyond Talia who might be able to help us. It has been done before.'

Isabel was rushing from the Art room to her next lesson when she nearly tripped over the little red pouch. She picked it up, fascinated; it looked like a prop from a school play.

It was made of soft crimson velvet, held together at the top with a drawstring – just the kind of purse full of coins that someone called Roderigo would toss across the stage to someone called Valentino or something in a Shakespeare play.

Isabel hefted it in her palm. It definitely did have something inside and she couldn't resist opening the string to see what it was. But it wasn't coins at all; it held tiny silver squares that she recognised straight away as mosaic tiles. 'Tesserae' they were called, and Isabel had thought she was the only person in the school who was interested in them. Who could it possibly belong to?

The only student who came to mind was Sky Meadows, the gorgeous butterscotch-coloured boy who sat next to her in Art and was going out with a girl called Alice. Isabel heaved a huge sigh. Sky hadn't taken any more notice of her than anyone else at Barnsbury, but she had often thought it would be nice if he did.

She dragged her mind back to the pouch of little tiles, her feet taking her in the direction of her next class without any conscious decision on her part. Sky was interested in Italian art but Renaissance sculpture was his thing; his Related Study on Donatello had been the only one with a higher mark than Isabel's. There wasn't time to take the pouch back to the Art room now – she would ask him about it at break. And if it wasn't his . . . Isabel pushed the red velvet bag deep into her pocket. She supposed she'd have to show it to the Art teacher, but she found the pouch oddly appealing. It was nice just closing her hand over it in her pocket and feeling the little tesserae through the velvet. She didn't really want to hand it over to anyone else.

Sky's reaction to the pouch at break time was a definite improvement on past contact with him. He said it wasn't his, but he was certainly taking notice of Isabel now.

'You say you just found it lying near the Art room?' he said, almost caressing the velvet, as if he knew something about it.

'That's right,' said Isabel, feeling embarrassed now that those brown eyes were at last fully focused on her own. 'It's tesserae inside,' she added. 'I looked. You know – little pieces for making mosaics.'

'You're interested in mosaics, aren't you?' he said. So he *had* paid some attention to her before.

'Yes. I love them,' said Isabel, feeling stupid and uncool even as she said it. But Sky didn't seem to mind; he just nodded.

'I'm more into sculpture myself. Don't know much about mosaics. But don't you think this bag or purse or whatever it is looks sort of Italian? It's got a kind of Renaissance feel to it.'

'Well, it made me think of the sort of Italians you

get in Shakespeare plays,' said Isabel. 'But yes, I suppose that's Renaissance in a way.'

She didn't want this conversation ever to end. Sky reluctantly handed the red bag back to her. And Isabel just as reluctantly took it to the Art teacher in her dinner hour. But Ms Hellings didn't know anything about it either. She suggested taking it to Lost Property. Isabel didn't say she would, she just nodded as if agreeing it was a good idea. But she had already decided to keep it.

Discover a thrilling new adventure from the author of the STRAVAGANZA series

Sixteen-year-old Silvano da Montacuto has wealth, good looks and a new hawk. But when a man is murdered, Silvano is accused of the crime. For his own protection, he is sent to a Franciscan house, where he poses as a novice monk. But murder seems to have followed Silvano, and soon several more bodies turn up. . . .

Fans of Mary Hoffman's critically acclaimed Stravaganza series won't be disappointed in the romance, intrigue and rich, marvelous setting of Renaissance Italy.

Discover a world of music, danger and romance

When Elinor discovers she is to be married to a much older man, she flees her comfortable life as a noblewoman to travel with a group of minstrels. Disguised as a boy, Elinor performs for nobles in southern France and hopes that one day she will be reunited with Bertran, a handsome troubadour she pines for. But as crusaders invade France, both Bertran and Elinor find themselves – and their entire society – in great danger.